THIS IS WHAT THEY SAY

*Martina Cole's No. 1 bestsellers – at time of press she has
spent more weeks at No. 1 than any other author

MARTINA COLE

THE GOOD LIFE

HEADLINE

First published in Great Britain in 2014 by
HEADLINE PUBLISHING GROUP

First published in Great Britain in paperback in 2015 by
HEADLINE PUBLISHING GROUP

This edition published in paperback in 2016 by
HEADLINE PUBLISHING GROUP

6

'The Good Life'
Music: Sacha Distel
French lyrics: Jean Brousolle
English lyrics: Jack Reardon
With the authorization of Prosadis

Cataloguing in Publication Data is available from the British Library

ISBN 978 1 4722 0097 6 (B-format)

Typeset in ITC Galliard Std by Palimpsest Book Production Ltd,
Falkirk, Stirlingshire

Printed and bound in Great Britain by Clays Ltd, St Ives plc

Papers used by Headline are from well-managed forests and other
responsible sources.

MIX
Paper from
responsible sources
FSC® C104740

HEADLINE PUBLISHING GROUP
An Hachette UK Company
Carmelite House
50 Victoria Embankment
London EC4Y 0DZ

www.headline.co.uk
www.hachette.co.uk

For my beautiful granddaughter Natalia Noonie
Whiteside, her nanny's little Maget!

Thanks to Yvonne and Osman – you were absolute stars.
PS It should have been me.
No cravats please!

For Canim Boo.

Prologue

There is love of course. And then there's life, its enemy.

Jean Anouilh

Jenny woke up early. She lay in her bed for long moments, savouring the warmth before suddenly remembering why she was so anxious. Today was the day she had been waiting for for a long time. Now it had finally arrived, she wasn't sure how it was going to go, what to expect and whether, at the end of it, she would regret the choices she had made all those years ago. She felt physically sick, wondering if she had made the right ones. Truth be told, she was terrified – terrified but also excited.

She stroked her body, feeling the softness of her skin, cupping her breasts which were still full even without the firmness of youth. The last time he had held her felt like a dream. She had always been so in love with him she had felt it was like a mania. Cain Moran had been everything she had ever wanted. He still was – but would he feel the same after so many years away from her, away from the real world? Would he still carry the guilt over the brutal death of their boy, his namesake? Would it always be there between them?

She missed her boy every day; it was like a vicious wound that never completely healed. A song, a word, an image, brought the pain back in seconds, each time bigger and more heartbreaking than before. She knew it had to be discussed, finally be put to bed, but it wasn't a conversation she was looking forward to. In the prison it had been too difficult to talk openly about it, and at the funeral there had not been time to discuss it properly. They were both so full of grief, so full of heartache. Even though they had spent one precious night together, and he had done murder for her that day, part of her had held a grudge for what he had cost her. Would they get past it? Could they really take up their lives again after all this time?

Well, tonight she would know the answers. She got out of her bed and went through to her kitchen. As she put the kettle on she looked out of the window; dawn was breaking and lighting up the sky. How different her view was now from when she was a girl growing up on an East London council estate. In those days, there was no escape from looking into other people's homes and lives, as they had looked into hers. She had watched so many petty dramas play out: fights, arguments, police raids, lovemaking and, of course, children of all ages playing and living their lives as best they could – as she had herself. A drunken mother and a father she had never once clapped eyes on didn't make for the greatest of upbringings.

But then she met Cain Moran and everything had

started to make sense to her. She had fallen for him in such a big way, and he had been her life ever since, even though he had not been an actual part of it for many years.

She had lost so much – her only child, her youth – but while she had Cain – or the promise of him – she had been able to cope. Now, faced with the reality that he was finally being released, the fear had set in. Would he find her old? Would he feel the need for a woman with less baggage and tighter skin, who still had the freshness of youth on her side? Because he could easily find one. Men like Cain Moran were magnets to certain women – she knew that better than anyone. Twenty-five years was a long time to be apart, but it had passed. That was the thing – eventually the time did pass and, now it had, Jenny prayed that Cain would still want her as she wanted him. Because, God, how she wanted him.

Caroline Moran was tall, heavy breasted and dangerously fat. She loved her food and she wasn't ashamed to admit it – she was always eating something. People seeing her now for the first time in years would be amazed at the change. As a young woman she had been magnificent – long dark hair, hazel eyes and a slender body with curves in all the right places. She had been a head turner in every way.

Now, as she sat in her transport café, eating a huge fried breakfast, shovelling the food into her mouth, her son Michael watched her with distaste. She was colossal but no one had the guts to mention it any more; it was pointless anyway – she just lost her rag. Food was Caroline's only pleasure, and she wouldn't listen to any kind of criticism or warning about her health. As far as she was concerned she was fine; Michael had learned long ago not to rock *that* particular boat. The strange thing was, she still looked after her skin and her hair. Her make-up was always perfect, her nails manicured, and painted her signature red. If she dropped the weight, no doubt she would still be the beautiful woman she once was.

Caroline finished chewing her food before saying aggressively, 'So, God Almighty is coming home today, is he?'

Michael nodded. Taller than average, with thick dark hair and deep blue eyes, he had the handsome, Irish look about him just like his father. He couldn't disguise their similarity in looks which he knew must be hard for his mother. She loathed his father, a man who had dumped them without a backward glance when he had found something better.

'Are you going to be OK, Mum?'

Caroline snorted. 'Fuck him! He means nothing to me, the two-faced filthy rat. He made his choice – for all the luck she brought him! I told him that God pays back debts without money, and look what happened. It all went wrong for him when he met her.'

The venom in her voice wasn't lost on her son; he

knew that no matter what she said, deep down, she still loved the man. It was the weakness of women. There had never been another man for her and at first it had not been for want of suitors. They had come thick and fast. She had had a lot to offer – not just in looks, but because she was also very well set up. A good businesswoman, she had revamped this café, turning it into an American-themed diner, even down to the red leather booths and iconic Wurlitzer. The place was always packed – not just with the usual lorry drivers, but also with families who came there to drink in the atmosphere and enjoy the excellent food. And the food was top notch – Caroline made sure of that.

Caroline buttered more toast and spread it thickly with jam. Taking a large bite, she chewed it thoughtfully for a few seconds, before saying seriously, 'I bet you he comes to see me. I bet you he can't help himself and, when he does, I am going to tell him a few home truths.' She sounded almost pleased at the prospect, and Michael Moran simply sighed, resigned to her delusions.

David Hannan had been up since the dawn, and he sat nursing a pot of coffee until it was time for him to leave. He was thrilled to be the one chosen to pick up Cain Moran – the man was a legend! He had been banged up for years, but before that he had been one of the hardest men in the Smoke, amassing a fortune that no one seemed able to find. He was David's idol growing up, and his father had told him many a story of the man's heroic exploits.

In honour of the occasion his suit was freshly cleaned, and his shirt and tie were brand new. He knew he looked good – a keen body builder, he took care of himself in every way. The birth of his first child – a little girl called Mae – had given him an added impetus to do well for himself. Today he'd be in receipt of a big wedge for a few hours' work. Even so, he was nervous. After all, a man changed after years behind the door. It was only natural, David supposed. Away from family and friends, living in a vacuum, it must have been hard. Even in the poke, Cain Moran's legend had still grown. The man had thwarted two attempts on his life, and each time he had come out on top. Not an easy thing in such a controlled environment, especially one ruled, more often than not, by the people incarcerated there in the first place.

David hoped Moran was up for a few words; it would be fabulous to get his advice on life and how to best present yourself. But either way, he was just glad he'd be able to tell his grandkids that he had spent some time alone with the great man – that in itself was worth a fortune to him. He knew it would raise his profile, make people take notice. He was determined to make sure he did a good job, and prove himself worthy of the trust placed in him.

Joe Biggs was annoyed. Even though he had always known this day would come, he wasn't happy about it. If ever a man should be dead it was Cain Moran – God knew it wasn't for want of trying. He was like a fucking cat – lives coming out of his arsehole. Joe had to sit back and see how Cain was going to react to his new-found freedom, and if he was going to try and re-establish himself as a Face to be reckoned with. There were still plenty of people willing to stand behind him – his rep made sure of that. He had sat out a big lump and that alone demanded respect. Even Joe had to give him credit for that.

He had arranged Cain's pick-up; he had a good young lad called David Hannan on the case – he wasn't going to send some old lag to pick him up – and he had arranged a drink in a local hostelry. Joe had to do this – it was expected from him as the main Face about town. But having to kowtow to that fucking old has-been rankled. The man had taken everything from his family once; he had never forgotten that, and he never would. Fucking piece of dirt, he was. He had his own personal beef with Cain 'High and Mighty' Moran. The man was a fucking piece of shite, but he was also a very charming and enigmatic piece of shite. Men and women loved him – he was both macho and good-looking – but he was still a piece of work when he wanted to be and people had forgotten that. But not Joe. He would never forget just what he was dealing with in Cain Moran.

He was not about to let everything he had strived for be taken away – he had worked too long and too hard to let that happen. He would play it by ear for the time being, see what the man's intentions were, and then decide the best way to proceed. After all, Moran was a wily, strong old bastard, and not someone to be dismissed in any way, shape or form.

Joe Biggs might be a lot of things, including vicious, vindictive and violent, but he was also capable of great patience when the time called for that. It was now time to sit back and see what occurred, keep his ear to the ground, and wait his opportunity. He could wait – after all, he had already waited long enough. So what was another few months?

Cain Moran had packed – not that he had much to take with him. Most of his stuff had already been distributed around his fellow cons. All he had left were a few books and a small amount of clothing. He couldn't admit it, of course, but he felt a trickle of fear at being allowed home. After so long he knew this was natural. But fear was an alien concept to him, and he felt it acutely.

He *wanted* to get out, that was a no-brainer, but it was how the world would be now that bothered him. He had been away a long time and he had not had access to the outside world except through visitors and going to his boy's funeral.

It was a completely different world he was going back to. He had read the papers, educated himself, absorbed every piece of information that he could lay his hands on, but the bottom line was he had no real idea of how the world had changed. How could he? It was a never-ending sameness in prison, each day merging into the next. TV wasn't enough to prepare him, and the probation service had not allowed him any weekend leave. A few days ago he was just told to pack because he was on the out – simple as that.

There was such a lot to look forward to, most of all his Jenny, his beautiful Jenny. He couldn't wait to hold her in his arms again; it had been what he missed the most, just holding her close. It wasn't even the sex – just being near her, the smell of her, the softness of her skin. He closed his eyes in anticipation; that at least he could look forward to – a night together at last. No sounds of men groaning in their sleep, no clattering of POs as they made their rounds, no more lying awake looking at nothing, willing the dawn to break so he could get out of his cell, dreaming of decent food and a drink in a real pub, wondering what the rest of the world was doing, wishing he were still a part of it.

Now it was here – what he had wanted for those long years – and he felt ambivalent. Part of him was raring to get out, while the thought of what he might find was holding him back. Still, he had no choice now; he was on the out. He just had a few debts to pay – both good ones and bad ones. He had to see Joe Biggs and sort out what they were going to do about the situation they found themselves in.

That was the first thing on his agenda – make the

bastard pay if he didn't toe the party line. The thought instantly made him feel better, made him feel powerful.

He was whistling as he went to the day room to make himself a final cup of coffee.

Book One

Oh, the good life, full of fun
Seems to be the ideal
Mm, the good life lets you hide
All the sadness you feel

'The Good Life'
Music by Sacha Distel and lyrics by Jack Reardon

Chapter One

Cain Moran was fit to be tied. His anger was legendary even in a world where a legendary temper was a requisite. He turned now and faced his antagonist.

'He fucking *blinded* him?'

Johnny MacNamara, affectionately known as Johnny Mac, sighed. He saw exactly where all this was going. 'Only in one eye, Cain . . .'

Cain Moran laughed at that, a deep, sarcastic laugh. 'Oh, why didn't you say that before! He's only *half* blind, then? What a cunt I am, eh? There was me thinking that my mate's boy was blinded completely, but it was *only* in one fucking eye.'

Johnny Mac instinctively stood in front of Sean Bowers, attempting to defuse the situation, but Sean, a nice enough lad prone to talking before he had fully engaged his brain, said plaintively, 'You told me to teach him a lesson, Cain. That lesson was well and truly administered. End of.'

Cain Moran was shaking his head in utter disbelief.

Johnny Mac stepped deftly out of the way of Cain's fist, and it landed heavily in the centre of Sean's eyes, sending him careering across the office, landing heavily against the iron filing cabinets. Johnny Mac could only look on helplessly as Cain administered a well-earned beating, culminating in Cain picking up a heavy cut-glass decanter filled with brandy and crashing it on to the unfortunate man's head.

'You fucking idiot! Do you know the fucking aggravation you have caused me? Do you? His dad is my fucking mate.'

Johnny Mac went to the door and motioned for two young men, both looking severely uncomfortable, to remove the offending object. Sean was covered in blood now, and was having difficulty breathing. It was a definite hospital job.

When the man had been removed, Johnny Mac poured two large whiskies and gave one to his friend. 'He meant well, Cain, he was just trying to impress you.'

Cain laughed. His shirt was splattered with blood and his knuckles were grazed, but Johnny could see that his temper was subsiding.

'Oh, he did that. Fucking moron. He blinded Vic Malone's lad. I know he took the piss, owed a couple of quid, but that wasn't any reason to fucking remove the poor little fucker's eye. Now I have to placate fucking Vic, one of me oldest mates!'

Johnny sighed. 'Fuck Vic, he shouldn't have let it get this far.'

Cain laughed. 'Oh, Johnny, it was fucking *Vic* who requested the lesson in the first place. He wanted his lad to realise the seriousness of getting in over his head.'

They both started laughing at the irony.

'Well, look on the bright side, Cain – lesson well learned there, I'd say.'

They both dissolved into loud laughter again.

'Let me change this fucking shirt, I hate the smell of blood. I'm going to have a quick shower. Get someone to clean this place up, will you?'

Cain left the offices and made his way up a rickety flight of stairs to his makeshift bedroom and bathroom. He had made sure he had these facilities for just these kinds of encounters – encounters that were becoming more and more prevalent, if he was honest.

Chapter Two

'Ooh, look at you all done up like a dog's dinner! On a promise, are we?'

Jennifer Riley looked good and she knew it, but the way her mother spoke it was not a compliment she was offering her daughter but an accusation.

'Don't be so silly, Mum. I'm going out with Bella.'

Eileen Riley snorted in derision. She had been drinking steadily all day, and the effects were not pretty. Her flushed face still held traces of her former beauty, but her hands were shaking and her eyes were bloodshot. Even her hair looked drunk, in its mass of knots and dark roots.

'You're a fool, Jen, giving it away to fucking schoolboys. You could make a fucking fortune I tell you, girl.'

Jenny could hear the disgust in her mother's voice but she deliberately ignored it – she wasn't getting into a slanging match this late in the day.

'Have you eaten anything, Mum?'

'"Have you eaten anything, Mum?" Can you hear

yourself, Jen? Fuck off out if you're going, and keep your fucking questions to yourself.'

Jenny shrugged. 'I'll take that as a no, then, shall I? Well, there's bread and milk – at least have a slice of toast.'

Eileen Riley pointedly refilled her glass with cheap wine and said emphatically, 'Fuck off.'

Jennifer Riley didn't need to be told twice.

Chapter Three

Jenny and Bella Davis were sitting in a pub in Dean Street, both dressed to the nines, and sipping vodka and tonics as if they did it every day of their lives. In truth it was their first real foray into Soho and, at sixteen, they were both completely unaware that they were basically sitting targets. If there was one thing a predator in Soho liked, it was a good-looking girl with no real understanding of the world. Young girls craved excitement, and there were men willing to do everything in their power to see that they got it.

Bella Davis was tiny, with long dark hair and hazel eyes; she had good legs and she knew how to make the best of herself. Jenny Riley, however, was a completely different kettle of fish. Tall for her age, she had the body of an old-time film star, long thick blond hair, and deep blue eyes. She was a real head turner, and men had been looking at her all her life. It was something she accepted now, even though it made her very uncomfortable.

The girls had been smiled at by some good-looking

young men, but mainly by *not* very good-looking older men, who had propositioned them into the bargain. While finding this wildly amusing, both were also becoming a bit scared as the night wore on. They had slipped into this pub in the hope of looking glamorous and sophisticated. The barmaid, a strange-looking woman in her forties with non-existent breasts and a suspicious-looking five o'clock shadow, had been watching them like a hawk since they had come in.

The place was livening up, and a tall man wearing a crumpled suit and a practised smile came and sat beside them. He was balding, had tobacco-stained fingers, and smelled like a week-old ashtray. He also sported a gold tooth and a scar that ran from his right eye down to his lip.

'Hello, ladies, can I get you a drink?'

They both shook their heads in unison.

'Don't be shy, girls –' he placed his hand on Jenny's knee now – 'I won't bite you. Well, not unless you ask me nicely anyway.' He laughed at his own humour.

'Leave them alone, Doug, they're only kids.' The barmaid was motioning with her head for the girls to leave as she spoke.

Doug gripped Jenny's thigh harder as he shouted angrily, 'Keep out of it, you fucking freak, and bring another round of drinks.'

Jenny tried to remove his hand but it was like a claw. 'We don't want another drink, thank you. In fact we were just going.' She tried to sound in control, but she was frightened now, and Bella was pale with fear.

'You stay there, madam. If you come in here like a couple of fucking tarts, then you should expect to be treated as such. This is Soho, darling, and it's a different world. Now, if you were thinking of joining the tart brigade I am the very man you need. It's what I do, see. I *recruit*.'

Jenny swallowed noisily, unsure how to answer. The barmaid brought the drinks over and sighed at the two girls as if to say 'I tried'. 'Drink up, girls, next stop Club Louise, eh? DJ Rudy's in tonight.'

Doug pushed the barmaid away roughly. 'Why don't you go and find someone to give a blow job to, and leave us alone, you fucking bender.'

'Doug, for the last time, they are just kids, leave them alone.'

Doug stood up menacingly, and the barmaid made a hasty retreat. 'Fucking animals! Men dressed as women, against the laws of nature. Fucking freak.' The last two words were said loudly, and with as much disgust as he could power into his voice.

Jenny and Bella were truly frightened; their little foray into Soho had turned into a nightmare. Why didn't they just go to a club? Why did they have to go walking around looking for excitement? No one else in the pub seemed bothered by their obvious distress; in fact, most of the men were trying to act as if they didn't exist. They sat mutely, neither of them knowing how to extricate themselves from the situation they'd found themselves in.

'Well, drink up then, girls, the night is young!'

Chapter Four

Johnny Mac listened intently as Cain Moran explained the complicated terms he expected for putting up the money needed for a new business venture by Jack Barton.

Jack's eyes, Johnny noticed, were glazing over with boredom. Not that it would stop Cain – he insisted that people knew beforehand exactly what he expected from them so that way there were no surprised faces anywhere along the line.

'My percentage of your profits is guaranteed up to three years from the term of the loan. If you're agreeable, Jack, then the money's yours.'

Jack Barton was nodding away; he had no idea what the fuck he was agreeing to but, as long as the money was handed over, he didn't really give a shit.

'Thirty grand is a lot, Jack. But I know you will pay me back with interest.'

There was an underlying threat there and even the thick-headed Jack Barton couldn't help but notice it. He was all attention suddenly, as the enormity of what he was asking was finally hitting him.

'Every penny, Cain, I swear.'

'Come on then, let's hit the boozer and have a couple of drinks to seal the deal.' The telephone on his desk rang and Cain picked it up quickly. 'Hello, Caroline, how's the house? Did the new beds arrive?'

He listened intently for a few moments, rolling his eyes at his audience before saying, 'Look, darling, I've got a lot on here. I'll ring you before I make me way home, OK?' He ended the call quickly. 'Her and that fucking house! Five bedrooms for three people. Take my advice, Jack, never agree to anything the wife says while you're pissed!'

They all laughed.

Chapter Five

Doug was enjoying himself; these two little girls were prime meat as far as he was concerned. The young ones thought they were something special with their cheap bags and heavy make-up. But he had been in the Tom game for many years and he knew that they had maybe eight good years before the Life would begin to take its toll on them. Youth dried up – it was the law of nature. He had forced two drinks down them and now they were on their third. When they were pissed enough he would make a quick call and get them picked up. Once they were out of here they were his.

As Cain Moran and Johnny Mac walked in the pub with Jack Barton in tow, the barmaid, Jasmine, as she liked to be called, breathed a sigh of relief. When Cain got to the bar, she said breathlessly, 'Just the man! Mr Moran, that Doug Havers has earmarked two lovely little girls, and they ain't Tom material, only kids. Could you . . .' She left the sentence open.

Cain sighed. 'Do I look like a fucking social worker to you, Jas?'

Jasmine fluttered her eyelashes at him. 'Pretty please! They are good girls, I can tell, and they are fucking terrified. He's forced three drinks on them already, large ones and all. Be on their backs in some sleazy hotel before they know what's happened to them. He's fucking scum.'

Johnny and Cain looked over to where the girls were sitting and, as he saw the really good-looking one trying to extricate Doug's hand from near her crotch, Cain sighed heavily and went over with Johnny close behind him.

'Leave the girl alone, Doug. Take your fucking hands off her.'

Doug looked up in surprise at Cain's words. 'Look, Mr Moran, I work for Kenny Barker, and Kenny don't like his business being interfered with, if you get my drift.'

Cain started to laugh. He could sense the two girls' fear as if it was tangible. 'Kenny Barker, that fucking fop. Ooh, I'm fucking shitting it.' He picked up Doug by the scruff of his neck and marched him out of the pub, throwing him into the gutter. 'You tell Kenny my offices are just up the road and my fucking door is always open. If I don't see him by tomorrow with an apology for making threats, I will be coming to visit him. You got that, you fucking imbecile?'

He went back into the pub where Johnny was already sitting beside the little dark-haired girl with the big eyes, holding a steady arm around her shoulder as she cried with relief. The other one, the blonde, was staring at him with a white face that looked so terrified he thought she might faint. Sighing heavily, he sat beside her and, smiling a little, he said lightly, 'Don't worry, you won't be hearing from him again, love.'

Jasmine brought over large whiskies for Cain and Johnny. 'On the house, boys, for saving our little damsels in distress.' Looking at the girls she said seriously, 'Stick to the clubs in future. Much safer, OK?'

The two girls nodded and tried to smile. Johnny put a finger under Bella's chin and pulled her face towards his, saying, 'What these two need, Cain, is a bit of food inside them to soak up all that alcohol.'

Cain sighed. Johnny was his best mate and he loved him, but he was always on the lookout for strange. Caroline would kill him if he was late home tonight of all nights. But he was peckish so, swallowing down the whisky, he said resignedly, 'We can take Jack with us. Let's go to the Italian around the corner.'

He had to help the blonde to stand up, annoyed that he had been put in this position in the first place. In all fairness she was a lovely looking girl – young, but still a stunner. Even half pissed and with her make-up smudged, she was a definite nine on anyone's scale. He thought of Caroline and sighed. He hadn't wanted this new house. She was the one who thought they needed a great big fuck-off place, so he let her deal with it all. The last thing he needed today was her mother Jane and her aunt Dolly scurrying about like worker ants.

He half carried Jennifer Riley out into Dean Street and manoeuvred her to the restaurant with the help of Jack. He was being a good Samaritan and, as his old mum always said, you have to help people when they are vulnerable and in need.

Despite his protestations, he knew what he would like to help this one with, young as she was.

Chapter Six

Caroline Moran looked around her new home with satisfaction. It was big and beautiful, befitting the Moran Clan, as she liked to call them. Trouble with Cain was he didn't understand that an up-and-coming businessman like himself needed to let people see his status. In many ways, he was a child where the real world was concerned. That was why he had married her, or one of the reasons anyway – being pregnant with young Michael being the main one, of course.

She smiled suddenly and it lit up her beautiful face. She loved that man, as irritating as he could be at times. He would be happy living in a flat, if truth be told. But she knew how to get what she wanted from him – that was the main thing.

Oh, she was well aware he took the occasional flier with another woman. That was OK; you couldn't have a man like Cain Moran and not expect some kind of competition. When Cain was out and about with another woman he usually snuck into her bed, half pissed and smelling of shampoo and expensive soap.

And, as long as he didn't flaunt them in her face, she was happy to turn a blind eye. They were always very pretty – and very short-lived. Cain loved her – she was his wife, after all, and that was what really mattered.

She walked into her brand-new kitchen and sighed with happiness. This house was just another investment in their futures, and one day he would thank her for insisting they buy it, even if he was a bit peeved with her about it at the moment.

She plugged in the electric kettle and set about making another pot of tea, humming to herself as she relished the sights and sounds of her new home.

Chapter Seven

Jenny Riley woke up and didn't know where she was for a few moments. Her mouth was dry and she had a deep ache behind her eyes. Sitting up, she was glad to see that she was fully clothed and in her own bedroom. She had no memory of how she got there. She had to take deep breaths to stop the feeling of nausea washing over her. This was her first hangover, and all she could think was, how could her mother wake up feeling like this every day of her life?

The evening before was a blur. She sat on the edge of the bed, vaguely remembering trying to eat a bowl of pasta. She closed her eyes tightly until the room stopped moving around her, and finally she made her way to the bathroom. Stripping off her soiled clothes she stood underneath the cold shower until she felt relatively normal. All the while flashes of the night before were moving before her eyes, but she couldn't make head or tail of any of it.

The bathroom door banged open and her mother's voice sliced through her skull. 'Up then, are we?'

Jenny closed her eyes in distress. This was going to be a long day.

Chapter Eight

'If I never see that ponce's face again it will be too soon!'

Cain Moran laughed at Johnny's words. 'You sound like your mother!'

Johnny grinned, because it was true. One of his lads, big Paulie Jameson, opened the office door and said quickly, 'Kenny the Pimp's downstairs and said he needed to see you.'

Cain and Johnny exchanged startled looks, then both started to smile remembering the excitement of the night before.

Johnny turned back to Paulie. 'Send him up, Paul.'

Cain sighed. 'That's all I need, Johnny, but I suppose it has to be done!'

'Lovely little pair though, weren't they?'

'What the girl or her tits?'

Johnny grinned. 'Both.'

Kenny the Pimp walked into the room like Uriah Heep on Valium, the fear on his face was visible and, as he looked at Cain Moran, he attempted a smile.

Cain Moran knew how to play the game and he just stood there towering over the other man and looking seriously menacing.

'You wanted to see me?'

Kenny nodded. 'I heard about last night, and I can assure you that I have spoken sternly to Doug. He realises he was out of order. Blames the booze – you know how it is.' He was warming to his theme now, and carried on in the same vein. 'I've told him to be careful, make sure he don't step on anyone's toes, but what can I say, Cain? He's a cunt.'

Cain laughed. 'Lot of them about, Kenny.'

The insult was taken on board, but there wasn't going to be any retaliation, they all knew that. This was an exercise in diplomacy, nothing more.

Cain went and sat behind his desk and, lighting a cigarette, he blew the smoke out in a long stream before saying, 'The thing is, Kenny, Doug had earmarked a pair of nice young lasses. They were pissed and scared but he wasn't fucking bothered. If I hadn't intervened they would have woken up in a hotel some-where stinking of sweaty blokes and that would have been just the start of their destruction. If I ever fucking see that cunt within a five-mile radius of this street, I will kill him. Hand on heart. Then I will pop in my car and I will drive to Brixton and kill *you*. Because it's cunts like you that's causing the huge police presence in Soho and the surrounding areas. You've got to take your business off the streets and start using your loaf.

It's nearly the eighties, and it's a different world here now. It's *my* fucking world. Don't fuck it up.'

Kenny the Pimp swallowed deeply; one thing that could be said for Cain Moran was that he never made idle threats. Kenny cleared his throat noisily, his nerves in shreds. 'Fair enough, if that's what you think is for the best.'

Cain Moran stood up quickly and saw the man flinch. 'I *do* think it is for the best. So fuck off.'

Kenny the Pimp scarpered, the laughter of the two men following him down the rickety stairs.

'I hate ponces, Johnny. Living off women like that. They are scum.'

Johnny nodded in agreement. Like Cain, his mother had been a Tom, and that was why their friendship had blossomed all those years ago. It was a terrible stigma to live down, but it was the truth and there was nothing anyone could do about that. Johnny remembered how hard it had been for them, and so did Cain, although it wasn't something they discussed very often. It was normally late at night, when well in their cups, that they broached the subject and discussed the finer points of their upbringings. But both worshipped their mothers – that was the main thing. They understood the times and the pressures and the lack of money for single women left with kids.

Cain had always been the bigger of the two. At junior school he had towered over the other lads. Johnny, on the other hand, was small for his age and black, which didn't exactly help his situation in those days. But between them they had conquered their particular world and their friendship was true and lasting. Johnny loved Cain Moran and he knew the feeling was reciprocated; they were closer than most brothers. There wasn't anything he wouldn't do for the man.

'I felt so sorry for those girls last night, but what I said was true – the new laws are going to clamp down on prostitution – well, for the younger girls anyway. The shrewd Toms rent a room and advertise as a model, or offer French lessons. The thing is, people like Doug and Kenny are a dying breed if they only knew it. They have to change with the times. I mean, if he invested in a house, he'd basically be legal. You can do what the fuck you like in a property you own. That's how the letter of the law works. But that thick cunt can't see it.'

Johnny put his jacket on. 'Come on, Cain, we're due in East London in an hour. Richie Jakobs is bringing his mate to offer us this marvellous business deal.'

Cain sighed. 'I suppose we have to go, show a bit of willing, but I don't trust that fucker.'

Johnny grinned. 'No one trusts that fucker, but he can earn, and that's all anyone really cares about.'

Cain nodded in agreement but he was still wary. Jakobs was a slippery bastard and, as such, needed to be watched closely. Cain Moran knew he wasn't a man who could put that much effort into another person, especially not one like Jakobs. But he'd agreed to the meet, and so he had to go and at least hear what the man had to say.

Chapter Nine

Jenny Riley picked up the phone quickly, the ringing torture to her pounding head. She was still feeling the effects of the night before and every now and then she would remember the man who had saved her and her face would burn with humiliation. All the way back to her house he had lectured her on the perils of being a young good-looking girl, and the trouble that could get her in if she wasn't a bit more savvy. The whole evening had since come back to her in stunning clarity and now she wished she could just forget it for ever.

'Hello.' Even her voice sounded fragile.

But instead of Bella as she hoped, it was the local publican Paddy Cartwright shouting that she had better come and get her mum or he was calling the Old Bill. Slamming down the phone, she grabbed her jacket and hurried out of the front door.

It was early evening and the weather was cold, but it cleared her head and, as she made her way to The Highwayman public house, she cursed her mother under her breath. She hoped Paddy didn't phone the police; her mum was only inches away from a custodial sentence for brawling, drunk and disorderliness and shoplifting. The judge was sick of seeing her – this time he would bang her up no trouble. Paddy was a good bloke though – he tried to look out for her mother, Jenny knew that.

But as she approached the pub she sighed in distress. She could hear her mother's big gob even from a distance, and she was in full fighting mode. Jenny ran as quickly as she could to try and defuse the situation; she was good at it because she had been doing it for as long as she could remember.

'Mum! What the hell is going on?'

As Eileen turned to face her daughter, she still had hold of a dark-haired woman's throat; she had been shaking her like a terrier and the woman was terrified.

'Put the lady down, Mum.'

'Will I fuck! She nicked me fucking drink.'

A small crowd had gathered to watch the debacle and Jenny turned to them shouting, 'Had your fucking look? Grown men watching a drunken woman fight and you didn't even step in to help?'

One of the men shouted back, 'Eileen Riley don't need no help, love, she fights like a man!' Everyone laughed at that.

Jenny extricated her mother's hands from the weeping woman's hair, and tried to pull her away. But Eileen was having none of it. Knocking her daughter back, she set about the woman again, this time dragging her by the hair and raining punches down on her head.

'I'll fucking teach you a lesson, you thieving cunt.'

Jenny pulled herself off the floor just as the police arrived. It was chaos. Getting out of the car was PC Magnus Billings, a big man, running to fat to the extent that he looked like he was going to burst out of his uniform. He was much disliked, not only by the locals but also by the police force in general.

Jenny's heart sank when she realised it was Billings who had come to break up the fight; he hated her mother with a vengeance bordering on mania. Eileen had once emptied a bucket of piss over him and he had never forgotten it. Neither had anyone else. It had gone down in the local folklore as those kinds of incidents generally do. Even his police colleagues referred to him as Pissy Bill, not a name he relished.

When he grabbed her mother in a chokehold, Jenny could see that he was really hurting her and, without thinking, she rushed to her defence.

'All right, hold up a minute, you're harming her.'

He laughed nastily. 'Piss off. She's fucking nicked.'

The other PC was a tall lanky young lad with dirty blond hair and bulbous blue eyes. He was attempting to help her mother's victim who, it turned out, was even drunker than Eileen.

Jenny stood her ground. 'You're hurting her! She can't even talk your hold's so tight.'

Eileen Riley did look distressed. Billings was holding her at an awkward angle and it must have been agony.

'If I've managed to shut this fucker up then that can only be good.' He looked at the crowd for confirmation but they weren't laughing now. The Filth were their natural enemy and, as bad as Eileen was, there was a strange affection for her. She brightened up many a dull day with her antics. Plus, if she was flush, she was always open-handed and willing to share her good fortune, even if it was earned on her back.

But now the police were involved, Eileen Riley was seen as the victim not the aggressor. A tall man with a bald head and a drinker's belly shouted angrily, 'Let her go!'

Billings retaliated by dragging her forcefully towards the patrol car, shouting over his shoulder loudly, 'You want to fucking join her, mate? Because that can be arranged.'

Jenny launched herself at the man who was trying to force a kicking and fighting Eileen into the patrol car. Without thinking she jumped on to his back and, using all her strength, she dragged him away from her mother. Letting go of Eileen, Billings turned around and pushed her forcefully to the ground. Eileen, seeing this, launched herself once more at the officer, knocking his hat off and grabbing at his hair, cheered on by the crowd of onlookers who wanted to see Pissy Bill get his just deserts. Which he did, with honours.

Chapter Ten

Cain Moran had driven to Stratford for his meet and, as he parked outside The Highwayman, he saw a sight he didn't think he would ever see. The lovely – *quiet* – girl of the night before was having a fight with a policeman.

Johnny Mac laughed. 'That's that little bird, ain't it?'

Cain sighed. 'So it would fucking seem. Not such a wilting violet after all.'

Cain and Johnny got out of their car and made their way over to the foray. Cain grabbed PC Billings and pushed him away from the fighting women. The man actually looked relieved.

Then he realised who had dragged him away and wished he had never answered the call.

'What the fuck are you doing? Fighting with women? Get in your fucking plod car and leave.'

The crowd were thrilled. This was added excitement. A local Face turning up was the icing on the cake as far as they were concerned.

The two policemen did as they were bid and left the scene quick sharp.

Jenny was mortified that the man who had been her saviour the night before had once more come to her aid. She could feel the burn of humiliation on her face. She must look like a complete headcase. One minute she was being groomed as a prostitute, and the next minute she was brawling in the street.

'Hello, young Jenny. You do have a flair for the dramatic, don't you, darling?'

Jenny Riley was so mortified she burst into tears. Eileen, who was sobering up by the second, was amazed that her daughter, her lovely looking Jenny, could know someone like Cain Moran. Especially on a first-name basis.

Cain put his arm around Jenny's shoulders and, motioning to Johnny, he walked her back to his car. Johnny Mac grabbed Eileen and they all left the scene together. Eileen Riley had once more provided the general populace with not just excitement, but also gossip. She was a girl all right.

Chapter Eleven

Cain looked around Jenny's home and his heart sank. It was a typical Tom's house – empty bottles everywhere, the residue of half-eaten food and overflowing ashtrays. He should know; he had grown up in a place just like it. He could see there was an underlying cleanliness that he guessed, rightly, was from young Jenny trying to bring some normality to her surroundings. He felt heart-sorry for the girl. What chance did she have with loony Eileen, as she was affectionately known, as her mother?

He felt a deep sadness settle over his heart. He had suffered the humiliation of a mother on the game, and he had learned to fight at a young age. Whatever his mum might have been she was still his mum, and no one was going to say anything detrimental about her, even if it was true. Most soft Toms like his mum, Eileen, and Johnny Mac's mum, were victims of their own looks and apathy. It was easy money, and you could drink and smoke into the bargain. It was a social job in a way, where you were out with other people. And it helped pay the bills and put the food on the table.

Johnny put the kettle on and hunted through the cupboards for clean cups. One thing with Johnny Mac, he could make the most awkward situation seem normal. Eileen was repairing the damage to her face, and Jenny was just sitting there, white as a sheet.

It really hit her hard, how these kind men, who had been so good to her and Bella, must see her and her world. For the first time, she was viewing her life as others perceived it. It wasn't a good feeling. Sometimes she hated her mother even as she loved her.

Johnny clapped his hands together loudly. 'Cuppa's on the way. Any biscuits?'

'Look what that fucker's done to me! Scratched my neck all over, and I'll have a black eye. Fat fucker, he is.'

Cain and Johnny laughed.

'You've had worse I should imagine and, look on the bright side, at least you ain't been banged up.'

Cain took two twenty-pound notes out of his wallet and passed them to Eileen, saying, 'Go to the chemist, get some salve or whatever it is you put on bruises.'

Eileen took the money, then she looked from him to Jenny thoughtfully and she smiled. 'Give me a lift, would you, Johnny?'

Johnny looked at Cain who nodded imperceptibly, and the two left the flat.

Cain poured out two teas and he placed one before

Jenny, her face still a white mask of humiliation and horror. Like him, she had realised her mother was offering her only child to a strange man. Fucking Eileen Riley, mother of the year as usual.

'Drink that up and you'll feel better. I put lots of sugar in it.'

Jenny didn't move, just sat there like a statue, staring at her hands. Cain Moran was annoyed with himself. Why was he bothering with this? What was the attraction of this young girl?

But he knew what it was all right. She affected him in so many ways. From her sad eyes, to her big full breasts, she had somehow entered into his psyche, and he couldn't stop thinking about her. He had a wife and a handsome son – true, he took the occasional flier with a bit of strange – nothing significant.

But what he felt for this girl was different to any feelings he had ever had before in his life. It didn't make any sense. He'd only met her twice. And each time she had caused him nothing but aggravation.

'Has your mum ever done this to you before? Left you alone with strange men?'

Jenny stirred to life then as she said indignantly, 'No, she hasn't. How could you even think that? I'm not like her! I'm *nothing* like her.'

'All right, all right, keep your hair on.' He believed her and he was inordinately relieved that she was a nice girl. 'Are you going to be OK, love?'

She shrugged, and he noticed how slim her shoulders

were; they didn't look capable of holding up those enormous breasts. She really was a stunning-looking girl. She nodded. He noticed she had relaxed a bit now she knew his intentions were honourable. She finally looked into his eyes and his heart constricted in his chest. This was trouble he really didn't need.

Chapter Twelve

Richie Jakobs was fat in every way, from his huge belly to his double chins; even his hands were pudgy. But he was surprisingly light on his feet and, even though he looked like he was six seconds behind everyone else, he had a razor-sharp mind. He was, in truth, a mathematical genius and, if he had been blessed with a different set of parents, he would have taken his brain to university and learned how to put it to good use.

Instead, he was a haggler. He had bookies, and he was used by everyone to work out percentages. His main fault – and they were legion – was he could never resist a scam of any kind, especially one where the odds were in his favour. He was wary of Cain Moran – who wouldn't be? He had a fearsome reputation.

But with the likes of Jamie Jones beside him, Richie felt that he was in a much better position. Jamie wasn't a mug by anyone's standards. In fact, he had a good reputation when it came to looking after himself. Jamie Jones was also known as a man who could earn, and earn well. He was tight-lipped and cunning, the qualities needed for the type of work they engaged in. They could make a formidable team.

There was a lot of talk about Jamie Jones. Years before he had been the recipient of a serious hammering, and had been hospitalised for four months. But he had come out with nothing to show for his sufferings except a scar across his right eyebrow. Rumour at the time was he had tried to have over the Moody brothers from Canning Town. But no one was saying anything, so it was pure speculation.

Frank Moody had been found bound, gagged and beaten to death on Southend seafront. His brother Gerald had never been seen again. It was a mystery all right, but the general consensus was that Jamie Jones had been behind it and, as such, his rep had shot up into the stratosphere.

The fact that no one knew the truth was just how Jamie liked it. He wouldn't give his size in a shoe shop, he was so close-mouthed. So, all in all, Richie Jakobs was pleased with his choice of partner.

When Jamie walked into the pub, Richie watched him for a few moments. He definitely had a presence, good-looking despite his scar. He was softly spoken, but when he did talk, people listened to him.

Richie hailed him loudly, as if he had just come back from five years abroad. 'You missed all the excitement! I do believe Cain Moran's going soft in his old age.' He quickly filled Jamie in on the story that was already doing the rounds.

Jamie listened carefully and, when Richie had finished, he murmured, 'The man's a gentleman.'

He could see that was not the answer Richie had expected. But Jamie was a shrewdie; he liked Cain Moran and everything that he had heard about him. Cain was only twenty-eight and already he was more or less at the top of his game. That was no mean feat, especially these days when the courts were handing out outrageous sentences. Jamie wanted this meet, and he wanted it badly. He also hoped that he could swerve this fat cunt Richie into the bargain. He didn't like him and he didn't trust him, but he couldn't get this deal off the ground without involving him, at least at the beginning.

Richie was unimpressed with the way Jamie had come to Cain Moran's defence so he said carefully, 'Never liked the schoolies myself. She's only about sixteen. Looks older though, in fairness.'

Jamie knew exactly where Richie was going with this, and he said in his usual careful manner, 'You know something, Richie, I had you down as a lot of things, but a fucking village gossip wasn't one of them.'

One good thing about Richie Jakobs was he knew when to shut his big mouth.

Chapter Thirteen

Cain picked up on the tension between the two men as soon as he sat down. Johnny was at the bar getting the drinks in, and Cain shook hands with Jamie, not bothering to do the same with Richie, which was noted by all.

'Sorry for the delay, guys, seems I walked into a Keystone Cops style situation.' He made light of it, but he knew there was already talk about why he had bothered to defend Eileen Riley and her daughter. 'People forget this is my stomping ground, and I hate the Filth, especially that fat wanker Billings. If ever a man needed a fucking smack it's him.'

Johnny Mac laughed. 'She is funny, though, that Eileen. I remember years ago when she beat up that bloke, what was his name? You know, Cain, short, fat Greek with a bald head . . .'

Cain laughed too, remembering. 'Fuck me, I'd forgotten all about that. Costas, that was it. Used to have a café on the High Road. He didn't pay her, she used to go out the back with him while his wife was at work. He would fuck a fence, that cunt. Woman mad. She gave him the hammering of a lifetime, and then told his wife everything.'

Richie laughed loudest before he said nastily, 'Never trust a Tom, eh? Fucking slags. Any bird that earns a living like that can't be trusted.'

He had genuinely not thought through what he was saying, but the faces of Cain and Johnny reminded him just who he was talking to.

Cain sipped at his whisky, saying smoothly, 'Fuck me, gents, we are sitting with a man of the world! Who would have thought it? By the way, Richie, my mum was a brass, and so was Johnny's, as I am sure you know. It wasn't exactly a secret, like.'

Jamie couldn't resist a little smile at the big man's predicament. This suited them all because it wrong-footed Richie and that made it easier to push him out of this deal once it was laid out. Jamie had a sneaking respect for Cain Moran; he had taken his opening and used it beautifully. He would enjoy making this bloke's acquaintance.

'I think after that faux fucking pas the next round's on you, Richie.'

Richie Jakobs jumped out of his seat and hurried to the bar. The other men smiled at each other in perfect accord. Then they got down to business.

Chapter Fourteen

'He's after you, Jen, and you'd be a fool not to take your chance.'

Eileen was still getting over the shock of the day's happenings. Not the fight – that was not an unusual part of her week – but Cain Moran turning up like that and obviously knowing her Jenny by name? That was the shocker for her, all right. She hugged herself with the knowledge that her daughter had given them guaranteed kudos by her connection with Cain Moran, however tenuous it might be. He was a handsome fucker and all, the jammy little cow. But, in fairness, her daughter was a beauty. Like her, she had the looks that sent men crazy, and she also had the body to go with it. Eileen didn't want her to waste that like she had.

Jenny Riley felt a faint stirring inside her belly at her mother's words. 'Don't be so silly, Mum, he was just being nice.'

Eileen wasn't fooled for a second. 'Look at you doing a cherry! You look like a Belisha beacon.

Seriously, Jen, if you're going to aim, aim as fucking high as you can. Youth don't last that long, take it from me.'

Jenny got up from the sofa; she had tidied up after Cain had left and wished she had tidied up before. The place was a dump, but at least now it was a clean dump.

'He's just a nice man, Mum, you know? Kind.'

She told the story of her and Bella up in Soho and watched with a certain satisfaction as her mother's eyes stretched wide in disbelief.

Eileen laughed at the end, though, saying, 'Fuck me, Jen, you've always been a bit too good and then overnight you nearly end up on the bash in Soho. Thought I was bad enough!'

They both laughed at the absurdity of it.

Then Eileen said seriously, 'Look, Jenny, you are your own woman. I knew that years ago. All finicky and nice – fuck knows where you got that from. But, for all my faults, I do care about you, darling. If he comes sniffing round, you think long and hard about knocking him back. He's a catch – a married catch – but that don't mean fuck-all these days, love.'

Jenny smiled, and didn't answer her mother. She loved her but she had a mouth bigger than the Blackwall Tunnel. There was no way Jenny would admit she had agreed to meet Cain Moran for dinner. She kept the knowledge to herself. For the first time in her life she was going out with a big handsome man – who had a wife and child. He had explained that to her and, even though she knew it was wrong, she didn't care. For the first time in her life, she was falling in love.

Chapter Fifteen

Cain picked Jenny up at Knightsbridge tube station. She looked absolutely gorgeous – and completely out of place. He drove them to a small Greek restaurant in Beauchamp Place; he often took his paramours there, as it was the last place he would come across anyone he knew.

One part of him was excited, the other half ashamed at his feelings for someone so young and so fragile. But he couldn't resist. There was something about her and, whatever it was, he knew he would not miss this date for anything in the world.

He had left Johnny Mac with Richie and Jamie to tie up the loose ends of the deal, and then he had driven here with a feeling of anticipation inside him that he had not felt in years.

She looked stunning, even in her cheap market clothes and shoes. As he ushered her into the restaurant, he saw the looks she was getting from most of the men in the place and he felt an inordinate pride that she was with him. He pushed his wife Caroline and his son Michael to the back of his mind. Once he had fucked her she would lose her appeal, he was confident of that. It was the conquest with him more than the sex.

Her youth did give him pause, but he consoled himself with the fact that if she was brought up by Eileen Riley she wasn't going to be a raging virgin. She was sixteen and he was twenty-eight – only twelve years between them – and in another few years, that wouldn't seem so great an age difference. It was all relative, as his old mum used to say.

'Want a glass of wine? I think we know you're not a vodka girl by now.' He laughed at his own wit and was surprised to find he was actually feeling nervous. It was her eyes, so trusting, so fucking lovely.

'Please.' She was clearly even more nervous than he was and his heart went out to her. He wondered if he was getting soft in his old age.

'I'll order a bottle, darling, a good one.'

She nodded compliantly, unsure how to answer him. This was so far out of her usual life she just didn't know how she was supposed to react. She was scared, if truth be told.

Cain Moran was all good-natured bonhomie but he could see that this was a girl completely out of her depth. What had seemed a wonderful adventure was frightening her, so he kept topping up her wineglass. He was going to get his leg over tonight if it was the last thing he did on this planet. She was exquisite, and he wanted her more than he had ever wanted a woman in his life.

When she laughed at one of his jokes, he realised the wine was finally doing its job and now all that was left was for him to do his. Happy days.

Chapter Sixteen

Jenny looked around her at the apartment Cain had brought her to. She was half drunk, and she knew in her heart that she should never have agreed to come here with him for a last drink.

The room was beautiful – velvet curtains and antique furniture. She was overawed by her surroundings, and she perched precariously on a leather sofa. Cain handed her a glass of brandy, sat beside her and pulled her into his arms. She settled against him and, as he felt the contours of her body, he was almost breathless at the prospect of what was to come. She looked up into his eyes and he saw such trust there that he felt a momentary pang of guilt at what he was doing to her. He lowered his head and kissed her; she tasted of brandy and garlic – not a bad combination at this particular moment. She smelled of cheap scent and deodorant, and he wondered at how she had such a spectacular effect on him, making him feel fifteen again.

'Do you live here? I mean, is this your wife's home too?'

He laughed. 'You're joking, darling! If my wife knew I was here with you I'd be looking for someone with a bollock donor card! No, this is my little pied à terre, for when I'm in town and can't get back.'

She smiled, the wine making her even more mellow along with the brandy. 'So this is where you bring your girlfriends, then.'

He leered at her saucily. 'Got it in one, darling. I don't think my old woman would be too thrilled if I brought them round the house!'

He was beautiful, and she didn't care if he was using her. There was something about this man that made her feel like never before. She felt looser somehow, but she guessed rightly that was the wine and the brandy as well as Cain's company. If all she got was one night then that is how it had to be but, for the first time in her life, she was aware of herself, and the power she had over someone. Men had looked at her all her short life, and she had been wary. Knowing her mother's life would never be for her, she had fought to be respectable.

But tonight she didn't care about any of that. Tonight she wanted this man with a vengeance. He made her feel fantastic, and she could happily look at him for hours, admiring him. He was, quite simply, beautiful.

Standing up, she said softly, 'OK then.'

And, lifting her dress over her head, she stood before him in her cheap underwear from Romford Market and her plastic leather-look high heels. He had never wanted a woman more. She was stunning, a real one-off, and he felt as if all his birthdays and Christmases had come at once. Picking her up, he carried her happily to the big bed that was waiting for them so patiently.

Five minutes later he realised she was a virgin, and his whole world collapsed.

'Why didn't you fucking tell me you were a virgin?'

Jenny was so caught up in the moment she wasn't sure how to react. 'I assumed you knew.' Then the rot set in her head and she said angrily, 'Oh, I get it. You assumed I was like my mum, and your mum, if what you said is true. Well, sorry to disappoint you, but I've never been with anybody.' She felt so humiliated; she had given herself to him and he had shouted at her!

Cain was in a quandary. Jenny had moved the goal-posts and, as he looked down at her lovely face, he made a decision. Taking a deep breath, he said quietly, 'It's an honour, darling.'

As he kissed her, he wondered just what he was getting himself into. But, fuck it, he was a man and what man could resist this? And her a virgin to boot. It would take a much stronger person than him to walk away.

Chapter Seventeen

Cain was in a very good mood and, as he swung his four-year-old son into the air, he was well aware of just why he was feeling like this. He kept getting flashbacks to the night before. That Jenny, what a raver she had turned out to be! He couldn't believe his luck.

Oh, he loved Caroline, and he adored his lad, but there wasn't that excitement there with his wife. Caroline was a lot of things, but she wasn't pliable or dependent on him. That had been her attraction in the first place; she was very good-looking and she was hard as a rock, which is what you needed if you lived this lifestyle. If the house was raided she would take little Michael out of the way, and keep her trap shut, no matter what was said to her. She knew the score and she accepted it.

His Jenny, though, was a different person altogether. She was vulnerable and she was gentle and he knew she trusted in him completely. It was heady stuff to a man like him.

He wondered briefly if he was falling in love with

her. Over the last few weeks he had seen Jenny as often as he could, meeting her all over the Smoke. He had also given her money to buy new clothes although she had refused it. She could be a really indignant little mare when the fancy took her. He had even organised a job for her at one of his mate's offices so she could earn a few quid.

Johnny knew about her, but no one else. Johnny Mac could see the attraction, but he had also cautioned Cain; he knew the trouble women on the side could cause.

Especially with a wife like his Caroline. She was a wonderful mother, a brilliant housekeeper, and a blinding cook. Caroline was a beauty as well, but then that was a given – he wouldn't want her otherwise. She was good in that she accepted he had indiscretions – she was a realist – but a permanent fixture she would never tolerate. She was too powerful a personality for that, had too much pride and who could blame her? She had a mouth on her, and she could use it; half the fun of their marriage was the making up after a good set-to. Caroline gave as good as she got, and she didn't take any shit from him or anyone else.

Well, he wanted them both. What man wouldn't? They were like chalk and cheese, but each one held an attraction for him. But there was no denying Jenny Riley had got under his skin, and he couldn't envisage his life without her. The die was cast.

Chapter Eighteen

Once Jamie Jones decided on something he saw it through to the bitter end and, right now, he was a man on a mission.

This was his first foray into the world of clubs, and with it came the necessary introduction into the drugs trade. It was a lucrative business and it needed to be controlled properly on the premises. That meant bouncers who were alert to unauthorised dealers getting in on the game, and making sure the dealers you did use were only providing the drugs you provided for them. It was a fraught business, but very lucrative. He knew he would need a good team, and he was hand picking the men himself. With Cain Moran's OK, of course.

He liked Moran, and his funny sidekick Johnny Mac. Best friends since they were kids, they were more like brothers, even though Johnny Mac was black. His huge Afro made him look amiable but it was a mistake to underestimate him. He was wiry, but he was a strong little fucker and there was a hard streak that ran through him; anyone who didn't see that was a fool. For all his smiling and clowning around, his eyes were everywhere and he missed nothing.

There were rumours that he swung both ways – boys and girls. But that was just speculation, and not anyone's business except his. What he did in the comfort and safety of his own home was his affair. Still Jamie knew that in their circles that could be perceived as a weakness. Too feminine a trait for the men around him. Most of the people in their world were there because they were overtly masculine – it was what made them so feared. Personally he couldn't give a flying fuck what people did in their private lives; Christ knew, everyone had their secrets, him included.

Now that ponce Richie was off the scene they could settle down and start making some money. The first step was to persuade Micky Platt to take over the drug operations for him, leaving Jamie free to sort out every-thing else. The hardest job was going to be convincing people to part with their premises, or take them in as partners. Cain Moran was confident that everyone would see the sense in doing what he called the right thing, but Jamie wasn't so sure. Asking people to give them an in, or take their businesses outright, wasn't going to be easy, and it would need tact, diplomacy and, in extreme cases, a sawn-off shotgun.

But it could be done and, once it was over, Cain Moran would be the number one and that was ulti-mately what this was all about. Control the pavements, the clubs and the drugs, and you controlled your world. It was as simple as that.

Taking over from competitors wasn't unusual; it happened all the time from taxi ranks to burger stalls. It was about having the monopoly – if they had the main clubs under their guidance it would be like printing their own money. This new generation wasn't like their forebears. They wanted a night out, they wanted to spend money and they wanted the best DJs and the best bands. And, of course, the best recreational drugs.

On the plus side it meant no heroin or opiates would be in the mix. They were street drugs and not for the youngsters who were looking for a good time. They wanted amphetamines and grass, either green or on the block, Afghan Black, Lebanese gold. And, of course, LSD for the real ravers.

No, this was going to be a real cull. In one fell swoop they would be controlling everything in London and the surrounding areas. Southend alone was worth millions, that went without saying. It was a clubbers' paradise for the kids of Essex and they were nearest to the docks so always had the first refusal of the drugs brought in. They were used to the best and knew a rip-off when they saw it. Speed, especially, had been cut more times than a samurai soldier by the time it hit the London clubs.

Tonight they were having their first meet with Micky Platt, known as Micky Two Fags because he smoked like a chimney and only ever had two fags in his packet – whether by design no one was really sure. But it was a name that had stuck since his school days. Micky Platt didn't like Cain Moran; in fact, Micky Platt didn't like anyone. He was a hard, pig-headed individual, so this wasn't going to be an easy sell. But it was what it was. Only time would tell.

Chapter Nineteen

Micky Platt had never been so insulted in his life. How dare that cunt Cain Moran offer him an out from his own club? From his own premises? Outrageous was the only word for it.

'You must be on something, Cain, if you think I will just roll over and give you my fucking livelihood without a fucking fight.'

Cain had been expecting this reaction so he let the man vent his spleen.

'You come waltzing in here like you already own the place, telling me what I can and can't fucking do? Can you hear yourself?'

Cain looked at Jamie Jones and Johnny Mac: both men were tight-lipped and following his lead as he knew they would. Micky Two Fags was going to be the hardest nut to crack, but once he had capitulated all the others would follow. It was why they had approached him first.

'Listen to me, Micky. This is non-negotiable, mate. I'm not asking you to sell to me – I'm telling you. I will pay you the fair market price, for goodwill et cetera. Unfortunately for you, I need your premises, and that's the bottom line. Harsh, but I am just being honest. You *will* sell to me eventually. Because I'm determined, Micky.'

Micky Two Fags was almost apoplectic. 'Oh, no, I fucking won't! I don't care how many fucking thugs you bring with you. I saw the others getting out of the cars, your little show of force. Well, you don't fucking scare me, you lairy cunt.'

Cain stood up and, sighing heavily, he said calmly, 'Well, I should scare you, Micky, because I always get what I want. And I want this place.'

Johnny Mac and Jamie Jones stood up then too, and Micky Two Fags saw what he was up against. But he didn't care. This was his club and it would stay that way.

'Fuck you, Moran.'

Cain grinned nastily. 'Not even if you asked me extra nicely. Be seeing you, Micky.'

After the men left, Micky found that he was shaking – how much was in anger and how much was in fear he didn't know. What he *did* know was that losing his club was inevitable; it was just whether he would fold sooner rather than later. Picking up his Benson & Hedges, he opened the packet and it was empty. Screwing the box up in his hand he threw it across his office, cursing Cain Moran into the ground as he did so.

Chapter Twenty

Cain snuck into his house at twenty-five past three in the morning. As he tiptoed through the giant hallway he got the fright of his life to see his wife sitting on the large staircase waiting for him.

'You're home, then?'

Cain knew that tone of voice and his heart sank. Caroline was up for a fight, and one of her fights could go on till the next day. If only he could delay the row until after he had had a few hours' kip. If she was pissed, then fireworks were guaranteed even over something trivial, but he had been out of the house for thirty-six hours. Even though he had not exactly expected a brass band welcoming him home, he had anticipated her being tucked up in bed.

Holding his hands up as if she was pointing a gun at him, he said reasonably, 'Calm down, Caroline.'

She started to laugh hysterically. 'Calm down you say? Aren't you Mr Reasonable And Kind?'

Then the expensive crystal wineglass she'd been nursing whizzed by his head and she was off the stairs and launching herself at him, all the time screaming expletives and attempting to claw his eyes out.

'Who is she? Who is it can keep you out this fucking long?' She was enormously strong, so great was her anger. 'I will fucking kill you and then her. So come on, clever bollocks, tip it up. Who is she?'

Cain grabbed her hands and pulled her into his arms, enveloping her in a great bear hug, using all his considerable strength to try to keep her still, despite her kicking and struggling. Eventually, after about five minutes, she started to calm down.

He had not said a word to her, knowing his voice would be like a red rag to a bull at this precise moment in time. He could feel her heart beating fast, and he was genuinely sorry for causing her so much distress. She was sobbing against his chest now and he hugged her to him, kissing her hair and neck. She always smelled so nice, did Caroline. Her thick hair was loose and he enjoyed the feel of it on his face.

She didn't deserve the grief he was giving her, but he couldn't help himself. God forgive him, even now he wished he was holding his Jenny in his arms and, as disloyal as that was, he had to acknowledge the truth of it.

'Where have you been, Cain?'

Judging it safe to release his hold on her, he looked down at her face and said as honestly as he could, 'I've been working, Caroline. I've got a delicate deal going . . .'

Before he could finish his sentence she had kneed him in the groin with all her might. As he bent forward in agony she spat in his face.

'I will get to the bottom of it, Cain, and if you have a bird *bird*, you will regret it to your dying day.' With that she turned and went up the stairs to her bed.

Left in the darkness of the hallway, Cain knew that he had to cool it with Jenny – at least for the time being.

Chapter Twenty-One

The following day, Johnny Mac thought the story was the funniest thing he had ever heard.

'It ain't that funny, Johnny, she nearly removed them from the sac. Fucking painful, I can tell you.'

'Well, Cain, you knew she was a spirited girl. That's why you had that great big expensive wedding, remember?'

Though Johnny Mac was laughing as he spoke, there was a note of censure in his voice and Cain asked him outright, 'Do you think I'm being a mug, Johnny?'

Johnny thought for a few moments before he answered his friend. 'Truth be told, Cain, I like Jenny. She's a lovely young girl – emphasis on the young – but you have a wife and a little boy. You know and I know that once Caroline gets the bit between her teeth she will move heaven and earth to find out the truth. All I am saying is, are you willing to take the flak? More to the point, is Jenny worth the trouble she is going to cause? It's your funeral, mate. But think on this. You've got a lovely home, a lovely wife and a great little kid. That will all be up the Swanee if Caroline ever finds out the truth.'

Cain knew his friend was speaking sense. He needed to cool it with Jenny for the sake of marital harmony – and his nuts. But it was proving harder than he had thought it would be. The more he saw of Jenny the more he cared about her. When he was with her nothing else really mattered.

Johnny Mac watched the conflicting emotion crossing his friend's face and felt a second's sorrow for him. He was a man in love all right – the most dangerous emotion in the world.

Chapter Twenty-Two

Cain Moran had put the hard word on Eileen and, as much as she would have liked to brag about her daughter's boyfriend, she knew it was a no-no. Cain would launch her into outer space, and in a way she understood that; after all, he was a married man. But it was hard not to have even a little show-off.

Cain was shrewd enough to compensate her for her silence with good hard cash. Money spoke louder than words in Eileen Riley's life. Now, as she looked at her daughter all upset and flustered, she said gently, 'Look, love, you have to see it from his point of view. He's a married man, and that wife of his is hard as nails, by all accounts. All he is saying is, let the dust settle for a bit.'

Jenny nodded. 'I know, Mum, but it's been a while now and I really do care about him.'

Eileen rolled her eyes in annoyance. Young love! If she knew anything about it, it wasn't love that was keeping Cain Moran in the picture, it was her daughter's obvious attractions. Not that she would say that to her Jenny, of course; she was still living in cloud cuckoo land, where the fairies sang sweetly and men left their wives and children for young girls.

'If you really care you will do as he asks, love. You have your whole life in front of you.'

Jenny made herself a coffee and took it to her bedroom. She sat in front of her makeshift dressing table and looked at her reflection in the old mirror. She missed Cain with a vengeance; she physically ached with sorrow at not seeing him. Every day she got up and went to work in that stupid office that didn't really need a secretary, then she came home, ate her tea and waited by the phone all night in case he called. It wasn't a life, it was just an existence.

But if this is what it took to have a few hours with Cain, then she knew she would accept that. She would be seventeen in one week. She hoped she would see him on her birthday. That was all she wanted – just to see him, even if only for an hour. As wrong as it was to want him – a married man with a little boy – she couldn't help herself. Young Jenny had discovered not only love, but also the powerful emotion of lust. She yearned for Cain Moran with her entire being.

Chapter Twenty-Three

Micky Two Fags was not about to give in to the inevitable without a fight. His club in Southend was his pride and joy, and there was no way he was giving it up without at least a show of defiance. He had bought the premises in 1974. It had been a rundown shithole, but after nearly six years of hard graft it was finally a success.

He had thought long and hard about what options were open to him and he had come up with only one: he had to enlist other club owners before the same thing happened to them. His was the biggest in terms of money and prestige, so he needed to see to the next one on the list and that was owned by a man called Jimmy Banks, otherwise known as Jimmy Boy.

Jimmy was a headcase and that was exactly what was needed to go up against someone like Cain Moran. Word on the street was that Jimmy Boy Banks had taken out an Iranian drug dealer single-handedly. Jimmy Boy dealt in skag which was now a very lucrative business for clubs. You couldn't move nowadays for stoners. It was pathetic – Micky blamed the punk rock movements and hippie parents. He wouldn't tolerate it on his premises – it was too dangerous. The last thing anyone needed was a dead kid in the toilets on a busy Saturday night. No, that business was for the pubs, the shittier pubs anyway. It was a mug's game as far as he was concerned – for the dealers *and* the junkies. He did a great business with the softer recreational drugs, and now that cunt Cain Moran wanted to just walk in and take it from him. Fucking scandalous, that's what it was, and he would fight him as best he could.

The trouble was, Cain Moran was a man to be reckoned with; nothing moved in the South East without his express say-so. He had Filth, judges and local politicians on his payroll, so he had plenty of clout. No one could take that away from him and he was to be applauded for his acumen. But this . . . this was a step too fucking far, and Micky instinctively knew he wouldn't be the only one thinking along those lines. This was an out-and-out piss-take.

As Jimmy Boy Banks walked into his office Micky Platt felt that in his darkest moment there was still a glimmer of hope.

Chapter Twenty-Four

'Listen to me, Cain Moran, I am your fucking *wife*. Remember the vows we made in front of the priest? Well, I took them seriously even if you didn't, you filthy rotten slag.'

Cain rolled his eyes at the ceiling. 'Always with the drama, aren't you, Caroline? Can't have a row, it's got to be a knock-down, all-out fight. Then you wonder why I play away. It's nice sometimes not to have to watch every fucking word that comes out of my mouth.'

Caroline laughed sarcastically. 'Oh, really? Well, fucking *fuck you*. I'm amazed they can even hold a conversation. From what I've heard they are just on the left side of duelling banjos. Walk them about on leads, do you, your fucking dogs?'

Cain Moran really wanted to slap his wife across the mouth, but he wouldn't. Didn't stop him feeling like it, though.

Caroline was near to tears now. 'I swallow a lot with you, and you know I do. But if you have a regular bird I will not tolerate it, do you hear me? I will *not* allow you to humiliate me like that. I still have some fucking pride. I'll never forget what you put me through when I'd just had little Michael. Some bleached-blonde trollop had the gall – the fucking gall – to knock on my front door shouting the odds. In front of my mother and all!'

Cain knew he was fucked to argue with that; he had definitely been in the wrong with that one. She had seemed so quiet. Who fucking knew, eh? Lovely looking girl, though, no doubt about that.

'Here we go, bringing up ancient history as usual. I said I was sorry, for fuck's sake.'

Caroline really lost her rag now as she screamed, 'Ancient history? We have only been married five years, Cain.' She was sobbing and he went to her, holding her tightly to him.

'Look, Caroline, I admit I'm a fucking nightmare, but I don't mean the half of it. You know what I'm like. If it's on a plate. . . I'm only human, darling.'

She looked into his handsome face. She loved this man as if her life depended on it and, in a way, it did. She was completely helpless without him in many respects. She had lived through the humiliation of lipstick marks on his dick of all places and the smell of another woman's perfume on him. She had been prepared to swallow that for the main prize: he was her husband and those girls had never truly meant anything to him. They were no competition because he always came home to her and Michael. She had had to resign herself to the fact her husband couldn't be faithful if his life depended on it.

Cain was like a big kid, always wanting the new toy. But this time it felt different – *he* was different. Whoever this bitch was, she was a threat. Caroline's world was crumbling and she didn't know how to make it right again. She pushed him away from her and walked into the kitchen.

She had never refused him sex, had never questioned him in any way until now. And for what? To be treated like nothing, like a nobody by the man she loved more than her own life. He genuinely couldn't see how much she was hurting, and that was the hardest thing to accept.

She was shaking with anger and upset, but the fact that he didn't follow her into the kitchen spoke volumes.

Chapter Twenty-Five

'Honestly, Jimmy, you'll be next. He wants all the big clubs in the South East under the Cain Moran banner. Fucking outrageous. If he gets what he wants we are fucked. He will control everything.'

Jimmy Boy Banks was not a big man, but what he lacked in size he made up for in plain and simple lunacy. At fifteen he had been put away for manslaughter when everyone, including the Old Bill, had known it was murder. The man he had stabbed fifty-four times had been a local Face who had taken up with Jimmy Boy's mum. Jimmy's mum had been a beauty in her day and she had always attracted men who were not exactly the whole ticket. She thrived on violence and rough sex and she had found it with a man called Reg Pointer. Reg had tortured her son for six months before he had retaliated. It was six months longer than anyone else would ever be given.

Jimmy had done his time in Borstal and come out hating the world. He had carved himself a good reputation and a good living and there was no way that

Cain Moran was going to walk in and take it from him – not without a fight.

Micky Two Fags had gone to the right man, there was no mistaking that. Jimmy Banks had been so up in arms he even frightened the man who had come to him for help – and that wasn't an easy thing to do.

Jimmy Boy looked at Micky and said dangerously, 'I'll sort this if it's the last thing I do.'

Chapter Twenty-Six

The first thing that Jimmy Banks did was call a council of war. He knew he was going to need all the help he could get if he was going to bring Cain Moran down.

There were five men at the meeting in Jimmy's offices in Barking. Jimmy was there, as was Micky Two Fags, also Richie Jakobs and a huge black guy called Elvis Munro. To complete the line-up was a small dapper man of indeterminate age who went by the name of Denny Gunn. No one knew if that was his real surname or if he'd acquired it because he'd provided guns to whoever wanted them since the 1940s. No one cared any more; he was a quiet man but he could come by anything in the line of firearms or explosives. Also rumoured to be in with the IRA, his reputation was guaranteed.

Everyone except Richie owned lucrative nightclubs and all of them were determined to hang on to their property. Richie was there because he had kicked the whole thing off and now he needed to extricate himself from his skulduggery by helping the men involved understand exactly what Cain Moran was after and why.

Richie knew he needed these brownie points badly; he had, after all, been the brains behind the whole thing. Consequently the men were wary of him. As was their right – even he had to concede that much. In effect, he had been the catalyst for this – him and his miraculous brain.

Now he was at panic stations in case they turned on him like Cain Moran had. It still rankled that he had made him such a wonderful proposition and Cain had taken it, then fucked him over like he was nothing, promising him a good drink for his efforts.

'So you think we're going to be able to talk him out of it? We all know Cain Moran is like a dog with a bone when he decides he wants something.' Elvis Munro liked Cain Moran, and he was sensible enough to know that if Cain Moran was determined in this endeavour that nothing – short of death – was going to prevent him achieving it.

The men in the room nodded at Elvis's wise words. Elvis was an anomaly in their world. Everyone treated him as an equal, and that was unusual as most races kept as far apart as possible within their own particular haunts in London. Brixton and Tulse Hill were where the Jamaicans hung out and dealt their particular trades.

Elvis had crossed the barrier because he was such an astute individual, and he always made sure he kept on the good side of everyone he dealt with. Coupled with the fact that there was not a man in London who could take him in a fight – and he was known to bear a grudge – he had carved out a very lucrative and respected career for himself. He had the one thing all good villains needed – the likeability factor. It was a requisite that few people cultivated. You couldn't dislike Elvis and he would have been mortified if he thought you didn't like him. He prided himself on being a nice bloke and the voice of reason, unless you upset him, of course, and then his good intentions went out the window, resulting in all-out war.

He liked Cain Moran because he was a good bloke but also because his best friend, Johnny Mac, was another Jamaican. It was a very unusual combination and yet it worked for them. Probably because of their shared upbringings with brasses for mothers. Birds of a feather, as the old saying went.

Elvis was the one person here who was not only needed, but also the Achilles heel. Jimmy Banks had known that, but he had taken a chance on appealing to Elvis's better nature, otherwise known as his earning capacity.

Micky Two Fags was almost beside himself with excitement; he had been right to go to Jimmy Banks. Jimmy had the creds that he himself lacked in as much as Jimmy could keep a lid on his temper if needs be, whereas Micky was a loose cannon. Plus, Jimmy Boy had the gift of the gab and that was essential in these types of fraught situations.

Micky said seriously, 'Look, Elvis, we all know Cain is a fucking charmer, but he is after our livelihood, for fuck's sake. Everything we built up and strived for he wants on a fucking plate. That's fucking abominable! Who does that cunt think he is?'

There was a murmur of general agreement, but no one was saying anything outright. Jimmy knew the score; no one here would utter a word until he had outlined his plans. He didn't knock them – he would have done exactly the same thing in their position. What he needed to do was bring them around to his way of thinking. That would take something Jimmy Banks was in short supply of: tact. As long as he didn't lose his temper he was in with a chance.

Denny Gunn piped up, 'From what I can gather he's willing to take over the clubs or accept fifty per cent ownership. We still own a stake and our money goes up – he cuts us in on everything he's doing. It seems like a win-win to me. We get the poke and he gets the aggravation. There's nothing to say we can't open up somewhere else. The way I see it he's after the established clubs. He's a fucking earner for sure – no one can take that away from him. Midas touch, if what you hear about him is true.'

Jimmy Banks was having trouble keeping a lid on his anger, but he swallowed it down knowing he had to be seen in a reasonable light.

'OK then, so what happens when you take his dosh and you reopen and make another fuck-off club? You really think he won't want that too? It's long term we need to be looking at. If we capitulate now he will own everything of significance in the South East, from the cabs to the bookies to the clubs. What will be next? He will control the drugs . . .' he paused dramatically before adding, 'He will basically own our world.'

Everyone digested what Jimmy was saying but none of them was willing to show their hand first. Such was the nature of this particular game. It was a very delicate situation. The wrong word either way could literally be the death of you, and that was a chance none of them was willing to take.

Elvis was the first to respond. 'So what do you think is the solution then?'

Jimmy grinned, an unusual occurrence at any time. 'What do I think, Elvis? I think we should drop the cunt. End of.'

Richie Jakobs heard the combined intakes of breath and felt the urge to laugh. His nerves were almost jangling; he had more to lose than any of them because Cain Moran would know he had given them the tip-off.

Micky Two Fags could not contain his excitement any longer. 'That's the most sensible solution. I mean, think about it. He has an army at his disposal – no one has ever had more men on their payroll than that flash cunt. He's like Hitler; he needs to be cut down now before it's too late. Coupled with the fact he is in on this with Jamie Jones . . .'

Jimmy Boy closed his eyes in distress. He had expressly told Micky to leave Jamie's name out of it. No one quite knew what Jamie Jones was capable of.

He was tighter than a nun's snatch, and he wouldn't phone the fire brigade if his house blew up. Now Micky had dropped his name out there, that had put a completely different complexion on things. This was three murders they were talking about now; of three very powerful individuals.

Micky Two Fags missed the signs of trepidation from his partner; he didn't understand the word subtle and Jimmy Boy realised that he never would. He was a moron.

Instead Micky said triumphantly, 'Three down, none to go! Think about it!'

All of them stared at Micky Two Fags like he had just grown another head in front of their eyes. Elvis was looking on in abject disbelief. Cain Moran and Adolf Hitler were bad enough, for fuck's sake. Now it was turning into a bloodbath, and that was the last thing any of them wanted. Jamie Jones was true Irish; there was talk that, like Denny Gunn, he had an in with the terrorists. It had been rumoured he negotiated deals for the Irish workforce in London – rumours that were unfounded but made sense. He was a loner, but he was also a dangerous man in his own right. Everyone with an ounce of sense knew that.

But apparently that was everyone except this thick fuck sitting in front of him beaming like a five year old. Denny Gunn caught Elvis's eye and shook his head in amazement. It was enough for Elvis – his mind was made up.

Chapter Twenty-Seven

Jenny lay in the big bed with Cain and smiled happily. He was resting on his elbow looking down at her naked body, and she could feel the power that she had over him. It was unusual for her to be this free with him after they had sex – normally she was shy. But tonight, with the help of a few drinks, she felt different. She realised she could reduce this beautiful man to a quivering wreck and she suddenly understood the power of sex – and love. Because he did love her. She could sense it enveloping her – feel it in his touch, in his gentleness. If someone had told her she was capable of such volcanic emotions she would have laughed at them. But that was before she had realised what life and love was about. Even a few stolen hours like this were worth more to her than a lifetime with someone else, someone who was free. When she wasn't with Cain she thought about him constantly. He was like a drug.

The phone on the bedside table rang and he picked it up with a sigh, fondling her as he answered, and she closed her eyes, enjoying the feel of his touch, savouring the last few moments before they had to go their separate ways.

Suddenly he sat bolt upright, his erection deflating in nanoseconds as he screamed, 'Are you fucking joking, Johnny?'

Seconds later, he slammed the phone down, saying curtly, 'Get dressed, darling, I've got to go.'

Then he was out of bed, dressing himself, swearing and making threats under his breath all the while. Turning back to her and slapping her thigh none too gently, he shouted, 'Come on, get your arse in gear! I ain't got all fucking night.'

Sighing, Jenny did as he asked.

Dropping her off at her house, he grabbed her face in his hands and kissed her deeply, before saying seriously, 'I am sorry, Jen. I know it doesn't seem like it, but I do love you, darling.'

She smiled softly and got out of the car. She was pleased to see that despite his hurry he watched her till she went to her front door; he was a gentleman like that.

Chapter Twenty-Eight

Caroline Moran was somewhat placated by her husband's re-found commitment. He was like a new man. Her fears were groundless – she understood that now – and she felt that even though it had been a tough few months she had made him realise what was really important. She wasn't a fool – she was a realist, and she knew that men like her husband had it laid on a plate for them on a daily basis. It was par for the course really, and she was willing to overlook the odd indiscretion. But she would never countenance a fucking regular bird. She had her pride even if he didn't.

But, in all fairness, he was making the effort and, knowing him like she did, that was hard. Cain was a man who had always lived by his own rules – she had known that from day one – and that made it more of a triumph. She loved her life, loved her house, the cars, the constant stream of money but, more than anything, she loved being Mrs Cain Moran and the kudos that gave her. Caroline was not going to let that go without a fight.

The phone rang and she walked across her huge kitchen to answer it.

Ten seconds later she was like a woman demented, her screams bringing not only her little son to her side, but also her mother-in-law, who was staying for a few days to admire the new house.

Chapter Twenty-Nine

Elvis Munro was a lot of things, but a fool wasn't one of them. He had thought long and hard about the meeting and had come to the decision that only an out-and-out fucking nut-job would try and take down Cain Moran. He basically had an army on his payroll, and he inspired a loyalty that was unusual in their game. He recruited youngsters who would do anything for him because he was such a role model to them. It was an honour to be a part of his crew.

Cain Moran understood respect and the enormous advantage it could give him. He had grown up just like these young men and he knew how, more often than not, it was all they had and everything they strived for. Growing up in neighbourhoods where money was tight and schools were barely adequate, where brute strength guaranteed you a place in your society, respect was a completely different animal in this world. For most of these young men there were two choices: the armed forces or a life of villainy. The only other possibility was low-paid work and that just wasn't good enough. They wanted the clothes, the cars and the money – good money, *serious* money. They wanted to be seen as people of importance and that was what Cain Moran offered them. If you worked for him, you were not only guaranteed a fucking good wedge, you were also guaranteed the respect that came with it.

Cain Moran had seen the potential in an army of young people with no jobs, no prospects and limited education, but who were naturally cunning and after the Good Life. It was the seventies and there were no jobs, there was no hope and no one cared. Cain Moran gave them money, prestige and his loyalty and they gave themselves back one hundredfold; they basically worshipped him. Cain Moran had provided them with hope, and that was something these lads had never dreamed possible.

Plus, Cain Moran had guaranteed peace; there were no more shootings in public or over-the-top bank jobs. He made sure everything ran smoothly and, for that, the Filth were overjoyed. It was a shame the newspapers didn't realise that the black economy was always going to be there and it was better for everyone if it was overseen by a man of Cain Moran's calibre. Until Cain's emergence into the upper echelons of their world, it had been like the Wild West – only in London there weren't any fucking sheriffs with the balls to sort it out. Shootings had been rife, knife fights, extortionate loan sharking – you name it and Cain Moran had modified it and made it almost respectable. People listened to him, and his ideas had made for a better working environment for all concerned.

Now that he had been challenged, Elvis knew that all Cain's hard work to garner his reputation had been worth it. Even combined, there weren't enough men to take him on and win. If they killed him they would have to kill Johnny too, and that again would be no easy feat. Drop Jamie Jones in this mix and you had a recipe for disaster. Well, Elvis knew whose side he would be coming down on and it wasn't that two-faced, treacherous fucker Jimmy Boy Banks's. He was like Micky Two Fags, a fucking parasite that used everyone around him; if he ever got to prominence there would be murders – literally. If he took out Cain Moran and Johnny Mac, he would crow about it from the rooftops.

One thing had amazed Elvis, though. Sitting through that meeting it occurred to him as he listened that not one of the men there was willing to work out the problem on his own – and that alone told Elvis all he needed to know.

Chapter Thirty

Jane Harding, Caroline's mother, lost control of her car on the A13 just outside Basildon. Cut from the car by a fire crew, she died at the scene.

If Caroline Moran loved anyone it was her mother – she was everything to her. More like a sister and the voice of reason in her daughter's chaotic life. She was the only person who could tell her what to do, and she made sure her daughter listened to her.

Jane Harding knew that Cain Moran was the best thing that had ever happened to her Caroline. She also recognised that without a firm hand Caroline would push and push and push until her husband walked away from her.

Jane loved her daughter, but Caroline could be a serious pain in the arse. She loved drama, especially when she was at the centre of it. Jane used to joke that her daughter was the star of her own life story, and it was true. Even as a child Caroline had been subject to tantrums, fits of pique and had displayed almost murderous rages. When she lost it, she really went for it. Caroline created scenarios and she acted them out. She had grown into an argumentative woman, with a very elevated opinion of herself. Jane knew that if she wasn't curtailed, Cain would eventually walk because he wasn't a man who enjoyed the aggravation of having a wife who needed continual reassurance and validation.

Now Jane was lying dead and her daughter had lost not only the real constant in her life, but also the only person who could actually keep her under control. Caroline Moran had suffered the worst blow of all. And she was not handling it well.

Chapter Thirty-One

'Well, Elvis, we did see this coming – we thought it would just have been Micky Two Fags who tried his hand. I admire Jimmy, though, for going to the main players. It displays a cunning I didn't think he possessed.'

Elvis shrugged at Cain's words. 'He's a cunt. Micky's bad enough, but Jimmy Boy? He is like a leech, you know? Sucks the life out of everyone around him.'

Cain and Johnny nodded in understanding.

'So we're all getting shot, are we?' Johnny Mac's voice was full of humour at the thought and Cain laughed with him.

Elvis was nervous but it didn't show. He had come to them to prevent a bloodbath, but it wasn't just because he liked these men. Elvis was interested in keeping the peace and keeping hold of what he had. He had an ulterior motive though – one he felt Cain Moran and Johnny Mac would understand. He was already willing to give up fifty per cent of his club – why wouldn't he? He would get his money back and more besides. He was also the supplier of most of the puff in the South East so, in many ways, it would benefit him in the long run.

'It seems we need to take out Jimmy Boy and those ponces Richie and Micky. On the upside, I don't think Lily Law will be investigating their disappearance, which is exactly what must happen, I think. They need to disappear. The others concerned aren't cunts. They realise the significance – and they won't be offered the fifty per cent ownership after this little display of temper, that's for sure. I'll take the clubs off them *and* teach them a valuable lesson in life: never bite the hand that feeds you.'

Johnny nodded his agreement. 'I have just the place for them, Cain. I know a geezer who has a business providing industrial acid. He's into us at the bookies for a good wedge. What better way to get rid of them permanently?'

'Sounds perfect, my old mate. That's that sorted then. I'll get a few lads to pick them up and you arrange the rest.' Cain looked at Elvis and smiled. 'Don't worry, you did the right thing. I can't see this as grassing on your mates – none of those ponces are anyone's mates. Except I always liked Denny Gunn. I'm glad he agreed with you on the best step to take. He is a hard old fucker. But Jimmy was always his own worst enemy.'

The phone on his desk rang and he picked it up quickly. 'All right, all right, calm down, Caroline. I am on my way now . . . For fuck's sake, darling, I swear I am on my way . . .' Cain stopped and looked at

Johnny. His face had lost all its colour, and Johnny was immediately on red alert.

'What's up, Cain?'

Cain shook his head in amazement as he said seriously, 'It's Jane, Caroline's mum. She's dead. Totalled her motor on the A13.'

All three men were silent for a few seconds before Johnny Mac jumped up and said, 'Come on, mate. I'll drive you home.'

Cain waved him away saying quietly, 'No. You set the other stuff in motion. The sooner those three go on the missing list the better. I'll call you later, all right? I want to see those fuckers grovel, and watch them as they die. It's the cheekiness I can't fucking abide, the sheer gall of it.'

Listening to Cain Moran, Elvis Munro felt the relief of a man who had just dodged a bullet. Which – if they were all being honest – is exactly what he had done.

Chapter Thirty-Two

Caroline Moran was heartbroken, and even Cain had to admit that this display wasn't her usual posturing – she was genuinely grieving. His own mum Molly was doing the best she could, but the relationship between his mother and wife had never been that strong. Molly was happy enough taking care of little Michael though, and that was a big help.

Caroline had never looked after that child for a full day on her own since he was born – it was like Jane lived with them. But that had suited Cain because it gave Caroline company when he wasn't there. As he took his wife in his arms he wondered what the future would hold for them now. Even at this moment, with her grief so raw and her needing him more than ever before, he was comparing her to his Jenny. It was wrong, but he couldn't help it.

Jenny had got under his skin like no one else and that was dangerous even as it was reassuring; she was a very calm person and, after the frenetic way of living with Caroline, it was nice to feel so unfettered. With

Caroline it was all about *her*, what *she* needed, what *she* wanted. Jenny, on the other hand, wanted nothing from him except his company. He could feel her love for him and it was like a balm – so uncomplicated and easy.

As if she could sense his thoughts, Caroline pulled herself from her husband's arms and, stomping into their en-suite bathroom, she slammed the door so hard it was a wonder it didn't come off the hinges. Cain sighed heavily. This was going to be difficult, but he had known that from the off. She would milk this for all it was worth.

Chapter Thirty-Three

Molly Moran had put her little grandson to bed and was adding the finishing touches to a stew she had made for the next day. It was very late and, much as her heart went out to her daughter-in-law, she was honest enough to admit she found it very hard to like the girl. Caroline looked down on her and that was evident.

Now her mother Jane had been a different type altogether. How she had raised that obstreperous mare was anyone's guess, but in fairness to the dead woman, she had done her best. God made the back to bear the burden, as her own mother used to say, and there was a certain truth to it. Although you would need a broad back to put up with that mare up the stairs! She blessed herself at her unchristian thoughts at such a time, but her daughter-in-law would try the patience of Saint Job himself. Even her mother's death was all about *her* and not the poor woman scrambled to death in her car, dying on the roadside like a hedgehog. Not that she would say any of this, of course – she didn't want to cause complete Armageddon in the household.

Molly heard her son coming down the stairs and poured him a generous glass of whisky – he would need it. She topped up her own glass and, seeing him enter the kitchen, she smiled at him happily. Cain hugged her as she sat in her chair. He loved the smell of her – a combination of Avon perfume, fags and her own particular sweet aroma that always took him back to his childhood. He sat opposite her and raised his glass in a silent toast.

'How is she?'

He shrugged. 'The usual.'

Molly sighed. 'It's a hard time for her, son, to be fair she's just lost her mother . . .'

He nodded his agreement. 'I know, Mum. How's the little man?'

Molly perked up at the mention of her grandson. 'Oh, he's all right, son. A gorgeous little fella, and clever as a bag of monkeys. Reminds me of you when you were a boy.'

Cain smiled his thanks, and swallowed his drink in one mouthful. She immediately poured him another.

'I'm sorry, Mum, for the way she treats you.'

Molly flapped a perfectly manicured hand at him. 'Oh, you don't need to apologise, son, she's a funny fecker and no mistake. I don't know what you saw in her,' she said bitterly, 'but she does love you, you know.'

He sighed once more. 'To be honest, Mum, that's the trouble.' He closed his eyes in distress. 'That girl

I told you about? For the first time ever I can't fuck and run. I have never felt like this before, not even about her upstairs.'

Molly leaned across the expensive glass-topped table and grabbed her son's hand in hers. 'Don't make any decision yet, son. Some things need to be thought through long and hard.'

He had told her about this Jenny, but she saw now it was more than a passing fancy. This would cause untold ructions if it was to come out – especially with everything going on. It grieved her that he had inherited her own capacity for loving too much. If truth be told, that was her only real mistake in this life – loving people too much. And the wrong people. Always the wrong people.

Chapter Thirty-Four

Jenny knew that Cain's wife needed him and she was happy enough to take a back seat for now. What had thrown her was this visit now from his mother. She let her into the flat, pleased that it was clean and tidy and her own mother wasn't in. Thank God for small mercies.

Cain made sure her mum had a regular income nowadays and that had lightened Jenny's burden considerably. It meant that there wasn't the continual shortage of money that caused Eileen to become so erratic, and it also meant there was less chance of strange men being there in the mornings. He had promised Jenny a flat of her own too, but she would wait and see if that materialised.

What he didn't seem to realise was that she didn't want anything from him – she never had. She was happy just being with him – that was more than enough for her. She felt at times, though, that it wasn't enough for him, that he was the one who wanted more.

Now here was his mum on her doorstep and she wasn't sure how she was supposed to react. She brought

Molly through to the lounge and offered her a seat. Jenny had never been so nervous in her life; when Molly had introduced herself on the doorstep she had almost fainted with fright. Cain's mother was here, asking if she could talk to her.

Molly looked at the beautiful girl before her and wasn't surprised that her son was infatuated with Jenny. Not only did she have a very calming way about her that was attractive in itself, she was utterly exquisite – that was the only word – and those eyes would make any man fall off the wagon, so to speak.

Molly sat down on the battered old sofa, and smiled at Jenny's palpable anxiety. 'Sit down, child. If I was here for a row it would have been well on by now.' She smiled to take the edge off her words and saw the girl physically relax.

Jenny decided she liked Cain's mother even if she had come to read her the riot act. She would just accept whatever the woman had to say – what else could she do?

'Would you like a cup of tea or something?'

Molly nodded happily. 'That would be grand.'

She followed Jenny into the little kitchen and watched the girl carefully as she prepared a tray for their tea. She almost felt the urge to cry at the sight of this child – because that is all she was – trying to make things look nice. A tea tray in a house like this! It showed her mettle if nothing else. This was a girl who wanted more out of life. Molly knew about the mother, but who was she to judge? After all, she hadn't been much better in her heyday.

The quiet wasn't menacing like it was with Caroline. Jesus, she could be in the house an hour before an offer of a drink came her way. Caroline loved everything about her husband except her – his mother. Caroline tolerated her – that was the best word she could use for her daughter-in-law's treatment of her. If it wasn't for Cain bringing that poor child round to see her she would never lay eyes on him. That would suit Caroline; the ex-prozzy granny was best right out of the picture. But she would learn you have to get on with your life as best you could, especially now she had lost her mother. Jane Harding had been a lovely woman, and where she got that awkward bastard from was anyone's guess.

Jenny placed the tea tray on the table, and suddenly Molly felt a great tenderness for her.

'Do you take sugar?'

She was gentle, elegant even. Jenny was in the wrong life – if she had been born into money there was nothing she couldn't have achieved, Molly thought.

Settled with the tea, Molly sipped hers and said sadly, 'Caroline's mother died last night. Car crash, God rest her immortal soul.' She crossed herself instinctively.

'That's awful. I am so sorry to hear that.'

'Well, I'm here to tell you that your man, Cain, will need to be there for her. Do you understand what I'm saying?'

Jenny nodded almost imperceptibly. 'Of course I do. I hope she is OK. It must be terrible to lose your mum like that.'

Molly agreed. 'Died on the hard shoulder, she never stood a chance. But, you see, Caroline isn't taking it well – that's understandable – but she has a very temperamental nature, if you get my drift.'

Jenny smiled diplomatically; everyone knew about Caroline Moran's temper and her snobbery. She didn't come from much – certainly no better than anyone else – but she acted like she had been born into the nobility.

For all her faults, Caroline was still her son's wife, and that meant Molly had to do right by her, even if the woman was like a thorn in her side. She had been Cain's choice and now he had to live with that – and, unfortunately, so did she.

'Did he send you round here?' There was desolation in the girl's voice.

Molly shook her head. 'He told me about you, Jenny. I came to try and make you understand that you need to let them be for a while. Caroline has had a terrible shock to her system, and she will need to be handled carefully. She's grieving.'

Jenny swallowed down her disappointment. 'Of course. I understand. How is Cain?'

Molly smiled at the question. It changed her whole face, and Jenny caught a glimpse of the woman's past beauty.

'Well, he's got his hands full with everything that's going on, and little Michael is only four so he doesn't understand his nana's gone. He saw her every day of his life. That's what will be so hard for Caroline, you see. Jane was not just her mother, she was her only real friend. They were very close.'

Jenny sipped her tea daintily, unable to believe that Cain's mother was sitting opposite her and chatting as if this was normal.

'I hope everything goes OK for her.'

Molly smiled and grabbed the girl's slim hand in her own. 'He does care about you, Jenny. Too much, if truth be told. But give them this time, child. He has enough on his plate as it is.' Then smiling to take the edge off her words, she said brightly, 'I don't live far away, you can come and visit with me. How would you like that?'

Jenny smiled a wide heartfelt smile. 'I'd love that, Mrs Moran.'

Molly gave a loud hearty laugh. 'Jasus, child, I was never married in my life! Molly will do fine.'

Chapter Thirty-Five

Caroline had finally been sedated, and Cain had left her with her aunt. Dolly Harding had never married – and not for want of trying. She had the face of angel and the mouth of a docker. Like her niece, she was of a temperamental nature and could have a fight in an empty house. She had a heart of gold though, and she was devastated by her sister's death. She loved Caroline like she was her own child, and she adored little Michael.

As much as he knew his wife needed him, Cain had other fish to fry. Business needed to be attended to and he was determined to see that it was sorted out sooner rather than later.

It didn't stop the feelings of guilt though. He could still hear her now: *'Don't leave me, Cain. This house is too big to be alone in.'* He had nearly told her she shouldn't have bought the fucking thing then, but he didn't. He had given her sleeping pills and left promising that he would return as soon as. Strangely enough, she had believed him. She knew that even he wouldn't be that callous – not at a time like this.

Trouble was, she irritated him now. Being in her company was a chore for him, and he resented her. It was like everything she did drove him up the wall. He knew that was unfair, because she had done no wrong. But his mind was full of young Jenny, and he couldn't help himself when it came to her. She was like a mania with him and he couldn't understand why. He had never felt like this before about a woman, and it was an alien, uncomfortable experience. He had always put his life into boxes; Caroline, God love her, had been one of those boxes.

When they were first together he had relished the big explosive fights – and the even more explosive making up. Now it just depressed him. She was high maintenance and her jealousy, which had previously been a reminder of her love for him, now just got him down. They had built a good life for themselves, but he had always been aware that it was his capability to give her that good life which was his real attraction for her. Their marriage was the complete opposite to the life she had come from, and she strived to get more and more possessions, believing all the hype that you needed the latest fridge freezer to be happy, or the newest style of shoes. She loved him in her own way, but her love was like being in a war zone.

He hated himself for his disloyalty to her, but he couldn't help it. Jenny was like a breath of fresh air in comparison – not that she was that much of a pushover, oh no. She was a realist, as young as she was, in a way that Caroline would never be. Jenny accepted her role and was just glad to be there with him. There were no histrionics if he couldn't make it, or he was late. She didn't ask him for anything either, and that alone was a new concept for him.

Sometimes when he came home and saw Caroline leafing through catalogues, looking for another expensive must-have, he felt the urge to brain her. He went along with it because it not only kept the peace, but also because it was easier to give in and avoid the drama.

Caroline judged his love for her by what he spent on her; Jenny just loved him. There was a big difference.

Caroline would take it hard if he left. More than anything she craved the prestige of being married to him and a divorce would turn into a knock-down, drag-out fight.

He slowed his car, amazed at the thoughts he was having of the consequences of divorce. He shook himself mentally, admonishing himself that he had a young son he adored, and who adored him. He had a good life with his wife and child, even if it was often fraught with contention; that was part and parcel of his Caroline.

Still, it had thrown him that he had even considered the possibility. Caroline would cut his nuts off and send them to him first class through the post if she knew what he was thinking. One thing was certain: Caroline Moran was not a woman who would easily be scorned.

Chapter Thirty-Six

Johnny Mac had brought together a small crew of trusted workers. They were young, large, strong and close-mouthed – exactly what was needed for this little episode.

They had picked up Micky Two Fags and Richie Jakobs earlier in the day and stashed them at a warehouse in Essex. Elvis Munro and Denny Gunn were off the hook, and secretly Johnny was pleased about that as he liked them both. The only one left was Jimmy Boy Banks and that fucker would be difficult to snatch. Luckily Jimmy Boy's brother-in-law, a certain Hank Barber, hated the man. He had treated his sister like shit for years and was a bullying father and husband. Hank Barber had sold Jimmy up the river without a second's thought.

Johnny parked the car outside Jimmy Boy's girl-friend's house. Typical Jimmy Boy – he had a little unmarried mother on the side with big tits and the brain capacity of an ant. Some men never changed.

From what he could gather, Jimmy usually went

into her place at seven in the evening and came out just after nine, no doubt after relieving his manly itch while her kids were in bed. It made sense when you thought about it. Some young girl grateful for a few pounds now and then, all the time unaware that she was nothing to him except an easy lay with a grateful demeanour.

When Jimmy exited the small house, they were waiting for him. As he approached his car, they surrounded him, subdued him and bundled him into the boot of Johnny Mac's car. The three main players were now out of the game.

Johnny Mac congratulated the boys on a job well done and they made their way to Essex, aware that the traffic from Stratford would be heavy at this time, but secure in the knowledge that Jimmy Boy's cries of rage would go unheard in the general noise of the A13.

It was a good day's work all round.

Chapter Thirty-Seven

Richie Jakobs and Micky Two Fags were aware that their number was up. Both men were terrified – they had backed the wrong horse this time. They were tied up in a warehouse that was full of oil drums and the stench was making their eyes water. They knew that before long they would be joined by Jimmy Boy and their fates would be sealed.

It was dark out now and they were getting more and more fearful as the hours passed.

Thirsty, hungry and frightened, they were almost glad to hear a car draw up outside. Neither of them was expecting to be saved, but there was always a chance of talking their way out of this difficult situation.

Cain Moran walked into the large warehouse with a carrier bag and, looking at the two men trussed up like chickens, he saluted them in a friendly way. He looked immaculate as always, even dressed casually in 501 jeans and a Fred Perry T-shirt, he looked every inch the burgeoning businessman. He opened the carrier bag and took out a bottle of Scotch, a pack of paper cups and then he removed a large pair of pliers and some bolt cutters.

The men's eyes widened at his antics, and he smiled at them amiably. 'You didn't think you were going to get off scot-free, did you, lads?' He grinned, enjoying their discomfort. 'Your mate Jimmy Boy, the other murdering bastard, will be here in a minute. Got myself a hat trick, ain't I? Feel like Geoff Hurst.' He poured himself a large Scotch and drank it down in one. 'What a day for England that was, eh? Fucked the Germans again.' He laughed at his own wit.

He could see the men eyeing the bottle greedily and, pouring himself another large drink, he saluted them again. 'To a happy death!'

A few minutes later they heard another car pull up, and they knew their time was up.

Cain laughed loudly, the whisky already taking effect, and he shouted, 'It's showtime, folks!'

Chapter Thirty-Eight

Molly had gone back to her own home knowing that, even in these circumstances, her daughter-in-law would rather she left them to their own devices. Her presence would probably make the girl worse; Caroline wasn't exactly subtle with the way she treated her husband's mother. It was hard for a mother to be sidelined so deliberately by her son's wife, but it was the way of the world, and it rankled. At least Cain brought little Michael round to her – that had to be enough.

As she sipped her whisky and ginger ale she pondered on the young girl her son seemed so enamoured of. She had liked her a lot. But what would be the upshot if her son walked away from his wife and family? Caroline Moran would never sleep another full night in her bed, she knew that much. She would move heaven and earth to make sure that Cain never had another happy day in his life.

Molly had warned her son on numerous occasions that he was making a rod for his own back, but he had never listened to her, and why would he? He was his own man, and he had married Caroline despite the warning signs. Men! Looked after all their lives – they just went from their mothers to their wives.

Molly was surprised by how much she had taken to Jenny Riley. There was an innate honesty about her that belied her tender years. She was a woman in every way, and a good woman at that. She emanated kindness and that was something few people truly possessed.

Christ Himself knew she wished her son had picked a wife she could at least like. That was an impossible emotion to feel when you dealt with Caroline on a daily basis. Molly had been invited to Christmas dinner once; it had not been a success and, after that, she had been glad to be left to her own devices. The day had been fraught with tension, and she had felt her daughter-in-law's resentment the whole time she had been there. It had been hard to swallow her dinner, even though she was the one who had cooked it. She had slaved all day, and not a word of thanks from Caroline, though her mother Jane had been at pains to make her feel welcome.

That silly mare had always seen her as a rival for Cain's affections, which was laughable really considering she was his mother. She hoped that having had a child – and a son – Caroline might have understood the relationship better but it never made one iota of difference. Molly would always be the terrible old whore who had dragged up her son, and who was to be ridiculed and sidelined for the rest of her days. Molly felt the sting of tears at the thought – the truth was often far more painful than people realised.

Cain, at least, loved her with a vengeance; he didn't see her as an ex-brass – he saw her as a victim of circumstance. That was true in many ways. She had been the victim of her own naïveté and the fact that she had been a very good-looking girl. Men were always her downfall – she never picked the right ones.

Something about Jenny Riley appealed to Molly, maybe the fact that she had encountered a kindred spirit: another person who loved Cain Moran with all her heart.

There was a knock on her front door and, surprised to get a visitor this late, she went to unlock it with the usual trepidation in her heart. Was it the Old Bill telling her that her son was nicked or, worse still, that he was dead? That he had been murdered?

She opened the door with a trembling hand so was pleased to see Jenny Riley standing on her doorstep.

'I know it's late, Mrs Moran . . . Molly . . .'

Then she burst into tears, and Molly Moran, being Molly, took the girl into her arms and hugged her tightly, all the while whispering endearments. She had turned up unexpectedly and eased her dreadful loneliness. To Molly Moran, this girl was like a gift from God Himself.

Chapter Thirty-Nine

Micky Two Fags was crying silent tears of despair, and Cain found them almost endearing. He was aware that the three men knew that their fates were sealed, but it fascinated him that they were still holding out hope for some kind of divine intervention. It was the old adage, he supposed. Where there's life, there's hope. Well, not for any of this lot. They were well and truly out of the game.

Cain and Johnny were enjoying themselves; this was what they did best and how they had made their first step up. Torture was something that most people just weren't capable of. It wasn't for everyone, and it didn't come naturally to the majority. For Cain and Johnny Mac, it was something they did as a matter of course, and it was why they had been unchallenged so far. It was only used in extreme circumstances, and this qualified as extreme to them.

Cain still couldn't get over the utter cheekiness of these men thinking that they could take him out so easily. They thought he would be fool enough to let them capture him without a fight? It was an insult of mammoth proportions.

Cain Moran called his lads in; there were times in life when only an audience would do. Though these bodies would never be seen again, it was important that at least *some* of the story got out for public consumption, and the only way to guarantee that was to make sure it was a public execution of sorts. Without a body, the Old Bill would be hard pushed to make a case. And, considering the people involved, Cain believed they wouldn't bother trying anyway. Whispers were all they needed now – and that was just what they were going to create.

Picking up the bolt cutters, Cain set to work on Jimmy Boy Banks. He took his fingers and toes off first, making the pain last as long as possible.

Cain and Johnny knew that the true torture was watching it happen to someone else – and that was the real frightener. Though the lads chosen for the night's work were good kids, loyal and true, both Johnny and Cain knew that if this night was over-the-top it would be leaked out at some point. The brutality of what they were doing would be talked over by these young observers. In their cups, they would discuss it in hushed voices, wondering if it had really happened. Extreme violence did that to the onlooker – it made them doubt their own eyes. It was exactly what Cain was counting on.

Cain looked at one of the lads and said seriously, 'Bring me the acid from the car.'

The wait was interminable for everyone concerned. There was blood everywhere from the bolt cutters and Jimmy Boy was groaning in pain. Richie and Micky Two Fags were almost delirious with terror and that all added to the excitement.

One of the boys, Peter Parkes, brought in a large bottle of sulphuric acid and handed it to Cain. They watched as he opened it carefully, before placing it on the ground.

'Do you see this cunt here, lads? He wore a fucking cravat to my wedding. A *cravat*. I knew then that he was a complete cunt.' He poured himself another drink and swallowed it down quickly. 'I mean, in this day and age, who would wear a fucking cravat?'

The boys were grinning now, getting into the swing of things.

'My wife nearly pissed herself laughing, but I said to her, "Don't laugh. He has his creds." I realise now that she was right. Because this cunt was a joke then, and he is an even bigger fucking joke now.'

Jimmy Boy Banks was in agony, lying on the floor with blood flowing out of his body, knowing that it wasn't enough to kill him quickly. All he had to look forward to now was death, and the peace it would bring him. He was squirming in agony, trussed up like a kipper, his ferret-like face contorting in agony, knowing there was much worse to come. He had already lost his fingers and his toes. It was over for him no matter what. Cain removed the gag, and looked down at the man's face before saying seriously, 'This is where the pain really starts, mate.'

As Jimmy Boy Banks opened his mouth to scream, Cain picked up the acid and poured it into his mouth, dissolving his tongue and incapacitating his ability to make even a sound. The stench was overpowering, and Cain and Johnny were pleased to hear a couple of the paid heavies gagging. It meant they were doing their job properly.

Cain started to kick the man in the head until it was obvious to everyone there that he was dead. Then Cain took a step back and let Johnny loose on Micky Two Fags.

When Johnny had finished, they offered Richie Jakobs to the young men they had handpicked, and watched as those same lads tried to outdo each other with their cruelty. Johnny had chosen well; these lads had the makings of a good crew and they enjoyed their work once they got into it. It always amazed Cain that the ones who had seemed the most squeamish at the off were often the most vicious once they were given free rein.

When it was all over, they had the boys clean up and pack the bodies in the burlap sacks they had ready. Then they let the lads leave, and Johnny Mac and Cain disposed of the bodies personally. They were placed in a huge tank in West Thurrock and then a thousand gallons of caustic soda were poured on top of them. It had been a good night's work.

When they were driving back home, Johnny started to laugh uproariously. 'When you cut Jimmy Boy's big toe off all I could hear was retching and when I looked at the crew I could see them white-faced and disgusted. It's like a war, I suppose – they just needed to be blooded. Because by the end of the night they were like baying hounds!'

Cain laughed with him. 'Keep your eye on that young Peter Parkes – he has the makings of a great torturer. Fuck me, once he got into it he really pushed the boat out.'

Johnny laughed again. 'I know, tell me about it. I wasn't that surprised though, considering the family he's from. His dad's just coming out after an eighteen and his older brother is in for murder. It is definitely in the genes there.'

Cain nodded sagely. 'He will go far that lad, you mark my words.' Then he laughed again, as he said seriously, 'Beware of cunts in cravats. I told you that was an outrageous way to dress in this day and age. I knew it would come to no good!'

They were both laughing, high on adrenaline, as they travelled towards their respective homes.

Chapter Forty

Jenny Riley was still chatting to Cain's mother.

'There is a kindness in him that most people don't see. But I do, Molly. I feel his goodness every time I see him.'

As much as Molly Moran loved her son, she wasn't so sure but she kept her own counsel. She knew her son was capable of literally anything if he was in a tight corner or felt he was being mugged off.

'I know about his reputation, but I see a different side to him, you see.'

Molly smiled sadly. 'Jenny love, what has brought you here really, darling?'

Jenny looked at Cain Moran's mother and she started to cry again.

Molly sighed heavily and, pouring herself another stiff drink, she said lightly, 'When's it due?', all the while thinking that this was the last thing any of them needed.

Chapter Forty-One

Things had never been so good for Cain Moran and Johnny Mac. Word on the street was they had taken out Jimmy Boy Banks and two others, namely Micky Two Fags and Richie Jakobs, but it was pure speculation. Lily Law had not even bothered to give them so much as a sniff so they knew they were free and clear and ready for the next phase of their operation.

Peter Parkes had been given a boost up in as much as he was now operating one of their recently acquired clubs and, according to the reports, doing a good job of it. They were pleased with him as they were with life in general – everything they touched seemed to turn to gold and they had more money than they knew what to do with.

They had found a crooked estate agent who was helping them launder their black money by buying cash properties and then remortgaging them. They had also invested a lot of money over in Spain, and they were now property tycoons. It was taking off over there big time and Cain and Johnny were determined to be in on the ground floor. It was a profitable time to have disposable income. Opportunities were limitless, every day a new scheme evolved, and they were, naturally, offered their percentage as top dogs. It was as if they were being watched over by a benevolent god who was determined to see them succeed.

But while things were going well in his work life, Cain's private life was deteriorating on a daily basis. Since the shock news of Jenny's pregnancy, he had been a man on a mission to get out of his marriage. When Jenny had offered to abort the child to make things easier for him, he had seen the sheer terror in her face at the prospect of such an act. The fact she was willing to do that for him in any case told him all he needed to know. Every time he saw her he fell more in love with her, and the relationship that she had with his mother was the icing on the cake. There was no way Molly would be rowed out of this baby's life. His mother, the raving Catholic, condoning his adultery was mad enough in itself, but his mum and Jenny had a genuine friendship built on love and respect and it pleased him no end.

Jenny didn't care that his mum had a past because her mother's was so similar. He wondered if that was why they got on so well; both Jenny and Cain had lived through the humiliation of having been looked down on all their lives. They knew the pain that caused a child and how, no matter what, they still loved the offending parent in their own way. For all Eileen's faults

– and they were legion – Jenny adored her and he understood that because he felt the same about Molly. His mum, God love her, had taken to Jenny big time; they were always together these days. He could sense his mum's excitement at the thought of having a grand-child whose life she would actually be a part of. That was heady stuff after the way Caroline had treated her over the years. It made him feel ashamed, because he should have nipped Caroline's treatment of Molly in the bud but he had just wanted a quiet life. He had a feeling he would get exactly that with Jenny.

A part of him hated himself for the way he was willing to abandon his marriage, his lawful wife and even his first-born child. But Cain Moran wanted Jenny Riley more than he had ever wanted anyone or anything before in his life. Every time he touched her, even heavily pregnant as she was now, it was like a revela-tion. It was as if this was what he had been put on this earth for – to be with this girl and share his life with her.

Loving Jenny Riley was the easy part; it was telling his wife he wanted a divorce that was going to be the killer. But tell her he must, and sooner rather than later. It was still only months since she had lost her mother, and that was making things difficult for everyone. Caroline was milking her mother's death for everything it was worth. She was like someone from a Victorian novel, lying around all day, comfort eating. She was gaining weight and blaming Cain for it.

He wiped a hand across his face as if to banish the thought of her. Then, getting up, he walked into the en-suite bathroom as quietly as possible; the last thing he needed was Caroline awake at this hour of the morning, shouting the odds. But luck wasn't on his side and he heard her voice as he started his early morning piss.

'What time did you finally roll in?'

He rolled his eyes with annoyance. 'Yeah, good morning to you too, Caroline. You know I was at a meet last night. You spoke to Johnny about it.'

He heard the grunt of disbelief that told him she still thought Johnny Mac was a part of some conspiracy against her. If only she knew that Johnny was about the only person who counselled him to think long and hard before he broke up his marriage. He was Caroline's sole supporter.

'You getting up today?'

He heard her sigh heavily.

'Why? What is there to get up for? You tell me that.'

He gritted his teeth and said as evenly as he could, 'Little Michael, how about him? Your auntie Dolly can't stay here for ever, can she?'

Caroline sat up in the huge bed and yawned loudly. He looked at her as he walked back over. He was tired having been out late the night before but, instead of getting in to have a longer sleep, he bent down and picked up his jeans off the floor, slipping them on quickly. She was getting to be the size of a house. He saw the chocolate wrappers on the night table on her side and knew she must have had a midnight feast. Her face was fuller and, even though she was still a good-looking woman, her permanent expression of discontent was marring her features.

She had suffered a blow, he accepted that. But she had so much else in her life and she was just wasting it. Wallowing in self-pity, she had become a fucking nightmare – and she hadn't been all that easy to start with, temperament-wise.

'Actually, Cain, she *can* stay here. I've already asked her and she's over the moon.'

He bit back the retort he wanted to make, because in some ways Dolly moving in would make things easier for him in the long run.

'Shouldn't you have discussed that with me, love?'

Caroline pulled herself from the bed and padded to the bathroom quickly.

'Now why would I do that, Cain? Since when have I had to have your fucking permission to do anything pertaining to this house and our lives? It will make my life easier having her here. Little Mike is a handful and I need to grieve.'

He could hear her taking her Valium – he hated the sound of that pill jar opening. She was eating them like sweets and they zonked her out. She needed a swift kick up the jacksie, but no one was going to do that any time in the near future. Everyone around her allowed her to do what she wanted, even at the expense

133

of living their own lives. She moaned constantly, but she had always been a complainer. Caroline dripped negativity; it seeped out of her pores and it infected everyone around her. When he thought back now at how she manipulated every situation, he was amazed that he had never comprehended it before.

He made his way downstairs where Dolly was already giving Michael his breakfast. He was a handsome boy, and he smiled widely at his dad as he walked into the kitchen.

'I've got boiled eggs, Dad.'

Cain kissed him on the top of his head. It would be hard to leave his little lad; he loved him with all his heart.

'Lucky boy.'

Dolly, in a flowery dressing gown, was making a pot of tea and, smiling kindly, she said, 'Sit down, I'll do you a bit of egg and bacon.' She placed a mug of tea in front of him and he sipped it gratefully.

'So, I hear you're moving in then.'

Dolly turned to face him, the smile gone. 'I think it's for the best, don't you?'

The air was loaded with tension suddenly and he realised that she knew about Jenny.

'She will go fucking ballistic when she finds out and, if you value your life or that girl's life, you had better make sure she don't get her hands on either of you. Pregnant or not pregnant, Caroline will hammer the fuck out of her.'

Michael was looking over his father's shoulder and, as he shouted, 'Dad!', Cain felt the full force of his wife's fist hit the side of his head. She was strong and he felt himself lifted out of his seat. As he crashed heavily to the kitchen floor, she was on him. Little Michael was wailing, Dolly was screaming and Caroline was almost incoherent with rage. She was straddling him now, tearing the hair from his head, and he had to use every ounce of his considerable strength to buck her off him.

After a while he managed to hold her down and, when she finally stopped struggling, he relaxed his hold a little. She spat into his face, a huge globule of spit. It smelled of minty toothpaste and he left it there, not willing to loosen his hold on her any further. Caroline could fight like a man and she was angry enough now to be capable of anything.

'Who is it, Cain? Do I know her?'

He looked down into his wife's wild eyes, and said gently, 'I'm so sorry, mate.' He meant every word he said and it pained her even more to know that.

'And it's pregnant, is it? How many months?'

'Nearly seven. Honestly, Caroline, I never meant for any of this to happen.'

She snorted nastily. 'You really want this bird so much?'

He nodded.

Suddenly it was as if the fight left her body and she slumped on to the floor. There were no tears in her eyes, no emotion in her voice, as she said wearily, 'You better go to her then.'

The only time he smiled that day was when he went into the offices in Soho and Johnny Mac, taking in his black eye and split lip, said airily, 'I take it Caroline's found out?'

As they laughed together at the absurdity of it all, Cain felt the pressure leaving his body. The word was out, and now he could look to the future. His future with Jenny.

Chapter Forty-Two

Jenny Riley could not believe what had happened. She was standing in her mum's front room staring at Cain Moran, wondering if she was imagining the whole scenario. She had dreamed of this moment, never believing for a second that it would actually come true.

Eileen grinned. 'She didn't take the news well then?'

Cain gingerly touched his swollen face. 'I've had worse.' He tried to make light of his condition, of the whole situation. Jenny was white-faced as it was – no need to go into the gory details.

Eileen surveyed him shrewdly. Against her will, she had a sudden respect for him; she had been convinced he was bullshitting her daughter about being with her one day. Fuck knows she had heard it all before, but it seemed her Jenny had the magic touch. She only hoped he was worth it in the long run – most men weren't. Once the sex dwindled, it was like going to work; men were a job you had to do every day of your life. Still, that was for Jenny to find out for herself.

She went out into the hallway and shrugged on her coat, calling out, 'I'll leave you two lovebirds alone.'

Cain looked at Jenny, his lovely Jenny, and, as she slipped into his arms, he felt the happiest he had in years. He still couldn't believe that Caroline had let him go – he would make sure he did right by her and his boy. He felt the baby kick and laughed delightedly. 'Seems little Junior here is fed up of his cave already.'

Jenny laughed with him. 'He takes after you, Cain, keeps nightclub hours.'

'Come on, pack a bag, you're moving into the flat with me.'

Jenny Riley didn't need to be told twice.

Chapter Forty-Three

Peter Parkes was an ambitious man, and he understood the business instinctively. He knew who to trust, who to avoid and, most important of all when you ran a nightclub, he knew who had the real money to spend.

He always treated the high-rollers well, even putting in a VIP bar on the top floor. It was a good money-maker, but it was also perfect for private meetings, for separating people who held grudges against each other, and for impressing the constant array of little birds he was knocking off.

Tonight, being a Sunday, it was being used for a very important meeting and Peter Parkes was thrilled to be the person arranging it. A big Face from Liverpool had requested a meeting with Cain through Peter, and he had brokered it, feeling like a million dollars to be approached by such a name as Lenny McAvoy. The man was a living legend whose name could inspire fear in the most valiant of hearts. He had the reputation as a torturer of his enemies, and he was also known as a man who dealt with friction personally – a lot like Cain Moran.

Peter Parkes assumed that was why they were in the position they were. He wanted to be a part of the upper echelons of villainy just like them. After tonight, he was already on his way, and that excited him.

Cain and Johnny Mac were the first to arrive. Peter stood behind the pristine bar and got ready to make them drinks; he already had a good bottle of Scotch on the counter, anticipating Cain's choice of beverage. Peter Parkes now drank Scotch himself in homage to his idol. He knew he had to create a persona – it was the main requisite for a Face. He had taken up smoking too, for the same reason.

He poured Cain and Johnny their whiskies and watched as they settled themselves at a table by the doorway. Peter noticed that both the men were packing guns, which surprised him. This was supposed to be a friendly meet. He had liked the sound of Lenny McAvoy in their phone conversations; he had come across as all right. But, as he had to remind himself, this was nothing to do with him and, until Cain or Johnny asked his opinion, he would be wise to keep his thoughts to himself.

When Lenny McAvoy arrived, Peter was taken aback by the man's size – he was enormous. Cain was tall even for a man, but this bloke towered over him. He was also very pale, with light blond hair, white skin that would burn in the summer sun and, most notice- able of all, he was loud. His voice was booming and, as he shook hands with Cain and Johnny, his two goons, who were nearly as big as Lenny, went and sat at a separate table.

'So, Cain, great to be down South for a few days. Fucking crazy place, this London! How the fuck do you manage to get around with all the traffic?'

The men chitchatted for a while, and Peter Parkes served them drinks, leaving the bottle of Scotch on the table for the men to help themselves. Peter watched everything going on. He noticed that the two goons were not drinking, but were surveying the scene with shrewd hooded eyes. He knew things were not as hunky-dory as was being made out.

Cain was laughing at a joke that Lenny had told about an Irishman and a German shepherd, when he said suddenly, 'I hear you were down here a few months ago, Lenny.' There was a steeliness in Cain's voice that didn't go unnoticed by anyone in the room.

Peter saw the two goons sit up that bit straighter at the change of tone. Johnny Mac turned in his chair and eyed them quickly. 'Sit there and don't fucking move unless you want me to get annoyed.' The men took the warning and relaxed back into their seats.

Johnny had a way that made even the biggest of men take heed of him. A lot of it was due to the fact he could fight like a fucking drunken navvy and that he always won. Peter had heard a story that the secret of Johnny Mac's success was that no one could put him down and keep him down – he just kept getting up and going back at the fight again. Cain joked that Johnny just tired his opponents out; they let him win so they could go home and have their dinner. Johnny Mac had always laughed the loudest at that. Now Peter was seeing that Johnny Mac was a real force to be reckoned with.

Cain carried on, 'Don't walk in here giving me a load of old fucking fanny, OK? I know who you saw and what was said. Now I want to hear it from you.'

That Lenny McAvoy was taken aback was an understatement; he was genuinely stunned at the other man's knowledge of his movements. He knew he needed to acquit himself well or he was in big trouble.

The atmosphere was charged now, and there was a sense of fear creeping up Peter Parkes's backbone. He was impressed with Cain Moran and Johnny Mac; they were the fucking nuts there was no doubt about it.

Lenny McAvoy picked up his whisky and drained it in one swallow before pouring himself another good shot. 'Well, I've had a right capture here, ain't I?'

He sounded contrite, and Peter saw Cain start to relax. His hand remained inside his suit jacket though, so he was still handling his gun.

'You have at that, my old mucker. Now stop fucking about and start talking.'

'I had a meeting with Jackie Cliff – I provide his pharmaceuticals, as I am sure you know. It seems though that you have your own supplier and that is not Jackie. I earned a lot of money from him, and we had it sewn up tighter than a nun's cunt, Cain. Now I am getting fuck-all. Hence this meeting.'

Cain laughed then, a real loud belly laugh. 'Let me tell you about Jackie Cliff, educate you for a moment here. I wouldn't use that treacherous cunt if my life depended on it. He was cutting your stuff to nothing and doubling his money while screwing you out of yours. He also gets stuff from the continent – not just drugs but hard-core porn. The lorry drivers bring it for him. He promises payment to people and then reneges. There are more than a few people out there who would like a private word with him and a baseball bat. I don't use him, or the people he associates with, because he's a fucking grass. No one can do what he does so blatantly unless they are protecting themselves. Any rivals seem to get nicked pretty quickly, if you get my drift. So now you know why you were rowed out in favour of a more profitable, but less dangerous, supplier. Me and Johnny here control everything this side of the Watford Gap, and you, my friend, would do well to remember that. You come visiting in future and you make sure we know about it long beforehand.'

There was a definite threat there and Lenny McAvoy accepted it; in fact, as Cain remarked later on, he took it on the chin, and he respected that in any man.

'I see. I can only assume you know what you're talking about, Cain, and I bow down to your superior knowledge of the situation. But the fact remains I am still without a very lucrative earn.'

Peter felt a sneaking admiration for Lenny; it said a

lot for a man when he was faced with this kind of opposition to still press his suit. And, in all fairness, he did have a good point.

Johnny Mac as always deferred to Cain and it would be his decision regarding the matter. Cain poured them another round of drinks, and flashing his disarming smile, he said seriously, 'I reckon we can come to some kind of arrangement, Lenny. But on one condition.'

Lenny was obviously happier now he had the chance of an in. 'And what would that be?'

'We get a percentage of your earnings up North.' It was a brazen move, and one that would either be accepted or would cause a war.

'Why would I do that, Cain?' There was definite sarcasm now.

'Because, my old china, me and Johnny here are going to be your new suppliers. We can get better stuff, and not only is it cheaper, it is also safer for all concerned because we're dealing with the Colombians and the Jamaicans direct. There's no middle man, and with the quantities we are dealing in, it's worth everyone's while to take advantage.'

Lenny McAvoy was thrilled. He picked up his glass and raised it in a toast, before they swallowed their drinks. Lenny was mentally counting up his profit in his head, wondering why he'd not had the foresight to meet up with this fellow before. It was true what he had heard – the man was a walking fucking cash register and, what was more, Lenny decided he liked him. Moran had no side to him, and that was always a bonus in their game. And that was something he could take advantage of.

'Oh, one more toast. I just remembered.'

Everyone looked at Cain and he refilled their glasses before ostentatiously checking his Rolex, and saying heartily, 'To the recently departed Jackie Cliff. Who shrugged off his mortal coil about forty-five minutes ago.'

Everyone laughed.

Chapter Forty-Four

Jenny had a backache, and she was lying in a hot bath, drinking a cup of weak tea. She had never thought anyone could be this happy. She had to pinch herself at times to make sure it was really happening. Cain was so good to her, he looked after her as if she was made of glass. She could feel his love in everything he did and said, and oh, how she loved him back. She adored the man.

She was carrying high with hardly any spare weight and, unlike for a lot of women, her pregnancy had been virtually trouble free. She still looked wonderful – blooming, as Cain was forever telling her. He treated her like a queen, insisting she had money, new clothes, whatever she wanted.

Now they were getting a room ready for the baby and she was having the time of her life planning the décor and the colour schemes. It seemed as though she had stepped into her own personal heaven.

She felt the baby moving and with that came a tiny stab of fear; she was terrified of the birth itself. As she was only seventeen, the midwife said that youth was on her side when it came to having a baby. Well, it was going to happen whether she wanted to do it or not, so she would just have to get on with it.

As she pulled herself out of the bath, she saw herself in the mirrored tiles on the wall, and couldn't help smiling. She had a small bump, but other than that she looked more or less as she had before, though her breasts were much heavier and tender. She wrapped herself in the luxury of a huge white bath towel and, walking slowly, she went through to the kitchen where she would wash up her cup. She cleaned obsessively; the flat was so nice she couldn't bear to see anything out of its place. She was forever plumping up cushions or dusting the surfaces so the whole place gleamed. She knew it pleased Cain – he liked her to be 'house-wifey', as he called it.

It was in the kitchen that she sensed something was wrong, but she couldn't place what that might be. As she turned to walk out, her head exploded into a thousand flashing lights. Her knees buckled and she dropped to the floor, her hands and arms instinctively cradling her belly to protect her unborn child.

'You fucking whore! Did you think you would get away with it, eh? Did you think I was going to roll over and just let you walk off with my old man?'

It was Caroline kicking her as she spoke, and Jenny could feel the hatred dripping out of the woman. Jenny was terrified. A particularly hard kick in the kidneys sent a spasm of pain through her back, and she groaned loudly. The towel had fallen away and her exposed belly and breasts seemed to enrage Caroline more.

Grabbing her hair, she kept banging Jenny's head on the floor, and Jenny was screaming for her to stop when suddenly the front door was being hammered on and Caroline realised that someone must have phoned the police.

She looked down at the bloody mess at her feet, and closed her eyes in despair. Next she heard the wood shattering as the front door was kicked in. She was praying it was the police and not Cain, because she knew if he saw this scene he would surely kill her stone dead.

Chapter Forty-Five

'Jesus Christ! I will fucking *murder* that bitch.' Eileen was beside herself with anger and fear for her daughter.

Molly Moran placed a hand on her arm, saying sensibly, 'Hush now, Eileen, I am sure that Cain is sorting the situation out.'

It was a warning and Eileen heeded it, but she was overwhelmed with grief. If Jenny lost that child she would never be the same; that child and Cain Moran was all she lived for at the moment, and look what that had got her. What kind of scum attacked a pregnant girl? No matter what the provocation, pregnant women were out of bounds. End of.

Caroline had given Eileen's daughter the hiding of her life, there was no doubt about that. Jenny's face was swollen up like a football, and there were bruises all over her body. Her eyebrow had been stitched as had her lip, and she was bleeding badly. The baby must have taken a battering too, if the bruises on her abdomen and back were anything to go by.

Cain had walked into the hospital, taken one look at

Jenny, spoken to the doctors and then left immediately. Molly Moran had taken out her rosary beads and began praying. Not just for Jenny and the child, but for Caroline, because she didn't want her son put away over trash like her.

Chapter Forty-Six

Sergeant Crammer had been expecting Cain Moran, but he had not been looking forward to the visit. As Cain burst into the police station he looked like a man on a mission to murder. Everyone was more than aware of who he was – considering most of them were on his payroll that was hardly surprising. Still, this was a delicate situation, though Caroline had of course been taken into custody. She was cooling off in one of the cells. They were just waiting to know what Cain Moran's plans were.

'Where is she?'

The sergeant looked at the man in absolute terror; Cain looked apoplectic.

He bellowed, 'Where the fuck is she?'

Johnny Mac had arrived at the station a few seconds before Cain and he motioned to the sergeant to open the door and take Cain through to the holding cells. Seeing Johnny Mac there, Crammer decided it was safe to do as was requested, and he unlocked the door. Cain was through it, banging it open, and knocking the sergeant nearly on to his ample behind in his hurry. A couple of CID followed Cain down to the cells, and one of them pointed at Caroline, who was sitting on a bunk looking angrier than ever. Cain and Caroline glared at each other for long moments.

'Open the fucking door.'

DI Royston Marchant said sensibly, 'Come on, Cain, this isn't the time or the place.'

Cain rounded on him, and he seemed to have swelled to twice his considerable size, as a voice, filled with venom, called out, 'I hope that baby's dead. I hope it's brain damaged . . .'

Caroline was enjoying herself, and none of the men knew what to do. 'Mind you, if it takes after its mother it would be hard to tell, wouldn't it? I hear she is as ignorant as shit. Mind you, she's only about fifteen, ain't she?'

'Open this cell door or I will fucking rip it off its hinges!'

Suddenly Caroline was frightened; she didn't think he would get to her in here. This was a police station, for Christ's sake. Surely they wouldn't dare.

'You can't let him in here! You cannot let him in here!'

Johnny Mac said emphatically, 'You should have thought of that, love. Open the door, guys, or there will be fucking ructions.'

The cell door was opened and Caroline, seeing Cain's face, had shrunk back on the lone bunk and was pressing herself against the cell wall as if trying to force her way out.

'You can't let him in here! He will kill me!'

Cain was on her in seconds. Grabbing her by the throat, he practically lifted her one-handedly off the bunk, and up against the wall, all the time squeezing her neck as she tried to fight him off. She was strong, there was no doubt of that, but he was stronger and his anger was such he could easily have snapped her neck without a second's thought.

'You vindictive fucking bitch! That you would harm an innocent child. You fucking hateful witch.'

Johnny Mac was pulling him away from her now; he had the sense to know that Cain had to confront Caroline to get his anger out. But he mustn't kill her no matter what she had done. This was a friendly nick to them, but it wouldn't be friendly for long if there was a murder on its premises.

'Come on, Cain, don't give it the satisfaction.'

Cain dropped her like a sack of potatoes and Caroline crumpled to the floor, holding her throat, gasping for breath.

'You're right, she ain't worth doing time over.' He looked down at her and his voice dripped poison. 'You're a sad, fat, vicious-mouthed cunt, and I must have had shit in my eyes when I met you. All you ever do is fucking moan, piss and moan. Nothing's ever good enough for you, is it? You, who was brought up above a fucking tobacconist's shop, giving yourself airs and graces. Well, that Jenny, *my* Jenny, is worth a hundred of you. She is kind, she is nice, and every minute of every day ain't about her. You brought this on yourself. No man will ever stay with you because you're too discontented, Caroline. You don't know how to be happy or how to make others happy. But this is the final straw. You were getting the earth from me, and now you will get the bare fucking minimum. I will hit you where it hurts – in your pocket, darling. You might even have to get a job. That will be a laugh! You're capable of nothing. But mark my words, you ever go near her again and I will kill you, I take an oath on that. If she loses that child you better have a plane ticket out of here because I won't be responsible for my actions.'

Johnny Mac and the other men stood watching in absolute silence. This was so out of their comfort zone it was embarrassing to watch.

'Keep her here. Lock her up and throw away the key. I couldn't give a fuck. She's nothing to do with me any more.' Cain walked away.

'I'll never let you go! Do you hear me, Cain Moran? You just try to divorce me. I will fight you with my last breath!'

Even as Caroline's screams became increasingly hysterical, Cain never looked back.

It was the talk of the station for weeks.

Chapter Forty-Seven

Cain and Jenny's son, Cain Junior, was dramatically brought into the world that night by Caesarean section. They were told there would never be another child because Jenny was too badly damaged from the internal injuries caused by the beating. But little Cain thrived from his first breath, and Jenny Riley fell madly in love for the second time in her life.

Cain looked down at his son's mother and felt the urge to cry. He knew that this was his fault, that if he had been a different man, a better man, he would never have pursued a relationship with such a young girl, especially when he was married. But God knew he loved this girl with a power he had not experienced before. It was like she was everything he had ever dreamed of come to life, from her hair, her beauty and grace, to her kindness and her sense of peace that was so different to the women he usually knocked around with. She had an inner strength, and she wasn't a pushover, but where he was concerned, she thought the sun shone out of him and she bowed to him without a murmur. There were no screaming matches if he was late, no snide comments, or mind games with Jenny. No ulterior motives. She was sunny, that was the only word for her. She had a happy disposition and she could make the best of any situation. How could he not love that in her?

Now she was lying there, battered, bruised and left with only the little boy to show for their great love and it was his fault. She wasn't even eighteen yet, and she had been through more than most people would experience in a lifetime. Yet she still tried to smile at him, show him she was all right, that she would be OK.

She was thrilled with their son, and she was trying hard to make Cain feel better, telling him that she couldn't blame Caroline, that he had to try and remember that she was hurting too. It was laughable how good this woman could be. Jenny wanted to keep the peace; he was more inclined to a 'Don't get mad, get even' mentality. And he *would* get even with that bitch if it was the last thing he did in this life.

After what Caroline had put Jenny through, he felt that the gloves were well and truly off for both of them. If she wanted one of her spectacular fights over this divorce then that was exactly what she was going to get.

Chapter Forty-Eight

Dolly was looking after little Michael and she was tired out. She loved being in this beautiful house and she loved being the main carer for Michael, but she was finding it increasingly difficult to cope with her niece and her mood swings.

No charges had been pressed, although the police had kept her for three days, and she knew that was down to Cain, more than likely for his son's sake.

Now Caroline just slept and ate, and it was getting harder and harder to communicate with her. The divorce papers had already been served, and Cain was holding her over a barrel, threatening her with court action over the assault if she didn't toe the line. Who could blame him? It had been a serious attack, but then that was Caroline all over – she never did things by halves, and she was hurting plenty.

As much as she felt sorry for her niece, Dolly acknowledged she had gone too far this time. There had been an element of compassion for her generally over the Jenny situation, but the girl had nearly lost her son and, from what she could gather from the local gossips, she would never have another child now. No one could forgive a stunt like that. The general consensus was that God paid back debts without money, and Caroline would get hers with bells on.

Little Michael was missing his father and that wasn't a situation that she had control over either as Caroline made his visits as difficult as possible. She supposed Caroline was a good mother in her own way, but she wasn't hands-on – she wasn't a cuddler or comforter. Dolly knew that if she left now Michael would have no one in his corner, because Caroline was so obsessed with her own dramas that she often forgot the boy even existed for days on end.

How she missed her sister Jane! Jane had known how to handle her volatile daughter. Usually by giving in to her, admittedly, but she was also the only person who could in any way reason with her. Now with the pills and the drink, Caroline was out of control. Dolly was at her wits' end, and she didn't know how to make it better. She could hear Caroline lumbering about in her bedroom. It sounded like an elephant was above her; she was eating for England and getting bigger and bigger by the day.

She had been such a beautiful girl, inclined to curves, but she had always controlled her weight and looked fabulous. Now she looked years older than she was, and she had lost all interest in herself or her life.

Dolly heard a loud crash and raced up the stairs to find a drunken Caroline passed out on the bedroom floor. Picking up the phone she did the only thing she could think of. She phoned Cain Moran.

Chapter Forty-Nine

'He is absolutely beautiful, Jenny. I'm not just saying that because he's my grandson either.'

Jenny grinned. Her mother had come over all maternal and it was weird seeing her doting on the baby. She could never remember her doting on her. But for Cain Junior, as he was being called by everyone, the attention could not be lavish enough. He was absolutely adored by everyone in his orbit.

'You look a lot better, love.'

Jenny sighed. 'I'm OK. It is what it is, Mum – there's no way I can have another baby so the sooner I get used to it the better. Anyway, this one is more than enough for me!'

Eileen could hear the sadness in her daughter's voice but she knew better than to pursue the conversation. Jenny was right; it was what it was, and that was that. But she had taken a terrific beating; that in itself was traumatic enough and it had changed her. She was quieter, more reserved. She had always had a calmness about her but now it was enhanced. Cain adored her no matter what – Eileen couldn't fault him for that. She had been sceptical at first, but there was no way she could criticise that man where her daughter and grandson were concerned. He was already buying a house for them all; the flat was beautiful, but now, of course, it held only bad memories for Jenny.

When Molly had cleaned the place up she said there was blood everywhere. Every time she thought about it, Eileen felt the urge to hammer that Caroline herself. Cain had arranged for her to go into a private medical facility, and now she was being helped by professionals. She was definitely off her trolley. All this just proved that she was even more unstable than previously thought. Since the news had got out about what she had done to Jenny, it seemed everyone and their dog had a story about how crazy she was. It was that poor child Michael that she felt sorry for, having a nut-job like that as a parent. Eileen, being Eileen, didn't see any irony in her thoughts.

Jenny put her son to her breast, looking the epitome of glorious motherhood. As he suckled contentedly, she wondered when they could move to the new house. She hated living like a gypsy, and she wanted her own world where Cain and Cain Junior could live properly with her taking care of them. She was young and she was healthy – well, almost healthy – and she wanted desperately to get on with the next phase of her life. She loved motherhood and she craved normality, both things she thought she would never really have.

Now, despite what had happened, she had everything she wanted in abundance, but since the attack she had started to wonder if you had to pay a higher price for happiness than she had anticipated. And the happiness she had now had come at an awfully high price.

Chapter Fifty

Johnny had seen Cain go through so much in the last few months and it was obvious that, like Jenny, he was changed. He was harder somehow; the gossip and the talk had affected him more than he could have imagined. He had a steely glint in his eye as if looking for slights or disrespect, and it was being noticed by everybody they dealt with – especially the workforce. Peter Parkes had made the mistake of enquiring after Jenny's health only to have his head proverbially bitten off. Cain needed a talking to and Johnny was the only one who could do it, hence this late meeting together in Soho.

He poured himself a large Scotch and, when he heard Cain's familiar tread on the stairs, he poured one for him too. Cain burst through the door, and Johnny offered him his drink.

Cain took the glass and looked at it for long moments before downing it in one. Then, settling himself in a chair, he looked at his old friend and said, 'That bad, eh? I need a stiff drink first.'

Johnny Mac smiled, and his face transformed; he had beautiful teeth and high cheekbones. In repose he looked different, fearsome, but his smile was like liquid gold, and it certainly attracted the ladies.

'More than one, mate, and the same goes for me too.' He poured them each another generous measure. 'You've got to get your head back to normal, Cain. This has been a bastard few months but you must have known when you embarked on this that Caroline was not going to roll over. You have to take some of the responsibility, mate.'

Cain looked at his oldest friend and for a few seconds he experienced an anger that he had never felt towards the man before rising inside him. But he swallowed it down. Johnny Mac was the only person in his life who would – or indeed could – criticise him. Cain accepted the man would only do it if he felt it was important. And, deep in his heart, he knew that Johnny Mac was only doing this out of friendship.

'I never thought she would go so fucking bananas.'

Johnny smiled gently. 'I did. I tried to warn you she wasn't the whole fucking ticket. Always a bit erratic, for want of a better word. But that was part of the attraction, as far as I could see. She tried to rule you and you loved it. At first.'

Cain conceded the truth of that statement.

'But she was never the full ten shillings – even her mother tried to tell you about her. Look how she acted towards your poor mum. She treated her like dirt, and you went along with it. What's the nut doctor said? Is it true they want to plug her into the national grid?'

Cain laughed at that despite himself. 'They talked about shock therapy, but what she needs is a fucking good slap. Spoiled rotten she is, and always has been. Even the quack there thinks she is suffering from too high an opinion of herself. She's half the size of a house these days too. Fucking hell, you should see her, Johnny. If eating was an Olympic sport she would get the gold. But they say she will be home soon. At least she's off the fucking Valium, so that's something. But it's what she was capable of that I can't get my head around, you know? The police said they found a vial of acid in her car, that she was probably going to throw it in Jenny's face.'

Johnny listened quietly. Cain needed to get it off his chest to a sympathetic ear. The acid didn't surprise Johnny Mac, Caroline was a drama queen through and through. He had tolerated her because he had to, but that didn't mean he couldn't feel sorry for her. She was incapable of holding a man like Cain Moran; deep inside she knew that, and it had chipped away at her. She was what the Yanks called a 'control freak' and that was why the two of them had started out so passionately and ended so tragically.

'That's Caroline all over – the big dramatic gesture. Now, though, she's had a fright and hopefully it will sort her out once and for all. Do the doctors think she will ever get back on an even keel?'

'With medication but, as far as I can see, that's what sent her over the edge in the first place. To be honest, I really don't know what to think, mate. But you are right, Johnny – I have to accept some of the blame. I caused this and now I have to deal with the fallout. I just never thought it would be so outrageous.' He drank his whisky down in one. 'What if that baby had died? And now look at Jenny – no more kids. She's not eighteen years old and she has had to contend with this and it's my fault. All my fault.' He put his head into his hands in despair.

Johnny Mac said half-jokingly, 'Oh, Cain, for fuck's sake, have a day off, will you? Can you hear yourself? You sound like you should be writing to Marjorie Proops! It's happened, wipe your fucking mouth and get on with it. We have serious business to contend with and I can't do it on my own, mate. Deep down you knew that you wouldn't walk away from that mad bitch unscathed. It was hard, I admit, but you did it. Now you have to accept the consequences.'

Cain Moran nodded his agreement, but he said sadly, 'I know that, I ain't a complete cunt, Johnny. But it's my Jenny who has had to pay the real price.'

Johnny Mac shrugged nonchalantly. 'She is a lot stronger than you give her credit for, Cain. Anyone brought up by Eileen Riley has to be streetwise; it stands to reason, don't it? You both got what you wanted, and that is an end to it. Now can we talk actual business?'

Cain Moran grinned. 'OK then, if you insist.' He felt better already; trust Johnny to know exactly what he needed to hear. It was over – at least he hoped it was anyway.

'One last thing, Cain, don't scrimp on the divorce. It will backfire in the long run, and there is still little Michael to think about. You have made your point, now be magnanimous. It will be the last thing she is expecting and one day you will be glad you caved.'

Cain didn't answer him.

'How is he anyway, my little godson?'

Cain shrugged. 'Dolly is doing a great job, but I know that I can't ever bring him into Jenny's life. That would send Caroline off her trolley again.'

'Well, be fair – you would feel the same if the boot was on the other foot.'

Cain saw the sense of what Johnny was saying but it still rankled. He loved his son – he loved both his sons. But Michael was Caroline's only family after Dolly, and if he took him away from her it would be cruel. Now he had to live with the fact that he had walked out on Michael for Jenny and that was not something he had ever thought himself capable of.

Johnny Mac saw exactly what was going through his friend's mind; he knew him so well he could write the script for him. Cain needed to sort everything out for himself and this was Johnny Mac's attempt at helping his old friend through a learning curve. He hoped it would work, because they really needed to focus on the business in hand. They had a lot of fingers in a lot of pies, and they needed to be keeping an eagle eye on their assets and workforce. Cain Moran had had his drama, and now it was over. Time to get back to reality.

Chapter Fifty-One

From the moment Jenny Riley had driven through the electric gates and seen the big old Georgian house she had fallen in love with it. It had been refurbished by the previous owners with no expense spared, and it sat in two acres of gardens with a swimming pool and tennis courts. She couldn't believe it was actually theirs, and she kept walking around touching the walls to make sure it was real.

Cain enjoyed watching the pleasure she took as she looked into each room. He had bought the place, furniture and all, offering well over the asking price to get it, but it was a good investment for their future and it got Jenny what she wanted: a home of their own. It was a wonderful property, but the real attraction was the ten-foot brick wall surrounding the place. With that and the electric gates, he knew Jenny would feel much safer. He sensed she wasn't relaxing as she should, that she half expected Caroline to leap out from behind a lamp post or a bush. This place, he hoped, would give her the security she needed to finally let her guard down once more.

The kitchen was huge, and he could imagine that Jenny was picturing them sitting down to dinner and being a family. Truth be told, that is exactly what he wanted too.

'You like it, then? If you don't like the furniture or whatever, just change it. I just wanted us to be able to move in as soon as possible, see? You do like it, darling, don't you?'

Her face split into a wide grin as she shouted excitedly, and with some of her old verve, 'Love it? I fucking adore it. Oh, Cain . . .'

Then she was crying, and he held her tightly to him, as he soothed her with loving words and stroked her beautiful hair. She was trembling and he hated that he had done this to her, made her a bag of nerves. But, as his mum said, she had just had a baby and been through a dreadful ordeal, and he needed to be patient with her. She would get over it eventually; these things just took time.

'We will be happy here, darling, I promise you.'

She nodded into his chest, and held on to him like her life depended on him. Which, in many ways, it did.

Chapter Fifty-Two

Michael and his mother sat in a park with his auntie Dolly and, as he played in the sandbox, he could hear his mother talking angrily and it frightened him.

'Great big fucking house he's bought her in Essex. Two acres of grounds – not gardens, mind – *grounds*. Just the thing for Eileen Riley's daughter.'

Dolly sighed heavily. 'He's promised you your house free and clear, in your name only. You won't do too badly out of it all, considering. Don't you think it's time you just let him go?'

There was a definite edge to Dolly's voice and Caroline's face revealed she didn't like it one bit. 'Never,' she spat.

Dolly shook her head; this was an argument they had almost daily. 'Well, let's get the lad back home, shall we? He'll be ready for his lunch, I imagine, by now.'

Caroline stayed seated on the bench and watched as Dolly went to tidy up Michael before putting him in the car. He was his father's double but then, by all accounts, so was the new son. She felt the tightening of her belly as she thought of that whore's child; if she had only managed to kick it out of her. How dare he humiliate her like he had! Who did he think he was?

She would fight the divorce every step of the way. And, what's more, she would wait, and she would plan, and when the time was right, she would take them down, and she would enjoy every second of it. It was what got her up in the morning, and what she thought of last thing at night. He wanted the Good Life, but she would make sure that it didn't last for either of them.

Smiling now, she stood up and went to her son and aunt.

'Lunch. Good. I'm starving.'

Book Two

You won't really fall in love
For you can't take the chance
So please be honest with yourself
Don't try to fake romance

'The Good Life'
Music by Sacha Distel and lyrics by Jack Reardon

Chapter Fifty-Three

1988

'Honestly, Johnny, I was flabbergasted myself. I mean, who would dare to intercept one of our shipments?'

Johnny Mac was wondering the exact same thing himself. It didn't make any sense.

'How much did we lose?'

Peter Parkes shrugged. 'About a hundred grand's worth. It was the take for Liverpool. You know they love their fucking Persian rugs up that end of the country.'

Johnny Mac couldn't believe how relaxed Parkes was being about this outrage. 'This all happened at the services?' he demanded.

Peter nodded his head. 'Yep.'

'What guns were they using, just out of curiosity?'

Peter Parkes seemed surprised at the question. 'I don't know, Johnny.'

Johnny Mac finally lost his temper then and bellowed, 'Well, go and fucking find out!'

When Peter had gone Johnny sat back in his chair and

lit a cigarette, drawing on it long and deeply, seriously unimpressed with Parkes. It was a melon scratcher all right. Surely, there was no one that would dare rob off them. Not even the young, up-and-coming crews – plus they always put them on an earn, and that kept insubordination to a minimum. Everything felt wrong. Once he found out what weapons they had, he would call on the gun dealers and see who had purchased those particular models in the last few months, and that would narrow the search considerably. But it was such a blatant piss-take, and that was hard for him to bear.

He picked up the phone to talk to Cain and see what his take on the situation was. He was in Spain with Jenny and Cain Junior, so he would not be best pleased to have his holiday interrupted. But needs must when the devil drives.

Chapter Fifty-Four

Cain Moran Junior adored his father, especially when he had his undivided attention like now. He was a natural water baby and loved nothing more than being in the swimming pool. He loved Spain and the sprawling Marbella villa that they called home while they were there. He was doing his best dives and his father was egging him on. He could see his mum Jenny lying on a sunbed reading, but he knew she was watching his more spectacular efforts.

He loved this family time. In England his dad was nearly always out somewhere; he had a very important job. Cain Junior wasn't exactly sure what that was, but it was important because his mum had told him so. Also, people were always especially nice to his dad, and he liked that as well.

Jenny watched the two men in her life as they played together and she felt the usual contentment that being with her family gave her. She thanked God every day for this wonderful life of hers. She knew how lucky she was; Cain adored every bone in her body, and they were still, all these years later, as happy as they could ever be. They lived like royalty but, as Cain always joked, villainy was recession proof, so they didn't have to worry like everyone else. It was these times that she loved the most, when they were alone and she didn't have to deal with Caroline and her latest demands.

She did feel sorry for young Michael; he was caught between a rock and a hard place, and it was difficult for him to have any real relationship with his father. It grieved Cain, she knew. Considering it was nearly ten years ago, for Caroline it was like it had all happened yesterday. She had been true to her word and fought the divorce for all she was worth. One day she'd agree if Cain gave her what she wanted; as soon as he did, she changed her mind or issued another demand. It was a never-ending battle.

Throughout it all, Jenny remained the calm, gentle woman Cain had fallen in love with. No matter that she wanted to be his wife more than anything else in the world; she was determined to give Cain the peaceful life he had never had with Caroline. And, anyway, they belonged together; wedding ring or no wedding ring. Despite everything, Jenny felt blessed.

She signalled to Rosa, her Spanish housekeeper, to set the table for lunch. It still amazed her that she had a housekeeper! Who would ever have dreamed that she would have such a wonderful life? It frightened her sometimes that at some point there would be a forfeit for this happiness. Her mum said it was just Catholic guilt and she should enjoy her life and fuck everyone else. That was a philosophy that seemed to work for Eileen Riley, but Jenny wasn't so sure it would be the same for her.

Ten minutes later, as they sat down in the shade to eat lunch, chatting about their day, the villa was rocked by a large explosion.

In London at the same time, a bomb went off in their club in Wardour Street. There were no fatalities but that was put down more to luck than anything else.

It seemed someone was sending them a message. The only question was, who?

Chapter Fifty-Five

Jenny's ears were still ringing even after they had arrived back in England, and she wondered if it was psychological. The shock of the explosion had really hit her hard. The terror in the aftermath of seeing her son with his hair covered in plaster and blood on his face was something she wouldn't forget.

She had never in her life been near such a thing as a bombing, not even when the IRA were at large in London. It was something that happened to other people, like car crashes or AIDS. It happened to people you saw on the news or read about in magazines. It didn't happen to you or yours.

But this time it had and, from what she had garnered listening to Cain's phone calls, it was something that had been planned in detail to harm them. The London club bomb had gone off earlier than expected; it was supposed to have exploded much later when the club would have been packed with young people trying to have a good time. It was sheer luck, she supposed, that had tripped it so much earlier when there had been no one to harm.

She felt sick; she was feeling like this a lot and she knew it wasn't because she was pregnant again – that boat had sailed a long time ago. It was delayed shock the doctor said. Well, of course she was shocked! Someone wanted to kill them – that in itself was a frightening thought.

Molly was waiting at the house for them. Cain had arranged for extra security and his friends in the bomb squad had swept the house and the other premises such as the club's offices. But she was still nervous – suppose they had missed something? She swallowed down her fear once more, and accepted the mug of tea Molly had made for her.

'Come on now, Jenny, you need to stop worrying. Cain has it under control.'

Jenny looked up into Molly's eyes and said seriously, 'You think?'

Cain Junior was sleeping with her and that was just how she wanted it; she didn't want to let him out of her sight. She closed her eyes in distress as she heard Cain's voice bellowing from his office – it was just off the kitchen and normally she couldn't hear anything – but he was so angry, and it was a fury that she had never seen in him before. He was almost spitting his rage, and she knew it was because he could not believe that anyone would dare to interfere with him like this and, more to the point, involve his family. Family was off limits. They were civilians. They were the reason he would kill everyone involved in this debacle stone dead.

He was screaming like a banshee now. She closed her eyes and tried to blot it out. For the first time in her life she wished for the death of someone and she felt bad about that. But she wanted whoever had tried to harm her family to die. It was a sobering experience.

Chapter Fifty-Six

Johnny Mac and Cain were in a small Portakabin in Manor Park; they had decided that it was probably the safest place for them to meet at this particular time. It was a recently acquired scrapyard which they had taken over in exchange for a gambling debt. They had every intention of selling it on, but for now it seemed like a good little meeting place. Few of their workforce knew about it, and they had been compelled to recognise that whoever was behind these attacks had someone on their payroll giving them information.

It was unbelievable, but it was a viable option they had to consider. It bothered them more than they cared to admit. They had always seen their workforce treated well, money-wise especially. So this would have to be a vendetta for whatever reason, real or imagined. Who did they have a barney with? No one they could think of and they had racked their brains. There was nothing or no one they had crossed in any way, shape or form. It was a fucking mystery all right.

Cain poured them each a stiff drink, and settled himself behind the small makeshift desk. The night-watchman and his Dobermans had been surprised to see them; Cain had slipped him an onner to keep the dogs quiet and alert them if anyone approached. The nightwatchman was thrilled with the extra couple of quid and was determined to do his best.

Cain sipped his drink and said on a laugh, 'Poor old fucker! He's got to be eighty if he's a day, and he is looking out for us. One fright and we'll be paying his old woman compensation!'

Johnny Mac laughed with him, glad that they could at least joke about the situation, before he asked soberly, 'How bad was the villa damaged?'

Cain sighed. 'Nothing we can't sort out. It was a car bomb and not a very good one. Bit of a damp squib, to be honest, but it did some damage. If we had been eating inside though we would have been in trouble, put it that way.'

Johnny Mac nodded. 'How's Jenny and the lad?'

Cain shrugged. 'Not good. She is a nervous type anyway, you know that. She loathes violence. Though being brought up by Eileen Riley, I know that sounds like a contradiction in terms.'

They both laughed again.

'What do you think, Johnny?'

Johnny told him about the take being robbed and that there had been a few events that he had not really put any credence to.

'The thing is, some of the people we take from on the weekly have complained that they have been approached by an outside party to pay them, not us. The people concerned told them to fuck off and that seemed to be the end of it. To be honest, I didn't really give it much thought either way. Just some youngsters chancing their arms, you know? The usual. But now, I ain't so sure. I think I should have investigated.'

Cain grinned. 'Well, hindsight is a wonderful thing. Why would you? Who in their right minds would take us on? I tell you now, Johnny, it can't be anyone we deal with. This is someone inside our crew. It has to be. No one else could have the information needed to co-ordinate all this. The club alone has a better security system than the crown jewels. This is personal.'

Johnny nodded; he could see the logic. But it still would take a better fucking man than any they had working for them.

'Or, look at it this way: someone has infiltrated, recruited some of our better workers and got the information needed from them. Money is a powerful incentive, as we both know, Cain.'

'Has anyone complained? Said they feel sidelined, unappreciated? Has anyone come to you for a raise?'

Johnny shook his head. 'No. But if we can nail that, it's bound to lead to the fuckers behind the bombings.'

A car pulled up outside and its headlights made the room appear brighter for a moment. Johnny Mac looked out of the window and said airily, 'It's that fucking prat from the bomb squad, and he has Denny Gunn with him.'

'Denny Gunn is old school. He deals with the Irish so he will know if it's a regular bomb or army.'

They ushered the men into the small offices and settled them with a drink. The tension was almost palpable. Detective Inspector Frank Harper had been on the payroll for years, but this was the first time his presence had been requested and he was none too happy about it. He loved getting the extra money – he had just never thought his particular expertise would ever be needed. Now it was, he was nervous and he was wondering if he was doing the right thing.

'So, Harper, what's your opinion?'

Frank Harper was good at his job, and he was used to a certain degree of respect from his colleagues. He was also a greedy, two-faced, double-dealing wanker but no one had said that to his face as yet. He sipped his whisky and said pompously, 'I can't give you an *exact* opinion – this is not really an *exact* science.'

Cain butted in then. 'Well, I wish you had explained that to us years ago, before we started paying you the national fucking debt for your services which, I might remind you, we have never used until now.'

Johnny and Denny both tried to contain their smiles.

Frank Harper realised he had just dropped a serious bollock. He tried to redeem himself by saying,

'One thing I can tell you, Mr Moran, is that it wasn't the Irish.'

Denny Gunn laughed. 'That, Mr Harper, is why I am here. I could have told them that.'

Frank Harper was nonplussed, not sure how to handle the situation.

Denny sighed heavily before saying, 'Fucking amateur night, Cain. No real use of detonators, a kid doing O-level chemistry could have managed it. But it's not a professional, I would stake my life on that. If it *had* been a professional, you would not be here now.'

That was a very sobering thought.

'But, by the same token, they did the job. The bomb in the club in Wardour Street had a dodgy fucking timer, it went off far too early.' He sounded grieved by this; he loved his weaponry and he hated to see it used in such a terribly poor way. He saw bombs and guns as things of beauty, albeit dangerous beauty. 'Oh, and before I forget, you asked me, Johnny, about the guns that were used for the robbery. Well, I can tell you that a young man called Shane Dwyer purchased those same guns three weeks ago from one of my lads. Now, he isn't exactly IRA but he is connected – his brother is in the Maze doing life. He's a very erratic young man from Belfast. Good Catholic boy, and a staunch Republican, but not what you would call stable. He has never joined the firm, so to speak. I reckon you find him, you find your fucking mole. He is a little gangster, a gun for hire. You know the type. Reckless. No fucking brain capacity whatsoever. Now his brother Eamonn is a great lad – I had the privilege of meeting with him on more than one occasion. One of your own, and a great soldier. Knows his way around a fucking circuit board too.'

Frank Harper was listening to all this with eyes like flying saucers. He was anti-terrorist and it had only just occurred to him just what he had got himself into.

'Shane Dwyer.' Cain grinned. 'He must be a loose cannon if even the IRA won't have him.'

Denny Gunn shrugged. 'You've dealt with them, you know they are a real military operation. They won't take any chances, and who could blame them?'

Cain and Johnny nodded in agreement.

'So, any idea where he might be?'

'Myself, I would scout Kilburn first. It's a big Irish community, and the IRA can hide there working on the builds. Nowadays, though, they are mainly collecting for the cause.' He laughed his head off then. 'Mark my words, young Gerry Adams will be in the parliament one day.'

Cain laughed along with him. 'Please my old mum anyway. Thanks, Denny, you've been a real star, mate.'

Frank Harper just looked on in amazement, wondering why this man Gunn knew more about the terrorist situation than he did. He felt as if he had been slapped in the face. All the time and effort that had gone into covert surveillance operations and the only thing they had really needed to do was ask a gun dealer from North London what the real score was. It was fucking laughable.

Chapter Fifty-Seven

It took twenty-four hours to locate Shane Dwyer, but they didn't get hold of him the way they thought they would.

Shane turned up at their offices in Soho large as life and twice as ugly. He looked like the type of person you crossed the road to avoid.

He was tall, with powerful shoulders, but very skinny legs. His head was bullet-shaped and his gleaming white teeth were crooked. But it was his eyes which told people that here was a man who was definitely not firing on all cylinders. They were large and a very pale grey colour, so thickly lashed they should have been beautiful, but there was no spark of life in them. He looked out with a dead-eyed stare, rarely blinking. Together with his sandy hair and sparse eyebrows, he seemed like the poster boy for the mentally challenged.

Cain and Johnny Mac didn't know what to make of this man's sudden arrival. He was grinning from ear to ear and he seemed pleased to have caught them on the hop, so to speak.

'I hear you are looking for me?'

Johnny and Cain just stared at each other in shocked amusement. This bloke had to be a Grade-A headbanger.

'You heard right.' Cain's voice was dripping with sarcasm now, the enormity of the man's actions shaking him out of his disbelief.

'Well, here I am, Mr Moran. I hate to disappoint.' He had a deep, musical voice, with the clipped Belfast tones of his home city.

Johnny Mac wanted to laugh; this was just too surreal.

Cain sniffed loudly before saying seriously, 'Your mum should have called you Daniel, because you just walked into the lion's den, mate.'

Shane Dwyer grinned in delight at that. 'Ah, now I like a man with a sense of humour.'

Cain motioned to Johnny Mac who then pinned the man's arms behind his back as Cain punched him unconscious. When he was out for the count they dropped him on to the floor, and then both burst out laughing.

'What a fucking twonk, Johnny. Got to give him creds for sheer balls. If he survives this we should put him to work on the firm!'

Johnny Mac was shaking his head in amazement

saying, 'Fucking unbelievable' over and over. They had him trussed like a chicken and in the back of a van within ten minutes. Shane Dwyer was going to tell them what he knew if it was the last thing he did on this earth.

Chapter Fifty-Eight

Jenny and Molly were both wondering what was going to happen next. It was obvious that this was far more serious than Cain was making out, especially as the London bombing had made it on to the news. It certainly wasn't a gas fault, even if the news crews weren't aware of it. Molly poured them a glass of chilled white wine each, and Jenny, who rarely drank, swallowed half the glass in one mouthful.

Molly grinned. 'Looks like you needed that.'

Jenny nodded. 'I can't stop worrying, Moll. No matter what Cain says, I feel like something's going to happen, you know? There's a dread hanging over my head. I can't explain it.'

Molly sipped her wine thoughtfully. She recognised the feeling – she had it herself.

'Well, you know Cain, and you know what kind of a life he lives, darling. This is part and parcel of being with a man like him.'

'I do know that. But it still frightens me. We could

have been hurt as well, me and Cain Junior. It sort of brings it home to you, I suppose.'

Molly poured more wine into Jenny's glass and said seriously, 'He's done a good job keeping the peace for so long. In the old days London was a law unto itself, especially after they put away the Richardsons and the Krays. The streets were anyone's suddenly. It was a fecking free for all. Believe me, those were dangerous times. Cain and Johnny Mac have given the pavements back to the honest in many ways. Now someone is after what they have – it's the nature of that particular beast. Knowing my son like I do, I don't hold out much hope for the perpetrators.'

Jenny sighed heavily. 'That's what worries me, Molly.'

Molly didn't answer but kept her own counsel; she was as worried as Jenny, but she couldn't let the girl see that – Jenny was a bundle of nerves as it was. There was definitely something very suspicious going on, and it was clear that, despite outward appearances, her son was worried too. Once people went after your family – a definite no-no in their world – it indicated that they meant business and were willing to do basically anything to achieve their ultimate goal. That goal, of course, was taking what Cain and Johnny had.

Chapter Fifty-Nine

The music inside the Parakeet nightclub in Ilford was so loud the building was shaking. It was disco night and Sinitta's 'Toy Boy' was blaring out of the speakers. The dance floor was packed with revellers and the tills were clanging up a small goldmine.

In the attic of the club, a soundproofed room kept aside for dirty work, Shane Dwyer was tied to a chair and still chatting amiably in his sing-song voice as if this was the most normal thing in the world.

'Do you ever fucking shut up?'

Shane laughed once again. 'I even talk in my sleep or so I've been told anyway.'

Johnny and Cain, against their better judgement, actually couldn't help liking the man. He was so off the wall, and so honest. It was quite endearing in a strange, David Cronenberg kind of way. He seemed so eager to please, but he was definitely not the full ten bob. Shane Dwyer was like an overgrown schoolboy. Granted, a very dangerous overgrown schoolboy, but there was definitely something about him that caught people off guard. If he didn't have such expressionless eyes he could be really likeable.

'So, Shane, I hear your brother Eamonn is a good bloke. Has he got anything to do with what's been happening?'

It was the logical place to start; the Irish were always interfering in someone's business.

Though, according to Gunn, they had no real interest in Cain, otherwise he would have heard about it well before now. Cain liked and trusted Denny Gunn and he was willing to take his word, but he still had to ask.

Shane shook his head. 'No, you're barking up the wrong tree there. He's in for the duration, mate – he won't be out till there's either a united Ireland or he dies.'

Johnny Mac sighed heavily. This bloke talked like a complete cunt, and expected everyone to go along with him. Johnny Mac had finally reached the end of what was normally for him a pretty long tether. He punched Shane with all the strength he possessed in the side of his head, nearly knocking both the man and the chair he was tied to on to the floor. It hurt Johnny's fist, so it had to have hurt Shane Dwyer. Shane took the blow as best he could and was still smiling, even if that smile was dripping blood.

Johnny Mac bent down and shouted into Shane's face, 'Where is our fucking money you robbed? We know it was you at the services. You bought the guns and we traced them back to you. You might as well give it up before this gets really nasty.'

Shane Dwyer just carried on smiling his maniacal smile. 'I can take whatever anyone doles out to me, fellas. I'll be just grand.' And he was grinning again, a bloody rictus grin that told Cain Moran and Johnny Mac that they had their work cut out for them.

Sighing, Cain lit the blowtorch. This man was going to take persuading, and that would obviously involve a lot of pain. But there was one thing Cain and Johnny knew for sure: this loony wasn't going to give up anything without a fight first. Shame really, because they had both taken quite a shine to him.

Chapter Sixty

Denny Gunn was exhausted, and he was looking forward to getting into his bed.

Denny was a real loner, with no wife or family to hinder his solitary lifestyle. That was what suited him, but he took an occasional flier with a pro every now and then to settle his manly urges. He decided to get himself one tonight, take the edge off him. It had been a while, and he could do with the exercise, if he was honest.

The last girl he had bought himself had been a young Russian – Svetlana? Irina? One of those names. She had badly dyed hair, pretty eyes and tits like concrete. But she had a nice way about her – even if her thighs were on the larger side. That was down to the diet here he reckoned, and why those girls were making their way to London in droves for a better way of life, more money and opportunities. She wasn't cheap, but she wouldn't break the bank, and she was up for almost anything.

Inside his flat he phoned her number, and arranged

for her to visit him within the hour. He had been forced to promise her double but he was willing to pay that. Now that he was thinking about her, he was quite looking forward to the encounter. She worked for a couple of Turks out of South London; they were two brothers who were sensible but also very fair-minded where the girls were concerned. They could also lay their hands on pretty good weaponry for the right price, mainly Russian guns out of Iran and Iraq. Good market for that kind of hardware. Cain had put him on to them. And Denny was cultivating them for a future relationship, one that would be to all their benefits.

He wondered briefly what was happening to Cain and Johnny Mac, and he couldn't resist a smile. They were clever lads; he was sure they would find the bastard behind recent events. He wouldn't want to be in his proverbial shoes when they did.

Ten minutes later he answered the door with a wide smile on his face, but it wasn't who he had thought it would be.

Chapter Sixty-One

Shane was more or less dead on his feet, but he hadn't caved. He had been tortured well beyond the pain threshold of normal individuals and, even though he had lost his teeth to a set of pliers, he was still trying to grin at them. Neither the blowtorch to the soles of his feet and scrotum, the removal of his teeth and fingernails with pliers, or a drill forced through his ankle had made him say anything of note.

'This is, without a doubt, the hardest fuck in history.' There was genuine admiration in Cain's voice, even though he was feeling irritated by the man's sheer strength of character. That he could go through all that without so much as a whimper was scary and weird. But then nothing made sense to him lately – why should this be any different? 'Let's kill him and dump him. See if anything comes through from that.'

Johnny Mac nodded his agreement. 'I feel bad. In fairness, he was a fucking star – not a fucking peep out of him.'

Cain pulled the man's head back by his hair and cut

his throat quickly as he said to Johnny Mac, 'Couldn't agree more, mate. Shame. Fucking shame.'

Then they both had a drink and wondered what was going to be the next move.

Chapter Sixty-Two

It was nearly last orders and Caroline was very drunk, slumped in the corner of the pub. That wasn't unusual for her – she limited her drinking to the evenings these days. Her stints in hospital had taught her to be much more canny about her alcohol because of the medication. She rarely drank around her son now, and that fooled everyone, herself included, about how much she needed it.

She had continued to fuck around with Cain and Jenny by issuing her demands – which she claimed were always for Michael's benefit – before dashing their hopes that she'd sign the divorce papers. She had heard about their problems and she was over the moon. It was true what people said – what goes round eventually comes round, and it seemed that those two treacherous fuckers were getting it back with bells on. And so they should! They had destroyed her life and her son's life and they owed a debt of honour that she wanted paid ad infinitum. They could never suffer enough, as far as she was concerned.

The fact that Cain was offering to give her whatever she wanted didn't make a dent in her hatred. Instead, it grew bigger by the day. And as for that Jenny Riley, she was a coward, and what Cain saw in that milksop she didn't know. It was as if she had bewitched him somehow.

Caroline Moran would take no responsibility for her own part in her downfall. As she knocked back her wine, she revelled in their suffering, glad that for once their life wasn't like some kind of fairy tale. It had grieved her for years that, despite the fact they hadn't been able to marry, it was always a sunny day for that pair, and that her life was so bad in comparison. Her son had, in effect, been sidelined, and that was something she would never forgive. He was Cain's first-born, and how she wished she had called him Cain Junior. But she had never believed in family names; she felt they stunted a child.

Now Cain had his fucking namesake, and *her* son was relegated to second position. It was absolutely outrageous. She had made him pay and, oh, how she had made Jenny Riley pay as well for what she had stolen from her and stolen from her son. As for poor little Michael, she had no intention of him ever spending time in Jenny Riley's company. It was never going to happen. Not then, and certainly not now.

She had opened herself a transport café, and it was doing fabulously well. She had done that on her own, and she felt it was a great achievement. It was very successful too. That was a punch in the eye for her husband and his fucking whore – that she had an actual head for business and had made a really good success of her café.

She couldn't admit that without Cain she would never have got the premises or the funding for her little enterprise. That she had a house, mortgage free, and a generous allowance, and that Cain paid the bills and her son's private schooling meant nothing to her. As far as Caroline was concerned, it was her right, her due. She didn't allow herself to admit that she had destroyed herself and her only son in the process, that she was now obese and her son was stunted from her hatred of his father. She had taken a lovely lad and made him into a handsome but morose individual whose whole life was tainted by her hate and her bitterness. He had no idea that his father loved him and would do anything for him.

When the man sat down beside her she hadn't even hesitated. She was willing to help bring Cain down in any way she could.

Now that she knew there was big trouble coming to Cain and Jenny, she could not be happier. It was as if she had been waiting for this all her life. God Himself knew she had prayed for this, prayed for his downfall every night since he had left her for that tramp, and finally, *finally*, her dreams were coming true. It was sweet revenge. She was going to take away the Good Life he had given that whore, and that he had taken from her and her son.

Chapter Sixty-Three

Denny Gunn was amazed that someone he had thought of as a friend would actually come to his house and threaten him. It was outrageous, in fact, but when he told him so he laughed.

Denny had liked Peter Parkes from the first time he had met him. So this was a big shock, especially the kicking he'd given him – surely he knew that he did not have to go that far? He was a paid-up member of the IRA, for fuck's sake. He was fucking royalty as far as fucking villainy was concerned, and here he was being hustled by a fucking berserk! It was the ultimate piss-take and he told him just that.

Peter sighed in annoyance. 'Look, Denny, this isn't personal, mate. I've already tried to explain that. A lot of people think that Cain Moran and Johnny Mac have had too big a bite of the cherry. It's time they were taken out to let everyone else have a piece.'

There was a truth to that, but Denny believed that the current peace in London was better than in the old days where there were far too many factions vying for the same earn.

'You can't get away with this, Peter. Listen to me, mate.'

Peter shrugged. 'I don't want to kill you. That wasn't on the agenda. I'm just here to make sure you don't fuck anything up. You think you've got the Irish? Well, so have I. This is all Lenny McAvoy's doing, mate. He wants to break those fuckers' hold on London and the North. So do I. Cain and Johnny Mac have run things for too long.'

Denny Gunn felt like he was stuck in a nightmare. Lenny McAvoy was a Face in the Irish community, but he must have offered a really good deal for them to countenance this. Although, in fairness, Lenny was a big supporter of theirs. Liverpool and Manchester had big Irish communities. This would have taken a great deal of planning.

Suddenly Denny felt a great sorrow for Cain and for Johnny Mac – they were gone no matter what. It was a shame, but it was life as they lived it. It was a brutal existence that spat you out as quickly as it raised you up.

'Can I get you a drink?'

Denny was fucked, he accepted that. He had to swallow his knob, wipe his mouth – it was the only thing he could do.

Chapter Sixty-Four

Cain and Johnny were taken as they left the club. No one would have believed how easy it had been. They were surrounded in the car park, and there was nothing they could do. They were convinced they were safe, invincible – neither of them had seen themselves to be vulnerable to treachery.

It was as if they were written out of history in minutes and, in many ways, that is exactly what happened.

They were transported to a warehouse in Slough that they had acquired many years before and forgotten about. Once they were there, it was as if the whole world had gone mad.

When he woke up on that cold concrete floor, Cain remembered being beaten but, much worse, he remembered seeing Johnny shot to death, his body taking each bullet as the force of the ammunition blew him across the filthy flooring.

And Cain remembered being shot himself. And what's more, he knew who the perpetrator was, knew it was someone he had treated like family. But he was helpless. When he lost consciousness he had never expected to wake up.

But against the odds he did. The old boy who was the nightwatchman had arrived late, but he had phoned the ambulance and the police. He had saved Cain's life. But it had been far too late to help Johnny Mac.

Chapter Sixty-Five

Jenny, Eileen and Molly were at the hospital. Cain Moran was hanging on by a thread. He had five bullets in him and a surgeon was operating but it didn't look good. Johnny Mac was dead, and it looked like Cain would be joining him. Jenny was beside herself with worry and the fear of losing the man she loved more than life itself.

After five hours in theatre, the surgeon came out and told them that if Cain lasted till the morning he was in with a chance. He was a strong man, and what was needed now was not just physical strength but mental strength too. Jenny was thrilled by the news. She was convinced that Cain had what was needed to stay on this earth, and she told the doctor that.

It was while they were celebrating this that the Filth turned up. That was when the real trouble started.

Chapter Sixty-Six

Cain Moran had regained consciousness five days later and was promptly arrested for fraud and the murder of not just Johnny Mac but also Micky Two Fags, Jimmy Boy Banks and Richie Jakobs. Shane Dwyer was tacked on as a victim before the case got to the Old Bailey. He was, as Molly said, sewn up like a kipper. The big shock though was that the witness for the prosecution was Peter Parkes. He had the starring role.

Jenny lost everything, and she could do nothing about it. The police had been quick to acquire any proceeds from the alleged crime. Cain Moran had been royally set up. He should have seen it coming but, like most people who thought they were at the top of their game, it had never occurred to him that anyone would tuck him up.

Jenny had had the sense to keep cash hidden away; as Cain had explained to her over the years, you never knew what might happen and cash was cash, plain and simple. She had to leave their home, and everything in it except for her clothes and her photographs. It was as if someone had slammed a door on the life she knew and loved. But she didn't care about anything except Cain.

All Cain had cared about was that Johnny was dead. Losing the man he had loved like a brother had really affected him. He knew when he was beaten and he knew that he had to swallow his knob to guarantee Jenny and Cain Junior's safety. He had been visited in hospital and the situation explained to him in graphic detail. He had his life – which was a result whatever way you looked at it – but if he wanted his loved ones to stay alive he had to do as requested.

He had become too powerful and that was something that had had to be addressed. In his own way, he understood that too. Cain had no options left – if he had to go away without a fight for Cain Junior and Jenny he was willing to do just that. Every now and again life kicked you in the nuts. His life as he knew it was over; all that was left was the formality of the court hearing, and he had already known how that was going to turn out. It was a guaranteed guilty.

The trial itself had been a showcase for the Metropolitan Police and it got great press coverage. Cain Moran's picture was everywhere, and he was depicted as a brutal crime boss who ruled his empire with a violent and bloody hand. He was portrayed as the stuff of nightmares, and his every deed, real and imagined, was splashed across the papers and relished by the readers. His torture of prisoners was written in all its gory detail, and old Faces came to the fore once more with their own tales of Cain Moran's derring-do. It was an abortion, but Cain could do no more than live with the consequences, and endure his trial day by day.

He was escorted to the Old Bailey in a meat wagon with motorbike outriders and a stream of police cars; there were even police helicopters overhead. The jury were to be left in no doubt that this was a very dangerous man indeed.

The judge had said in his summing up that Cain Moran was a particularly nasty character whose reign of fear and terror was thankfully over. The people of London could now sleep safely in their beds. He sentenced Cain Moran to twenty-five years behind the door. In other words, Cain would not be eligible for parole until he had served the twenty-five years. The papers once more had a field day, and Cain Moran had left the Old Bailey to go back to the Scrubs awaiting his time till he was dispensed to a maximum-security prison. He was treated well in the Scrubs by his fellow inmates, who were all aware that he was the victim of his own success.

But Cain Moran had respect, and that was something no one could take away from him.

He knew this was his life from now on and he swallowed down his hatred and his desire for revenge against the bastards who had brought him down for the sake of his Jenny and Cain.

But when all the lights were out and the prison was dark and only the whispers and the clanking from the other cells could be heard, he put his pillow over his head and finally cried.

Chapter Sixty-Seven

Jenny looked around and, satisfied that everything was tidy and clean, she turned off the lights in her kitchen and made her way to her bedroom, stopping only to make sure her son was asleep. Cain Junior was lying half out of his covers, and she gently put him back into bed and covered him up.

This flat was small but it was in a decent block; Cain had seen to that and she was grateful to him. It was supposedly owned by a third party, but it was hers really and she had no mortgage on it. She also received compensation from Peter Parkes and that was the hardest to bear. That he had turned on Cain after all he had done for him – it just didn't bear thinking about.

The only good thing to come out of it, and what she consoled herself with every night, was the fact that now her son would grow up outside the world of villainy. That at least gave her some comfort.

Molly had taken the turn of events very badly, as had Jenny's own mother. Jenny, to all outward appearances, was stoic – at least in public anyway. Alone, she mourned for the man she loved more than her own life.

But it was Caroline who had hurt Cain the most. She had stood in evidence against him accusing him of threatening her, beating her, dumping his child and forcing her to take part in different nefarious activities. It was well planned and complete bullshit. To cap it all, she had finally signed the divorce papers, claiming she had no desire to be tied to a 'violent criminal' and that she would do everything to shield her son from such a father. Caroline had her five minutes in the spotlight and was given the opportunity to pay her husband back for leaving her for the woman he loved more. Of course, that was the one thing Caroline could never rewrite – he had loved her more. It was still eating away at Caroline like a cancer and Jenny was well aware it always would. That was at least small consolation for her – it was what had kept her going through these times.

Jenny's real fear was for Cain. He was looking at twenty-five years behind the door, and that was a long time. She was twenty-five now and she would be at least fifty by the time she could hold him once more in her arms. At least she was on the outside and could still have a life of sorts, but his would be a Grade-A, top-security existence. It would mean the police coming to her home after she had sent a photograph of herself in to prove that she was who she said she was. It would mean being searched and being treated like a criminal. It would mean twenty-five years of short visits and trying to keep some kind of life going for them even though they were so far apart. It would mean her son growing up knowing of his father's incarceration, and only seeing him when the visiting orders allowed.

She felt the sting of tears and hastily wiped them away. Whatever happened she was determined to keep her family together, and she would stand by her man. She had experienced the Good Life. Now it was time to pay the price – the price she had always believed would one day be demanded from them. Cain had laughed at her when she used to worry about it, but it had been true. You couldn't have too much, it was wrong – it flew in the face of God. At least, that's what she believed. And she knew that her priest did too.

She had gone back to the church during the trial, and prayed to God for guidance. Molly had been pleased, she had always been a religious woman. Molly was so strong; she joked that Mary Magdalene had been a whore, so Jesus couldn't be that against women of the horizontal persuasion. Against her better judgement, even Jenny had laughed at that one. Molly was such a firebrand, and she was glad she had her in her life. Jenny knew she was going to need her as the years wore on.

She finally climbed into her bed and, as always, she had laid one of Cain's shirts on the pillow beside her. She could still smell his scent and it gave her a great feeling of peace. It would be so long before they could lie side by side once more. She often tormented herself remembering him making love to her and how wonderful it had all been. It was strange that even when they had accused Cain of torture, of murder, of every heinous crime they could think of, she had never once doubted her love for him, even though she had believed some of it. *That* Cain had been a different man to the one who came home to her at night. Her Cain had been a loving and gentle man who adored her and adored his son. That would be the Cain she remembered, the man she would educate her son about. The man she would wait for and who would always be the love of her life.

She pulled the shirt towards her and buried her nose in his smell. She felt the sting of hot tears at the waste of a life, and the waste of time before she could hold him again. Like Cain, she cried for what was, and what could have been. Like Cain, she wondered deep down if their love could survive all those years to come. It was a frightening thought, but she had to acknowledge it, even as she hated herself for a moment's doubt. She was still a young woman, and that was something she couldn't change, no matter how much she might want to.

He had more or less told her to go and make another life for herself, that he would understand, but she couldn't leave him. The idea frightened her. She shook the bad thoughts away, sat up in her bed and lit herself a cigarette. She smoked it in the darkness, listening to the traffic outside her window, picturing the man she loved alone, thinking about her just as she was thinking about him. He had given her the Good Life. And now she had to wait twenty-five years before she could have that Good Life given back to her.

She cried once more.

Book Three

It's the good life to be free
And explore the unknown
Like the heartaches when you learn
You must face them alone

'The Good Life'
Music by Sacha Distel and lyrics by Jack Reardon

Book Three

Chapter Sixty-Eight

1998

Prison was a strange place in many respects. The men who ended up there had only two choices: either get your head down and get through it, or fight the system for all you were worth. Cain Moran had decided on the former and it was working for him. He had enough creds to make sure he was left alone, and the circumstances of his sentencing were so outrageous that ninety-nine per cent of the villains incarcerated with him felt he had been done down. He had a natural ability to make people like him, and that was invaluable when you were banged up. It was a harsh regime, but he was managing; he lived day to day as that was the only way to really serve a big lump. It was the thought of his Jenny and Cain Junior that kept him going at his darkest moments.

The sheer monotony was the worst, especially as it encouraged some of the men who were inclined towards creating excitement just for excitement's sake. Slights were carefully nurtured and brooded on for weeks before a final violent showdown would be demanded.

It was easy in prison to lose your life for something so trivial it was not even worthy of consideration. Imagined offences or a piece of dope going missing could become major battles between two people who normally got on like the proverbial house on fire.

Cain was still in Parkhurst and he was on one of the two wings that held category prisoners. M Wing was the smaller of the two and Cain found it almost liveable, as they were out of their cells for most of the day. He was in there with a mixture of terrorists, murderers and high-stakes bank robbers. They even had a five-a-side football team which caused all sorts of rivalries. They had their own kitchen too and Cain was now an expert cook; he had found to his utter amazement that he actually liked to create meals for himself and, more often than not, he was serving up to the other men confined with him.

Best of all he had his own cell; it was a luxury he didn't take for granted – he had paid enough for it. He could read whenever he wanted, and the screw who was supposed to turn out the lights at 8 p.m. was well paid to keep them on until late in the evening. He had a good radio too and, like most lifers, he had become a devotee of Radio 4; it was educational as well as uplifting for the men inside.

Cain Moran had made a life of sorts for himself despite the odds. He still had a lot of bird to do, but it was all about getting your head around the situation and making the best of it.

Some of the men on big lumps had cut ties with their wives or girlfriends, believing that they would do their time easier without the worry of who was now doing the dirty with the woman they loved. It was a sad but inevitable fact of life for a lot of the men. They understood it was tough on the outside too. They just didn't want to be the ones to be dumped by a woman who loved them and had their kids, but needed human touch on a daily basis. They couldn't get that from an hourly visit in a room watched over not just by other prisoners but by the screws as well. It was a hard life for a woman whose husband was banged up; they suffered even though they had done nothing wrong.

Jenny had been a star – she still loved him unconditionally. Cain wished that the British penal system was like the American one, where conjugal visits were encouraged to keep families together. He missed the feel of her and her touch more and more every day, and he knew she felt the same. At the back of Cain's mind there was always the worry that she would be snapped up before he made it out. She was still a beautiful woman, and she was also a woman who needed loving, and needed that loving often. It was bittersweet to remember how much she had enjoyed their lovemaking, and how much he had enjoyed it too. The only thing he was glad of was the fact he had never once done the dirty on her. He had often quoted the old Paul Newman saying: 'Why go out for a hamburger, when I can have a steak at home?' He had really believed that and he still did. He wished he could have married her all those years ago when Cain Junior had been born. But Caroline had put paid to that. It had taken pulling a lot of strings, and a significant amount of time of 'good behaviour' but he finally had the green light to marry his Jenny and give her his name. That they would be married in the prison chapel wasn't ideal, but it was something they both wanted more than anything. He pretended to the other inmates that it was all for her, but inside he was overjoyed he would have a legal claim on her finally.

While thoughts of Jenny and Cain Junior comforted him, his thoughts of Johnny Mac plagued him, broke into his dreams and upset his peace of mind. The fact that no one believed that he had been fitted up for his murder was what really rankled with Cain. Everyone knew that, as bad as he was, he could no more have harmed Johnny Mac than he could have harmed his own child. But there was nothing he could do to right that wrong – not banged up in here anyway – plus his priority now was to keep Jenny and Cain safe, and if that meant he had to keep his head down and do his time, he would do it for them.

He walked into the kitchen – or two cells that had been knocked into one and fitted out; it was a shithole but better than nothing. He opened the fridge and took out a large pack of minced beef. He was going to cook everyone on the wing spaghetti Bolognese – it was a favourite of the men – and he was going to make garlic bread and, for a few of the diehard Northerners, hand-cut chips to go with it.

Cain liked this time of day. It was late afternoon, and the knowledge that another day was nearly over was a good feeling for most. It was another twenty-four hours closer to getting out. Not that any of them talked about that, of course, but it was always on their minds. Even something as mundane as cooking was a pleasure when it utilised your time, and helped you get through another few hours.

Cain started to pull out the pots and pans needed when a PO came into the kitchen with a carrier bag. He opened it and took out a bottle of Scotch, three litre bottles of red wine and, with a flourish, a bottle of grappa.

Cain grinned and put the bottles under the sink. 'Well done, my old son. Fucking grappa will go down well!'

The man grinned in agreement. He was a friendly screw – which meant he could be bought – and it was things like that which made this place easier to bear. He was paid on the outside so that no money changed hands on the actual premises. It was the only way they could get alcohol or drugs inside; even if they didn't search family members visiting, they couldn't bring in enough drugs for the whole prison system – and they certainly couldn't bring in alcohol. The POs were seen as whiter than white no matter what, but who gave a flying fuck, as long as they got what they wanted from them?

This particular PO was called Tommy West and he was a decent bloke who genuinely thought that the men locked up like they were for the long haul should have at least some form of recreation. He wasn't a PO who believed that the men needed a second sentence; after all, the judge had already given them one and it was a harsh lesson. Tommy West felt that losing your liberty was punishment enough. He was a well-liked and well-respected man who did what he could to lighten the load. And, of course, for a price which paid for his own little luxuries. He made a point of doing his damndest to make the men inhabiting M Wing feel like they were still part of the human race.

'Listen, Cain, I don't want to speak out of turn, but there's a new guy on his way in and, from what I have heard, he has paid out a lot to get on this unit.'

Cain felt the familiar hand of fear creeping up the back of his neck. He knew the prison jargon and he understood what this man was trying to tell him. All the same, he just smiled amiably. Cain Moran knew exactly how to play the game. He was getting a heads-up, and if this man was laying it on the line for him out of friendship, then it was important.

'Who is that, then?'

Tommy West liked Cain Moran a lot. He thought he had been given a fucking hard sentence considering he had not done all the crimes he was convicted of. Cain Moran's circumstances were very well known in the justice system. The general consensus was, the bigger you were, the harder your fall would be, and he had fallen big time.

'It's Jimmy Boy Banks's kid. He's after retribution for his old man, or so I hear.'

Cain Moran closed his eyes for a few seconds. This was the last thing he needed – a young, up-and-coming bruiser looking to gain a reputation. It wasn't as if Jimmy Boy Banks had even had a second for any of his kids – by numerous women he would add. He had been known as a slag. He fucked them, gave them kids, and moved on. But this boy was willing to defend his father. It was laughable, but not unexpected. There had been a few youngsters over the years who had confronted him, hoping to make their reputation by giving Cain Moran a hammering. Well, he had hammered them first and shown them that it took more than willing to put a man down – especially a man like him.

'When is he due in?'

Tommy sighed. 'Tomorrow, late afternoon. He is being shipped from Durham. He's paid a good wedge for this wing, but I felt you had a right to know.'

Cain smiled easily. 'Thanks for the heads-up.' Then he set about the preparations for the evening's dinner.

Chapter Sixty-Nine

Caroline was in her diner, and she was eating as usual. As her son came inside, she smiled at him. He was his father's double and taller than most of his peers. He would be like Cain, and young Michael Moran was sick of hearing it. He hated his father for abandoning him – especially for abandoning him to this woman who he loved and hated in equal measure, depending on her state of mind.

When she was drinking he loathed her with a passion so acute he could almost taste it. He felt the same when she went on one of her long tirades about his father and his utter contempt for his faith, for his marriage and for his family. And once Jenny Riley's name was brought into the mix she was like a woman possessed. In his heart of hearts, he wished she would just let it go once and for all; it was ancient history now.

'Have you heard the latest, Michael?'

He shook his head. It was typical – not even a hello

or a greeting of any kind. This meant the news had to be about his father.

'He is marrying it in prison.' She said this last bit with a flourish. Then she laughed nastily, as she said, 'A jailhouse wedding! Just about her fucking mark, that is.' She was still laughing as she continued, 'No fucking honeymoon either!'

Michael nodded. He had learned a long time ago that when she was in this kind of mood the best way to deal with her was to keep quiet and let her get it out of her system.

She carried on eating; she was working her way through two pies, a pile of chips and a huge mound of peas, topped off with gravy, and a mountain of bread and butter. He eyed her critically. She had to be twenty stone at least, yet her hair and make-up were always perfect. It was as if she couldn't see the rest of her body, the fat ankles that spilled over her shoes, or the huge pendulous breasts that hung to her non-existent waist. It was such a shame that she had allowed herself to get so big, because it wasn't good for her health, or her peace of mind.

'Well, what have you got to say?'

He shrugged as if he wasn't bothered. 'It had to happen someday, Mum. I don't know why you let it bother you so much. Who cares what that pair of wankers do anyway?'

He was trying to ease her tension, but she went

behind the counter and poured herself a glass of red wine. As she knocked it back, he sighed. This was going to be a long night.

Chapter Seventy

'Oh, Jenny, that is beautiful, darling.'

Molly was admiring the white suit and little lace hat that Jenny had purchased for her wedding day. It was understated, well-cut and she looked a treat in it. She still had her killer body and Molly mourned for the years Jenny had been forced to sacrifice without Cain by her side. It was a powerful love that would make a woman so determined to have her man and no other, no matter what. She never missed a visit and she never acted hard done by, she was always cheerful and happy. But Molly knew she was lonely, desperately lonely. It took a certain kind of woman to wait so long for a man, and she knew how lucky her son was to have found one.

Little Cain wasn't so little any more. He was tall and handsome, he had his father's build and his father's good looks, but his mother's disposition. Jenny had high hopes for him, especially as he was such a genuinely nice boy. He had always just got on with whatever he was asked to do, no dramas, no teenage angst.

Cain was proud of him; considering he had grown up visiting his father as a Grade-A prisoner, he took his father's predicament in his stride, and, as Molly was forever pointing out, kids were resilient. Cain Junior certainly was – he accepted the situation, and he lived with it. He supported his mother, and he loved his parents. It broke Jenny's heart to see him sit every Sunday night composing a letter to his father about his weekly doings. It was so important for Cain to get those missives, but it was also important for her son to keep up that contact with his father, especially as Michael had no contact with him whatsoever. Every letter Cain had sent to Michael had been returned unopened, and that had broken his heart, though he would never have admitted it.

For Jenny, life had fallen into a pattern – she lived for her son and for her visits to Cain on the Isle of Wight. He had left her provided for, and she appreciated that, but it had cost them dearly to keep him from being shipped all over the country. He liked M Wing, and he enjoyed the company of the men there; that was good enough for her. All she wanted was his happiness, and she would move heaven and earth to help him achieve that. It was hard enough for her, and she was on the out, able to do what she wanted, when she wanted. It was different for Cain. She never let herself forget that – it was the mainstay of their relationship and her whole life was devoted to making him feel better about his position.

She was made up that they'd at last been given permission to get married. It was all she'd ever wanted. She would finally be Mrs Moran and they would chase away the ghost of Caroline, the first wife, the only wife. Until now.

Chapter Seventy-One

James Banks Junior was a strange man; he had more of his father in him than he realised. Not that he had really known the man, of course. There were a couple of photos of his father holding him as a baby and that was about it. His mother told him everything he needed to know and, despite her best efforts, he continued to idolise him. In fact, it was what kept him going as he grew up, trying to emulate the man who had spawned him and then cruelly rejected him. He looked just like his father which didn't help either – he would catch his mother watching him at times, and he could see the naked loathing for the man whose child she had produced.

James Banks's story was pretty typical. He had started out getting into trouble at school. And then school stopped. So he ran wild on the streets, and pretty much descended into violent crime.

It had not been easy, but he had wangled himself to Parkhurst so he could finally take out Cain Moran, right a wrong, and gain a reputation as the man who had taken out a legend. It would guarantee him respect and admiration, both of which he craved. He wasn't a complete fool – he knew that Cain Moran wasn't going down without a fight, but he was willing to give this his all. It was make or break time for James Banks Junior. And he was almost looking forward to it.

Chapter Seventy-Two

Word was all over the prison about James Banks Junior and his sojourn on M Wing. He had his own cell too, so it seemed that he already had a few friends in high places.

Cain Moran was monitoring the atmosphere, and he didn't like what he was feeling. The younger men were already siding with James Banks. Cain could understand that to a degree, but it was the reaction from some of his own peers that rattled him. Prison was a strange place – the normal rules and boundaries didn't exist. This would be making for excitement, something different; it was such a monotonous experience that it was amazing what constituted entertainment.

He dished up the dinner and everyone ate it with gusto. As the wine and the grappa flowed, the talk turned to local matters.

It was Frankie White, a huge bear of a man doing a thirty for drug and arms dealing, who said what everyone else was thinking. 'How do you feel about your nemesis arriving, then, Cain?'

Cain shrugged indifferently. 'What can I do? He'll be here tomorrow afternoon. I just have to wait and see. Could be something or nothing.'

One of the younger men, a nice lad called Benny Pyle, said carefully, 'You did kill his dad, though.'

Cain barely suppressed a grin at the boy's words. 'Well, Benny, I think we can safely assume that old Jimmy wasn't exactly a fucking choirboy. Someone was going to take him out and he happened to get up my nose first. I ain't apologising for the past, son. Fuck him. It was a mercy killing. If ever there was an argument for abortion, Jimmy Boy Banks was it.'

The older men laughed. They agreed with him in principle, but there was still an edge to the atmosphere around the table. Violence was always simmering away somewhere in the prison system. It was a real, raw emotion, and it was also a way to get things off one's chest. There was nothing like a good riot to put everyone into a good mood. Failing that, a decent punch-up could do the trick.

Young Benny waited for the laughter to die down before saying carefully, 'Just seems a coincidence him turning up in the same wing as you.'

Cain poured himself a large glass of grappa and knocked it back in one swallow. Then, grinning, he said to Benny loudly, 'You fallen in love with me or something? Very concerned for my welfare all of a sudden, aren't you? Is there something you're not telling us?' Cain fluttered his eyelashes like a girl and the men cracked up laughing, but the insult had been delivered – Cain was warning him off in a nice way. 'The day I start to care about little fucking wannabes is the day I listen to the fucking Spice Girls, OK? Now stop worrying about me, son, and if you're really good I will let you hold me hand in the shower!'

Everyone was laughing once more, and the tension eased. But it told Cain what he needed to know about young James Banks and his entrance into the criminal fraternity of M Wing. The lad had a few supporters, and that was natural, but it seemed he would have to take the fucker out sooner rather than later. Although any trouble and he would lose his wedding privileges – that was not something Jenny would take kindly to. She was over the moon about this wedding, even if it was a prison do. It was the least he could give her when she asked for so little and did so very much for him. It was a fuck-up all right, this James Banks turning up now, in more ways than one.

Later that evening, Frankie popped into Cain's cell and in a quiet voice, he said seriously, 'You never heard this from me, but there is a hidden agenda with this kid, so just watch out.'

Cain nodded. He didn't sleep much that night, just lay there and pondered the best way to deal with the situation. He was still awake when the sun finally crept through his cell window. He would have to box clever to try and resolve the issue with the minimum of fuss. The wedding was the important thing at the moment, and he daren't do anything to fuck that up.

Chapter Seventy-Three

One of the screws was a big Scot who answered to the name of Jock McFarland, liked and respected by fellow POs and prisoners alike. He was the one to keep order, and he had a natural ability to lead. He was also on the take, as were most of the other officers. They all took money for different reasons, for different services rendered. McFarland had brokered the deal that had brought young James Banks on to M Wing. He had not questioned it too closely; well, he wouldn't, would he? It was for a flat fee, and it was a popular wing to be on – especially if you were doing a lot of bird.

Now, though, he was in a quandary and he wasn't sure what to do for the best. This was a very delicate situation, especially considering the two protagonists involved. Cain Moran was a man with a big lump still to do, and a temper that could bring untold slaughter on the wing if pushed, whereas the younger man, James Banks, was just that – a man with a score to settle and a reputation to make. It could only end in disaster. This could end up a kill-or-be-killed situation, and that would not be good for anyone. The governor would not be impressed, this was worthy of TV news coverage, and that was the last thing anyone wanted. The prisons liked to keep their heads down these days. It was such a powerful subject for the politicians, and no one actually had to deal with these people hands-on except the prison service. It paid off all round to keep certain prisoners happy – in the long run anyway.

He would have to order a cell search, something that he hadn't done for years. Most of the men would be found with various sorts of dope or prescription drugs – contraband was accepted as part of the monetary system of a prison. Debts were paid, certain things could be purchased, and it gave the men a feeling of wealth and security. Now they would have to instigate a huge search for weapons, because he would lay his last pound on there being at least one dangerous one already floating about – probably more. Shivs were the easiest – a Stanley knife blade in a toothbrush was a quick and efficient weapon, as was a billiard ball in a sock. But he would put his money on a knife of some description, and a stabbing either in the showers or a cell. It would be quick and brutal, and it would cause him untold fucking aggravation. He needed to monitor the situation, and keep his eyes open.

He had a feeling, though, that there was more to this story than met the eye, and it would be a while before he would even manage to scratch the surface. He had called a meeting of his fellow officers to try and find out what they each knew individually, and see if he could piece together a fucking resolution that didn't involve coffins or intensive care units.

As the officers trooped into the common room, McFarland sighed heavily. This was going to be a long old day. Half of these were only in the prison system because the army didn't want them, or because they weren't suited to any other kind of work. It took a particular breed of men to want to lock up others; that was something he had learned over the years. Not all of them were doing it for the right reasons either. It could easily turn nasty – things like this caused factions to divide, unsettled behaviour and death. He was hoping that somehow he could minimise the damage. But he wasn't holding his breath.

Chapter Seventy-Four

'Sometimes I wonder what planet you're on, Mum!'

Jenny and Eileen were arguing about the wedding, and Jenny was not about to give in to her mother's demands.

'You're my only daughter and I want to see you married.'

Jenny laughed. 'And you can, only you are not wearing that outfit. I'm sorry, Mum.'

Eileen looked down at her new suit and felt the familiar resentment at her daughter's deliberate attempts to turn her into a washed-out version of Molly Moran.

Jenny didn't even bother to answer her, just made a vague gesture in the mirror with a roll of her eyes.

Eileen carried on admiring herself; she loved the suit she had chosen – it was a cerise miniskirt and bolero jacket. Personally, she thought it looked good on her, but obviously her daughter had different ideas.

Jenny held up a pale green dress and coat set; it was silk, fully lined and looked like something an old granny would wear.

'I'll look like your mother in that!'

Jenny grinned, exasperated. 'But you are my mother, remember?'

Eileen dutifully tried the ensemble on, and had to admit it looked much better on than off. Which in itself was very annoying – her daughter had a knack of choosing the right clothes for every occasion. It galled Eileen, even though she knew it was unfair. She was actually looking forward to seeing this daughter of hers married at last, although if she was honest, she thought Jenny should have cast her net a bit wider and got herself some proper companionship. There had been no hint of scandal attached to her girl, and there was a part of Eileen that thought she was unnatural. Sex and living life was for the young, and a twenty-five-year wait seemed to Eileen Riley a very foolish thing to endure. She was entitled to a bit of companionship, for want of a better word. There were plenty of men willing to take up the slack and, as her old mum used to say, you don't miss the odd slice from a cut loaf. The girl should have some fun before it was too late. That was Eileen's attitude anyway – not that Jenny took any notice of her of course. Hell would freeze over and Christ Himself would be risen before that ever happened.

Jenny was genuinely admiring of the outfit she'd chosen for her mother. It really suited her, and she looked a lot sexier in the green silk than she did in the cerise miniskirt ensemble! If only her mum understood that sometimes less is more.

'You look lovely, Mum, really lovely.'

Eileen smiled. It was true – she did look nice. Jenny had chosen well for her. She could have anyone she wanted, her Jenny. She would put a bit of temptation in her daughter's way; she didn't want her to waste her entire life waiting for Cain Moran. She needed a bit of life for herself now and again. Everyone did.

Chapter Seventy-Five

James Banks Junior was already settled in his cell; he was liking the wing. He had been nervous at first but that had passed quickly. The other young men were friendly and eager to make him welcome – he was a novelty and someone new was always welcome in a monotonous place like this. He had news, stories of mutual friends and enemies. It was hard to keep track of people when they were in different prisons all around the country, so he would be in demand for a few weeks until he had exhausted his supply of gossip.

Cain Moran had greeted him cordially and James had been taken aback at the sheer size of the man – he had what was called a presence. Moran was clearly not in the least bit worried about seeing him; he had shaken James's hand firmly, his grip a clear indication of his strength. James Banks knew he had his work cut out here. Cain Moran had to go down, and go down quick. If he managed to get up, then James was finished.

He was now observing Moran in the gym. He was standing with the other older lags, and he still looked like he could give anyone younger a run for their money. His reputation as a violent fucker was obviously well-deserved. But nothing was going to deter James; this was an opportunity he had thought about constantly for the last few years. The plan was to take Moran out, put himself in his place, and then sit back and reap the rewards. He would be established overnight and, as he would have all the rights to Cain Moran's enterprises, that would set him up for life when he got out.

Now he had to plan his attack, and it had to be a good plan. Cain Moran was older, and he was certainly much wiser. But one of the things James Banks had inherited from his absent father was not just a big nose and a psychotic personality, but his innate cunning. He would watch and wait, and then, when he was sure of his bait, he would pounce.

It was a shame in some ways – everyone agreed that Cain Moran's cooking was exceptionally good; he had to give him credit where it was due. His Sunday roasts would be sorely missed, but such was life. This was James's big chance and he was going to take it. Whatever his old man had been, he was still his old man, and that had to count for something, surely? James liked to think that when he had been sent down for this big lump, his dad would have stepped up to the breach and looked after him if he'd been around. It would have made him proud – he really believed that. Such was the mentality of James Banks Junior.

Chapter Seventy-Six

Eileen Riley knew that Freddie Marks had always had a crush on her daughter. He was a small-time Face – and a good-looking man – so she had arranged for them to bump into one another at the pub on a few different occasions. What was the harm?

It wouldn't take a blind dog long to sniff out that the man was crazy about Jenny. He was big, dark and blue-eyed just like Cain – definitely her daughter's cup of tea. Eileen didn't see this as being unfaithful – it was just a diversion while the love of her daughter's life was otherwise engaged for what was a fucking long time by anyone's standards.

Eileen knew the score with men like Cain; he would be chasing youth once he got out, and she saw it as her maternal duty to make sure her daughter had some fun in her life before it was too late. She appreciated that Jenny was so loyal – something she'd not inherited from her, that was for sure! But it was wrong to see that girl waste away for the best years of her life.

Eileen had given Freddie Marks a heads-up that her

daughter was actually going to meet her in The Highwayman for a drink; he was clearly over the moon at the chance to be in her orbit. Eileen, being Eileen, had basically said that her daughter was up for anything he might want. Not strictly true, of course, but it would give the boy a bit of encouragement – he was like a greyhound waiting to get out of the trap. He was a handsome, nice fella, and, most importantly, sensible enough not to mouth off about anything that might happen. He didn't want to find himself dead one night through a leaked conversation. As far as Eileen was concerned he was a perfect candidate for her daughter's affection; if she got a bit of the other now and again it would do her the world of good. It wasn't natural to be without for so long – that was Eileen's take on life.

As her daughter walked into the pub Eileen felt a wave of fondness; she was a good girl, and how she had turned out so fucking well was a mystery to everyone, not least her own mother. As Jenny sat down, Eileen looked her over. One thing with her Jenny, she had never let herself go because she didn't have a man in her bed. She kept herself nice for the man who she adored, even though he was as far away from her as the moon. It was a crying shame.

She went to the bar and got them both a drink, making sure her daughter's was triple, and encouraged her to drink it quickly. After a few of them, Jenny became soft and silly; unlike her mother, Jenny didn't drink heavily on a daily basis. Just a glass of wine at the end of the day, she had never made a career out of it. Moderation in all things was her girl; whereas Eileen was more take what you can get – you might never get it again. Now, though, Jenny was rocking, and that was going to help matters along considerably. Eileen was pleased to see that her Jenny had a bit of her mother's DNA in her after all.

When Freddie Marks joined them it seemed perfectly natural. Jenny was welcoming, and there was no doubt he was pleased to be seeing her and that he was basking in her company. Eileen sat back and watched Mother Nature working her magic. As the two of them reminisced about their school days it really was a sight to see. Her work here was done.

Chapter Seventy-Seven

The POs were on edge, and it showed. Every time Cain or James went anywhere, they followed, even if they were going in different directions. On a wing that wasn't very big, it was getting irritating. But it was necessary and there was not much anyone could do about it.

Today Cain was trying his hand at something new – fish with roasted vegetables and, of course, the mandatory chips! Most of the older lags wouldn't eat anything else – chips were a staple in their diet, especially the Northerners, who drenched them in gravy whenever possible. He was keeping a close eye on young James, who was, in turn, keeping a wary eye on him, as Cain was wielding a particularly large knife for most of the afternoon.

Bobby Vincent, a forty-five-year-old con from Essex, found the situation quite amusing. He was the wing wag, always ready with a funny story or a joke. He was also a violent criminal who was doing thirty years behind the door for murder and drug dealing. He would do the thirty, mainly because of the drug dealing – anything to do with property and money always took precedence in the courts over human lives. Bobby was a known bruiser, but he was also well liked and an integral part of the wing's group. He could often be an unlikely arbiter between feuding parties – his sense of humour often defused very tense situations.

Now he was lounging in the kitchen, chatting to Cain as he cooked. 'Cocky little cunt that James.'

Cain grinned. 'Nice enough kid – just a bit misguided!'

Bobby burst out laughing. 'Misguided? He couldn't find his cock with a compass. Cheeky little bastard. Fucking take him out!'

Cain laughed too. 'It's not for me to make the first move, is it? I mean, I ain't got any row with him. He seems to have one with me, though, I will grant you that.'

Bobby smirked, then said seriously, 'How can he defend that piece of shit, Cain? The man didn't even fucking give him the time of day. He should be shaking your fucking hand for doing everyone a favour, especially him.'

Cain shrugged. 'Maybe he feels that's all the more reason to repay that particular debt. He at least thinks he is doing the right thing.'

Bobby didn't answer him for a few moments. 'Well, you were always a fair man, but I've got to say, if it was me, I would give him a fucking good hiding, and put him out of action for a few months. I fucked his mum once – met her at a party in Blackheath. Not the greatest shag I ever had, but willing after a couple of lines of coke, got to give her that. I was going to mention it to him, but he seems the type to hold grudges . . .'

Cain was still chuckling when Bobby left him to go to the gym, but he knew Bobby had a point. Maybe he should give the lad a talking to, at least attempt to clear the air a bit. There was no real animosity between them, but Cain Moran knew that meant nothing in the world they inhabited. It was why they were all Grade-A on this unit – they were all what was called 'unpredictable'. They were men in for serious offences who could look after themselves should the need arise. They lived a kind of life together here, but it could be rocked at any time. Cain Moran knew the others were wondering what the outcome of this situation was going to be – he wondered it himself. He just felt he should let the lad make the first move. He was the harbinger of the trouble, not Cain.

Later that day at dinner, young James said to Bobby in a friendly manner, 'By the way, Bob, my mum says to tell you hello.'

It was said in all innocence and when Bobby and Cain started to crack up laughing they could see the poor lad's confusion at what he had said that was so funny.

Most of the older men sussed it out straightaway,

but it wasn't a joke they should have shared together in public. It was the piece that cemented James's resolve. One of the other lags explained the joke to him later that night, and he was not a happy little bunny. You could more or less say anything to a man in prison, but never denigrate his mother. It was bad enough Cain had murdered his father, without adding insult to injury. Jimmy felt he had been humiliated, even though he would be the first to admit his mother could be quite free with her favours. He had had more uncles growing up than all his mates put together. But whatever she was, she was his mum and he loved her.

The damage was done, and there was no going back.

Chapter Seventy-Eight

Freddie Marks had driven Jenny back to her place, and she had invited him in for coffee. It had been a lovely night, and she had enjoyed his company enormously. It had felt good to unwind, be out of her home for a while and enjoy some adult conversation. It felt odd having the place to herself, but Cain Junior was staying at her mum's – she was taking him up the Roman the next day to get some bits and pieces, and treat him to his favourite pie and mash.

Freddie Marks had been her friend since they were in infant school, and they had both tried to outdo each other with their recollections. Suddenly names and places she had not thought about in years were as real to her as they had been way back when. Teachers long forgotten were discussed – and taken the piss out of for the most part. It had felt so good. Freddie was a handsome man, and she was aware he had always had a crush on her; she had liked him too in those days long ago. But then along came Cain, and there would never be another man, not for her anyway.

She poured them both another coffee and said on a whim, 'Fancy a brandy?'

Freddie was more than ready to prolong their evening. Jenny was stunning, and he was knocked out by how nice she was. She had no side to her character, what you saw was what you got. She dressed well too – without flaunting everything as if she was on sale, but he liked what he was seeing well enough. He had had a big-time crush on her since they were teenagers and part of him couldn't believe he was in her flat, drinking brandy and listening to her laughing as she regaled him with another story of their youth.

At the back of his mind was Cain Moran, but it was hard to worry about a man who still had a good fifteen years before he would be a problem. Clearly Jenny loved the man – she had kept telling him that all night to the point where he had nearly asked her who she was trying to convince, him or herself? He didn't, of course – he would do nothing to alter her mood. He loved listening to her, being with her. He liked the way her breasts moved when she laughed, and how she looked at him with that pretty half smile as she listened to him. And she did listen which was unusual in a woman, as far as he was concerned. He was used to the lairy, laughing, everything's-a-joke kind of women who he usually attracted. Until, of course, he realised they thought they meant something to him, then he would end up on bad terms and arguing for England, when all he wanted was a nice little fuck and a good night out. But Jenny Riley had a way of concentrating when you talked to her that really made you feel what you were saying was valid. It was a wonderful feeling, and he knew he was falling for her hard.

Freddie had briefly lived with a girl, and they had a little daughter who he adored, but within months he had known her mother was not for him. Andrea was pretty, bubbly, he supposed, and she had a body like a porn star. Unfortunately, an original thought in her head would die of fucking loneliness – she was basically as thick as shit. Unfortunate turn of phrase, but apt in her case. She could chatter for hours and still not have a real opinion on anything and it had driven him to distraction. His three-year-old daughter could have a better conversation and, as much as it had hurt Andrea when he left, he knew there was no way they could ever be together for any length of time.

He was ambitious and he knew *this* was the type of person he needed – a calmer, self-assured woman who would not be intimidated by him, who would hold her own if he challenged her beliefs. For the first time in years, he was excited about being in a female's company, and it was even better because that woman was his first love. All he wanted to do was kiss her, strip off her clothes and make love to her. But he was a sensible man who recognised she needed to be handled with care. He had to wait until the right time presented itself.

Coming back to earth, he suddenly realised what

she was saying, and he interrupted loudly, 'Sorry, Jenny, can you repeat that, mate?'

Jenny laughed. 'I said, I'm getting married in one week! I'm marrying my Cain at long last.'

He tried to plaster a smile on his face, even though he could have cried. 'Kept that a bit secret, haven't you?'

She shrugged. 'I didn't want a big fuss. It's just a matter of getting it legal, you know?'

He nodded sagely, while stifling the urge to scream with frustration.

'What with his ex-wife still causing trouble, you know? We thought it would be best to keep it low key. Not rub her face in it.'

He didn't know how, but he was still smiling at her. Then he said boisterously, 'Caroline Moran causing trouble, who'd have thought it?'

Jenny laughed with him. 'She's a fucking nightmare, honestly!'

'Well, it's been a long time coming, Jenny, and you deserve some happiness.'

'Thanks, Freddie, that means a lot.'

'Cain still has a big lump ahead of him, though, I mean, are you sure you're doing the right thing, mate? You're still a young woman.'

She smiled at him, appreciating that he was concerned for her. 'I know what I'm doing, Freddie. He is the only man for me. Has been since I met him when I was sixteen!'

She launched into the story and, as she told him about her first run-in with Cain Moran, all Freddie could think was, *what a fucking waste of a life.*

But he smiled anyway, because he didn't know what else to do as she told him how much she loved her husband-to-be.

Chapter Seventy-Nine

A young con named Stevie Harper was closeted with James in his cell. It was time for James to put his plans in motion, and he had recruited Stevie to help him. He was negotiating with James about getting him a blade that would be delivered to the gym the next afternoon. It wouldn't be a problem getting it back on the wing because he had a cousin who would take care of that end too – for a hefty price.

James Banks had decided he needed a decent blade and not a shiv because he had to take Cain down in one; if the man got up he would be up shit street. He would never underestimate a Face who had got as far in life as Cain Moran.

Stevie was happy enough to be the provider; he knew that no one would hold it against him however it might turn out. He had a living to earn like everyone else. Personally, his money was on Cain Moran – you would need a fucking seriously early start to get the better of him. On the other hand, young James Banks was a determined soldier, and you never knew what might go down in these kinds of cases. The book was already open, of course; the older men and a few of the younger ones were laying money on Cain, but no one was writing James off, so that was a compliment to him in a way. It would be a bit of excitement at least and that alone was something in this place.

'When you going to do it, James?'

Stevie was genuinely interested, and James believed he wasn't trying to find anything out for reasons detrimental to him, as they were already good mates.

He shrugged. 'I need to have a good think, you know, Steve? I don't want to fuck it up, like. In the next few days, though.'

Stevie nodded sagely. 'Well, I wouldn't leave it too long either. He'll know you're tooled up. It's the way of this place. He's been fair, I think. I mean, he has access to basically anything he wants, especially in the kitchen. You were right not to use a knife from the unit – that could cause untold aggro especially if that's the reason the kitchens close. You would really make a few enemies then, believe me. The cooking of food has become the prime fucking interest in this place!'

They laughed together.

'I ain't a cunt. I want Cain Moran, but I don't want to take on all-comers!'

Stevie grinned, before saying seriously, 'I admire you, James, and I don't want to tell you what to do, mate, but the general consensus is you would be better off trying to resolve this without violence. No disrespect, but your old man wasn't what could be called popular. You know what I mean?'

James nodded in agreement. 'That's it though, Stevie – whatever he was, he was still my old man. Laughing about my mum and all, that's fucking out of order. I know she was a bit of a girl, but she's still my mother. She's stood by me through thick and thin. No matter what I've done she's been there for me, without question.'

Stevie smiled. 'Enough said. You will have your tool tomorrow.'

They shook hands and left it at that.

Chapter Eighty

Cain Moran was lying on his bunk wide awake. It was late and most of the other lags would already be dreaming of their own particular heaven. He got up quietly and, pulling out his bunk, he took off the mattress cover and felt inside until he found what he was looking for. He had owned this for over seven years and he had kept it in the sure knowledge that one day he would have to use it. Now it seemed was the time.

He weighed it in his hand – it was heavy and it was dangerous. It was a real boning knife, the kind used by fishermen. It was honed to perfection, and it would easily slice up anything from a rampaging elephant to a human being, such as young James. He was sorry he was going to have to use it, but the options were either strike the first blow or defend himself. Cain still wasn't sure what it was going to be.

He placed the knife back in its hiding place and remade his bed. Lying down again, he debated whether to kill the kid once and for all, or whether to just maim him enough to keep him away for the duration. He was leaning towards the latter option, but his sensible head was telling him if he was going to do this he had to do it right – finish it and send a message of sorts. Cain Moran had an inkling that there was more to this than James Banks Junior was letting on. It was a melon scratcher all right.

For the first time since he had been banged up, Cain fell asleep thinking of someone other than his Jenny.

Chapter Eighty-One

A wise man once said that a prison was a place of revenge and retribution. The man in question was doing thirty years and had already served twenty-eight of those, so he knew what he was talking about.

Young James seemed to have quietened down, and some of the men breathed a sneaky sigh of relief; a murder on the wing would cause a lot of fucking aggravation. Others believed the lad was biding his time and waiting for his opportunity, so there was a general feeling of expectancy in the air too. It was certainly colouring the men's days, and the POs were in a state of nervous exhaustion into the bargain. Young James was acting as if all was well with his world and Cain Moran was not showing any sign of concern. It was everyone around them who seemed to be the most troubled.

In truth, Cain was on red alert. His big fear was that if it went off too soon, it might affect his wedding, and that was something he did *not* want to happen. It was only three days away and he wanted it to go off without a hitch of any kind. This was Jenny's big day and it had to be as fabulous as possible, given the circumstances and where it would be taking place. He had taken it upon himself to weigh out a serious wedge to make sure there was a decent cake, good flowers and to top it off one of the POs had even promised him an hour with his new bride. That was something he was *really* looking forward to.

He could smell cannabis and knew without looking that Stevie Harper had come into the kitchen, Stevie liked to do his time stoned. Lots of the younger men were inclined that way. It was considered one of their five a day – it was green and could be mistaken for a vegetable, he supposed. Cain wasn't averse to the odd puff himself, though he would never understand the heroin used by so many of the younger men. But they were entitled to do their time in their own way, and no one could deny them that – especially the POs who brought it in at greatly inflated prices.

'All right, Stevie lad?'

Stevie was really stoned today; his eyes looked like pools of piss in the snow. Still, he was an amiable boy and rarely any trouble. 'I've got the fucking munchies. Anything sweet about?'

Cain couldn't help laughing at him. 'There's still a bit of cake from Blokko's birthday.'

Stevie was thrilled. 'You are a fucking veritable Escoffier, mate. That cunt could cook and all.'

Cain grinned. Only mad Stevie would know about

a French chef. He was a mine of useless information – he read voraciously and had a brain like a sponge. The men were forever telling him he should do a degree, use his time inside wisely. But he had no interest. Stevie said he went on the rob rather than to school, so he wasn't going back there now. It was a crying shame because he was a clever lad when he bothered.

'Listen, Cain, I know I shouldn't be telling tales out of school, but watch your back tomorrow, mate. He's eager and he's determined.'

Cain stopped his food prep and turned to face Stevie. 'Could you do me a favour? Would you ask him to leave this until after the wedding? I just want to get that out of the way, you know?'

Stevie nodded. ''Course. Can't see why he wouldn't. It's all a fuck-up anyway. On a death wish, if you ask me.'

Cain didn't bother answering. He thought he might talk to the lad himself and see if he could sort this out – at least in the interim anyway. Jenny was so looking forward to taking his name and being his wife – it was all she wanted in her life. It wasn't really much, when you thought about it. She was a fucking star. Cain wondered if he deserved to be loved with such loyalty. She just saw this as a blip; on the nights when sleep escaped him, this seemed like a fucking big blip to him. He knew how lucky he was that she was happy to wait for him. He couldn't bear the thought of her with anyone else; just the idea of someone else touching her was enough to send him nearly demented. He had expected it at first, even as he prayed it never happened.

He had seen the effect a wife finding an alternative sex life and pay packet could cause to men in his position. It was harder for them at times because they were men who were respected for not showing weakness. They couldn't reveal the pain of betrayal. They left behind beautiful, vibrant women still in the peak of their physical fitness, who were far better looking than they deserved. If they hadn't been villains the women would never have given them a second fucking look. How could they be blamed if they got fed up of waiting around and found another meal ticket?

So many young women used sex as a bargaining tool to make sure the men they targeted left their wives and children for a better fuck and a supposedly better life. They provided a quiet haven with no kids, a decent Scotch and a firm pair of knockers, heady stuff to the men they had set their caps at. Men had walked away from the mothers of their children for less. Loyalty might be everything in a villain's game, but when it came to wives it was a one-way street. They expected it, even if they didn't give it.

But young girls weren't about to spend the best years of their lives visiting a man old enough to be their father. They loved the name, the money and the prestige they garnered from their association with the criminal they had shagged like their lives depended on it. But once the said criminal got a lump and a half there was some rethinking on the part of the young female. They tended to go on the trot before the end of the trial. Karma was a bastard.

Cain Moran was one of the lucky ones. It was more than just love with his Jenny – she was staunch and loyal and she did believe in fidelity. That was why he was so pleased he had never taken a flier during their relationship – it made him feel that he had been as loyal to her as she was to him. And it meant he could justify expecting her fidelity in the dark hours of the night when he wondered if she was really as good as she made out. That was another pitfall for the long timers – the night thoughts, when you questioned everything about yourself and your life, when you felt paranoia settle over you and you tortured yourself with thoughts that you knew were wrong but you couldn't dismiss. He would picture Jenny with another man, convince himself that she was laughing up her sleeve at him, making a fool of him, feeling the bitter tears of frustration and desolation wash over him, until the dawn light when he would finally manage to get a few hours' sleep, and the world could be put back on its axis again. Until the next time, of course. Night horrors were a part of prison life, everyone knew that.

So he had to make sure his Jenny got her day. She deserved a day to remember.

Chapter Eighty-Two

Blokko Barnes was a well-built man, covered in thick body hair that looked like a coat, with a smile that could disarm a concentration camp guard. He was a big part of wing life, in as much as he was always the first to hear, see or find out something. He could procure almost anything – except a woman. But he was working on that.

He was pondering the situation of Cain Moran and young James Banks. Blokko didn't like James. He had hated his father and he thought the boy was acting the goat with this macho bullshit. The long and the short of it was the boy wanted what Cain Moran had and he was out to get it. There was also a suspicion – only a small one – that made Blokko believe there was more to this than met the eye. The kid seemed to have an inexhaustible source of bunce. He wasn't a serious Face like most of the men in here, and he didn't have the income on the outside to bankroll his nefarious activities. So someone was obviously putting up the dosh and he was doing them a favour while he helped himself at the same time. This was something Blokko knew instinctively, and he was wondering why no one else had thought of it, especially Cain Moran, who was as shrewd as they came. But then, ten years in the clink did dull the senses somewhat.

Blokko had a tame screw who worked the gym. He was a handsome, muscular young man who would let Blokko use his phone for a price and who would drop down on his knees now and again and give him a blow job. Blokko was only queer on the inside, never on the out. It was another anomaly of the prison system. But needs must when the devil drives, as the old saying went.

He decided he would make a few calls and see what he could unearth. He liked Cain Moran, and people getting fucking murdered for nothing didn't sit well with him. It completely devalued the real killings that were performed for serious reasons; murder wasn't something that should be taken lightly by anyone.

As he wandered towards the gym, he saw Cain eyeing James's cell and he wondered if the boy would be dead come dinnertime. If that was the case, he would be well pleased. But he still wanted to know the score. Blokko could be quite nosy when the fancy took him.

Chapter Eighty-Three

'I've got his suit freshly cleaned, and Cain Junior's clothes are perfect too. Oh, I can't believe it's only two days away! I will finally be Mrs Cain Moran! Woohoo!'

It was a hen night of sorts, but it was enough for Jenny. They were in The Highwayman and they were having a lovely time. It was nice because people kept coming over and offering them drinks and congratulations. Jenny was a bit worse for wear and Molly was keeping a beady eye on her; she knew she wasn't a drinker as such. Unlike her mother, of course – Eileen was putting the drinks away like there was no tomorrow! God, that woman must have hollow legs.

Someone put some music on the jukebox, it was 'Gangsta's Paradise' and, as Coolio started to sing the lyrics, Caroline Moran suddenly appeared in front of Jenny, her enormous bulk intimidating in its sheer size.

It took Jenny a few seconds to realise who it was. When she did, she sighed heavily. 'What now, Caroline?'

Her voice sounded measured and bored; she had learned the hard way how to treat this woman.

'So he's marrying you, is he?' There was a threat in her words, but that was par for the course with Caroline Moran. She thrived on intimidation.

'Jesus! You must be hard up for a fight, Caroline, if you've ventured all this way just to state the fucking obvious.' This from Eileen who hated Caroline Moran with a vengeance. She had stolen her daughter's ability to have children and that was something no woman should have to endure. Eileen was standing up now and, as she grabbed a glass to use, if necessary, on Caroline's fat, smug face, Jenny pulled her back into her seat with a surprising strength.

'Sure it will get that far, darling? He might be dead by then. Or he might be on the block. A lot can happen in a few hours.' Caroline's voice was dripping venom, and her hands were shaking with her anger.

Jenny looked at the women she despised and wondered at a person who could maintain such bitterness for so long.

'Do you know something, Caroline? I felt sorry for you once. I know how I'd feel if Cain left me. But you just can't fucking leave anything alone, can you? You have to taint everyone and everything with your bitterness and your fucking bile. Yes, he is marrying me like he always wanted to. It would have happened years ago if you hadn't stood in the way. It won't be the wedding of the year, thanks to you, but that's the difference between me and you. He doesn't need to buy me. He never did.' Jenny was smiling now, her lovely face lit up with happiness. 'I will be a Moran too. Be like relatives, won't we? Now, take your fat fucking carcass and get out of my sight, because this time, lady, I'm going to fucking hit you back. You've done enough damage.'

The whole place was quiet – someone had even unplugged the jukebox. There was an air of menace closing in on Caroline and she could feel it. She knew she had no friends in this place – she had no friends, period.

As if on cue, Bella Davis walked into the pub, late as usual, and seeing the scene before her she rushed to her friend's side.

Molly stood up and, taking Caroline gently by the arm, she said kindly, 'Come away now, Caroline, this isn't the time or the place. . .'

Her voice seemed to spur Caroline into action. She pushed the old woman away and screamed at her, 'He was mine, Molly, and she fucking stole him from me! He was mine and I loved him.' There were tears streaming down her face now, and she was clenching her fists with frustration and rage.

Everyone was staring at the enormously fat woman, with the make-up and hair and the black silk muumuu. There were still traces of her former beauty beneath the fat. It was like seeing the destruction of a beautiful painting, she looked so obese and so bloated. But it was the perfectly made-up face that was so haunting, especially screwed up into a mask of hate as it was now.

'He was never yours, Caroline. You made sure of that with what you put him through. And look at how you're carrying on now. All these years later you're still holding a grudge.'

Molly sounded so normal, so sensible, that for a few seconds Caroline almost found herself agreeing with her. Then she looked at Jenny, beautiful, slim Jenny Riley, who would soon have her name and her son's name, and who would legally be the main woman in Cain Moran's life. That's when she launched herself across the table, and all hell broke loose.

Chapter Eighty-Four

'All right, James? Can I talk to you for a few moments? Nothing funny, I swear.'

James shrugged. "Course.' He was wary, though, in case Cain was going to go for him and get this over with.

'I need a favour from you, James. I know you think you have an axe to grind, and that's your prerogative but I want to call a truce until after my wedding. My Jenny is a great girl – she's kind and soft and a really nice person who wouldn't hurt a soul. I'm asking for her, really.'

James smiled suddenly. "Course, mate. I'm happy enough to do that.'

Cain Moran smiled back.

Chapter Eighty-Five

Jenny Riley was on top of Caroline Moran, battering her to within an inch of her life. The years of upsets and late-night phone calls spewing abuse, all the insults to her child and the aggravation and demands for money were finally taking their toll on Jenny. But it was the woman's battering of *her* that she really wanted to pay her back for. The beating that nearly ruined her life and that stopped her from ever having another child and that could have killed the only child she would ever have.

The people in the pub were as amazed as Molly, Eileen and Bella, as they watched Jenny give a woman at least three times her size the hiding of a lifetime. It was cold and it was calculating. Jenny was concentrating on her enemy's eyes and nose, which were bloody and raw already and, worst of all, it was done without Jenny uttering one word. Eventually Jenny was dragged off Caroline by Freddie Marks, who pushed her out of the pub with the aim of calming her down. He had hoped he might see Jenny there, but when he walked in on the scene before him he thought he was hallucinating. Lovely, gentle Jenny Riley was beating up that fat bitch and doing it like a professional. Wonders would never cease.

Jenny was struggling to get back inside and finish what Caroline Moran had started all those years before. She had never in her life felt so angry and full of hatred. They heard the police arrive before they saw them, and the car was closely followed by an ambulance. It was the sound of sirens that finally allowed the reality of what she had done to sink in, and Jenny slumped into Freddie's arms. Then the tears came. Freddie was quite happy to hold her and comfort her until it was time for him to deal with the authorities on her behalf. He felt like he was rescuing his very own damsel in distress.

Chapter Eighty-Six

Blokko was in a quandary. He wasn't sure what he should do with some new-found information. His telephone calls had uncovered a very strange scenario, one he had never imagined before. He was annoyed that someone else could be so fucking snidey. Snidey but clever – very, very clever. It was so calculated, he couldn't for the life of him work out how he could even attempt to rectify it without getting involved personally.

And personal involvement wasn't something he cared for. He was a lifer, and in a nick like this he was a sitting target – they all were. You only had to look at this shit with Cain Moran and that fucking moron Banks. Everyone acting like it was none of their business when, if they were on the outside, everyone would be telling Cain to shoot the cunt and get it over with. But in here real life was suspended, and it was all pretend niceties. That was what was wrong with this whole fucking set-up. They were living a life of pretence, forced to share their space with people they would cross the road to avoid on the out.

In here you had to be accepting, had to make allowances for people, like the youngsters skagged out of their tiny minds because they couldn't hack the boredom, and didn't know how to cope with their sentences. They had never allowed for the fact they might get caught and end up with a lump and a half, spending the best years of their lives in a top security prison, watching their youth fading away while their friends on the outside married, fathered children and went off every day to mundane jobs and had holidays in the sun.

He made his way to Cain's cell. He had to tell him the score. The man had been treated badly – he deserved a fucking break and, more to the point, a heads-up. This was far more involved than any of them had thought.

As Blokko walked through the unit, he looked around and sighed at the futility of a life wasted – and a life that was on hold for the foreseeable future.

Chapter Eighty-Seven

Freddie Marks was pulling in favours left, right and centre, and finally they were getting somewhere. The DI on the case was a woman called Kate Desmond, and she was obviously in full sympathy mode with Jenny. It seemed that Caroline Moran's knack of making enemies stretched to the police force as well. But it was Jenny he was worried about. She looked dreadful.

Molly and Eileen had been sent home in cabs; the last thing they needed now was Eileen sticking her oar in and causing more trouble. Freddie was happy to be left alone with her to help sort out her problems. He had rung a few mates and that had softened everything so far – there had been no charge as yet. It was up to Caroline now; if she pressed charges that was it. He hoped the few well-placed calls he'd made would dissuade her from that course of action.

What a fucking mess! Jenny had cried her make-up off, though somehow she still looked good; it occurred to him that he must really be on a love job. She was dangerous but he didn't care – all caution had gone out of the window.

Kate Desmond was in a quandary. She had, in her station, Jenny Riley – soon to be Moran if the rumour factory was true. Jenny was known as a good 'un – the fact she had battered the fuck out of that big-mouthed Caroline Moran was a shock in itself. And now she was being championed by Freddie Marks. Kate sighed heavily. The last thing she needed was the aggro of this kind of situation. They never ended well – and there was the obvious grudge match as they both wanted the same man.

Why did women want these kinds of men? It had always amazed her. She had raided houses where young girls, with their whole lives ahead of them, already had two kids and a black eye from the local bullyboy. It was heartbreaking knowing the kind of existence these girls had unwittingly signed on for. Old before their time, visiting various nicks, as their good looks faded and their men looked elsewhere for excitement and youth. Kids whose earliest memories were their mattresses being split open with knives in case the loving father had hidden drugs or guns in them. Christ, she had once taken a ten-inch blade from under a cot mattress. If the toddler sleeping in there had got hold of it . . . There was certainly no accounting for taste, she knew that much. When she thought of the shouting and screaming that accompanied these raids, from girls no more than children with a misguided sense of loyalty, she could scream herself.

Then there were the Jennys of this world, decent women who had genuinely fallen for the wrong man, who had not actively sought out the local nutter. And where had it got the poor lass? It had got her under caution while everyone decided the best way to handle this particular scenario, that's where. It had also got her into the clutches of Freddie Marks who, by all accounts, was fast turning into the new Cain Moran. Sometimes Kate hated her job. The only good thing was that everyone in the pub had said the same thing: Caroline Moran had thrown the first punch and caused all the aggro. Not that it made it any easier for Kate, of course. She didn't want to arrest any of them.

She sighed as she excused herself and made her way to the hospital.

Chapter Eighty-Eight

Caroline was in extreme pain, and she was also in extreme shock. Her sheer size usually guaranteed her the edge when it came to a fight, so to have that skinny little mare defeat her had really knocked her for six. It was a public humiliation, even though she knew it was her own fault. She had wanted to send that bitch to her wedding with two black eyes – that had been the reasoning behind her confrontation. Never in the wildest stretch of her imagination had she thought the girl would fight back at all, let alone so vehemently. It was still sinking in. She had been royally trounced, and the people who had witnessed it seemed to think she had got what she deserved.

She saw the nurse walk past her room and bellowed once more, 'Oi! Bring me a fucking mirror!'

She needed to see the damage. It hurt like fuck, she knew that much, and her nose was throbbing. That whore had actually broken it! She was a strong fucker, she could see that now. Jenny Riley had systematically battered her as if she had been waiting for years to do just that. Caroline knew in her heart that she had driven her to it, with all the obstacles she'd put in front of a divorce, determined to keep Jenny from getting the one thing of Cain's she had left – his name. There was a tiny part of her that was ashamed of her behaviour, even though she couldn't stop herself. It was like a mania with her – she'd never come to terms with the fact that Cain had left her for that council-house rat. God, she wished her mum was still alive. She missed her every day.

Just then her aunt Dolly came into the room with two teas and a small hand mirror. She did not look happy in the least. Caroline was well aware that she was on her last chance where Dolly was concerned; the woman was heartily sick of her and what she called her 'antics'.

'Well, she certainly made a mess of your boat race, Caroline.' Caroline didn't answer her, so her aunt went on in the same irritated voice, 'You are not to press charges, Caroline, do you hear me?'

Caroline didn't know what to say.

'If you press charges, this becomes bigger than it ought to be. You had your shot at the girl and she's kicked your arse. Let it go now, for fuck's sake. Just let it go.'

It was the horrified scream that accompanied her peep into the small hand mirror that brought the nurses running back to her room.

Chapter Eighty-Nine

Jenny Riley looked at her reflection in the mirror and was pleased with what she saw. The hotel was perfect. Close to the prison, it wasn't the first time a Face's bride-to-be had stayed the night. They knew the score and they didn't intrude too much, though they had sent her up a bottle of champagne and some chocolates. She didn't care that she was a prison bride, she just wanted to be a bride – Cain Moran's bride. She had waited so long for this day and now it had finally arrived. She felt the buzz of excitement as she sipped at her glass of champagne to settle her nerves.

Her mum and Molly were still getting ready and Cain Junior was waiting patiently down in reception in his new suit, looking handsome and gorgeous just like his dad. These were her last few moments alone, and she raised her glass to her reflection and toasted Cain silently. She felt the sting of tears, but she fought them back. This was a day of happiness and nothing and no one was going to ruin it for her.

Closing her eyes, she thought of Caroline. Even

after everything, she felt a wave of pity for the woman who she knew had been determined to destroy this day for her. In Caroline's warped mind, it was going to be Jenny with a broken nose and two black eyes, not the other way around. Jenny couldn't believe that she had actually broken the other woman's nose! It was so far removed from her usual behaviour that it still shocked her to think of it. But Caroline had asked for it – kick a dog enough times, eventually it will turn and bite you. That was an old East End saying but a true one. She had seen red that night, as if someone had turned on a switch inside her and she had just gone absolutely demented.

She was lucky to get away relatively unscathed herself before the wedding. A lot of ice and arnica on her knuckles in the past forty-eight hours had concealed most of the damage to her hands, and a good manicure had done the rest.

Thankfully, Caroline had refused to press charges and with Freddie Marks's help she had been well looked after. Freddie had proved himself to be a good friend, and she needed a friend these days. She could sense she and Bella were growing apart. They led different lives now, and the fact that Bella was too scared to come to her wedding spoke volumes.

Well, she wasn't going to think about that. Now Jenny just wanted to enjoy her wedding day and spend the rest of her life in peace and tranquillity. It had been a long time coming. She took another look at herself, satisfied with what she saw. She only hoped that Cain liked what he saw too. But she was sure he would. After all, he loved her as much as she loved him – that was all there was to it really.

Chapter Ninety

Molly and Eileen didn't always see eye to eye. Eileen in particular could be jealous of Jenny's closeness to Cain's mother. But today they had called a truce of sorts. Molly was dressed in a pale blue, well-cut suit that Jenny had chosen for her, and a small pillbox hat that looked sophisticated and cheeky at the same time. Eileen was in her green silk confection and the two women admired themselves as they stood side by side in the suite.

'You look lovely, Eileen, that green really brings out your eyes.'

Eileen smiled. 'I know. She can pick clothes, my Jenny. Fuck knows where she got that knack from – it certainly wasn't me.'

They both laughed.

'You look nice and all, Moll. That blue suits you a treat.' Eileen poured them both more champagne, and they toasted the bride and groom together.

Eileen sighed. 'I never thought my Jenny would be getting wed in Parkhurst.' There was an unusual note of sadness in her voice and Molly laid a comforting hand gently on her arm.

'Sure, she is a good girl and, whatever the circumstances, they love each other.'

Eileen nodded her agreement. 'I always saw her having the whole nine yards, you know? Church, bridesmaids, the lot. I know she wanted Bella to be here but she couldn't do it. Bella is scared of all this, bless her.'

Molly sipped her drink and sat gingerly on the edge of the bed, careful not to crease her good suit. 'Well, that's as may be. But your Jenny has her head screwed on. I admire her so much. She has done a wonderful job with that lad, and she's always known what she's taking on. She's no fool. They'd have done it years ago if Caroline hadn't fought Cain at every turn. I swear that if I thought for one second Jenny was doing the wrong thing I would have said it to her. But, you know, I honestly believe they are meant to be together. I think the fact that they've let nothing drive them apart all these years just proves it. I have never known my son so enamoured of anyone for so long in my life. And I love Jenny like my own for the goodness in her, and the loyalty she has in abundance. You should be proud, you know, Eileen? You obviously did something right, lady.'

Eileen basked in the compliment, all the time thinking, *You would think that, you old bat. It's your son you're interested in, not my girl who's wasting most of her life waiting for a man who she can't even hold in her arms.* But she didn't say any of that – she wasn't a complete moron. Instead she raised her glass, and said sweetly, 'To the bride and groom! God help them.'

Chapter Ninety-One

Cain was showered and primed, amazed at how excited he felt. It was due mainly to the fact he had had the nod to say he would get an hour alone with his wife rather than anything to do with the wedding itself. It was going to be worth the wait. His mind kept replaying Jenny naked and waiting for him. After all this time it would be a fucking thrill to feel himself inside her again. He was sweating just thinking about it. His Jenny, a room to themselves, and an hour that needed to keep them going for another fifteen years. It was a tall order but he felt up to the job. He closed his eyes and pictured his Jenny and groaned out loud.

Hearing the laughter of Blokko he guessed the man had sussed him out. He shrugged as nonchalantly as possible. The man had given him an invaluable heads-up about what was really going on with young James Banks. Blokko was a real mate, and Cain would always be grateful for his help. He had not expected such loyalty and friendship from him and it was all the more appreciated because of that. Now he knew exactly what he was dealing with and how to put an end to it. Blokko had certainly taken a load off his back, there was no doubt about that.

Cain had a few axes to grind, and this was the perfect excuse to get sharpening his chopper and pay out some much-needed retribution. He had swallowed his knob for ten years, because he had needed to protect his family. But this revelation put a completely different complexion on things. He needed to assert himself, let the people concerned know that he was back and not about to let them keep him down any more.

If the Irish were out of the game, and according to Blokko that was the case, then it was open season. And that cunt who had been holding him to ransom all these years would be the first the feel the effect of Cain flexing his muscle. He had taken over the use of a certain officer's mobile phone and arranged his own little party for *that* particular ponce and his grassing sidekick. All in all, Cain Moran was feeling life was looking pretty good.

Chapter Ninety-Two

James Banks Junior was as excited as Cain Moran – although for a very different reason. He was going to make his move sooner rather than later. He'd been thinking about it for days. Cain Moran thought he was getting a pass until after his wedding. But he wasn't. He wouldn't be expecting that – no one would be expecting that.

James rolled up the sleeve of his shirt and started to burn some H – just a little buzz to keep him calm and collected. Stevie had introduced him to the healing benefits of heroin and he was finding it did help the time to pass. As he fished a yellow jelly diazepam out of his little leather kit bag to melt with the powder, he imagined what it would be like to plunge the knife between Cain Moran's shoulder blades. He felt quite breathless at the thought. Nervous and excited at the same time. He would be set for life, and that's what he wanted more than anything in the world: to be somebody, to achieve a proper status.

It didn't occur to him that if this came off, *he* would

eventually be in the same position as Cain Moran. There would always be a youngster looking to off *him* so he could take on his mantle. That was much too forward thinking for young James Banks.

Chapter Ninety-Three

The pastor was a middle-aged Jamaican called Leon Sparks, and he was looking forward to marrying this couple today. He looked around the small chapel room and smiled happily; the place looked almost festive. He took in the expensive flowers and the ornate wedding cake that looked like it should be on the cover of *Hello!* magazine. It never ceased to amaze him what the cons were capable of in this place. Good luck to them too – he wasn't a man who thought they should be locked up every second of every day. He liked to do the weddings, it made a change from preaching to a church full of men who were only there to do deals or relay messages. He wasn't a fool – he knew the score.

Now, as his eyes swept the place to make sure nothing had been forgotten, he set about distributing the hymn books on the few chairs, and making sure that the music was in place in his little ghetto blaster. He was still smiling as he went through to reception to meet the blushing bride. He liked Jenny Riley, soon-to-be

Moran. She was a decent, steady woman who loved her husband-to-be with a passion that was painful to watch at times. But you played the hand God dealt you – that was all anyone could do.

Chapter Ninety-Four

The POs were still nervous about the situation regarding James Banks and Cain Moran. That something would happen was inevitable. They were each just hoping that it wouldn't be on their shifts – the paperwork would be fucking outrageous. Statements to be taken, local Filth swarming all over the place, treating them like they were no more than glorified fucking mall cops. It would be a nightmare.

The wedding had lifted the mood. There was good-natured slagging off going on at breakfast where the men had been drinking champagne and orange juice and Cain Moran had even made scrambled eggs and smoked salmon. The atmosphere had been good, everyone toasting the groom and making lewd jokes about his wedding afternoon; it was common knowledge he was getting the opportunity to be alone with her. The men were jealous and impressed by that in equal measure. One thing was certain, it would not have come cheap. Everyone had seen photos of her too, so there were definitely going to be a few marathon wanking sessions tonight. She was a good-looking piece, and so loyal too, never the hint of a scandal surrounding her.

Nevertheless, Jock McFarland couldn't shake the feeling of foreboding. He had spent a lot of time on this wing, and he knew when there was something about to erupt. He could feel an undercurrent of malice, hidden under the coating of camaraderie and jokes. There was something just a little bit off – nothing he could put his finger on, but it was there all the same. Until something happened, though, he could only advise his men to keep alert for the first signs of aggravation, and then to steam in as fast as possible. It would be over in seconds, but the reverberations it would cause could be felt for years.

Until that James Banks had wangled his way on to this wing, it had been a good place to work. They were hard men, admittedly, but sensible, wanting to do their time with as much comfort and ease as possible. Now the place had an air of tension underlying everything. Jock wanted it over with the minimum of fuss.

That aside, he still had a tenner on Cain Moran. After all, if it was going to happen, the least he could do was make a few quid off it. That was only human nature.

Chapter Ninety-Five

The car was a white Rolls-Royce and, as Jenny and her family piled into it, she couldn't help smiling as the other hotel guests waved her off in a friendly fashion. She wondered how many guessed she was going to a prison to make her vows. But she didn't care what they thought – all she wanted was to marry the man she had loved since she was sixteen years old.

She shivered as she thought of the hour together he had promised to bag them. She knew it would have cost in excess of twenty grand, but that was a small price to pay for the opportunity to feel his arms around her, feel him inside her once more. She had hardly slept for thinking about him and what they were missing. She tried not to let herself dwell too much on the physical side of their relationship, but it had been very important to them both and if she allowed herself to think of them together, making love, it killed her. God, how she missed him, the smell of him, the taste of him. She pushed the thoughts from her mind – this was neither the time nor the place.

She smiled at her son who was chatting away to his nanas, full of excitement at the day ahead. He was the best man and kept taking the rings out of his pocket to check he hadn't lost them.

Molly and Eileen looked great and she smiled at them, her stomach fluttering once more at the thought of soon feeling the man she loved holding her. She fought to blink the tears behind her eyes away.

Cain Junior looked at her, and said seriously, 'I feel like crying too, Mum. It's not every day your parents get married!'

Eileen and Molly laughed but they too had a catch in their throats. The lad looked so very happy, and he was obviously looking forward to the day. It was a bittersweet moment, and even hard-faced Eileen found she had a tear in her eye.

Chapter Ninety-Six

Peter Parkes had grown up a lot in the last ten years and he relished his status as a man of the world. Peter made his presence felt on every level. He was aware that his workforce didn't exactly like him, but he was at least respected as a fair, if somewhat hard, boss. If he had learned anything from Cain Moran it was that to stay at the top you always had to be one step ahead, not just of your competitors, but of any wannabe that might work close to you.

His part in Cain's downfall and the death of Johnny Mac didn't bother him in the least. He had never liked Johnny and the feeling had been mutual; he suspected that Johnny had never entirely trusted him – well, he had been right about that. He would have preferred Cain Moran dead too, and that was what he was working towards now. Cain Moran's reputation was ever more stellar inside than it had been on the out. That he had been badly treated was a common topic of conversation, and Peter knew that went a long way with the older men in the business.

Since the Irish had bailed, he had been given a much clearer idea of what Lenny wanted the organisation to be involved in. Drugs were the main earner, but that was par for the course these days. They still controlled the movement of all shipments and decided the prices. If working for Cain Moran had taught him anything, it was to always make sure everyone got a decent earn – that way, you cut down on people brokering side deals for themselves. Anyone caught doing that was punishable by death. That was the final word on the subject.

The only fly in his ointment was Lenny McAvoy. He was still living in the 1960s and that annoyed Peter. Lenny was a good bloke in many respects but he had passed his sell-by date a long time ago. The fact was, Peter didn't need him any more. Once Cain Moran was out of the picture for good – and that was providing that silly little cunt James Banks achieved his objective – Peter was going to out Lenny as well. He would disappear and that would be the end of it.

Peter Parkes's wife Lola was a tall, leggy redhead, with killer tits and a serious coke habit. As he walked into his house he could hear her shouting at their twin sons like a banshee. He rolled his eyes in annoyance and went through to the large state-of-the-art kitchen. His sons were only eighteen months old, and she expected them to act like adults; it was fucking laughable. He saw the mirrored tile on the breakfast bar, with lines already cut, and a rolled-up twenty-pound note beside the residue.

'Keep the fucking noise down, you silly bitch!' His two boys toddled towards him, glad to see their father. 'Where's the fucking au pair? What am I paying her for?'

Lola laughed nastily. 'The au pair has fucking been sacked, for fucking the boss as usual. Honestly, you can't keep it in your fucking trousers, can you?'

He closed his eyes in distress. He really had to stop shagging those young Swedish girls; it always ended badly for everyone concerned.

'The next one to come here is going to be short, fat and hairy. Even you wouldn't sink that fucking low.'

Peter didn't answer her; he really couldn't argue with that.

Chapter Ninety-Seven

Caroline was drunk – drunker than she had been in years. Her face was still a mass of bruising and pain, so the alcohol and the painkillers were making her even worse than usual. Michael tried to help her, but it was a pointless exercise.

'She will get her fucking just deserts, you mark my words.'

'Mum, it's early afternoon and you can barely string a sentence together. Why don't you go and lie down? Or at least eat something.' He never thought he would be asking her to eat, so it proved how far gone she was. Normally he was begging her to stop; he was convinced she would have a heart attack if she didn't sort herself out.

She was mumbling now, going on about how much she hated his dad, how he had dumped them for his new whore. It was a story he had heard since he could remember. It was funny, but he didn't really feel any animosity towards Jenny Riley. She was just as caught in the crossfire as he was, and he had made

305

it his business to look up his brother a few times. There was no doubt they had the same father and he seemed like a good kid.

It was his father he blamed for everything, because his leaving had turned Caroline into a shadow of her former self. She had been funny once, full of fun and laughter, but those times were few and far between. If only she could move on but, as Aunt Dolly had pointed out to him on many occasions over the years, she didn't *want* to get over it. She revelled in her sorry state and her life dictated that she could never experience happiness like normal people. She just moped around, and the only time she was even remotely normal was in the diner. There she generated a bit of her old sparkle, and laughed and joked with the customers, making sure the food was top notch and the atmosphere was good. It was the only success in her life and it clearly meant the world to her. But for his sake he wished she would just let the anger go. He wanted a mother, not a drunken bitch whose life was a constant stream of invective.

Michael remembered how it had been when his dad came home to *them* and not to Jenny Riley. He had been a happy kid then and lived for his father's attention, but he realised now that it wasn't enough. Cain should have been kicking a ball with him, coming to his school, but the fact was he never had done any of those things. He was always working, keeping nightclub hours most of the week, and he was rarely about except for on Sunday mornings after a heavy Saturday night. Michael remembered those long breakfasts, though, when his mum would push the boat out and they would have American pancakes with maple syrup, and bacon and eggs. That was another lifetime.

Still it was a nice place to visit in his head sometimes; he liked to remember the good times with his dad. There had been some – whatever his mum might think. But that was long ago and now the man was banged up. Good riddance to bad rubbish.

Well, his dad was finally getting his new family today, all signed, sealed and delivered. He hoped the new Morans fared better than the last lot. Because his dad had a fucking lot to answer for.

Chapter Ninety-Eight

'Nice suit that, Cain. Handmade?'

Cain nodded. It was a long time since he had worn anything other than casual clothes or gym sweats. The suit was a reminder of everything that he had lost, of a life gone from him, and that was putting a shadow over his day. If he wasn't careful he would become depressed. It happened to a lot of the younger men especially – depression and anxiety were reasons why drug and alcohol abuse was so rife. It was hard to keep upbeat and cheerful all the time. Someone once said that prison and doing time was a state of mind and they were right. It was about keeping in the moment, living day to day, and not dwelling too much on the past or the future. But Cain couldn't help mourning what he once had. He felt almost tearful.

'The last time I wore this suit was for a business dinner. Jenny was wearing a cream dress which showed off her cleavage to advantage. It was a good night.' He could hear the regret in his own voice.

Blokko laid a hand on his shoulder. 'Don't dwell

on it, mate. Listen, you got her today, by your side. She is one of the good ones. Don't fuck it up by wishful thinking.'

Cain laughed. 'You're right, mate. Besides, I'm feeling on top of the world. I've sorted out something that's been on my mind for years, and it's my wedding day.'

Blokko left him then, and Cain resumed his preparations for his wedding. He couldn't wait to see Jenny, and his boy, of course. He wondered how Michael was – he had written to the lad a few times but never heard back from him. Natural, he supposed, that he would take his mum's side.

Cain Junior had always written to him at least once a week, rambling letters about his life. He knew Jenny probably made it fun, sat with him and discussed what he would tell his dad. She was good like that – she could make anything seem like an adventure, even something as boring as writing a letter.

He was getting choked up again, and he had to fight back the tears. What was wrong with him today? He had to sort himself out – the last thing he needed was to break down. His credibility would never be the same again. He could just imagine the ribbing he would have to take from the others, but he couldn't help it. He felt very emotional today.

Last night at the stag party, he had cooked as usual and the men had all brought drink to the table. They had discussed marriage, women, sex, the usual male

309

ribald topics. But it had set him thinking about the future, and how long it would be before he could enjoy a real married life with his wife. Another fifteen years at least before he could even hope to get out. Suddenly it seemed so fucking far away, even though he was already nearly ten into his sentence. The knowledge that he would have to wait so long to be beside his wife hit him hard. He wondered once again if it had really been worth it.

Taking a deep breath, he settled himself to the tasks in hand. Regrets were for fools – what was important now was getting through the days, and that was what he had to focus on. Today would be a good day, he knew that much.

He heard someone come in his cell and, as he turned towards the noise, he saw the flash of metal, and realised instantly that young James had decided to take matters into his hands a little earlier than expected. The fucking idiot! If he had only waited as promised.

Bringing up his arms, Cain Moran knew he was in a fight for his life.

Chapter Ninety-Nine

Peter Parkes was sitting at his breakfast bar, drinking a cold beer, scanning the headlines of the *Sun*, when two men walked through his patio doors and shot him dead.

Lola heard the shots from the pool house as she watched her sons paddling in the baby pool Peter had installed a few weeks before. She instantly recognised the sound of the gunshots and knew they must mean bad news.

Scooping up her sons to go and investigate, Lola felt sure of what she was going to find. Having just sacked the au pair, she was irritated to think she would have to deal with everything herself. Really, some people were so fucking selfish. She popped the boys in their playpen and cleared away her drug paraphernalia before she finally called the police. One look at her husband had been enough to tell her it was too late for an ambulance.

Chapter One Hundred

Lenny McAvoy was in his office in Liverpool when the telephone rang. He picked it up and listened for a few moments before throwing the receiver across the room in fury.

'Fuck!' he bellowed. This news was not good.

He headed out, motioning to the two heavies standing guard to follow him.

'Come on, lads, we're going to London.'

As they got in the car and the driver turned the key, there was an ominous click.

Lenny desperately lunged for the door. But it was too late.

Chapter One Hundred and One

'I beg your pardon?' Eileen's voice was rising an octave a word as she tried to comprehend what the PO was saying to her.

Molly and Cain Junior were equally disbelieving and Jenny was white with shock as she demanded, 'Where is he? Is he OK?'

Jock McFarland was a soft touch where a pretty woman was concerned; he liked Jenny Riley and really didn't relish being the bearer of bad news. 'He's alive, Jenny, but badly cut up. It was a clear case of self-defence but, as the other man is dead, we'll have to hold an inquiry. It's such bad luck this had to happen today of all days.'

Jenny dropped into a chair and, putting her head in her hands, wept bitter tears. She couldn't believe it. Everything she had put up with over the years had been made bearable by the thought of this day. Now it was ruined. Once again, the consequences of Cain's lifestyle had destroyed something precious to her and, for the first time ever, she felt a huge wave of resentment towards him. She had never asked for much – this was all she had ever wanted for herself.

Now her dreams were shattered, and she was left like fucking Cinderella – all dressed up with no fucking ball to go to.

Molly Moran was beside herself with fear, and she wondered why Jenny didn't appear more worried after learning of his injuries. 'Can we see him? Can his wife at least see him?'

Jenny stood abruptly and said quietly, 'I'm not his wife, though, am I? You can see him if you like, Molly. Personally, I'm going home. I can't deal with this at the moment. If they let you in, tell him I said he can get fucked.'

With that, Jenny pulled her son towards the door, her mother following on behind in stunned silence. Eileen had not expected her Jenny to react like that.

Molly called after them, 'You heard the man, Jenny. It wasn't his fault!'

Jenny didn't even slow down as she said seriously, 'No, it never fucking is his fault, is it?'

Jock McFarland didn't know how to react, so he did just what his mother always did in an awkward situation and asked Molly Moran with forced cheer, 'Can I get you a cup of tea, darlin'?'

Chapter One Hundred and Two

Cain Moran was being stitched up in the infirmary; the cuts were deep and painful, but not enough to get him to the local hospital. He was fuming with James Banks Junior. The silly little fucker had ruined everything for Jenny, Cain Junior and his mother. Enraged, Cain had used all the considerable force he possessed when he plunged his blade into Banks's neck. If the stupid little cunt had waited a few days it would have been sorted. Once he had known Parkes was out of the picture, leaving him with no backup, he would have definitely folded. He wasn't a foolish kid; he would have understood he had no chance without support.

Now Banks was dead, and Cain's wedding day was completely fucked. His fury was such that he didn't even need an anaesthetic while he had the stitches. Instead, the pain felt good, real, and it took his mind off his troubles momentarily. Poor Jenny – she would be devastated, bless her heart. He loved that woman so much, and he had planned on showing her just how much in the room he had arranged for them; he could have held her and loved her once more for a precious hour. Now, thanks to that prize prat, it had all gone to shit.

If the little fucker was still alive, Cain would kill him all over again.

Chapter One Hundred and Three

'Are you sure you're all right?'

Jenny sighed heavily. 'Yes, Mum, I'm sure. It's happened and I can't do anything about it, can I? He killed someone on the morning of our wedding. If it weren't so fucking tragic it would be laughable.'

Eileen was trying her best to ease her daughter's broken heart. 'It wasn't his fault though – you heard that PO. Be fair, darling . . .'

Jenny drank her vodka and Coke in one long gulp and reached to refill her glass. 'Oh, Mum, you just don't fucking get it, do you? None of you do. It's not just the wedding, it's everything. I love him – God fucking help me – but I'm still young. I needed today; I needed to feel good, like any other woman on her wedding day. I was so looking forward to it, but it's like everything else with him – nothing is ever just fucking *normal*.'

Eileen was genuinely stumped at what to say. Usually, even hinting that Cain Moran might not be the god her daughter thought he was meant the outbreak of World

War Three. Now here she was defending him. She was well aware of how disappointed her daughter was, how much store she had set on this day. But Cain was banged up – he wasn't a fucking angel and that was a reality her Jenny had to face.

'Do you know, Mum, last night I lay in that hotel room in that big fucking bed and I cried for us. For what we've missed. Oh, I've accepted that if I want him, I can't have him for years still – not properly anyway. I've been so good about it, Mum, because I love him with every fibre of my being. But today I was reminded of just how fucking shit my life really is and it hit me like a kick in the teeth.' Jenny swallowed down her vodka again. 'And then to think of that Caroline gloating! She will fucking love this. She couldn't have planned it better, the fat bitch.'

Eileen was struggling to know what to say – she didn't recognise this Jenny. The Jenny she knew was usually so positive about everything, always trying to find the bright side no matter how hard it seemed. For once Eileen could tell that her daughter was actually seeing her life as it was – and she didn't like it one bit. She tried to console her once again.

'It was self-defence, darling – even the PO said that.'

Jenny wiped her eyes with a crumpled tissue and wailed forlornly, 'Only he would kill someone on my wedding day! The fucking idiot! It's always about *him* and what *he* wants and what *he* needs. I despair, I really do! Well, I'm done. He can do what he likes now. I've had enough. It will be in all the papers tomorrow and our son will have to live through another fucking scandal. Everyone will know my day was destroyed and that Cain Moran has killed again. I suppose they will drag up the trial again too . . .'

As the tears started to flow, Eileen tried awkwardly to comfort her daughter. 'Stay here with me for a few days, darling, till it calms down a bit, eh?'

Just as Jenny was knocking back another vodka, the phone rang. Eileen answered and then held the receiver out to her daughter. 'It's for you, darling.'

Jenny took the phone from her mother and her heart leapt in her chest. She hoped it would be Cain. The POs were good at Parkhurst – they sometimes let the men call on birthdays and anniversaries – or perhaps that PO Jock had let Cain use his mobile.

'Hello?'

But it was Freddie Marks. As he asked her how she was, Jenny knew she was on the verge of crumpling again. Taking a deep breath, she said with forced brightness, 'Why don't you pick me up and we can go for a few drinks?'

Eileen was aghast at her daughter's behaviour, though she welcomed it all the same. Lord knew this lass of hers needed a bit of fun in her life – especially after the stunt that bastard Cain had pulled today.

Chapter One Hundred and Four

Hasan and Ali Osman were brothers born in South London to parents from Istanbul. Hasan, the elder, in particular was a man of intelligence and tact. Ali was more unpredictable but still they both had their creds and ran the prostitution ring in the South East. Peter Parkes had been a thorn in their side for a while now so they were very happy that he was finally out of their hair. More than that, they had taken over all the businesses and had a very powerful sleeping partner in Cain Moran. All in all, it had been a productive day.

They were sitting in a Turkish restaurant in South London drinking raki and toasting their good luck. Hasan was particularly pleased to think of Parkes being taken out in his own home. There was a finality about dying that appealed to Hasan's sense of fairness. Parkes had always been known to settle scores in front of the offender's loved ones. It created added torture for everyone involved: a young son seeing his father beg for leniency or witnessing his mother in a chokehold. Parkes had just been a bullyboy who had only gone as far as he had because he had turned on Cain Moran – the man who had mentored him – when he'd been given the chance. He wasn't the sort of Face they wanted to do business with, and it was very satisfying that he had finally been given a taste of his own medicine.

Hasan had a hidden agenda too, and that was Lola Parkes, who he had liked for a long time. He would let her play the grieving widow for a while, then he would be straight round to the house to offer his condolences and, if he played his cards right, a quick blast on his banjo. She had great legs, did Lola, and he wouldn't mind having her in his bed till the next bird came along.

There was a new era coming for the Smoke, and the Osman brothers would be at the forefront, thanks to Cain Moran and his decision to step up and act like a fucking man at last.

The brothers were two men after the same things: power, money and pussy. And they would make sure they each got all three in abundance.

Chapter One Hundred and Five

Caroline Moran had been in a state of high excitement since the story of Cain killing James Banks Junior had hit the news. It felt as though God was finally answering her prayers. What she wouldn't have given to see that bitch's face when she'd realised the wedding was off because the groom-to-be would rather commit a murder than marry her. It was the best news she'd heard in years, and she was going to celebrate it.

She pictured Cain in his cell, stitched up and bereft, and she laughed with glee. Her own wounds were forgotten in her elation. According to the news he had been defending himself from an attack, so it wasn't as if he'd planned the incident. But just knowing the wedding was off was enough to lift Caroline's spirits. She had felt physically ill that morning at the thought of Cain marrying that vicious little mare and had actually prayed for something to happen. Never in her wildest dreams did she think that something might go this wrong for them. That Jenny Riley had lived a charmed life, but the boot was well and truly on the other fucking foot now! She was almost beside herself. To think that Jenny had arrived at the prison to be told her husband-to-be had killed again. It was almost too perfect.

Caroline poured herself another drink and savoured the taste of the champagne as it bubbled down her gullet. She was drinking a bottle of Cristal; this was an event that needed to be savoured and enjoyed to the full.

She raised her glass in a silent toast. To Jenny Riley. For Jenny Riley she still was and would be for the foreseeable future. Still not married to the man who had broken his real wife's heart and walked away from his first-born son. Well, at least Caroline had made sure there would be no more kids from her. If she had achieved anything, she had at least achieved that.

She ordered two takeaways – one Chinese and the other Indian. She was going to have her own wedding feast. That piece of dirt had taken everything she held dear, and no one could blame her for enjoying this night. She turned up the news and waited for the next bulletin about the Parkhurst prison stabbing. She couldn't get enough of it, and could only imagine Jenny Riley's humiliation. It felt so good.

The Good Life – that had always been Cain's mantra. Money and more money was all he was ever interested in. He had promised the Good Life to Caroline on their wedding night and she had believed him. She wondered if he had also promised it to his little paramour. Well, that was an irony best savoured by the ex-wife.

She felt so good that she actually experienced the desire for sex for the first time in years. She could not believe that Jenny Riley had been thwarted. For once that girl had not got what she wanted. It was such a wonderful feeling, and proved to Caroline Moran that sometimes all you had to do was bide your time. It seemed that God really did pay back debts without money.

She had loved Cain Moran through thick and thin, swallowing his birds, him staying out all night and his fucking complete disregard for family life. She had sat it out, believing that one day he would realise what he had and finally appreciate it, but it had never happened. She understood now that the only thing she had ever been to him was a trophy wife – she was the runner up. It was Jenny Riley he had truly fallen in love with.

She could never forgive Jenny Riley for taking her Cain away. But now it had come full circle and she felt no small glimmer of satisfaction in knowing that just once, that skinny bitch wasn't getting everything her own way.

Chapter One Hundred and Six

Freddie Marks couldn't believe his luck. Jenny Riley was lying beside him, naked as the day she was born, snoring softly. They had just had the most mind-blowing sex and he was still reeling. She had almost eaten him alive, in more ways than one! She had been drunk, but not so much that she didn't know what she was doing. He had never experienced anything like it before, and hoped he would be experiencing it again soon. No wonder Cain Moran had left his old woman for her! She was that rarity: a woman who was built for sex and loved every second of it.

He closed his eyes, letting his mind fill with all manner of images of the past hours, and he started to grow hard again. Never had he felt like that before – she had literally blown him away. She was sleeping now, her lovely face serene and her body relaxed. No one would think that there was such a wildcat beneath that ladylike exterior.

He had fallen in love, big time, with a woman who was not his to fall in love with. She belonged to Cain

Moran, and he would not take kindly to his woman being rogered as often as physically possible by the likes of him. Yet, even knowing that, he couldn't stop now. She was like a drug. He couldn't get enough of her, and was hoping their night together would put this relationship on a more permanent basis.

He pulled Jenny gently into his arms and, as she settled herself against his body, he kissed her hair, breathing in the scent of jasmine and Chanel. Christ, she was gorgeous, and she came like a fucking train. He didn't care how dangerous this relationship might be. He wanted her – it was as simple as that.

Chapter One Hundred and Seven

Cain Moran was lying on his bed, listening to the sounds of the prison around him. Through the thin walls of his cell he could hear someone coughing, a radio on low, the hum of chatter from the cons and POs. Prison was a noisy place, and at times like this a man really felt that he was indeed buried alive amongst it all.

The day had started out so fucking well but now he was stitched up and in pain, both physical and mental, with a hard-on like a baseball bat. He knew he had done the unthinkable – he had assumed that everything would go right. In this environment that was fool's logic – today had proved that anything could go wrong at any time. And Cain had murdered a silly lad who should have used his fucking noggin.

As he shut his eyes, he could see Jenny, with her thick, lustrous hair and her white skin. How many times had they lain together? It had always been fantastic. Today should have been the day he made love to her after nearly ten fucking years, but he had lost that chance the moment he plunged his blade into Banks's neck. He had rung her mum five times and on each occasion Eileen had told him Jenny didn't want to speak to him. Now he was angry with her too, even though he knew he had no right to be, but he just wanted to explain the circumstances of the day's events.

He didn't think he would be able to cope with his sentence if he lost Jenny. She was his reason for living – nothing made sense without her. The dread of her leaving him was overwhelming and the worst of it was he couldn't blame her if she did. She was still a young woman with needs and wants, and he knew it was asking a lot for him to expect her to remain faithful. But, so far, she had. Jenny was without guile and she didn't play games – what you saw was what you got. That was one of the reasons he'd fallen so completely in love with her. She was innately honest, and though they were polar opposites in so many respects it had worked for them because she didn't question him or his life. She totally accepted him and who he was.

But what would Jenny do after this fiasco? She had set such store on the wedding, and had written to him nearly every night telling him of her hopes and her dreams for their future together. The words had been like a balm for his tortured soul. The love she poured into each letter was what kept him going from day to day, while the nights were filled with memories of her face, and her body, when he would relive every inch of her in his mind. She remained his only weakness.

The fear of losing her was putting him on edge, and he wanted to pound someone or something. The pain in his arms was nothing compared with the pain in his heart, which actually felt like it was breaking. All he could think about was her with another man. The idea of her letting someone else into her body, into her life, whispering words of love and opening her legs to welcome them in was torture.

Well, he would see her fucking dead first. She would never be allowed to do that to him. It would be the ultimate humiliation. He would fucking rip her head off with his bare hands.

As the anger overtook him, Cain could no longer contain his frustration. The walls of his cell felt like they were closing in, and the knowledge of everything he had lost consumed him. He wanted to destroy something just as Banks had destroyed everything he'd hoped for today.

He finally demolished what was left of his cell at 4.15 a.m. It took three POs and two male nurses to subdue and sedate him. He was down on the block by 6 a.m.

Chapter One Hundred and Eight

Eileen was making lunch the next day when Jenny finally strolled in.

'Well, fuck me, girl, you have certainly nailed the just-rogered look!'

Jenny attempted a smile but she felt awful. The effects of the drink and the knowledge that she had slept with Freddie Marks were starting to take their toll.

'Oh, Mum. What have I done?' She burst into tears.

Eileen put her arm around her girl, and held her close. 'I'll tell you what you've done. You went out with a nice bloke and you got your leg over. It's hardly a hanging offence in this day and age. You were hurting, you'd had the worst day possible and you needed to escape your life for a while.'

'But, Mum . . . Poor Cain. I was so fucking angry and disappointed with him yesterday. Now I've gone and slept with someone else!'

'Did you enjoy it?'

Jenny nodded, feeling a flush of shame.

'Listen, girl, you ain't the first and you certainly won't be the last. Personally, I think it will have done you the world of good. A bit of passion never hurt anyone and he is a nice-looking lad. I would, and I'm nearly old enough to be his big sister!'

Jenny had to laugh then. Eileen could be funny at times and maybe she was right on this occasion. She had enjoyed it, and she wanted to do it again. So why did it feel like a betrayal? Freddie Marks had been so lovely, telling her all the things she needed to hear, holding her tightly and making her feel safe. She turned to go upstairs to her bedroom, but Eileen stopped her.

'By the way, Jen, you'll never guess who was shot to death yesterday in his own home.'

Jenny looked at her mother and shrugged. 'Who?'

'Peter Parkes! And I know I'm no fucking master-mind but it seems funny, all of this happening on the same day. It looks like your Cain is back to his old self in more ways than one, eh?'

Jenny couldn't quite comprehend what her mother was telling her. Peter Parkes was dead? Shot down in his own home? There was no way the timing was a coincidence; she knew that much was true.

'It was all over the late evening news – knocked your Cain from the top story, darling. Guns always top knives when it comes to the order of these things. So there are obviously a few things you don't know about this, darlin'.'

Jenny didn't answer her mother. She sat down at the kitchen table and poured herself out a cup of tea.

'He rang here last night. I said you didn't want to talk to him. He sounded fucking upset.'

Jenny rolled her eyes at that. The knowledge of what Cain had planned for what was to be their wedding day was just sinking in. Her anniversary would always have been the same date as Peter Parkes's death, and Cain didn't even seem to care. She felt a terrible coldness wash over her as she realised exactly what the man she loved was capable of.

She cried bitterly, 'I bet he was. Missed out on a fuck, didn't he? He paid twenty grand for a fucking hour with me. Now I've spent the night with Freddie Marks and, do you know what, Mum? It was *fantastic*. You were right all along. I need a bit of life. I want to live *my* life finally.'

Eileen shook her head. 'I've got to give it to you, Jen, you don't do things by halves!'

'I must have been mad, Mum. All these years I've lived in a vacuum. Everything I did was for Cain – trying to make his life easier while he was banged up. Writing to him, visiting him, telling myself that it wasn't that hard, that the loneliness was something I could control if I just kept my mind focused. And I was lonely, Mum – so fucking lonely – but I bore it because I knew he felt the same. Yet he'd planned to have a man killed on what should have been the happiest day of our lives. Jesus Christ, talk about having shit in my eyes. I never saw him properly, did I? I made him into the Cain Moran I wanted him to be.'

Eileen sat down at the table opposite her daughter and took her hand gently. Never had she heard her Jenny talk like this about the man she loved to distraction.

'Well, girl, the ball's in your court now.'

Jenny sighed. 'I know that now, Mum. I need to think long and hard about what to do with my life.'

Chapter One Hundred and Nine

Freddie Marks and Jenny were together in Freddie's flat. He was smiling at her happily as she sipped her glass of wine. Though it wasn't an ideal situation, he was willing to accept Jenny's pleas for secrecy. Freddie wanted to be seen with her; he wanted to take her out and spoil her. He wanted to be her boyfriend. But Jenny Riley knew that could never happen and, in spite of her anger with Cain over his antics, she'd come to the realisation that she would always love him and accepted the limitations that put on her. She had made it plain to Freddie Marks that if he wanted her, it would have to be on *her* terms, and on the quiet. Even though he'd made it clear he wanted more than that she wasn't going to change her mind.

Jenny Riley was in lust, not in love, and there was a big difference. The sex with Freddie was explosive and regular, and there was no denying she was enjoying it. But she was still in love with Cain Moran and nothing would ever change that. Once she had admitted it to herself, she felt resigned to the fact that

Cain would always come first, no matter what. These last few months had been a real learning curve for her, and even her relationship with Cain had undergone a massive transformation. She didn't accept anything at face value and quizzed him on everything. The shift in balance had been good for her, and she was determined not to be so gullible or ignorant any more. But it didn't matter what he had done or might do in the future – Cain would always be the love of her life.

The sex with Freddie Marks was physically fulfilling, but she was well aware she could never love him. What she and Freddie had would eventually run its course, then she would go back to the way she was before: waiting for Cain to come home.

As she watched Freddie now, Jenny felt sad for him, but it was only fleeting. Because now he was taking off her dress, and she couldn't wait much longer.

Sex really was the best medicine, and she had grown up enough to realise that sometimes you needed certain things in life. If she thought of Cain while she made love to Freddie Marks then that really was her prerogative. She couldn't have the real thing, so she was willing to settle for second best.

Eileen was right behind her, making sure she had the time she needed to enjoy her new-found freedom. It felt good to be needed, to be desired again. As she followed Freddie Marks to his bedroom she didn't feel the slightest shred of remorse. If she had learned one thing from Cain, it was that the only way to survive in this life was by taking what you could from every situation. She was simply putting his philosophy into action.

Chapter One Hundred and Ten

Cain was working out and, even though he didn't feel like it, he knew he had to do it. Sleep had been harder to come by since the events of what should have been his wedding day.

Jenny was a changed woman, and he only had himself to blame. She didn't come to visit as regularly as she had before, and when she did come, she was a lot less passive, talking about her own life rather than just enquiring after his. Before, she had hated telling him about her life because it was on the outside and she didn't want him to feel excluded. Now, he had every thought in her head thrown at him. It was certainly different, but how could he blame her? He had taken the piss in many respects and he rationalised maybe they were better off with this new relationship. They were equal partners.

Cain Junior had also changed, and wasn't as affectionate as he had been towards his father. Cain knew he would have read all sorts in the papers and heard plenty of gossip about him. But he was a realist and had always known his son would find out the truth one day. He'd just hoped he would understand. There wasn't much he could do about it banged up like he was now, so he would have to rely on Jenny to deal with the situation as best she could. It was frustrating to be so powerless when it came to people you loved.

In terms of Cain's power as a Face, though, he was far from helpless these days. Now that he'd had Parkes taken out, and had entered into a partnership with the Osman brothers, he was back on top. It felt good to be scamming again and using his brain, and it was easier than he had thought possible to get back into things from the inside. The Osmans needed his good name, and he needed them on the outside to help pile up the money again. He was back in the Life, and making up for lost time; though he could not change his sentence he could still earn a decent wedge. The Osman brothers were good blokes and, now he had a mobile phone, he was able to keep in contact with them easily.

This new technology was amazing, but it also made the men aware of just how much the world outside was changing. It seemed that every week something new was launched on the world at large, and they felt left out of the loop, unable to access any of it. It was changing the face of the crime industry, and this was just the beginning. He had always been on the ball, and he was catching up with it as quickly as he could. The younger men were more than willing to explain things, and it was good to keep abreast of change – especially now he was back in business.

The prison had ruled James Banks Junior's death as self-defence on Cain's part – there was no comeback, which pleased him no end. In some ways he would have enjoyed a trial as a way of getting away from these fucking four walls for a while. There was no end of inmates who would keep appealing their sentences, just to get out and about. All in all, though, Cain was so relieved he had finally got his Jenny back and he had some work to occupy his time, that was enough for him right now.

The lack of sleep bothered him though – he would often lie awake for hours on end. Blokko reckoned it happened to a lot of the lifers, and saw it as a form of depression. Maybe he had a point. One thing Cain did know was he needed to get some well-earned shut-eye soon because it was really starting to take its toll on his frame of mind. Working out would make him physically tired, and he hoped that by upping his regime he might just finally drop off through sheer exhaustion. It was worth a try anyway.

Chapter One Hundred and Eleven

Molly was exhausted; it was a long journey to the Isle of Wight, what with the drive down and the ferry crossing. It had been an arduous day, and she wasn't getting any younger. As usual she had accepted the ritual of being searched by a female prison officer and, after what seemed an age, she was finally able to go through to the visiting room.

She lived for these visits and, now that Jenny wasn't coming down at every available opportunity, she could see her son more often on her own. She preferred that – they could talk properly without having to worry about Jenny's reaction – and she knew Cain liked it too.

She bought two mugs of tea and a couple of Kit Kats and settled at a far table, awaiting her son's arrival. She sensed he hadn't been quite as chipper of late but he always had a smile and a wink for his old mum. He put on a good show for her, she knew that much. She loved the fact that the eyes of female visitors always followed him, responding to his good looks, and how the men always gave him a respectful greeting. It was a crying shame that her son was spending the best years of his life locked up.

As he made his way towards her now, he was smiling widely, and she felt the sting of tears at what she had to tell him. But she was his mother, and she had to do right by him. If there was another man in Jenny's life, then he ought to know. He wasn't going to be made a fool of, not on her watch. As much as she loved the girl, there were some things that couldn't be forgiven.

Chapter One Hundred and Twelve

Eileen was unloading her shopping from Jenny's car when she heard Caroline Moran's voice behind her.

'Feeding the five thousand, are we?' She sounded friendly, but her usual undertone of malice could be heard beneath the surface.

Eileen replied nonchalantly, 'No, we just thought we'd better be ready in case you popped in for a snack.'

The barb hit home and Caroline closed her eyes for a moment before saying carefully, 'I thought I would see how poor Jenny is doing these days – after the wedding fiasco and everything.'

Eileen turned to face her, ready for a fight if need be. 'She survived, and she and Cain are stronger than ever, darling.'

'Really? So all this talk about her and Freddie Marks isn't true?' Eileen's face paled, telling Caroline Moran all she needed to know. 'Well, who can blame her? I wouldn't think Cain will be so fucking forgiving though. Funny like that, he was. Slept with any old trollop who'd let him between her legs, but he always said he'd kill me if I did it. Food for thought, eh?'

With that she waddled away. As Eileen watched her retreat, she felt a rising panic. The cat was out of the bag. She needed to warn Jenny and, more to the point, Freddie Marks. Cain Moran might be banged up but that wasn't going to stop him retaliating. Freddie must have blabbed, the stupid fucking idiot. Now there would be hell to pay.

Chapter One Hundred and Thirteen

'Oh my God, what are you going to do?'

Freddie Marks was nonplussed for a moment by Jenny's words. 'What do you mean, what am *I* going to do?'

Jenny sighed in exasperation. 'Are you being deliberately obtuse?'

He shook his head. This was what he had wanted – they could be a proper couple now. He said as much and saw the way Jenny's face paled. 'Look, Jen, think about it. He's going to be banged up for years and we can move away. Abroad even.'

Jenny laughed then, nastily. Fear was hammering at her chest. 'Are you on fucking drugs, Freddie? Do you really think Cain will swallow the idea of you taking his woman? I told you from the get-go that I wouldn't ever love you. That I could never be with you. You agreed to that. You must have told someone. If Caroline Moran knows then so does the whole fucking world – they don't call her the *Romford Recorder* for nothing.'

Freddie was reeling. He had told someone, but it had been a person he really trusted.

'I swear I only told my mum.'

Jenny closed her eyes in dismay. Mary Marks was a lovely woman who lived for her nights at Mecca Bingo in Ilford, but she was also a loud gossip who spent all her time between games chatting with her table of cronies, one of whom was Molly Moran. This was getting worse and worse. She knew Molly cared about her but her loyalty would always be to Cain first. If Molly knew, then Cain would already know too. Her stomach clenched in fear, not just for herself, but for Freddie Marks.

'What are you, Freddie, eight years old? Telling your mum, one of the biggest fucking gossips in East London, that you're having an affair! What were you thinking? Cain will fucking *kill* us. I mean it, he will kill us dead.' She was close to tears at the enormity of what she had done.

As her words sank in, Freddie Marks was only just starting to understand the trouble he was in.

Three days later he was killed in what was reported as a hit and run – only the driver had reversed over him three times to make sure the job had been done properly.

Chapter One Hundred and Fourteen

Molly Moran watched Jenny as she walked into the visiting room at Parkhurst. The girl looked beautiful – there was no doubt about it – but there was a nervous edge to her today. Though Molly felt sorry for her, she still stood by her actions in telling her son. If she had forever damaged her relationship with this girl that was something she would just have to live with. Her Cain would always be the first priority, end of story.

When Eileen had accused Molly of getting Freddie murdered, it had been beyond the pale. That bastard had got what was coming to him – no more and no less. Molly had not brought up a fool for a son, and no one was going to get one over on him. Not on her watch.

As she waited in line to get the teas and the biscuits she observed Jenny sitting at the table, forlorn and frightened. She didn't seem to realise, as Molly did, that Cain could never hurt her. He worshipped his Jenny, and always would. She lingered in the queue so she could see the reaction of her son as he walked into the visiting room. Men could be funny creatures where women and sex were concerned, but he had sworn no harm would come to the mother of his child, and Molly had believed him.

She watched Cain walk over to Jenny and smile briefly before sitting down opposite her. Molly felt immediately relieved that there was no drama at his arrival and brought the teas over to the table before making her excuses. They needed to be left alone to sort out their differences.

'I'm so sorry, Cain. I was just so disappointed about the wedding . . . I was angry and lonely . . .'

There were tears in Jenny's eyes and though part of Cain Moran felt the urge to attack her, he restrained himself. He was tortured by the thought of someone else touching her, tasting her. It was so consuming that he couldn't eat or sleep. But he knew that eventually he would get over this. As his mum had pointed out, Jenny was still a young, vibrant woman. He had to find it in his heart to forgive her, though it was going to be very difficult, and right now he didn't know if he wanted to kiss her or kill her.

He hated seeing the fear in her eyes, but relished knowing she would now be too frightened to ever contemplate doing the dirty on him again. However forgiving he felt, he wasn't going to let her off easy though, especially knowing they were being watched by everyone else in the visiting room.

'So how was he then, Jen? Good, was he? Must have been doing something right all those fucking months.'

Jenny didn't know what to say – she was so scared of Cain at this moment.

He leaned in and whispered in her ear, 'Made you scream, did he? Tell you he loved you, did he? Fucking answer me!'

She pushed his head away and looked into his eyes before saying, 'It was good, Cain, because I was thinking of you. I think he knew that deep down, but he wanted me and I needed to feel wanted – really wanted – by someone.'

The brutal honesty of her answer brought Cain up short. He had expected tears and pleas for forgiveness; he had not expected her to tell him that she had wanted him so much she'd replaced him.

The POs looked on warily. There were never secrets in a prison, and Cain's bird playing away from home had been a hot topic of conversation for everyone. But if he killed her in the visiting room it would cause untold aggravation for all concerned, and Cain had been put through the indignity of a cavity search before Jenny's arrival. It was astounding what someone determined enough could ram up their arse.

'You destroyed me on our wedding morning, Cain. When you used that day to settle old scores and put yourself back into the Life, you ruined everything I had ever wanted. I did what I did out of revenge as well as loneliness and I am heart-sorry. But you have had your revenge too. You had him murdered. And even knowing that, I still love you and want you. I'm frightened of you for the first time ever, Cain, but I still can't see me loving any other man.'

Jenny dropped her eyes then, and didn't attempt to wipe away her tears, so Cain wiped them for her. Then he pulled her into his arms and held her tightly, kissing her hair and telling her he loved her. The whole visiting room could breathe again, and the POs who had been put on the duty roster for that morning in case Cain Moran had needed subduing were no longer on edge.

Jenny relaxed into Cain's embrace and, as they hugged, no one mentioned the no touching rule, least of all the Prison Officers.

Chapter One Hundred and Fifteen

Eileen Riley was still suffering over Freddie Marks. She wasn't sure she could ever forgive Molly Moran for bringing the information about his affair with Jenny to Cain's attention. Eileen had been the catalyst for that relationship, believing it would do her daughter the world of good to have a man in her life for a while. But now he was dead, and everyone knew why.

Guilt was not an emotion she had ever really felt before. Eileen had always been selfish, taking what she wanted without a thought to the consequences. Now, though, she was haunted by that man's tragic and terrible end and the knowledge that she had been instrumental in his death, even if it had never been her intent. She knew full well what Cain Moran was capable of, but the fact that he might act so quickly had never crossed her mind.

It was her Jenny who had really surprised her. Her lovely kind Jenny had been harder than she'd ever thought possible, shrugging off Freddie's death and putting her energy into winning back Cain Moran's love. It really was an eye-opener. She had thought her daughter would have run a mile from Cain Moran after what he'd done, but instead she seemed more in love with him than ever.

Jenny was visiting today for the first time since the incident and, in a strange way, Eileen hoped Cain Moran wouldn't want to have her daughter back. She was even willing to accept that their lifestyle would change drastically if this was the case. She didn't like the idea that her lovely Jenny – the kindest girl she knew – could so easily dismiss the death of a man who had loved her. Maybe that was why Jenny and Cain made such a good couple. Perhaps Jenny was more like him than either of them realised. It was certainly food for thought.

Chapter One Hundred and Sixteen

Jenny Riley lay on her sofa with a hot whisky and honey and a cigarette, going back over her time with Cain today. She had been terrified when she'd arrived – not of him hurting her, but of him abandoning her. She wished she could feel differently but she loved him and that was that. Even knowing that they had been to blame for Freddie Marks's demise didn't make her feel resentment towards the man she loved. It bothered her in some ways that she could never judge him and his actions in normal terms, but hers was a complicated love for a man who, as well as being a violent criminal, was to her also the kindest and most loving person she had ever known.

She had believed deep in her heart that he wouldn't hurt her – though he might have felt like it – nor would he have got someone else to do it for him. He loved her with every ounce of his being, and this latest episode just proved that to Jenny.

She questioned why she was able to remain un-affected by his actions against Freddie Marks, who was in reality an innocent in this. She felt truly sorry for him – it had been a brutal, vicious end to someone who had only wanted to be with her. But that still didn't result in her feeling any animosity towards Cain. She had always been aware of just how much he was capable of and so had Freddie Marks.

Her Cain had found it in his heart to forgive her, and that was all that really mattered. Coming so close to losing him had made her realise just how much she needed him. Without him she couldn't survive, she understood that now. She would never do anything again to make him question her, and vowed to channel her energies into keeping them together. At the end of her visit today he'd asked her to renew their wedding preparations. She was over the moon, and of course she had agreed to make a start as soon as possible. She wanted to belong to him more than ever. And if that meant spending the next fifteen years alone, it was a small price to pay in order to prove her loyalty to him. She wanted to be clean for him again, to be the Jenny he knew and loved.

She regretted her liaison with Freddie Marks so much, not just for the heartache it had caused but because it had given Cain reason to doubt her – something she would never forgive herself for. Well, she had had her moment of madness, and it had come at a terrible price. Now she would work tirelessly to give Cain the life she owed him, the life that she wanted.

He had promised her the Good Life together. It was still a way off, but it was there nonetheless. She would do everything in her power to make sure she was waiting for him to make good on his promise when he got out.

Chapter One Hundred and Seventeen

Cain Moran was lying on his bed thinking of Jenny and everything she had said to him in the visiting room. One thing he was sure of with her was that she wouldn't lie. When she had told him she'd been thinking of him while she was with Freddie Marks he had known immediately it was the truth – that she had been craving *his* affection all the while and not that cunt Marks's. Every time he thought of him he just wanted to murder him all over again.

Not that his feelings for Jenny were all sweetness and light either at the moment; he still felt hurt and humiliated by her actions. But, as the men on his wing had pointed out, she wasn't the first to go AWOL during a long stretch and she certainly wouldn't be the last. She had stood true for ten years and that in itself was a feat. After all, with her looks she wasn't exactly short of attention.

Cain had to control his emotions. He still loved his Jenny with a vengeance; he would always love her, just as she would always love him. They were meant to be, and he wanted no one else. Once the pain of her betrayal had subsided they would get things back on track. She had learned her lesson, and that was a good thing in itself.

He had asked her to marry him again as a way of proving he was willing to put the past behind them. They had survived so much – Caroline's bitterness, her vicious attack on Jenny, his long incarceration. They would survive this too, and they would come out stronger than ever. Theirs was an unbreakable bond.

Now Cain had re-established himself and his reputation in the Life, Jenny could be an invaluable asset, helping to relay messages and overseeing certain aspects of the monies collected. She wasn't a fool, his Jenny. It was just a case of putting her indiscretion to the back of his mind, which he was determined to do. She was still a young woman who needed to love and to feel loved, and it was up to him to ensure that she never felt neglected or lonely again. Marrying her would prove his love, and getting her involved in the new operations would be a way of making her feel part of that side of his life.

He would speak to the Osman brothers about it – and they could keep an eye on her at the same time. He might have decided to forgive her, but that didn't mean he automatically trusted her again. It was something that would take time, but he was willing to try, and that was the main thing.

Sleep was eluding him once more, and he lay listening to the sounds of the prison as he planned the next stage of his life. This was what most of the men did on a regular basis. It was late at night that you needed to tell yourself this couldn't go on for ever – that one day you would be on the out and living the Good Life again. It was what kept them going.

Book Four

Please remember, I still want you
And in case you wonder why
Well, just wake up
Kiss the good life, goodbye

'The Good Life'
Music by Sacha Distel and lyrics by Jack Reardon

Chapter One Hundred and Eighteen

2008

Cain Moran was on his mobile phone in the exercise yard while the other inmates played five-a-side football. He was talking to Hasan Osman and the conversation was getting very heated indeed. In fact, they were practically arguing and that was never a good thing. Over the last few months they had been party to their first big disagreement, and it was slowly festering into a full-blown row. It concerned a northern Face by the name of Jason Biggs – a built, loud-mouthed funny-man with a temper that was legendary if he was thwarted. He had three brothers who worked side by side with him, and they were not to be taken for mugs either.

Jason had made a name for himself over the last few years and now ran much of the drug and prostitution trades in the north of England. There was a lot of money to be made from sex, and there were plenty of girls from Eastern Europe and China needing an earn. In addition, there were many men willing to supply said girls; it was a ruthless and wicked industry, and one that was flourishing thanks to considerable supply and demand. Jason was dealing with the Russians for the girls, and up to now had been getting his drugs from the Osman brothers.

Recently, though, he'd been offered what he thought was a better deal by the Russians, and Ali and Hasan Osman didn't like it. Now, they were all for taking Jason Biggs out of the game.

Cain Moran, on the other hand, didn't think that was a good idea. He knew Jason of old and if he was murdered there would be too many people wanting retribution. It would get too personal, and that was the last thing anyone wanted at this juncture. They needed to be reasonable – to try and come to some kind of arrangement. It would avert all manner of trouble.

Cain had known from the off that the Osmans didn't like Jason very much. He was a man with a big sense of humour, often at the expense of other people. He could imagine that the Osmans would not like his brand of joke-making – especially young Ali who often took umbrage over any imagined slights. Still, this was a situation that could not be allowed to get out of control.

'Look, Hasan, I'm categorically saying no. You cannot take Jason down without causing fucking murders. His brothers will go all out for revenge and I don't think the fucking Russians will be too pleased either. Try to work with me on this. Let me talk to Jason and see what I can come up with.'

Hasan was being his usual cautious self. 'Let me talk to Ali, Cain, then I will call you back.'

Cain clicked off his mobile phone and pushed it into the pocket of his tracksuit bottoms before joining the kick-about. He had every reason to be worried. Things had been going well for a long time and this was something that, if ignored, could result in all-out fucking war. The Biggses were not a family to cross, unless you were willing to accept the untold aggravation they would be sure to give you. It was at times like this that being banged up brought home the limitations on the power you wielded in your particular world.

Chapter One Hundred and Nineteen

Cain Moran Junior was in his twenties, and was now the double of his father at the same age. He was also a very self-assured young man who had worked hard at school, gone on to college and carefully inveigled himself into his dad's business. It seemed that criminality was in his genes. He liked to think it anyway.

He had become a collector and general factotum for the Osmans and, on rare occasions, his own mother. It seemed Jenny Moran had a nose for the businesses she oversaw, which were booming just within the law. She needed a minder for certain meetings and, as her son was a big strapping lad, she often took him with her. The Osmans were pleased with him – he reminded people of his father, and that was no bad thing.

Cain himself was proud as punch that his son wanted to follow in his footsteps – he'd always dreamed of bringing him into the business. And, from the reports he had heard, his boy was good at what he did. He didn't balk at violence and never opened his mouth unless he had something useful to say. These were good attributes in their line of work. Cain Junior was a liked and respected young man. Cain Senior had high hopes for the team the Moran family would make when he got out. They would be unstoppable.

Cain Junior was about to meet up with a girl called Linda Lloyd – a petite redhead with deep blue eyes and a figure to kill for. They had met while he was collecting the take for one of his betting shops and he had been bowled over by her looks and fiery personality. Linda was nineteen, loud and funny, and she also very small-boned – only a size two shoe – and she had the smallest hands he had ever seen, perfectly manicured. Her red hair was a thick mass of curls as hard to tame as she was. This was only their third date but he was falling for her big time. As they sat together in the restaurant and she chattered on about her job, her life and her family, he felt happy as the proverbial Larry. She really was a special girl – always so upbeat and cheery. It was infectious.

To cap it all, Linda already understood the Life so there was no fear of her worrying about his late hours or what he was doing for a living. That was the problem with the straight girls – they really didn't get the economics of the criminal world. He wanted to settle down with someone he could relate to and who could relate to him, not someone he'd have to lie to about what he was really doing. Linda would have the brains not to ask too many questions; what she didn't know couldn't hurt her. He had really fallen on his feet with this girl – she was what his mother would call a 'keeper'. He wanted to keep her all right, for the rest of his life. Cain Moran Junior had fallen in love and it felt good.

Linda Lloyd, for her part, felt exactly the same. She'd had her eye on Cain for longer than she cared to admit, and he was her perfect man in every sense. She came from a local family, so she knew exactly who he was, who his parents were and what he did for a living. But this did not put her off – if anything it added to his allure.

She liked his dark hair and his fierce blue eyes, she liked his five o'clock shadow and the fact that when he looked at her it was as if he couldn't quite believe his luck. They were a match made in heaven and, as they ate their lunch together, each knew they had found their soul mate.

Chapter One Hundred and Twenty

Jenny Moran was tired out and happy to have reached the end of a busy run of meetings. As she walked around her flat turning on lights and putting on a pot of coffee, she sighed happily. This had been a really good day; she was looking forward to a light supper, a long bath and an early night. It was a bonus when she had a day like this, as it left her feeling genuinely weary and ready for bed.

She often had trouble sleeping; her brain seemed to turn itself on as soon as she switched off the light and then the oblivion she craved eluded her. It was natural she supposed. But she would never change her life. She made the best of her days, and enjoyed them for the most part.

Sometimes, though, she missed her husband so much it was like a physical pain. It seemed amazing to her that he had been away for twenty years. Occasionally time flew by, other times it crawled, but it always passed eventually. That was the thing she had to tell herself in the darkness of night, when everything seemed hopeless and she wondered if she was wasting her life waiting for a man she loved to distraction. When she had waited this long, what difference was another few years? That was the conclusion she always came to, usually as dawn was breaking, and she felt exhausted from another restless night.

Cain Junior had called to let her know he was going to be in for his supper. If she was proud of anything in her life it was her handsome son. Even though she had been reluctant to see him becoming embroiled in the Life, she had come to accept that it was what he wanted to do. She had little other choice; he was his own man and his father's son in more ways than one. He looked so like her Cain that it broke her heart to look at him sometimes.

Cain Junior had taken well to the Life and he was respected. He had a natural ability for his work and she suspected that was down to his father. They had become a lot closer in recent years – once he entered the business it was as if Cain Junior had recognised that he needed his dad – and that had pleased Jenny and Cain no end. She constantly reminded herself that she had a lot to be grateful for: they lived like kings, and rarely had to go without.

Even that nut-job Caroline had slowly started to leave them alone. Though there were still the late-night drunken phone calls to contend with, it was harder for her to get hold of their mobile numbers when Jenny changed them so often. It was a pain in the arse but what could she do? Caroline was not a woman to let things lie.

She sighed as she started to prepare a Caesar salad for her and Cain Junior. She just wasn't in the mood for cooking tonight. She'd much rather a glass of wine and a long bath, in that order. It would be nice to eat with her son though – it was rare to have him home at a decent time these days. She wondered if he had a bird in the offing; he had certainly been taking more time over his personal appearance lately and he was forever on his phone texting someone. Good luck to him. He was at the age where he needed to start thinking of settling down with a decent girl.

Cain Junior had started looking at flats to buy. He wanted to branch out on his own, and she could understand that. In some ways she couldn't believe he had stayed living with her for so long, but she knew it was mainly because he worried that she would be lonely. He was good in that way, and she appreciated that he looked out for her. They had spent so much of their lives together, just the two of them, and were so close. It would seem strange when he finally flew the nest, though she knew it was inevitable. Kids grew up and moved away – that was the way of the world. She just hoped he didn't go too far; he was all she had in many respects. He would go his own way, that was certain. He was his father's son, after all.

Chapter One Hundred and Twenty-One

Hasan Osman was coming round to Cain Moran's way of thinking, but his brother Ali wasn't so sure.

'Why the fuck do we need to step back, Hasan? Who the fuck does this Biggs think he fucking is? Are we expected to roll over while he treats us like cunts? Not happening.' Ali's voice was loud, aggressive and determined.

Hasan listened with growing unease to his little brother. Ali had a temper that defied logic. Once he believed something, nothing could dissuade him from his course of action. But this was a time when Hasan really didn't think his brother was looking at the big picture. He had a bad feeling and, even though he had no reasoning other than Cain Moran's opinion, he felt that this could all get completely out of hand and he didn't want that any more than Cain did.

Ali and Biggs felt a natural animosity for one another; it happened sometimes with people. From the second they met, there had been an element of dislike and, more to the point, distrust between the two of them.

Jason Biggs had made it evident that he didn't like dealing with the Turks – he felt they were always trying to have him over, even though it had never once happened in the years he had dealt with them. It was only Cain Moran's involvement that had kept the peace for so long. Now it was all falling out of bed and, once the talks broke down, it would be open warfare.

In Hasan's view, Cain was talking sense when he said there were too many Biggses on the scene for them to take out Jason without fear of retribution. They couldn't police the entire north of England in any case. That would be an impossible task, especially from London.

'Sorry, Ali, but I'm with Cain on this. You need to let things go on this occasion and see if we can come to some kind of understanding. Whether you like it or not, Jason Biggs is too much for us to handle at the present time. Our strength comes from being able to supply fucking good gear. That is what keeps us at the top of our game. I don't think the Russians will be too pleased if we go in guns fucking blazing and take out their new best mates. This is a compromise situation.'

Ali Osman looked at his brother as though he had just grown another head in front of his eyes, such was his shock and disappointment. They had never gone up against one another on anything before; they had always backed each other to the hilt. Ali was younger by five years and had grown up worshipping his older brother, but nowadays he wanted more of a say in their daily dealings. Hasan seemed to be thwarting him at every turn, and it was only now he was starting to realise how much that bothered him.

'A fucking compromise? With that cunt Biggs and his fucking brothers? Are you serious? All a ponce like him recognises is a show of force – if we don't get in there and give it to him first, we will have to deal with the fucking Russians. Is that what you want?'

Hasan rolled his eyes in annoyance. 'Truthfully, Ali? No, I do not want to deal with the Russians. They are too fucking organised for us, end of story. We need to salvage what we have and not push our fucking points across. This was inevitable – it was going to happen at some point. Get over it, will you, and use your fucking brains.'

Now Ali was insulted as well as angry.

Hasan sighed heavily. 'That is my final word. We'll arrange to go up there, have a meet with Biggs. See what kind of compromise we can come to. If we have to sell the drugs cheaper then we will, but I for one don't want the Russians getting their toe in the water up there. It is as simple as that.'

Ali was too angry to answer his brother. Cain Moran was banged up and yet he was still calling the fucking shots. There was a moral in this story somewhere but he was fucked if he could see it.

Chapter One Hundred and Twenty-Two

'She's beautiful, Mum.'

Jenny listened to her son extolling the virtues of Linda Lloyd and tried to suppress a smile. She knew young Linda; she was a beautiful girl, and a good little worker with the brain of an accountant. Numbers worked for her, which is why she oversaw big bets for their shops, as well as laying them off and working out the more difficult odds. She came from a nice family and she knew the score. Jenny's son had chosen well.

It never worked when straight girls were brought into the mix; they weren't familiar with the Life and that caused untold problems. If a girl couldn't understand why she wasn't told every detail of her boyfriend's life, and why he kept nightclub hours, their relationship would be fraught with difficulty.

'She is a beautiful girl, son, especially with all those red curls. Lovely nature she has too and her head's screwed on. I'm pleased for you.'

Cain breathed a sigh of relief. 'I know it's early days but I want to get engaged. We are off to Paris for the weekend and I am going to ask her there. No point hanging around – I know she's what I want and I think she feels the same.'

'Very romantic. She will love that, darling.'

Jenny couldn't help feeling a deep yearning inside – her son was thinking of marriage and here was she, practically a virgin. She had waited out the best years of her life for a man she loved, but it had been a very high price to pay. She hoped that this would never happen to her son and his girlfriend, because Jenny knew that women like her were few and far between.

'I'm sure she will say yes, Mum. Honestly, it's like we were made for each other . . .'

As her son continued to wax lyrical about his girl, Jenny felt tears stinging her eyes. She prayed that they had a much easier time of it than she had with Cain. She wouldn't wish her lonely existence on her worst enemy.

Chapter One Hundred
and Twenty-Three

Jason Biggs was in a club he owned in Manchester town centre and, as usual, he was the centre of attention. This was his natural habitat and he loved to be in the midst of the young girls and cronies, on show for the up-and-coming fuckers who needed to know that he wasn't going anywhere in the near future. A lot of villainy was about fronting everyone else out. He was a marvel in many respects. He looked and acted the part so well; no one in their right mind would challenge him.

Biggs had a wife called Bernice who was a small and dark Italian firebrand. It was said that once, in a temper, she had ripped the hair off the head of a girl twice her size, and it had taken three men to drag her away from the unfortunate female. It was also said that, even though he played away at every available opportunity, Biggs loved his wife with a deep and abiding affection. A few wags had also mentioned that he was scared of her, and anyone who saw Bernice lose her temper would agree with that statement. They had three young sons and a daughter, who were the light of Jason's life.

Tonight, though, he was just out for a drink and a look at the local talent. He had his eye on a tall blonde with brand new tits and an expensive set of teeth. Her only drawback was her Birkenhead accent. It wasn't adding to the package in any way, but he felt he could overlook it if it meant getting his hands in her lacy little drawers.

His three brothers, Jack, Joe and Jeremy, were all in attendance as usual, and he was regaling them with his usual brand of humour and exacting wit.

'I had me hand up her skirt and she punched me right in the face. I said, "Hold up, girl! What's your problem?" and she said, "Where's your fucking manners? Tits first!"'

Everyone cracked up with laughter, except for a few of the newer girlfriends, who felt the barb might have been aimed at them.

These days, Jason was a very satisfied man. He had wanted to get shot of the Osman brothers for a while, and it looked like that could be on the cards. He had always thought the world of Cain Moran. Cain was a man he admired – he had taken his knocks on the chin and he didn't fucking piss and moan about his situation, he just got on with it. His wife, that Jenny Riley as was, was a star and all. His own little Italian lunatic would be straight on the trot if he ever got a lump like that. It was a measure of Moran that his bird had stuck by him all those years; it spoke volumes about who he was and the kind of loyalty he could inspire.

Loyalty was a big thing to Jason Biggs. He had a devoted workforce and that was largely because having four brothers working in unity was a very powerful thing. It was about making sure that people knew the consequences of their actions – and a few kneecappings certainly sorted out the men from the boys. Jason Biggs had learned from very early on that there was no better way to instil loyalty into people than by making examples of those who did not make the grade. It was also about paying a good wage and keeping a good eye on your workforce – that much he had learned from Cain Moran. He had always refused to do business with that two-faced cunt Peter Parkes. There was a line, and that ponce had crossed it.

Now, though, Jason Biggs was confident that his life would be even richer. He was about to hold the Turks and the Russians to ransom, and that could only get him a better deal on the drugs front. Cain Moran was a realist – he would sort out the latest drama with the minimum of fuss.

He was well pleased with how he'd played this hand. As his old mum used to say when they were kids, 'If you don't ask, you don't fucking get.' He couldn't have put it better himself. Jason was no mug and he wasn't going to settle for anything less than life at the top.

Chapter One Hundred
and Twenty-Four

Ali Osman was in his flat in Soho with his current girlfriend. He loved blondes – real blondes with blue eyes – not the pretend ones with dark eyes and black hair everywhere but their fucking heads. He preferred them natural, not too tall, and well built in terms of tits and arse. His latest squeeze, Tiffany, was the real deal and, though she had little in the way of conversation, she was right up his street. Ali was in no mood to talk tonight anyway; he was out of sorts, still smarting from his brother's refusal to listen to him.

As they sat on Ali's black leather sofa drinking expensive whisky it occurred to him that he was gradually being rowed out. Cain Moran was taking his place at Hasan's side, and that was not a good omen for the future. Hasan seemed to be paying more and more attention to Cain's opinions rather than his own brother's. He was feeling distinctly left out of everything.

Tiffany watched her beau as he drank steadily. He

was practically ignoring her, but she wasn't bothered. She was a trophy bird and happy with that. When he stripped her off later in the evening, the fact that she was blonde both collar and cuffs would be enough to get her what she wanted from him as usual. It wasn't rocket science, and she had no interest in anything he had to say anyway. He was hardly Stephen Hawking.

Nevertheless, she was picking up a bad vibe and she couldn't tell if it was directed at her. Ali wasn't the best lover she had ever had but he was certainly willing. Anyway it was his reputation she was most attracted to. She watched him frowning, getting drunker and drunker, and she wondered if it was time to move on. She lit a cigarette, passing it to him, and he took it gratefully.

Ali was wondering if Cain Moran would be on the phone to his older brother at that very moment, telling him what they should and shouldn't do. It was galling to think of Hasan suddenly so enamoured of every word that came out of Cain Moran's mouth.

He took a wrap of cocaine out of his wallet and started to cut it on the glass-topped table before him. He noticed Tiffany buck up at this; she did like a line, did his Tiffany. It didn't occur to him that his cocaine use might be affecting how far Hasan was willing to trust his judgement. Since he had met Tiffany and discovered a taste for his own product, Ali had been acting in a very paranoid and secretive manner. Hasan had tried to talk to him, but he wasn't interested in what he had to say. He snorted two lines quickly, before passing the rolled up fifty-pound note to Tiffany who had a nose like a vacuum. She snorted a couple of lines herself, then watched as he started to recut the rest of the wrap. This was more like it, now the party was really starting.

But Ali wasn't a happy bunny, and when she took off her dress a little while later he realised that he couldn't raise a pint of Guinness, let alone anything else.

Tiffany went home shortly after with a frown on her face and her cab fare in her purse.

Chapter One Hundred and Twenty-Five

Jenny had picked up her dry cleaning, paid most of her workers and was now at home preparing a meal to officially welcome Linda into the family. Molly and Eileen would be coming too. This was such a milestone and she was thrilled to be doing it for them. It was bittersweet though without Cain there too.

Molly and Jenny were civil to each other these days, even if they had never managed to get back on the same footing after Freddie Marks's death. Though Jenny and Cain had moved on, she could never forgive Molly for what she had done. What had hurt the most was that the woman she had loved and cared about had asked her nothing about the situation before running to her son. The tales she'd told had nearly cost Jenny her relationship with Cain, and it had certainly destroyed the trust between her and Molly. She would never stop Molly seeing her grandchild, but to know that she had condoned the death of such a vibrant young man had shown Jenny where the woman's priorities lay. There had been a small chance that Cain might have taken Jenny out as well, and Molly had to have known that when she grassed them up. It was a difficult situation, but Jenny Moran made the best of it. The closeness they had shared was long gone, but Molly was still her mother-in-law and nothing would change that fact. Still, the affection that had once been between them had cooled considerably.

Eileen, in contrast, had become her daughter's biggest champion and ally in their world. She worked for Jenny now – or thought she did at least – as a bar manager in one of the nightclubs, which paid well. Everyone else knew the real manager was a young Irishman called Colm Holmes. He got an extra payment to run the place efficiently, and to let Eileen Riley think that she made the decisions. It had been a big boost for her; she was paying income tax for the first time in her life instead of finding herself at the mercy of the benefits system. The only thing that Eileen wouldn't do was move out of her council flat. She felt safe there with all her cronies around her.

Needless to say, Molly wasn't on Eileen's list of top ten people to mix with but, for Jenny's sake, she tolerated her whenever she had to. It was a shame that the family had become so divided, but what could Molly Moran expect? She had committed the ultimate piss-take and that could never be forgotten.

Jenny had cooked a roast beef dinner and, as she

carried the food into the dining room, she smiled expectantly at her son and his bride-to-be. Needless to say, Linda had accepted Cain Junior's proposal and he was beyond thrilled. This was going to be a real celebration for them all. Even though Cain Junior and Linda had only been together a few months, anyone with eyes in their head could see they were a wonderful match.

As she looked at them all around the dinner table, Jenny felt happier than she had in years. Her family was growing – what more could anyone ask for in life? Her only sorrow was that Cain couldn't be there to join them, though he would ring later and congratulate the happy couple. It wasn't perfect by any means but it worked for them. And soon they would be one big happy family together again. It was all Jenny could hope for in this life she had chosen.

Chapter One Hundred
and Twenty-Six

Cain Moran was having his own celebration of his son's engagement with the men on his wing. He had cooked a leg of lamb, accompanied by potatoes and vegetables, as well as the inevitable chips. He had never managed to talk the older men into healthier eating. For dessert he had made a cheesecake. There were a few familiar faces around the dining table, and some new ones who had been sentenced in the last few years.

Blokko was now up in Durham; the funny peace-keeper had battered a young Irish lad to within an inch of his life over a marrow of all things. It was an amusing enough story, but the ending had not been to anyone's satisfaction. On the plus side, Cain still had a few old cronies from his youth at Parkhurst to keep him company. He was back on top and that was something he would never take for granted. He liked that he had the respect and status he wanted once more and, as he neared the twenty-year mark, only another five awaited.

There was still a long way to go but at least he hadn't lost everything while inside in terms of his work and his life. And now he was well past the halfway mark – an achievement in itself.

All the same, it was hard to think that his son would be bringing his fiancée round tonight to officially meet the family without Cain there. But he would pop her name on a Visiting Order and meet her soon enough. Thank God she wasn't straight; fuck knew how that might have turned out. He had heard of men whose children's spouses had refused to visit them in prison, and even tried to stop their children from coming in. Obviously that kind of situation never got sorted to *everyone*'s satisfaction. Once the offending party had been given a serious talking to, the kids were usually allowed to visit.

He poured everyone a glass of Barolo wine and raised his own with pride. 'To my son's engagement. And to his lovely fiancée, Linda.'

The men joined Cain in his toast, but there was a feeling of sadness at the table – especially for those with young children, who were reminded that it would be years before they saw them on the out again. Like Cain Moran, they would spend the best part of their kids' lives imprisoned while the people they loved went on with their lives. It was a sobering thought in more ways than one.

'So how is it going to work? Have you spoken to your brief about compassionate leave for the wedding?'

Cain nodded. 'Oh, yeah. I've never been out, not even for a funeral, so he reckons I will get it. I hope so. I would hate to miss Cain Junior's big day.' He placed a large forkful of lamb in his mouth before continuing seriously, 'I ain't never even appealed before, have I? I've done everything I was supposed to do. I will tell the parole board when the time comes that I am sorry for any trouble I've caused, any old pony and trap they want to hear. It's the only way to survive – play the fucking game, abide by the rules.'

The men nodded in agreement.

'Then once you are back on the out, all bets are off!'

They cracked up at that.

Desmond Harker, a tall black Mancunian with a head full of dreadlocks and a winning smile, said jovially, 'I agree. The day the judge gave me the eighteen years, my mum told him, "It ain't my boy, it's the people he hung around with!" I fucking didn't live that one down for years. She still believes it as well.'

The men were laughing. It was even funnier because Desmond Harker was a criminal mastermind of the bank robbing persuasion. But he was a good bloke and very friendly with Jason Biggs, so his friendship with Cain on the inside suited them both. The fact that he and Cain were of a similar age and background had cemented their friendship almost immediately. Cain got insight into Jason through Des's knowledge of the man – and that was invaluable when dealing with him on a day-to-day basis. They were close mates now, who enjoyed each other's company. They were also the most senior men on the wing, which meant they were often the arbiters of petty squabbles, arranging for any contraband needed by the other men.

Tonight Cain Moran was feeling the effects of his long incarceration. It was always missing the family get-togethers that was the hardest to bear, Christmas and New Year being the worst. Cain Moran knew of a man who hanged himself for missing his only daughter's First Communion. A staunch Catholic, he had committed the ultimate sin while depressed and alone on the block. It was a scandalous thing, and the POs had been wary for a long time afterwards. They were aware that the other men blamed them for separating the bloke from his friends when he needed them most. He was being punished for nutting a prison officer, but what followed would not have happened if he had been given a few hours out to see his daughter on her big day. They could take men who were as hard as fuck, and bring them down so low they were willing to end it all.

That was why you needed to be strong and have the right people around you for times when it seemed fucking hopeless and a sentence seemed to stretch out endlessly. Cain had used his time as well as he could – he was now a proficient cook and he read voraciously. But none of that compared to being able to walk out your own front door for a pint any time you wanted to, or kiss your wife and children whenever you felt like it.

Cain served dessert and then phoned his family from his own private mobile, passing the phone around the table to let everyone wish the young couple well, or to catcall out about the wedding night. It was a jolly evening in many respects, but the men were very subdued when they went back to their cells. Sometimes there could be nothing worse than a reminder of real life.

Chapter One Hundred and Twenty-Seven

Hasan Osman was worried about his brother Ali. There was a distinct tension between them for the first time in recorded memory and Hasan knew Ali felt his opinion wasn't being valued. While he was sorry about that, he had to understand that sometimes the best course of action was to remain passive. Villainy was about using your brains, and aggression wasn't always the right way to go about things.

Hasan believed that Cain Moran had his head screwed on and, the more he thought about it, the more he could see where the man was coming from in his assessment of the situation. If everything he had heard about the Russians was true, they were formidable opponents who were willing to use extreme violence for the most trivial reasons. Hasan wasn't intimidated by many people but these adversaries seemed to be worthy of respect. He looked at Ali who was sitting hunched in his chair, every bit of his body language screaming out that he was not a happy camper.

'Look, Ali, listen to me just this once. Remember in Istanbul when we were young and we went up against the Cercezs family? We thought we had it in the bag but we didn't allow for the friends they had onside. This is the same fucking situation, mate. The Russians have friends in high places. We have to box clever for now. It's not over – once we know what we are dealing with we can act accordingly. Surely you can see that?'

Ali didn't answer.

'When we meet with Jason tonight I want you to play nice, OK? No matter what he says, don't rise to the bait. He is the type of bloke who will wind you up even more if he thinks it is getting to you.'

Ali sighed and looked at his brother with an expression of serious dislike on his face. 'Want me to kiss his cock while I'm about it or is that a step too far?'

Hasan rolled in eyes in annoyance. 'Do you know something? You can be like a fucking child sometimes. If you weren't shoving so much gear up your fucking hooter you might see sense in what I am saying. Remember the old saying: never buy from a dealer who uses more than you do. You are getting a bad rep. Everyone knows you spend every night out of your tiny mind. You are the one who will bring this business down, not that cunt Jason Biggs. Sort your fucking head out or find another fucking partner in crime because, honestly, I'm sick to death of you.'

Hasan had never spoken so forcefully to his younger brother before and the shock on Ali Osman's face was evident. He stood up, and Hasan readied himself for a fight. Ali also liked a knife, and he would need to look out for that too. He knew him well – better than he knew himself.

'Is that what this is all about? You and Cain Moran becoming best buddies and leaving me out of the loop? I feel like you and Cain Moran are taking me for a cunt. A Grade-A, prize-winning cunt.'

Hasan Osman was torn between love for his brother and a powerful urge to hammer him into the ground. Taking a deep breath to steady his growing anger, he said as reasonably as he could, 'Listen to yourself, bruv. You sound like a fucking whining girl. Now this is my last word. When we meet with Jason Biggs tonight I do not want a fucking word out of your mouth, no matter what. Do you get my drift?'

Ali Osman reluctantly agreed. He was still burning at the injustice of it all, and was convinced his brother and Cain Moran were colluding against him. He was too coked out of his nut to make rational decisions. He couldn't see that they were trying to stop a serious war erupting with enemies they knew nothing about. And he couldn't for the life of him see that all Hasan and Cain wanted was time to find out who they were dealing with before working out the next step. All he could see was that he was not being listened to, and in his book that was tantamount to mutiny.

As always, Hasan had to have the last word. 'I mean it, Ali, if you fuck this tonight you and me will fall out big time. This is the moment for sensible heads. So try not to vacuum up a whole eighth before the meeting, will you?'

Ali was so disgusted he didn't even answer.

Chapter One Hundred
and Twenty-Eight

Jason Biggs and his brother Jack were in the back offices of their nightclub in Manchester. This was their main place for meeting with people; it was soundproof thanks to the DJ in the main hall and it was very secluded. It also had a private staircase leading down to the basement which was often used when people became a bit too annoying for their liking.

Jason and Jack were very alike in appearance – both were good-looking men, always immaculately dressed – but whereas Jason was a live wire, Jack was the quiet one. Happily married with a couple of young sons of his own, he was the family brainbox – good with numbers and quick to grasp anything he was told. He was the acknowledged number two in the family and he and Jason were closer than close. You rarely saw Jason have a meeting without Jack by his side. Jack had a retentive memory and, in dealings where the detail was critical, his ability to reel back everything he had heard was crucial. Jason Biggs loved all his brothers but would be lost without Jack.

They were waiting for the Osman brothers, satisfied that Cain Moran had talked them into renegotiating the drug money. Cain wasn't to know that Jason Biggs had no intention of dealing with the Russians. Jason had already sussed that once those Russians got an in, they didn't give up till they had everything they wanted. And that generally meant everything you had. As far as Jason was concerned this was a win-win situation for him and his firm. He'd played this hand well and a better deal was in the offing. As they sat sipping expensive brandies and smoking even more expensive cigars, the brothers were pleased with a job well done.

As the Osmans were shown into the office, Jason was out of his chair and welcoming them like long-lost relatives. It was part of his considerable charm – when he could be bothered he was a very good host – and this had stood him in good stead in some very tricky situations over the years.

Ali and Hasan sat down and accepted the drinks, though they declined the cigars. Then Jason Biggs opened an office drawer and took out a mirrored bathroom tile covered in lines of cocaine and offered it to Ali with a flourish. 'I hear this is your preferred recreational drug, Ali.'

It was a genuine joke, but it could not have come at a worse time for Ali Osman, who took it as an insult.

As soon as Jason realised his little bit of fun had offended he laughed, saying, 'As my old mum used to say, "Don't take offence, take a gate." It was a joke, mate, fucking lighten up!'

Ali could feel his brother's eyes on him and said through gritted teeth, 'I'm splitting my sides, mate.'

Jason grinned, his natural humour coming to the fore, as he said lightly, 'You will be splitting the bridge of your nose if you don't ease up on the gear, mate. I know a bloke who had to have a steel plate put in. Whole thing collapsed. I said to him, "That's what you get for picking your nose too much."'

Even Hasan laughed at that; it was an old story but a true one. Ali Osman smiled. Though he had heard it before, what Jason had said still rankled. It was a piss-take, no more and no less. He knew his brother wanted him to play it cool – he would do that for him today but this was the last straw as far as he was concerned.

The negotiations started in earnest and, one hour later, Jason Biggs was thrilled with his new deal. Cain Moran had the right idea: never get mixed up with the Russians, though by all means use them to your advantage. They shook on the arrangement and the meeting was over.

Ali Osman, though, was still smarting from the earlier insult and he was determined not to let this one go. Jason fucking Biggs needed a reality check and Ali was just the man to give it to him. He would show his brother and Cain Moran that he was not to be treated like a fucking mug. Most of all, though, he would show Jason Biggs that sometimes you could push the wrong person too fucking far.

Chapter One Hundred and Twenty-Nine

Eileen tuned Molly Moran out as the silly old cow droned on about her marvellous son. She looked across the dinner table at Cain Junior and his lovely bride-to-be and felt a surge of pride. She'd be the first to admit that she had not been the greatest mother. Eileen wasn't what you would call the maternal type, and she knew deep in her heart that she could take no credit at all for the fact that her daughter had turned out so fabulously. She had often left her home alone as a kid while she went out drinking, she had brought all manner of men back to their home, and she wasn't what anyone would call a housekeeper. But in her own way she had loved her daughter, just as she loved this big strapping grandson of hers. Now, as he embarked upon life as a married man, she hoped to have more babies to dote on, even if she had never really doted on her own. Hindsight was a wonderful thing.

Her ears suddenly pricked up at something Molly

was saying and she asked her to repeat herself. 'Sorry, Molly, what was that again?'

Molly Moran looked straight at Eileen before saying slowly and sarcastically, 'I said – my son will be out before we know it. He's broken the back of his sentence now. Only another few years.' She looked at Linda then, who had already guessed that the conversation was about to turn nasty, and continued, 'Then you will see what's what in this family you're joining.'

Even Jenny took umbrage at that insinuation, and Eileen snapped quickly, 'What's that supposed to fucking mean?'

Cain Junior closed his eyes in dismay. Why did his nan always have to rock the boat after a few glasses of whisky? He reached for Linda's hand and squeezed it tightly.

'What I mean is, once my son is back in his rightful place as head of this household—'

That was it. Eileen was on her like a greyhound on a hare. 'Head of what fucking household? My daughter has kept this fucking place going for years, darling. She is also running his fucking businesses for him while he is banged up. When he finally comes home he will be down on his knees thanking her for keeping everything going so smoothly against the odds.'

Molly laughed at that. 'We all know exactly what she had running smoothly, as you so eloquently put it, and it wasn't a fucking business.'

'*Nan!* This is supposed to be my special night with

Linda. That is enough ancient history for one fucking night if you don't mind.'

Molly was astounded at her grandson's words. Never had she expected him to talk to her like that. But Cain Junior had really had enough.

'You're a bitter pill, Nan. You think I only know your side of that story? Well, I know both sides, so let it fucking drop. You naused up your place in this family and you did it with malice. No matter how many times you tell yourself otherwise, I know the truth and so does my dad. I've spoken with him about it.'

Molly turned pale with shock and no small amount of fear. What had they been saying to Cain about her behind her back?

'You've always got to put your ten pence worth in at every fucking opportunity. Well, it stops now, OK? My mum is the best in the world. She brought me up single-handedly and she gave me everything she could. I'll tell you something for nothing – I almost wish she would get herself a bloke sometimes. I know how fucking lonely it is for her on her jacksie and I wouldn't hold it against her, even if you would. I love my dad, but life is for living and my mother has never really lived her life as she should. That's because she loves your son, and if you can't see that then you are even more of a stupid woman than I thought.'

Everyone at the table was staring at Cain Junior in shock. Eileen was thrilled with her grandson's words;

they had needed to be said and she was glad that someone else was doing it!

Molly stood up unsteadily with tears in her eyes; her whole face was flushed deep red with embarrassment. That her grandson could say those things to her in front of that young girl was more than she could bear. She had been humiliated and, what's more, a little voice in the back of her head was telling her she deserved every word.

'Sit down, Molly – you're going nowhere.' Jenny's voice was quiet, but there was an edge to it that everyone at the table could hear.

'I will ring for a cab, Mum. There's no way I am dropping her home tonight. This was supposed to be a lovely evening to welcome my fiancée into the family. Well done, Nan, you've ruined it.'

As he left the room, Molly looked towards Linda who was bowing her head down to her chest. The embarrassment was radiating from her too.

Jenny shook her head sadly and said to Molly, 'Well, that was certainly a turn up for the books. You did ask for that, Molly.'

Molly Moran remained standing. Her humiliation was complete and she didn't know how to rectify the situation with her grandson and his fiancée. She knew it would always be between them now.

'Well, good on Cain Junior if you ask me,' Eileen said. 'You've caused a lot of grief in this family, Molly. By rights my daughter should never have let you back

through the fucking door after the stunt you pulled.
I'd have kicked your arse the length and breadth of
the fucking road. If your Cain had to choose between
the two of you, he would choose my Jenny just like
her son did. She is the one who has always loved them
both, always been there for them. Cain Junior got it
in a nutshell when he said he wished she'd had someone
in her life, even briefly. She strayed just once. Once in
twenty fucking years. If that doesn't tell you how lucky
that son of yours is I don't know what will.'

Linda looked up as Jenny said to her quietly, 'I'm
so sorry about this, Linda. Families, eh? You can pick
your friends . . .'

Linda Lloyd smiled nervously then and answered,
'Don't worry about it, Mrs Moran – my lot are just
as bad after a few drinks.'

Eileen laughed heartily. The girl had somehow lightened the atmosphere. 'Good to know. Your mum can
hold her own, I've heard.'

Linda grinned. 'Especially after eight Pernod and
blacks.'

Jenny stood up then and went to Molly, gently
ushering her back into her chair, and poured her another
whisky. 'Drink that, Molly. You've had a shock.' Then
she turned towards the door and shouted, 'Where's
that cab coming from – fucking Romania?'

Cain Junior walked back in. 'Sorry, I had to use the
little boy's room. It's on its way.' With that, he sat
beside Linda and poured them both some more wine.

Putting his arm around her shoulder he pulled her close. 'Sorry, darling.'

Linda snuggled into him and said gently, 'That's all right, Cain.'

As he squeezed her to him, he said, 'But that's the point, Linda, it's not all right.' He looked at his grandmother. 'I mean it, Nan. If you ever pull another stunt like that, I will never speak to you again. I'll not have you, my dad or King Street fucking Charlie criticising my mum. You remember that.'

Jenny was proud of her son for his words, but she also felt sorry for Molly. Inadvertently, she had broken the heart of the one person in the family who had genuinely loved her.

Cain Junior raised his glass and addressed the table. 'Here's to family. You can't live with them, and you can't live without them.'

Eileen raised her own glass and clinked it against her daughter's, saying happily, 'Amen to that.'

Jenny Moran turned and touched her glass to Molly's. 'And here's to Cain. Wishing he was here with us tonight.'

Molly smiled solemnly, relieved to have at least one person in the room throwing her a kind word.

Cain Junior raised his glass again. 'To my mum.'

Jenny and her son looked each other in the eye and as Cain winked at her she wondered what she had done to be blessed with such a wonderful, loyal and handsome son.

Chapter One Hundred and Thirty

Cain was working out in the gym in good spirits. He'd just heard that Hasan Osman had sorted things with Jason Biggs. It was certainly a weight off Cain's mind. Like Biggs, he believed that there might come a time when they would need to band together against the Russians. There were too many of them trying to muscle in on established operations. It was the nature of the beast, and a reason to keep on good terms with people you might need in the future. It was a different world these days, and the sooner people realised it the better off they would be.

Cain Moran had been feeling increasingly as though he was being slowly buried alive in prison. Even with the educational courses at Parkhurst nothing was the same as being out in the world and experiencing life for yourself. It was frightening how far technology had advanced. Cain had heard from Des Harker that Jason Biggs was recruiting for computer fraud operations, which sounded amazing. No real graft there – you just took money at the click of a button – and that was something that Cain Moran was very interested in. He wanted to keep Jason Biggs and his brothers happy. If he could partner with them properly in the future they could make some really big money together.

Cain had never liked dealing in women but there was no avoiding it these days; there were so many girls turning up from Eastern Europe, especially now that the Russians were so active. They would happily sell their own grannies if the price was right. Human trafficking was something Cain Moran had resisted up until now, but when times changed you had to change with them. That was the harsh reality of the Life.

The Russians who had come through the unit were hard men who had grown up in abject poverty. The inmates had been astonished at how tough their lives had been, especially those from the Ukraine. Even older men who had lived through the war and been brought up on bombsites were amazed at how those men were raised. Poverty bred criminals – it was as simple as that.

One thing that had struck Cain was how they used tattoos to let others know why they had been banged up, and just how much they were capable of. Certain designs could indicate that they were murderers for hire, or that they had killed policemen or other gang members out of self-defence or for profit. They were each covered in a network of inked tattoos that were as weird as they were colourful. These were the Russian equivalent of cockney rhyming slang – completely incomprehensible to the outside observer, but crystal clear to those in the know. They were dangerous fuckers who needed to be treated with extreme caution.

Cain had to admit, though, that he liked the ones he had met and admired their stoic acceptance of their sentences. From what they had told him, the British penal system was a doddle compared to the Russian equivalent, where the most basic amenities were few and far between. Even food had to be bartered and paid for – it was an eye-opener all right. They were clever fuckers for all that, and worthy of their reputations. Cain knew he had good reason to be wary of them, so was pleased that Hasan and Ali Osman had come round to his way of thinking, and now they had Jason Biggs on board for the future, which would work to their advantage.

Cain's son would be coming in later on for a visit, and he couldn't wait to see him. Cain Junior had made himself very useful to his father, liaising directly with those on the out on his behalf, and it was working even better than he had hoped. The lad had a natural affinity for the Life and he enjoyed the day-to-day which, at his level of the game, could be monotonous. Cain was a lucky man to have his enterprises looked after so well in his absence.

He had spoken to his Jenny earlier. He never failed to marvel at how much she still meant to him after all these years. He had long forgiven her for Freddie Marks, and rarely allowed the thought of him to spoil his days. Just hearing her voice was enough to give him a hard-on. She was still the sexiest woman he had ever laid eyes on, and he told her so constantly. He missed her so much, just as he missed his family life. From what he could gather, his mother had upset everyone at his boy's dinner party the other night, and he wished she could keep her fucking beak out of everyone's business. She was a loyal old bird, and he had to allow for that. Trouble was, no one else did, and that was something she didn't seem to grasp.

The past was the past and sometimes you had to leave it alone if you wanted to have a future. Cain finally felt the time was coming for that to become a reality, and it felt good. He had wanted the Good Life, and had had it for a while. Now he wanted a good life, and that was something completely different.

As he showered, he felt another tingle of excitement at the prospect of seeing his handsome son; he lived for the visits from Cain Junior and his Jenny. They were what made this fucking shithole bearable. They gave his life meaning, and provided him with a reason to get out of bed every morning. Without them, he didn't know how the fuck he would have coped all these years.

Chapter One Hundred and Thirty-One

Ali Osman was drinking in a small boozer on Old Compton Street. It was a private club owned by an ex-con and frequented by a legion of cronies and their associates for planning operations and discussing times gone by. It was also a place where you could drink alone and be sure that no one would bother you, unless you wanted them to.

Ali was there to meet a man he had tracked down through an old acquaintance – a well-known Face in his own day called Kevin Donovan. He was now retired and just did the occasional quick job for good financial gain, provided his involvement was kept on the down low. He was adept at planning things down to the last detail and was always in and out with the minimum of fuss. Kevin was sixty-seven years old – though he looked a good decade younger thanks to his healthy lifestyle and a new wife of thirty-two. He had a little boy of five who he adored, and a string of older grandchildren.

Ali Osman was determined to have his way over Jason Biggs and this was how he was going to achieve it; it gave him great pleasure to shake Kevin Donovan's hand and get on with planning the next move. If his brother Hasan couldn't see what was going on then, as far as Ali was concerned, it was a good job that he had it all sussed out for them both.

The two men settled in a dark corner with their drinks before Ali said quietly, 'It's a big job.'

Kevin grinned, showing expensive veneers. 'I'd sort of worked that out for myself.'

'It's a hit, and it's on Jason Biggs.'

Kevin Donovan sat back in his chair and Ali could see he was shocked. Kevin drained his entire drink before getting up quickly. 'Not in a million years, Ali. Sorry, son, but I plan to live a bit longer. If you want my advice, I would forget the whole thing before it gets out of hand.' With that he walked away.

Ali Osman sat there for a while, contemplating Kevin's words and wondering how best to move forwards. It didn't occur to him that if a man like Kevin Donovan wouldn't go near a proposition, it was unlikely anyone else would consider it lightly. Kevin was a hard man who would do literally anything for the right price. The very fact that he was walking away should have spoken volumes. But Ali Osman wasn't thinking straight. He had a blind spot where Jason Biggs was concerned and was still smarting from the man's attempts to humiliate him. He was also too coked up to rationalise his behaviour. Cocaine did that to the body after prolonged use. He was snorting first thing in the morning and suffering from nosebleeds and numbness in his face. His teeth were getting loose and his gums bled when he cleaned them. He also had regular headaches and panic attacks – all symptoms of long-term cocaine use. He was convinced that people were talking about him, laughing behind his back and trying to do him down. He saw his brother – who he adored – as the enemy when he didn't agree with him on every single matter they discussed. Ali Osman was an addict and, like all addicts, his habit would be sure to destroy not only him, but everyone else around him.

Chapter One Hundred and Thirty-Two

Cain Junior already had the teas and biscuits waiting when his father walked into the visiting room. Cain Moran always felt a surge of pride when he saw his boy – he was very good-looking and easily a head and shoulders above everyone else in the room. If the admiring glances he got from the women were anything to go by, Cain Junior also had his father's way with the opposite sex.

Seeing Cain Junior always reminded Cain that he had another son out there in the world. Cain had written many times to Michael, and was pained by the fact that he had never received a single reply. He continued to send him birthday cards each year, even though he guessed they would be thrown away. He wanted the boy to know he had not forgotten him, even if he had forgotten his father. He hated Caroline for her part in the loss of his first son, just as he hated her for ensuring that Jenny would never bear another child. Caroline had a lot to answer for and he hoped that when she got it, she would get it big time.

Cain Junior embraced his father briefly, and then they settled down at the visiting table. He had been doing this for so many years that it never felt strange to him. Seeing his father incarcerated had been something he had come to accept as his way of life – for the most part this had always been his reality.

'How are you, son, and how's that lovely girl of yours?'

Cain Junior blushed to the roots of his hair and his father grinned.

'Good, Dad. Actually, I have some news and I wanted you to be the first to know. She's pregnant – she's having my baby.'

Cain Moran was stumped for a few seconds. Then with a beaming smile he grasped his son by the shoulders and hugged him tightly, much to the amusement of the people sitting nearby.

'Congratulations, son. Fuck me – your mum will be over the moon. She loves babies. I don't know how fucking Eileen will take it though . . . She'll be a great-granny!'

They both laughed at that.

'My mum will be thrilled too. Don't be too hard on her, son. I know how you feel but when it comes to family they don't come more loyal than her. Never forget that.'

Cain Junior just nodded; he wasn't getting into that conversation today.

'I wanted to tell you first, Dad, because I know how hard it must be sometimes, always getting things second-hand. We're going to tell Mum tonight.'

Cain Moran felt a sudden urge to cry and had to blink away the tears. His boy had grown up to be such a kind and caring man, and that was because of Jenny. Christ knew, he couldn't parent him from in here – Jenny had taken on the role and here was the result: a decent, loving man.

'I appreciate that, son, and you're right. It is nice to be the first to know. I am so pleased for you, mate. A new baby, and I'll be a granddad! How's Linda doing?'

'She's grand – determined not to put on too much weight, eating the right food, all that fucking palaver. She's only a couple of months gone.'

Cain laughed at his boy's resigned expression. He could tell that this Linda already had him well under the cosh.

'We ain't told her mum and dad yet either. I wanted this to be yours alone. Everyone else can wait.'

Once again, Cain felt the urge to cry, and he wondered if this was part of getting older. He was much more sentimental these days, and he wished he had his old mate Blokko to talk to about it; Blokko always had an answer for everything to do with long stretches inside. Cain knew that this was a tough reminder of another big event he would only see from inside, and that was hard to take.

'I can only say that I'm honoured, son, to be the first to know. This is a real milestone.'

As his son outlined his plans and dreams for the future, Cain Moran marvelled at how much of a man his son had become. He was so proud of him and pleased for his news, but at the same time he couldn't help dwelling on the fact that the first time he held his grandchild would be in this shitty room, watched by every fucker in the place. But, as he had always told himself, it was what it was. He had chased the Good Life, and now he was paying the price.

Chapter One Hundred and Thirty-Three

Jenny and Eileen were in The Highwayman pub with Linda's parents, Sally and Peter Lloyd, when the happy couple announced they were having a baby. After the champagne had been ordered and glasses raised, Cain Junior told Jenny that he had shared the good news with his father earlier that day before he'd told anyone else. Jenny had never felt more proud of her son in her life; she knew how much that would have meant to her Cain. Being the first to know anything was unusual, even with his mobile phone!

'He's pleased as punch, Mum. A granddad, eh? And you'll be a granny too.'

Jenny looked at her mum as she said slyly, 'Just think, Mum, you will be a great-granny!'

Eileen retorted loudly with, 'We will have to fucking see about that!'

As they laughed and joked together, Jenny looked

up to see Caroline Moran standing near their table staring at them all, and her heart sank to her boots.

She was grotesque in size and her eyes, which had once been her best feature, fired hate.

'Oh, for fuck's sake, what do you want now?' It was Eileen who started the conversation off. She hated that bitch, and wondered if she had some kind of supernatural power. The fucker seemed to have a way of turning up and ruining everything.

'So he's going to be a granddad, is he?'

Cain Junior stood up and moved between the woman and his mother.

'Why can't you take yourself off to another part of the pub? This is a private *family* party.'

Caroline Moran laughed at that, and said nastily, 'You are your father's son all right – the spit of him – and you are like him in other ways too, I hear. I wouldn't be surprised if your kid spent the best part of its life visiting you in a maximum-security and all. Like father, like son.'

Eileen stood up immediately, shouting, 'Fuck off, you silly bitch! At least he ain't a fucking nancy boy like your Michael. I hear he likes the blond boys – is that true? No grandchildren for you by the sounds of it.'

'My boy ain't queer.'

'No, of course not – but all his friends are.' Eileen was laughing at her own wit.

'Sit down and shut up, Mum. And, as for you, Caroline, stop showing yourself up. It's been fucking donkey's years since he left you for me. It's time you got over it.'

Caroline could see how well Jenny looked – how youthful her figure had remained, and how beautiful she was. She envisioned herself ramming a glass into that perfectly made-up face and twisting it for maximum effect. But Peter Lloyd was ready for her if she made a move like that, and so was that handsome bastard who, unlike her boy, was a man's man. It was so unfair. This woman had stolen her life and yet she still came out of it smelling of fucking roses.

Peter Lloyd stood up and went over to Caroline. Taking her arm gently, he said in a placating voice, 'Come on, love, let's see you to your car, shall we?'

His tone instantly triggered something in her. 'Get your fucking hands off me! I am meeting a friend here. Who are you to fucking tell me what I can and can't fucking do?'

'Leave her, Peter, let her do what she likes. You can't hurt me any more, lady. Meet your friend, eat a fucking big dinner, I really don't care. Just leave me and mine alone.' With that, Jenny motioned for the men to sit and they resumed their conversation as if nothing had happened. But Jenny could see the fear in young Linda's eyes and she hated Caroline Moran for spoiling what should have been a really great night.

Caroline felt humiliated once again as she turned

away. Everyone in the pub was staring at her, and she knew her bulk was largely to blame.

Then Eileen shouted, 'Here, can I rent your dress? I want to go camping in France. Sleep six, will it, you fat cunt?'

That's when all hell broke loose.

Chapter One Hundred and Thirty-Four

Sally Lloyd and Jenny Moran were sitting in Eileen's flat while the men sorted out the police. Linda was shaken up but relatively unharmed. The pub, on the other hand, had been destroyed. It was amazing how quickly Caroline Moran could move considering that she was nearly twenty-seven stone in weight.

Everyone was seeing the funny side now, as was often the case. Eileen walked in with a tray of tea, announcing loudly, 'That poor man! When Caroline landed on him I thought she was going to fucking crush him to death. And did you see his wife's face!'

They all laughed again at that.

'It's not that funny, Mum. You fucking caused the whole thing with that tent joke.'

'Come on! Everyone in the pub laughed.'

Jenny grinned. 'Well, they soon stopped when Ten Ton Tessie fucking launched herself at you!'

'The weirdest thing for me was hearing her speak.

She had the most beautiful speaking voice.' Sally Lloyd had a deep throaty voice herself; and hated it. She never believed it when people told her it was sexy.

'You've got to give her that – even her swearing sounds posh.'

That led to another raucous outburst.

'There goes my door. I bet it's the lads back from the police station.'

Instead, Jenny answered the door to find Michael Moran, her husband's first-born son, standing there. You could tell instantly that he and Cain were related – there was nothing of his mother in him at all – and it was like looking at an older version of her own son. She looked him straight in the eye and said firmly, 'We don't want any trouble.'

He responded with a shrug. 'I don't want to cause trouble, I just came here to apologise for my mum.'

'Well, that's very good of you, Michael,' Jenny answered warily. She couldn't take her eyes off this man: her son's brother and her husband's first-born. What did he want? She hated to be suspicious but it seemed strange to her that he had come knocking after so many years of silence. Nevertheless, she led him into the living room to join the others.

'How is she? Your mum, I mean.'

Eileen was wide-eyed, watching with a look of scorn, but she knew better than to say a word.

Sally Lloyd, however, was the epitome of diplomacy and said quickly, 'Come on, you two, let's make another pot of tea.' With that she ushered them into the kitchen, closing the door behind them.

Michael Moran looked at the woman who had stolen his father away – she wasn't the monster he had expected. In fact, she seemed very nice indeed.

'Please sit down.'

As he took a seat on the sofa she noticed he had his father's hands.

'Is Caroline OK?'

Michael grimaced, 'She's in hospital. They keep a special eye on her you know, what with her drinking and her weight. I'm forever telling her to do something about it but she won't listen.'

'She is enormous, but surprisingly light on her feet considering.'

Michael smiled at that. 'I know. The thing is she has been getting help for years with her mental health. She has episodes . . . at least that is how the psychiatrist describes them. She's always been unstable apparently.'

Jenny didn't know what to say; she just nodded. This was so surreal.

'I just wanted you to know that if anything had happened to the girl having a baby I would never have forgiven my mum. I'm not making excuses for her, but she isn't all the ticket at the moment. I felt you were owed an explanation.'

'Can I get you a drink – a tea or something stronger?'

'Scotch would be nice.'

Jenny made them both stiff whiskies. As she handed Michael his glass, he smiled at her and she was reminded of Cain again.

'Mum drinks as well, and on her medication that makes her even more erratic. She can appear more or less normal for months, and then something sets her off and . . . Well, you can guess the rest.'

Jenny took a large gulp of whisky before saying, 'To be honest, Michael, tonight wasn't entirely her fault. My mother made an unfortunate remark about her weight.'

He nodded solemnly. 'So I hear.'

Jenny Moran could not believe she was defending the woman who had caused her such heartache. But there was something about this boy that made her want to ease his burden. He seemed a genuinely nice guy.

He looked at her sadly, before taking a deep breath and saying quietly, 'How is he?'

Jenny finished her drink and got up to refill both glasses. 'He misses you, Michael, I know that much.'

He looked into her eyes. 'I know. Every now and then I salvage one of the letters he sends me. But you know the score with my mum – if she thought I was anywhere near him she would lose the last ounce of sense she still possesses. For years I hated him, but as I got older . . .'

Jenny felt deep sorrow for this young man, left to cope on his own with that mad bitch. 'It's not too late, you know. He would be thrilled if you were to drop him a note.'

Michael laughed then, bitterly. 'According to my mum he wouldn't want to hear from a fucking poofta. Her words not mine.'

Jenny shook her head sadly. 'That would bother him no more than it bothers me. He would be proud of you, knowing how well you have looked out for your mum. He'd just like to see you and know that you're OK.'

Michael Moran raised an eyebrow inquisitively. 'You seem pretty certain about that.'

She smiled. 'That is because I am. He knows you're gay, Michael. You can't keep things like that secret for long. In his own way he has always kept an eye on you – through other people, of course. It's what he is like.'

'He knows?'

Jenny nodded again. 'It's not a secret, is it?'

He sighed heavily. 'I suppose not.'

Just then the men could be heard returning from the police station. Jenny Moran was thrilled at the thought of finally introducing her son to his older brother. It had certainly been a strange night.

As the room filled with chatter, Eileen's booming voice cut loudly across the group, 'Truth is, Peter, Michael is as gay as a Mexican tablecloth.'

Cain Junior closed his eyes in dismay and was about to apologise to his older brother when Michael piped up, 'At least I don't look like a fucking drag queen!'

Everyone started laughing at that, and somehow the terrible night began to take a turn for the better.

Chapter One Hundred and Thirty-Five

Cain Moran couldn't believe the news about his eldest son. After all these years it was impossible to think that Michael might actually be back in his life. Though it was something he had prayed for, he had never quite believed it would happen. It seemed that Caroline's hate and venom had forced her son away from his father. Now she had brought them back together again with that same hatred. The world was certainly a strange place.

Cain didn't care if his son was gay – that was Michael's business. It wasn't his place to express an opinion either way. All he wanted was for his son to be happy and if that meant being with another man then so be it. From what he could gather, it was Caroline who had the problem with it. She had convinced her son that his father would never accept him as gay, and that was something Cain would find hard to forgive. Cain may have done the dirty on her all those years ago but that should have been water under the bridge by now. Instead, Caroline had kept her hatred burning for all those years and it had affected Cain's relationship with his own son. He would hold that against her for the rest of his life.

As he showered and got himself ready for the day he felt a lightness he had not experienced in years. He had both of his sons in his life – what more could a man ask for?

Chapter One Hundred and Thirty-Six

Michael Moran felt a deep sadness as he listened to his mother raving to the doctors and nurses as they tried to help her. Caroline was accusing them of trying to poison her, refusing to eat any food other than what her son brought in especially. She had been in hospital since the incident in the pub, and this was one of the worst of her episodes that he had witnessed. He hated to see her in such obvious distress. If she got wind of the fact that he'd gone behind her back and made contact with his father and extended family it certainly would have tipped her over the edge.

He didn't regret it for one moment though. Things were working out surprisingly well now that he had taken that first step. Michael liked Jenny Moran. Her calmness was soothing, and there were no histrionics or mind games; what you saw was what you got. His brother, Cain Junior, was nice too – and his girlfriend Linda was a very sweet girl. Eileen was a scream and

Michael had really taken to her. His only disappointment was his grandmother, Molly Moran. He had guessed rightly that she wasn't well thought of by the rest of her family, though they were scrupulously polite to her in person. There had definitely been some kind of altercation at one point or another – he would lay money on it.

As he watched his mother cram food into her mouth, he leaned across and gently wiped her mouth. She seemed to think her son's homosexuality was inherited from his father's side of the family; she was forever pointing out there were no gays on her side. There were a number of mental illness cases, though, if what the doctors had told Michael was true. He sighed at the sadness of it all. If only she could take her tablets and stop drinking, her life could begin to take some sort of shape again. Some days she would be OK for a while and then it was like she went on a self-destructive bender – drinking all day, self-medicating, and eating a colossal amount. It was terrible to watch.

He wondered what it would be like to visit his father in Parkhurst. He was nervous and excited all at the same time at the thought of it. He only wished he had bitten the bullet and got in touch sooner. It felt good to be around people who didn't need looking after, and who were cheerful. Eileen Riley could make a cat laugh; she was always so upbeat about everything. Even when she referred to Michael's mother as 'the nut-job' he couldn't take offence. She said it in such a funny way, you couldn't help but laugh. He had also met her a few times at the club she thought she ran. It was a sight to see: Eileen Riley in enough make-up to sink a battleship, lording it over everyone and loving every second.

But it was his brother who Michael had really taken a shine to. Cain Junior had accepted him without a moment's hesitation. He said he had always wanted to meet him and was thrilled that it had finally come about. They chatted about everything, discussing their lives and the different paths they had taken over the years. Michael had explained to Jenny that his mother's condition – though not helped by his father's desertion – had not been caused by it either. There was nothing she could do to stop it from happening to her; she was unstable, and there was a chemical imbalance in her brain. It was no one's fault, but it was difficult to live with all the same. Jenny Moran told Michael she thought he was marvellous looking out for his mother as he did, and he had loved her for saying that.

Later on he would be meeting his new-found brother for a few drinks, and he was really looking forward to it. His life had certainly taken a turn for the better. Now he just wanted his mother to get well enough to go back home, even if he had a feeling that might be a long way off. The staff at the hospital were very good, though, and they knew his mum from old. When he took leave of her this time she didn't even acknowledge him, but he kissed her anyway.

Chapter One Hundred and Thirty-Seven

Cain Junior and Jenny Moran were together in the Soho offices; this was where Jenny did most of her accounting for the businesses they ran. The bets were booming and, the deeper the recession grew, the more people gambled. It was a strange but true fact. Everyone wanted a big payday and they wanted it fast. The clubs would always make money – that was a given – and other businesses were proficient earners all year round.

As they sat chatting over a coffee, the talk inevitably came round to Michael Moran.

'Your dad was thrilled to talk to him – he can't wait to get a VO sorted so he can see him in the flesh.'

Cain grinned. 'He's a really lovely bloke, Mum. He's had a fucking life of it with his mum, hasn't he? He's so patient with her. I really do feel sorry for him.'

Jenny shrugged. 'It's like he says: she can't help it. I wish I had known that myself all those years ago. I hated her for what she did to me, but in a way I feel I deserved it. I mean, I took her old man away.'

She was struggling to be fair, but it was hard. In the end Caroline Moran had taken far more away from Jenny.

'I know all about it, Mum, Nanny told me everything. I can understand why you hate her.'

Jenny sighed in annoyance. 'Her and her fucking big trap! She should never have said anything.'

Cain Junior smiled. 'At least Michael doesn't know. Mind you, he's always hanging about with Nanny at her club so in all likelihood he will find out eventually. He calls her his drag nanny and she loves it.'

Jenny laughed. 'He fits in well, bless him, considering the circumstances. Is he seeing anyone at the moment? He is a good-looking man.'

Cain Junior waved away the question. 'I don't ask him things like that. It's his business, though he does mention a friend called Alan quite regularly.'

Jenny laughed happily. 'Good, he deserves to have someone in his life. I can't believe how that poor fucker was brought up. Even his aunt Dolly took a step back years ago because she'd had enough.'

Cain shrugged again. He was so like his father and Jenny felt a sudden sting of tears.

'It's clear that you're brothers – you are both like the spit out of Cain Moran's mouth! It's lovely for me – a bit like having your dad back.'

'You really miss him, don't you?'

Jenny smiled the tight little smile she always reserved for such questions. 'I made my decision . . . I don't regret it. I love your dad with everything I am and I must have him in my life. I know people think I'm a mug, but the heart wants what the heart wants. I am not saying it has been easy, but I have made a life of sorts for us.'

'Mum, you are fucking awesome, and I really admire you. Linda loves the bones of you too. I can't believe we are having a baby – it's scary and exciting at the same time.'

'You've got a good girl there; you look after her.'

She meant every word she said – Linda was terrific. Jenny was so happy with her life at the moment; the only thing that could make it better was if her husband was back. But she was a realist, and had learned many years ago that it isn't always possible to get what you want. She laughed at that. The Stones knew what they were talking about.

'It'll be Christmas soon. Just think, Cain, this time next year there will be a baby to celebrate it with!'

Cain Junior laughed now in delight. 'God, I never thought of it like that! I hope it's a boy. I fancy myself as a footballing dad.'

'It'll be a while before you're doing that, mate! I wouldn't mind if it's a little girl – I always wanted a daughter.' There was a trace of sadness in her voice and, getting up from his chair, Cain Junior walked around the desk and hugged his mother tightly.

'Well, if we don't get one this time, maybe the next one will be a girl, eh? We like the idea of having a big family.'

They were laughing now as Jenny said, 'Well, just see how she goes after the first one. She might find she wants to wait a while before having any more!'

'I expect you're right, Mum. By the way, have you heard from Hasan or Ali Osman? I was supposed to meet them tonight for an update and I can't get either of them on the phone.'

Jenny shook her head, looking puzzled. 'That's not like Hasan. He's usually a stickler for meets. Maybe something came up. He will be in touch though – don't worry.'

Cain picked up his car keys and kissed him mum on the cheek before walking out of the offices and heading back to his work.

Chapter One Hundred
and Thirty-Eight

Hasan Osman was a very worried man. His brother Ali was completely out of control and Hasan had no idea what to do about it. He pulled into the lot of his car dealership and rushed into the building, seriously afraid of what he might find.

Ali was standing inside the dealership with the air of a mad man, his eyes blazing. He was surrounded by three men who were staring at the beaten and bloody figure on the floor in front of them. In his hand Ali held a large blood-stained wrench; he looked like something from a horror film. As Hasan took in the battered young man he sighed heavily. There was brain fluid leaking from his skull; Hasan hoped he'd died quickly. He went to his brother and gently took the wrench, then motioned for the men to clear the boy away.

'Who was he?'

The tallest of the three men answered quietly. 'Zafar.

He's newly over from Izmir. A mechanic, with two little kids . . .'

Hasan closed his eyes in distress. This was getting worse by the moment.

'What the fuck were you thinking, Ali?'

His brother was coming out of his daze and looked around as if he wasn't sure where he was.

'He was staring at me – fucking blatantly staring at me. Snidey cunt.'

Hasan was beside himself with anger. 'He was a fucking mechanic, Ali! A grease monkey. All of twenty-two years old and with a wife and kids he was trying to provide for. He was probably wondering if you were the full fucking ten bob. You look like a fucking mad man. When was the last time you slept?'

Ali stared at his brother, his anger building up inside him. 'Who the fuck do you think you are talking to? You might be my older brother but I've sussed you right out, mate. You and that fucking piece of shit Moran. I know exactly what is going on and I ain't got to listen to anyone. I will do what the fucking fuck I want, when I fucking want. You and your fucking boyfriend can lick Jason Biggs's arse all you want. Don't mean I'm going to be doing the same.'

Hasan was incensed with rage and frustration.

'Listen to yourself, Ali! You just can't get it into your thick fucking head that this is all for the best. Cain Moran is a shrewd man, and you would do well to listen to him occasionally. If he thinks Jason Biggs is worth cultivating then I think he is right. We might need him one day.'

Ali started laughing. 'Well, not me, Hasan. Not me.' With that, he exited the building, leaving his brother to clean up his mess once more. Hasan had just about had enough of his brother's antics and, following him outside, he called his name. When Ali turned to answer, Hasan Osman gave him the hiding of a lifetime.

After he had finished, he pulled Ali up from the floor by the collar of his jacket and said to him angrily, 'That was just a fucking taster. Get yourself sorted out and get off the fucking gear. Until you do, I don't want to see you. Now fuck off home and have a fucking wash – you stink.'

As Ali began to wipe the blood from his eyes, Hasan added quietly, 'Oh, and one last thing, bruv, you better sort out compensation for that poor cunt's wife and family. Fucking staring at you! Are you completely fucking stupid?'

The disgust in his brother's voice was worse than the physical beating Ali had just been given.

Hasan Osman went back into the building and started to organise the clean-up operation. This was the last thing he needed today: a needless murder by a brother who had lost himself to drugs. How he was going to hush this up he didn't know, but money usually had a funny way of shutting mouths. He was so disappointed in Ali. If push came to shove, he would have to take his brother out personally. The way Ali was carrying on, it was only a matter of time before someone would take it upon themselves to do the dirty deed. At least Hasan would do it humanely.

Ali was an accident waiting to happen, and if this little lot didn't make him come to his senses, then sooner or later someone else would.

Chapter One Hundred and Thirty-Nine

Jason Biggs was at his latest girlfriend's flat in Manchester city centre. She was a game bird this one, a bit older than his usual squeezes, but there was definitely something about her. Maybe it was her experience. She was up for literally anything and – more to the point – she enjoyed it as much as he did. She was also argumentative and, after the act was finished, she liked a cuddle and a bit of a chat. What she didn't appreciate was him having to get dressed and go home when it was all over; she didn't quite understand this part of shagging a married man. At least not when it suited her.

He was anticipating the fight of the night as he prepared himself to leave and, when his phone rang, he answered it quickly. It was his brother, Jack, calling to arrange a meet for later that evening. They would be seeing a crew from Liverpool who wanted to put a proposition to them. He arranged to meet at his club before putting the phone away.

Lorraine was lying naked on the bed, watching him distastefully. She had amazing eyes that could flash from bright blue to a steely grey in nanoseconds.

'Come on, Loll, you heard me. I have a meet to get to.'

She closed her eyes and took a deep breath as Jason Biggs pulled his trousers on as quickly as was humanly possible. He knew she had a penchant for throwing objects and the last thing he needed was a fucking dirty great cut-glass ashtray winging its way towards his head – she had good taste, he'd give her that. Biggs wasn't silly, there was no way he was going to chance a shower; he would have one at the club before the meet.

Lorraine sat up, lighting the remains of a joint and, as the hot cinders fell on to her naked breasts, he had to suppress a laugh. She jumped off the bed trying desperately to put them out; hardly the sophisticated look she'd been aiming for but he didn't mention anything. She wasn't stoned yet, and that meant she was still capable of a punch-up if the fancy took her.

He clearly liked the fiery natured ones – his wife was a prime example. She was another who could fight like a man when the fancy took her. He'd have to have a rethink on the bird front. He was getting too old for all this drama, and it was tiring into the bargain – especially after two hours of solid shagging. A fucking Olympic weightlifter couldn't raise it now, and he knew she'd want one last go before he left. She always did.

He was fully dressed now and Lorraine was lying

provocatively on the bed once more, her legs open and her smile telling him that the sooner he fucked her the better.

'I got to go, darling. It's been lovely . . .'

She got up, pulling on a short, black silk dressing gown that barely covered her perfectly round arse. He was getting tempted. Bending towards her, he kissed her long and hard before pushing her away firmly. He said gently, 'I've really got to go, babe.'

She made a grab for him then and he stepped away from her deftly. As he walked to the bedroom door he felt a wineglass whizz past his head and saw it smash against the wall in front of him. Red wine was every-where – all over his suit and on the floor.

'You can't just fucking use people, Jason!'

He turned towards her then, saying darkly, 'You have ruined my suit. Fucking red wine, you silly bitch.'

This was what she liked, what she craved, the excite-ment of fighting a hard man and seeing how far she could push him. She launched herself at him but he was ready for her, and the fight started in earnest. Lorraine threw punches and kicks left, right and centre, and Jason Biggs did his best to avoid the blows and subdue her. After a frantic five minutes he finally had Lorraine pinned back on the bed. Then she did her usual party piece and burst into uncontrollable sobbing. Though he was worn out, he did as was required, hugging her and kissing her, telling her he was sorry and that he would stay longer the next time.

'There won't be a next time. You can fuck off, Jason! I've had enough of you.'

He got up off the bed, annoyed to see the wine was spreading. A fucking grand the suit had set him back – grey silk – and now it was wrecked.

'Fair enough, Loll. If that's what you want.'

She knelt up and said, 'You know it's not what I want, Jase, but I hate it when you have to go. It feels like you only use me for sex.'

He could have pointed out that was exactly what was going on but knew better than to speak the truth at moments like this.

'I love you, Jason.'

That was the last fucking thing he needed. 'No, you don't, Loll. Come on, darling.'

He tried to sneak a look at his watch as he was holding her but she caught him in the bedroom mirror. The blow to his nuts was quick, hard and painful. Then the fight started up again, only this time it was him doubled up on the bed in agony and Lorraine had the advantage.

When he finally subdued her, she started to cry again and he sighed impatiently. During the fight, her dressing gown had come off and, as he'd held her down, he'd got a very good look at her in the full-length mirror beside the bed.

'I want you to fuck off out of my life, Jason Biggs, and leave me to find someone who cares about me.'

'All right then, Loll, I'll do that if it makes you

happy.' He let go of her carefully; she was capable of anything.

She turned on her side and wiped her eyes tragically. 'I mean it, Jason, don't call me any more. We are finished.'

'Really, Loll? I am over the moon. You see, I hadn't wanted to be the one to do it.'

With that barb he walked away and tried to get out of the bedroom door. At that moment an ashtray hit the mirror, sending it into a million pieces.

He turned back towards her, laughing. 'Fuck me, Loll, make your fucking mind up! I thought this was what you wanted. You knew from the off that I was married and that ain't going to change, not for you or for anyone else.'

She was kneeling on the bed screaming at him. 'Fuck off and leave me the fuck alone, you rotten piece of fucking shit!'

He stood there, the picture of innocence, his arms open wide and a smile on his face. 'I take it a fuck is out of the question then?'

He continued smiling as he fucked her on the leather sofa in her 'through lounge' as she called it. He did like the passionate fuckers – couldn't resist them. It would make him late for his meeting but this was far too good to pass up.

When he finally got out of Lorraine's flat he was an hour late and looked as though he had spent the night in a skip. His suit was ruined but he had to admit it had been pretty legendary sex! He had come like a train and now he was knackered.

He had just pulled into the car park of the club when he saw his brother, Jack, getting out of his own car. But before he could call over to him he spotted a very dishevelled-looking Ali Osman in the far corner of the car park pulling out a 12-gauge sawn-off shotgun. He watched in slow motion as Ali shot his brother Jack twice. The first shot lifted Jack into the air, his guts spraying everywhere, the second was straight to the head. All Jason could think was that their mother wouldn't be able to see her dead son properly before she buried him.

Ali was already back in his car, speeding off as Jason ran to his brother with tears in his eyes and terrible hatred in his heart. He knew the bullets had been meant for him, not Jack. They looked like twins, especially in the dark of the night. If he hadn't gone for round two with that cunt Lorraine he would have taken the bullet. He would have happily done anything to save his brother.

That fucking animal Ali Osman had shot the wrong fucking person and now he had an enemy who would not rest until he had tortured him to death. As he held his brother's mangled body in his arms, tears streamed down his face and he wondered how the fuck he would explain all this to his poor old mum. He kept replaying the scene – the sound of the shotgun, his brother's body flying into the air and the fucker going in for the final kill. This was a hit, pure and simple. It had to be because he'd threatened to take his drug business to the Russians. Well, he would make sure they all fucking paid a hefty penalty; he would make sure they knew to never fuck with a Biggs again.

He could hear the police and ambulance sirens in the distance as he held his brother in his arms. The revellers inside were all clamouring to leave; a nightclub shooting was never good for business.

Chapter One Hundred and Forty

Cain was told the news at 1 a.m. He could not believe what he was hearing and, even though Hasan assured him he would sort it all out, Cain knew it spelled the end. Jason Biggs would not let this go – why should he? And all the while Cain was stuck in his cell, confined to pacing the fucking floor and wondering what kind of retaliation Jason was considering.

Hasan Osman had told Cain he was going to take his brother out as soon as he had tracked him down. He could lecture all night about drugs, drink and everything else in between, but the bottom line was Ali Osman should never have been allowed to get into that fucking state in the first place. After years of working together, the goodwill between Cain and Jason Biggs had been destroyed in seconds because Ali fucking Osman couldn't take a fucking joke. If it wasn't so tragic it would be laughable. Cain had tried over and over to get through to Jason, but his phone wasn't even turned on. He would be too busy with appeasing the Filth and trying to console his mother and his brother's grieving widow. Jack had a couple of young sons, if he remembered rightly.

Cain poured himself a large brandy and, for the first time in years, he felt the urge to really harm someone. That someone was a cunt called Ali Osman. Jason Biggs was not a man to be crossed in any way, shape or form, but while Cain was banged up there was literally nothing he could do to alleviate the problem. It would be left to Hasan to do that. Though Cain loved Hasan, he knew he wasn't the man for the job. Not this time anyway. Jason Biggs would need expert handling, and that was something few people were capable of delivering.

Cain didn't sleep. He drank and stared at his mobile phone, willing it to ring; he had never felt so desolate in his life. Jason Biggs was a man capable of real cruelty – they all were in their own way. It was what made them who they were. But Jason Biggs had been known to hurt just for the hell of it; he had a penchant for violence. Now he would go all out for revenge.

Cain prayed to God for the first time in years, and asked Him to give Hasan Osman the gift of the gab. Because he was going to fucking need it – for all their sakes.

Chapter One Hundred
and Forty-One

Jack Biggs's death hit all the daily papers, and his family's connection to violent crime was picked over and digested by the nation. It was a hit and the papers loved it as usual, finding any excuse to rehash anything they could find that pertained to the family and their workforce. Jack's wife Maria was devastated of course, and her beautiful picture adorned all the front pages; the *Sun* had even managed to get a photo of them on their wedding day.

Cain shook his head in bewilderment at what people would do for a few quid. His heart went out to Jason, but it was three days now and still no word. He kept telling himself that no news was good news, but that was getting harder to believe as each hour wore on. Desmond Harker couldn't get through to Jason, or any of the Biggs brothers for that matter, either. He was 'incommunicado', as Des kept saying.

Meanwhile Hasan was still trying to locate that

fucking muppet Ali, and Cain had a terrible feeling that this was going to blow up in their faces. He was devastated for Jason's loss, but he had to get through to assure him it was nothing to do with him or Hasan. It looked like they had been trying to take Jason Biggs out – it looked like a hit.

Ali had thought he was going for Jason, there was no doubt about that in anyone's mind, least of all Jason Biggs himself. It was an abortion and needed sorting as soon as possible. Cain knew that a lot of the men on the wing were questioning his part in it all – even Desmond Harker.

This was when being banged up really hit home, because he was like a sitting duck in this dump. The waiting was killing him; he felt frustrated and helpless. Cain had to watch his back – with someone like Jason Biggs you had to try to pre-empt them. Think one step ahead. That was the only thing he could do now.

Chapter One Hundred and Forty-Two

Hasan finally tracked his brother down to an old girl-friend's council flat in Fulham. He had put a ten-grand price on a sighting and now he had him in view.

He waited until the woman left to take her kids to school before going inside. Kicking in the front door, he removed his brother from the premises with brute force, bundling him into a white Ford Transit where three men were waiting patiently to keep the fucker in line until they reached their destination. It was a small scrapyard in Tilbury, Essex. The man who owned it was renowned as someone who could easily dispose of unwanted items, mainly dead bodies. He would put them through the crusher with the cars.

Ali Osman looked terrified. He was rocking and Hasan realised that his brother – his baby brother who he had always looked out for – was using crack. Ali was crying now as he begged for his life. The paranoid cokehead had been replaced by a coward who just wanted to smoke a pipe of shit and get out of his head for a few hours at a time. Hasan Osman had never felt so ashamed of anyone or anything in his life. That his brother should end up like this, causing so much aggravation, was unbelievable to him. He blamed all those fucking whores he hung with, fucking cokeheads the lot of them, fixated on their next high. And where had that got him?

'Kneel down, Ali. Just kneel down.'

Ali Osman was in tears; he knew his brother was going to kill him and he didn't want to die.

'Please, Hasan, don't do this. I can go back to Istanbul or Adana. I can hide there . . .'

Hasan sighed. 'There is nowhere for you to hide, you fucking moron. Don't you understand? If Jason Biggs had found you first, you would have died long and slow. This is my last act of kindness. You have to go, *canim*.'

Being called 'darling' by his brother was the last straw for Ali and he cried like a baby. Gravely, Hasan shot him in the back of the head, execution style, then watched as the men loaded Ali's body into the boot of a Mercedes sports car that had lost its front body in a crash.

As the whole thing was lowered into the crusher, Hasan said sadly, 'He would have liked that – he always appreciated a nice car.'

He waited until the vehicle was completely crushed, then he wiped his eyes with a big white handkerchief and, motioning to the other men, climbed back into the van and prepared to leave. Hasan didn't know then that these Turkish men who worked for him were in awe of him for taking out his own brother in the name of business. Especially considering how close they had been.

On the M25, Hasan said to no one in particular, 'Fucking drugs, they make such a cunt of people.'

Chapter One Hundred and Forty-Three

Jenny and Eileen were worried. It seemed Cain was convinced that Ali Osman's actions would have far-reaching consequences. He had warned Jenny to be careful, to get all the premises swept for bombs and to stay away from the offices for the foreseeable future. Jenny thought he was being over the top and did her best to placate him, but he wouldn't listen to reason and kept telling her that Jason Biggs was a man who always paid his debts. Jason's brother was dead and he would be convinced that the hit had been planned for him. Which, of course, it was, but it had been Ali's idea and no one else's.

'Honestly, the way he is carrying on, Jen, you would think we were caught up in *The* bleeding *Godfather* or something.'

Jenny smiled. 'It's being banged up, Mum – everything takes on a significance of enormous proportions. Cain is a worrier, that's all. He thinks he is looking out for us.'

'Putting the fear of Christ up us, more like!'

'Try to understand, Mum. He's been away a long time and he feels like he can't protect us like he used to. Now let the fucking subject drop, eh?'

Jenny was cross because, if she was honest, her husband's paranoia was actually scaring her. He was a lot of things, her Cain, but he wasn't stupid. If he thought there was a threat then she would take him seriously – even if no one else did. She was aware, though, that she mustn't frighten her family with her worries. Linda was pregnant and the last thing she needed was to be panicking about something happening. But it would be Christmas soon and that would take everyone's mind off things.

Cain Junior was so excited about his first Christmas with Linda, and they would be spending it at Jenny's place. She was cooking for them all, Linda's parents and Molly included. She couldn't leave the poor old cow out, even though she was like the spectre at the feast.

'I tell you something, I think this Christmas will be a good one, Jen. I am really looking forward to it.'

Jenny smiled. 'So am I actually.'

'I always loved Christmas.'

Jenny didn't answer. She could remember too many Christmases where there had either been a strange man in the house or her mum had gone on the missing list. She didn't say that, though, as it was water under the bridge now. One thing she had learned over the years was that you couldn't dwell on the past. It was not worth the upset – all it did was break your heart again and that was a fool's errand.

Christmas was hard for Jenny; it was when she missed Cain the most. She liked to surround herself with people – it gave her a purpose – and she would cook and serve and tire herself out before going to bed and crying in private. She hated Christmas with a vengeance as it reminded her of just how much she had missed out on over the years. Not that she ever let on, of course. Her son needed good memories, and she had always been determined to give him just that. Good memories were what made life worth living. She should know – they had been keeping her going for years.

Chapter One Hundred and Forty-Four

Hasan Osman had travelled to Manchester to see Jason Biggs. He had no choice in the matter, and it was with a heavy heart that he sat in the hotel waiting for the meet. He was pleased to be in a public place, though he knew Jason was shrewd enough to understand that he wouldn't have come otherwise. This was Hasan's chance to persuade the man that his brother had acted alone and tell him that he had taken him out himself as a result. He only hoped he could be convincing enough to make Jason see the truth of the situation. It was his idea of a joke that had caused it in the first place – not that he would say that, of course. He would explain his brother's coke taking and his paranoia and hope for the best. It was all he could do.

In reality Hasan blamed himself. He should have taken better care of his brother; he had always tried to look out for him, but he was a grown man who had made his own choices. There was nothing anyone could do now. He missed him and was sad to think that he wouldn't even get a proper burial. Even though Ali had not been the most observant of Muslims, he still deserved at least that. But needs must when the devil drives and Hasan had done what he needed to do for the greater good.

Just then he heard someone speak his name and, as he turned to answer, he was shot three times in rapid succession. The shooter calmly dropped the gun and walked quickly away as pandemonium ensued. Hasan's last thoughts were of his mother in Istanbul and how she would cope with the loss of both sons within twenty-four hours.

Chapter One Hundred and Forty-Five

When Desmond Harker broke the news to Cain Moran, his heart went out to the man. He had already decided that Cain was on the up and up; no one was this good an actor.

He saw Cain close his eyes in genuine distress and said to him sadly, 'Jason's already taken over in London. I've spoken to him. I told him the story but he wasn't in the frame of mind to listen. He was very close to Jack. They were more like twins really – even as kids they were always together.'

Cain nodded. 'I don't fucking know what to say, Des. Now Hasan's gone as well, and he didn't deserve that. All over that fucking muppet Ali.'

Des smiled and said, 'Ironic really, when you think about it. A drug dealer dying over taking drugs. Always stick with the puff, that's what I say. It mellows you out.'

Cain Moran was in no mood to discuss the merits of different drugs and their effects on the human psyche. 'It will be me next. I'm like a fucking sitting target in here.'

'Best thing you can do now, Cain, is to get yourself put in the hole. That at least will give you breathing space and time to think through your next step.'

Cain nodded his agreement – the thought had already crossed his mind. 'I think you're right, Des. Jason will have a right hard-on for me now. It's only a matter of time.'

Des shrugged. 'In the meantime I will talk to the brothers and the workforce, see if I can convince them otherwise. But you need to remove yourself from this wing for a while all the same.' He gave him a wink as he added, 'No one likes that new Face Walker. Fucking hammer him, pick a fight, whatever. He's a flash cunt and he needs taking down a peg.'

Standing up Cain shook his friend's hand and, moving quickly to the recreation room, he picked up two billiard balls and slipped them into the sports sock he had just taken off, before making his way to Kevin Walker's cell. Once there, he proceeded to batter the man to within an inch of his life.

Cain was on the block within the hour, and Kevin spent the next six weeks in the infirmary. He wasn't liked by the cons or the screws – he was too flash for his own good – and Cain's little escapade wasn't really made that much of. Most of the men had worked out the whys and wherefores anyway; they thought it was a shrewd move on Cain Moran's part. Buying time, that was what it was all about.

Chapter One Hundred and Forty-Six

'Dad is on the block, Mum. Beat up some geezer called Kevin Walker. So no visits for a month.'

'Well, that's fucking Christmas ruined.' Jenny was close to tears.

Cain Junior hugged her to him tightly. 'Not necessarily – you've still got us. I'm sure he had his reasons, Mum.'

Jenny knew this son of hers would defend his father no matter what he did, and she was proud of that. But she wouldn't be happy now until Cain was back on his wing. She was well aware of what the block entailed: no books, no communication, no nothing. It was barbaric. And he would be there for Christmas too. As she watched people scurrying around buying presents and leaking goodwill, she often wondered why she bothered. The only thing she wanted to do was get into bed, pull the covers over her head and get up on New Year's Day when it was all over. But she couldn't; she had no choice but to carry on.

'You're right, son. He must have had his reasons and it's not like he was going to be with us anyway.'

Cain Junior hugged her again. 'That's the ticket, Mum. Never let the fuckers get you down! By the way, did you hear about Hasan Osman?'

Jenny shook her head in bewilderment. 'What about him?'

'He was shot dead in Manchester last night. Three bullets to the chest.' Cain Junior watched as his mother's face paled. 'Here, sit down, Mum.'

She allowed her son to lead her to the sofa. He poured her a whisky and watched as she drank it straight down.

'Fucking hell. I didn't think you liked him that much!'

She looked sad. 'It's just a shock, son. He was a good friend to your dad.'

'I know that, Mum, I dealt with him too. Ali's been on the missing list since Jack Biggs was shot.'

Jenny felt physically sick. It was all falling into place for her. This was why Cain had been in such a state. Jason Biggs thought that he and the Osmans were behind the murder of his brother. That's why he was now on the block – he had been buying time.

Jenny felt a wave of nausea wash over her. Cain had been right to be so paranoid. They were at the centre of a war, and most of them had no fucking idea what was actually going on. All she could do was watch and wait.

But the fear was taking over now, and she prayed that this would somehow be resolved. How ironic it would be if she waited all this time and then Cain died in prison. She had to calm herself and not appear worried. The last thing she needed was for her son to pick up on her anguish; it was pointless for the rest of the family to feel this pressure.

'Right, Mum, if you're OK I'm off to meet Michael. We're going to do a spot of Christmas shopping in Bond Street.'

She forced a cheerful smile. 'Sounds great – give him my love.'

'I will. Are you sure you're going to be all right? I can always ring and rearrange.'

She smiled again. 'Don't be so silly. You go off and enjoy yourself. It was just a shock hearing about poor Hasan.'

As Jenny watched her son leave, terror gripped her once more. She prayed to God, begging Him not to take her Cain from her; not when he was only a few years away from coming home. It would be too cruel.

Chapter One Hundred and Forty-Seven

Jason Biggs sat in church with his mum and dad, listening to their crying with a heavy heart. Outside a raft of press and TV cameras lay in wait, and it was all Jason could do to keep his temper with the reporters. He hated that his brother's funeral was no more than a fucking spectacle for people to come and gawk at. The idea of his family's grief as common fodder for the masses made a terrible situation all the harder to bear.

The priest was a nice bloke; he had baptised each of them and they had made their First Holy Communions with him. He had known Jack and liked him, so at least he could talk about him with a modicum of realism. There was nothing worse than a funeral where the priest had never met the deceased.

Their mother had always expected good church attendance from her family and she had got it. They all adored her – why wouldn't they? She had had their backs from day one, hiding guns and drugs whenever the police came knocking, and fighting their corners in court. Now she was burying her son, and the pain was etched all over her lovely face.

Jason felt rage building up inside him once more as he thought of the audacity of the Osmans and that cunt Moran, thinking they could fucking have him over. It was absolutely fucking outrageous that his brother was leaving little boys behind while that cunt Moran sat on the block in Parkhurst planning his next move. Well, there were other ways to skin a cat and Jason was going to hit that cunt right where it would hurt him most. See how he liked them fucking apples!

He glanced around the church and saw to his dismay that Lorraine was there, sitting at the back in an all-black get-up that wouldn't have looked out of place in a strip club. She caught his eye but the look he threw her would have been enough to put the fear of Christ up the hardest of men, and he was pleased to see her hotfoot it out of there as a result. She seemed to be under the impression that she had saved Jason's life and that he owed her. Well, he would soon disabuse her of *that* fucking notion. The silly whore! As if he wouldn't have taken a bullet meant for him if it could have kept his brother alive. What kind of fucking man did she think he was, for fuck's sake? He could feel animosity burning up in his chest and, looking at his two younger brothers as they each held one of Jack's boys on their laps, he felt the familiar urge to wreck the fucking place. But he knew he must keep calm, at least until this farce was over.

What a great fucking Christmas for his family. Even his wife had become subdued since realising the bullet had been meant for him. She had turned into a fucking poster girl for a Victorian wife. No more, 'Make your own fucking tea!' or, 'What did your last servant fucking die of?' Now it was all sweetness and light: breakfast in bed, tea at his whim, kisses and cuddles for no reason. It was like living with a Stepford bride. Still, at least he knew that she loved him. The strange thing was, he loved her too, even if she never believed him.

As Jack's wife broke down sobbing, her heart-wrenching cries hardened Jason's heart even further. Squeezing his wife's hand, he sat stoically through the service planning his next move. It didn't bother him that he was doing it in church; Jesus had been a prisoner too, as his mum was always pointing out. He was sure He would understand the need for revenge – for retribution. An eye for a fucking eye and all that.

Chapter One Hundred and Forty-Eight

Linda Lloyd was helping Jenny trim the Christmas tree and it was looking very festive. Jenny was worn out with pretending to be cheerful and excited for the holidays when all she felt was a terrible pressure inside her chest. But she was doing a good job; as yet, no one had asked her if she was OK.

Eileen came into the room with a tray of mulled wine and the smell was so overpowering it made Jenny feel sick.

'I thought this might put us in the Christmas mood. That's your alcohol-free one in the long glass, Linda.'

'Thanks, Eileen. Doesn't the tree look nice?'

Eileen stood back and pretended to observe it. 'Beautiful. I wish you would put up a few paper chains, though. Next year we'll do it at mine and then I will festoon the place with colour!'

Jenny smiled. 'Remember the year you put them up

while you were pissed? You fell off the kitchen chair and broke your wrist.'

Eileen roared with laughter. 'I'd forgotten about that! That was funny, wasn't it, Jen?'

Jenny nodded, though it had not been so funny to her – a visit to the hospital followed by cooking a Christmas dinner at nine in the evening while her mum spent the night drinking with a large black man who kept trying to put his arm around Jenny at every opportunity and give her a Christmas kiss. But she kept her own counsel; some things were best left in the past. That seemed to have become her mantra these days.

Jenny saw Linda looking at her sadly and guessed that this lovely girl had an idea of exactly what that Christmas would have been like. Linda was a good lass, and Jenny was pleased that she was with her son; they were a perfect match and they adored each other. She wondered again how her Cain was getting on, and if he was bearing up. When Des Harker had last called he had assured her that everything was in hand and that he was doing everything he could. She liked Des; he was a good bloke and he had put her mind at rest, for a while anyway. But she would be glad when this Christmas was out of the way.

Her mobile rang and she answered it with a sinking heart. It was Des and she felt ill with what he might be about to tell her. *Don't let it be bad news about Cain.* Her hands were visibly shaking as she walked to the kitchen to take the call in private.

'Is that you, Jen?'

'Is everything OK, Des?'

'I have great news. I've spoken to Jason Biggs and he has assured me that there is going to be no comeback for Cain. He swore to me on his children's lives that nothing would happen to Cain Moran. We can all breathe easy, darling. I think I managed to convince him that Ali was working alone.'

Jenny felt faint with relief and she sat down at her kitchen table as tears filled her eyes. 'Oh, Des, thank you. Thank you so very much. I will be forever in your debt . . .'

Des brushed it off lightly. 'He buried his brother today, so perhaps he thought there had been enough killing already. But whatever his reasoning, I've got his word that Cain will be safe in Parkhurst. So you stop worrying and enjoy your Christmas, OK?'

After thanking him profusely again Jenny rang off. She sat there and pondered what Des had said. If Jason Biggs had sworn on his children's lives, then he was being honest. That was the kind of promise that no Face would make lightly. She smiled suddenly as she remembered how Cain used to say to their son, 'I swear it's the truth, on a policeman's eyesight!' And Cain Junior would believe whatever it was he was being told.

She hugged herself with happiness. The fear had left her and she felt lighter than she had in weeks. She kissed her mobile phone reverently and then she closed her eyes and thanked God for hearing her prayer and protecting her husband from harm. This was going to be the best Christmas ever; she was determined to see to that. Her Cain would be home in a few years and they could resume their lives together. Michael was back in the family and there was a grandchild on the way. In many respects they were truly blessed.

Chapter One Hundred and Forty-Nine

It was Christmas Eve and Jenny was stuffing the turkey ready to put it in the oven on a low gas at midnight. It was huge and she had covered it in a pound of streaky bacon and a pound of butter. If it was dry then it couldn't be helped – she had done her best.

She couldn't remember feeling this happy for years. Since Des Harker had given her the news that Cain was in the clear she had felt almost carefree. The thought of losing Cain had nearly destroyed her, but now she could face the world again and get on with her life such as it was.

She could hear her mother and Michael chatting away; they were a funny pair really. They got on like a house on fire, and he genuinely loved her. Eileen now told anyone she came across that she was a bona fide Fag Hag and that she was loving it. Michael did have a point, though, about her mother's make-up giving her the look of a drag queen. He had even taken

Eileen out to a few gay clubs, and apparently she had been a huge hit with his friends.

She was pleased that Michael could join them on Boxing Day, even if he might not be able to make Christmas dinner. He would have to spend Christmas Day with his mother but from what he had let slip it was never the best of days for either of them. It was such a shame because he was a good lad and Caroline should have respected all that he did for her. She was drinking again by all accounts and that always made her more paranoid. Jenny sighed heavily. It was such a shame, but life wasn't always about getting what you wanted; often it was about being able to compromise. There was an old Irish toast that said: 'May we all get what we want, and *not* what we deserve.' She had never liked it, but her mother thought it was funny.

Jenny finished the bird and covered it in foil, then she cleaned up the kitchen quickly between sips of white wine. It was all feeling very festive, and she was looking forward to the big day tomorrow. For the first time in years she wasn't dreading Christmas Day; that was a turn-up for the books as far as she was concerned. She finished her tidying and, after one last glance around her kitchen, she joined the others in the lounge.

Cain Junior and Linda were on the sofa together; her bump was becoming much more noticeable, though she was still tiny really. The tree looked amazing, and there were presents piled everywhere. There were also a couple of jewellery bags hanging from branches of the tree itself and Jenny wondered what Cain had asked his son to get for her. She never needed presents, but she knew it made Cain feel as though he was a part of the day. God, she missed him. Christmas was a real family time of year and he was conspicuous by his very absence. But she pushed those thoughts out of her head; she was going to be happy tonight and tomorrow if it killed her.

'Oi, madam, I was talking to you!'

Her mother's voice broke through her reverie and she said quickly, 'Sorry, Mum. I was miles away.'

'You've been like fucking Dilly Daydream lately. You sickening for something?'

Eileen actually sounded concerned and Jenny felt a sudden rush of affection for her.

Holding out her arms she said with a laugh, 'Come here and give me a cuddle, you old bat!'

Thrilled and happy Eileen did just that and, as she hugged her daughter, she asked herself for the hundredth time how she had been so lucky. She was a lot of things, was Eileen Riley, but she wasn't a complete fool. She knew that any other girl would have blanked her mother for the start she had been given. In spite of everything Jenny seemed to believe that you had to make the best of things. Eileen loved this girl with all her heart, and it pleased her to know her daughter felt the same.

Michael catcalled them, shouting, 'Hugging a drag queen! Let me get a photo . . .'

Cain and Linda were laughing their heads off. Michael had a new digital camera and he was snapping away left, right and centre.

'It's nearly nine o'clock! Don't let me forget to put that fucking turkey in at midnight.' Jenny looked at Linda and asked, 'Are you still staying here tonight, darling?'

Linda nodded happily. 'Yes, if that's all right.'

Cain Junior hugged her. ''Course it's all right. You're carrying the next generation of Morans, darling.'

Linda laughed and went bright red with embarrassment.

'Who wants another drink?' This from Eileen who couldn't stand the sight of an empty glass.

The doorbell rang just as she went to the kitchen, and Cain jumped up to answer it. 'More fucking carol singers, I'll bet.' He searched in his pocket for a few pound coins as he walked out of the room.

When Jenny heard the first shot, she thought for a wild moment that it was a car backfiring. As soon as she heard the second shot she ran into the hallway screaming.

Cain Moran Junior was lying across the doorway, his lovely handsome face destroyed. Then there was more screaming and Jenny was on her knees, trying to bring her son back to life again. But it was never going to happen.

Chapter One Hundred and Fifty

Cain Moran had been miraculously released from the hole that morning. He was sitting with Des Harker and the rest of the lads at the kitchen table having cooked them all a large Bolognese with a salad and, of course, the requisite bowl of chips. They were all in a festive mood and looking forward to the following day.

'Thank fuck they let you out, Cain. We were dreading trying to cook that fucking turkey without you. The food has been shit lately, believe me.'

Everyone laughed. They each refilled their glasses and raised a toast.

'Another year out of the way, thank fuck for that.'

'I'll drink to that, mate.'

They were chatting among themselves when Des Harker's mobile bleeped with a text message. As he read it, Cain saw his friend's face change and, when he put his hand over his mouth in obvious distress, all the men at the table stopped talking and stared at him. Des shook his head in disbelief.

'Everything all right, mate?'

Cain put his hand on his friend's arm as Des gave him the phone, saying, 'I am so sorry, Cain . . . just so fucking sorry, mate. Jesus fucking Christ. The bastard . . . the absolute bastard.'

Cain looked down at the message; the rest of the men were bewildered as to what the fuck was going on.

'What is it? For fuck's sake, tell us.'

Cain looked around the table with tears running down his cheeks.

'Jason Biggs murdered my boy tonight. My Cain. Jenny will go off her head, he has a baby on the way . . . Oh, dear fucking God!'

He was sobbing bitterly and every man at the table was at a loss as to what to do. Des Harker put his arm around his friend's shoulders and held him as he cried, wondering all the while at how a man could be so cruel, no matter how justified he felt his actions might be.

Chapter One Hundred and Fifty-One

Michael Moran was still in shock. He sat holding Eileen's hand as they waited in the hospital to find out what would happen to poor Linda. Jenny had been sedated, thank God; her screams had been like a wild animal's. Linda's parents were with them too, and they all were waiting silently to hear if she was going to be OK. The poor girl had been in absolute bits.

Michael wiped his eyes again, and Eileen squeezed him to her. She was crying silently too, unable to believe what the night had brought on them. The cruelty of Jason Biggs waiting until Christmas Eve was something she could not comprehend. It was evil. But that was what the criminal world could be, and if you weren't able to allow for that you should not be a part of it. Still, to see her grandson blown away was not something she would ever forget. That handsome, kind boy with a baby on the way and his whole life ahead of him. It was evil all right, and it would finish off her poor Jenny for sure. Her only son – her only child – taken from her so brutally.

She was crying even harder now and, as she and Michael continued to hold one another, Jenny Moran lay in a hospital bed dead to the world, sleeping the sleep of the just. She would have to wake up at some point, though, and then the nightmare would begin all over again.

Chapter One Hundred
and Fifty-Two

Cain was handcuffed to two Prison Officers, but they at least had the decency to keep as low a profile as possible. Jenny looked awful and, as she cried into Cain's chest, he held her as best he could. The service had been beautiful and as they'd left the church it had begun to snow. It was a bitterly cold day and Cain was consumed with thoughts of making Jason Biggs pay.

Linda's parents were supporting their daughter as far as they could. The only saving grace was the baby was still there – if she had lost that too it would have been unbearable. But, as Jenny kept saying, there was still a piece of her boy in the world.

They made their way slowly to the grave and Cain looked around him, wondering how it could have come to pass that he was burying his treasured son. He felt the sting of tears again just as his son Michael put a hand on his shoulder, and he smiled sadly. Michael was a good lad; there was no doubting that.

As they approached the grave, Cain saw his mother being helped along by Eileen. She had taken the murder of Cain Junior really badly – they all had. How else could a death like this be taken?

'I knew if I waited long enough you'd get what was fucking coming to you!'

Everyone closed their eyes as Caroline stood spouting her usual hatred and vitriol.

'I prayed for this – for you to lose everything – and you have.'

She was laughing now, but the sight of her son Michael left her so shocked she couldn't say another word.

'Go home, Mum. This is not the time or the place.'

As he started to walk towards Caroline she backed away as though he had the plague.

'She got you and all, did she? She's taken everything from me and now she has taken my son too, is that it?'

Caroline was becoming hysterical. Everyone was gawping at her; this had not been on the agenda and they didn't know whether to laugh or cry.

Jenny stood staring at the woman who had been a thorn in her side for years, and eventually said loudly, 'Can you really blame him, you mad bitch? Just go home and let us bury our son with a bit of dignity.'

Michael started dragging his mother away from the graveyard; she was not happy to be going. Cain was shocked at the sight of his ex-wife, and couldn't understand how someone who had once been such a beautiful and vibrant woman could now look like someone from a Hammer horror film. It was proof of just how long he had been locked away.

He pulled Jenny towards him awkwardly and they resumed the walk to their son's graveside. The snow was coming down thicker now and the ground was frozen solid. Cain looked around and felt pleased with the turnout for his boy; it was a mark of how popular he had been. All his old schoolmates were there, as well as ex-girlfriends, work associates and the other men he had come to know over the years. It reminded Cain of the fact that he still was part of a community and he felt a strong sense of gratitude that he had not been forgotten – he still had a place in the world he had chosen all those years ago. There were flowers everywhere and the snow was starting to settle on them. There was going to be a blizzard by the looks of it. Cain kissed his wife's head and held her hand tightly as the priest started the final prayers.

Chapter One Hundred
and Fifty-Three

Jason Biggs had a new bird and her name was Jemima. She was very posh and owned a lovely cottage just outside Manchester, which suited Jason as it was away from his wife's prying eyes. Jemima also had a lot of money and plenty to say for herself – as per usual he had picked another nut-job. She was dark-haired with startling green eyes and small, juicy little tits. She also had the tightest snatch he had ever encountered and that was a big part of her attraction.

She was naked, on her knees, giving him a mind-bending blow job. He was in seventh heaven. She was new to the area and he could not believe it when she had come into his club and made a beeline for him. Not only did she have a voice like Princess Anne, but she could fuck like a train; she was everything he wanted, gift wrapped in a pale-grey Mercedes sports car. As he felt himself coming, he relaxed and let his mind wander a bit. He wanted to keep this feeling for as long as possible. So few birds enjoyed giving head, and when you found one who relished it you had to make the most of it. It was only manners, after all. But when he opened his eyes, he saw a man standing across from him with a gun. It was at that moment that he realised Jemima had set him up.

She was standing now, and she said in a broad cockney accent, 'Get it over with, for fuck's sake. I need to get back to Canning Town.'

The man was only too happy to oblige.

Chapter One Hundred and Fifty-Four

At Eileen's flat, Cain was negotiating a deal with the local Chief of Police, Geoff Dawes. They went back years, and had a grudging respect for each other. The snow was bad and Cain was hoping to persuade the Police Chief to let him have one night with his wife.

'Come on, tonight of all nights. Do you really think I could go on the trot and leave her in this state?'

Geoff Dawes was inclined to agree with Cain's request. Ten grand was a big sum to pass up and there was Jenny Moran standing with the cash in her hands. It seemed the two POs were happy enough with the situation; if Cain went on the trot they would be in the clear with two grand each, which wasn't to be sneezed at either.

'All right. But I want your word, Cain, that you won't get up to any funny business.'

Jenny looked sharply at her mother before she had

the chance to answer them with a ribald retort. Eileen looked suitably shamed.

'I am putting a couple of blokes outside, OK?'

Cain nodded and they shook hands on the deal.

When the police had left, Eileen tactfully retired to her bedroom with a bottle of vodka. Alone at last, Cain and Jenny looked into each other's eyes. Jenny began to sob as Cain held her tightly, glad that, if nothing else, he could be there for her tonight of all nights. The night they had buried their only son.

'It's done, babe.' She cried into Cain's chest as he stroked her hair, and continued gently, 'Jason Biggs is dead.'

She looked up at his handsome face and kissed him fiercely on his lips, her tongue slipping into his mouth, and he kissed her back deeply.

'Thank you, Cain. Thank you . . .'

With that, he picked her up and carried her to the bedroom.

Chapter One Hundred and Fifty-Five

Michael Moran was sitting with his mother, listening to her rant on as usual. Sometimes he felt as if he was living Groundhog Day over and over again.

'Look, Mum, he is my dad. I was supposed to bury my little brother today, but instead I am here with you. You have got to listen to me for once.'

Something in her son's voice broke through the fog in Caroline's mind and she looked at him expectantly.

'This can't go on, Mum, I can't live like this any more. I am going to move into my own place permanently and you're going to have to start taking responsibility for yourself. You've got to keep up your medication and stop drinking so much.'

Caroline remained quiet, afraid of what her son was telling her. She was terrified at the thought of being alone.

'You do so well in the diner – you're the star of the show there. Why can't you act like that all the time and be the star of your own life? Now, one of your staff members, Carole Borden, has said she is willing to move in here with you so you have a bit of company. You and her get on well, don't you? I've seen you having a laugh together at the diner.'

Caroline was nodding now, and her bloated face looked so forlorn Michael was almost tempted to change his mind. But he knew that if he didn't do this now he never would.

'She will see that you take your pills on time, and she can cook for you.'

He had a feeling that would be the clincher, and his mother was looking happier already. Her and her fucking food, it would kill her in the end.

'Michael . . . You won't leave me for them, will you? Promise me, darling.'

He shook his head and hugged her tightly. She smelled of Chanel No. 5 and stale sweat.

''Course not, but I needed to see my dad. Jenny is all right, Mum. She isn't like you would think.' He felt her stiffen in his arms then and he knew he had said the wrong thing. 'What I mean to say is that I tolerate her for my dad.'

Caroline Moran was terrified of losing this son of hers and she knew she had to keep him on side. The only way she could do that was to go along with whatever it was he wanted.

'God help me. I love you, Mum, but you can't half be hard work at times.'

She smiled at him then, and he wiped her eyes and brought her a huge piece of cake. He had said what he wanted to and the world hadn't ended. As he watched his mother eating he wondered if Cain Junior was in a better place now. He certainly hoped so.

Chapter One Hundred and Fifty-Six

Cain and Jenny were both spent as they basked in the afterglow of their lovemaking. Jenny could not believe that her Cain was here with her – that she could touch him and smell him like this. It was as though they had never been apart. She felt tears gather in her eyes and he held her even tighter.

'What a fucking day.'

Jenny didn't answer him. She didn't know what to say.

'That fat cunt turning up and all. Fuck me, I swerved a bullet there, girl!' Jenny laughed despite herself, as he had hoped she would. 'At least the baby is all right.'

Jenny settled herself so she could look into his face and said, 'If it's a boy she is going to name him Cain.'

'She's a nice girl, Jen, I like her. Good family too.'

Jenny nodded her agreement. 'He was lucky to have her, but – oh, Cain! – the pain I feel in my heart makes me think I will never know another truly happy day again.'

She started sobbing again and Cain held her and soothed her, willing himself not to cry too. He had to be strong for her.

'Only another few years and we will be back together for good. Keep your mind on that, darling. We have had our fair share of trouble, but we've got this far and we are still here and tight as any two people could possibly be.'

Jenny knew that was true. 'Cain?'

He kissed her head gently and answered, 'What, darling?'

'Can we give it all up now: the business, everything? Can we just be like normal people? We have plenty of money and I don't want this any more. It's taken you and our son from me. This isn't the Good Life, darling. It hasn't been for a long time.'

He digested her words before finally saying, 'If that is what you want, then that is what we will do. I will sort out selling everything off, OK?'

'Do you promise me?'

He looked into her lovely eyes and smiled as he said, 'I promise you, Jen.'

She was as lovely now as she had been when he had first seen her in that Soho pub all those years ago. If he had known then everything that would happen between them, would he have embarked upon the same course? The answer to that question was simple: he would not change a day. He loved Jenny with all his heart and soul, just as she loved him. They were meant to be and that was all there was to it. They fell asleep finally in each other's arms and, for the first time in nearly twenty years, they held each other like a normal couple.

Chapter One Hundred
and Fifty-Seven

Eileen lay in bed alone and wondered at her daughter
and Cain together in the next room. She knew she
could never have waited that long for anyone. It wasn't
in her nature; a six-week romance was enough before
her eye would start to wander and she was on to the
next one. She felt so sorry for her Jenny today, burying
her only child. It was a terrible thing for any woman
to have to do. At least there would be a grandchild
– that was something.

Eileen welled up as she remembered Cain Junior
climbing on her lap when he was little, always holding
her hand or giving her a kiss. He had been such an
affectionate child. She thought of how her Jenny had
loved him and played with him. Eileen had actually
enjoyed being with the child, and that was something
that had never appealed to her before. She wished that
things had been different while Jenny was growing up,
and that she had understood sooner a child's need for

parental love. Jenny had put up with her mother's drinking and her bringing men back for money and had even been taken into care on occasion. Yet that girl still wanted her in her life, and still gave her the affection that she now craved. Life was a funny thing all right, there was no denying it.

She picked up her grandson's photo and kissed it lovingly. At least she had done right by him, even if she had struggled to look after her Jenny. She was rightly proud of her for coming through the worst the world could throw at her and surviving it all. It was no mean feat. Eileen Riley liked to think her daughter had inherited that strength from her. After all, she must have got it from somewhere.

Chapter One Hundred and Fifty-Eight

Jenny had made Cain and the POs a huge cooked breakfast before Cain had to leave and go back to Parkhurst. After the men had departed, Jenny ran herself a bath and locked the bathroom door before gratefully easing her tired and aching body into the hot water. She lay back with a large mug of tea and a packet of cigarettes, savouring the memories of the night before. She knew they would have to keep her going for a long time. It had been so wonderful to breathe in Cain's smell – to feel his touch all over her – and it had taken some of the heartache out of a terrible day.

She closed her eyes and, thinking once more of her gorgeous son and the life he had lived under her care, she cried bitter tears. She knew, though, that as long as she had Cain Moran beside her she could cope with anything life might throw at her. He had done the one thing she had asked of him, taking out Jason Biggs, and she hoped that bastard had died in the knowledge that it was retribution for her boy's murder. For the first time in her life she'd wanted revenge and Cain had made sure she'd got it.

There was a part of her that blamed Cain for their son's death, though she knew she could do nothing about it. There was no denying that his lifestyle had been the cause of every major upheaval in their lives together. Now she needed to concentrate on healing. That was what she had learned as a child under the erratic care of Eileen Riley: if you waited long enough, things generally got better. At the very least, they couldn't get any worse. It would take time but she trusted that eventually it wouldn't hurt so much and that life would go on.

Epilogue

God shall wipe away all tears from their eyes.

Revelation 21:4 (*King James Bible*)

David Hannan was a happy lad. Cain Moran had been quite friendly and talkative as they had driven away from Parkhurst, asking the young man questions about his mum and dad and his beautiful daughter Mae. It had been a dream come true to be entrusted with picking up the infamous Cain Moran from the nick. They had arrived at Joe Biggs's offices so Cain could pop in to thank the man for the lift.

Joe Biggs felt nervous as he heard Cain Moran walking through the office. He was being hailed by all and sundry and that annoyed him. This was his business now, not Cain's, and it had been since the cunt killed Jason. He kept a smile plastered across his face and tried to look calm and business-like.

Cain walked into the office as if he owned the place and Joe was amazed at the sheer size of the man. He seemed to fill the entire place with his bulk. It was all muscle too, old as he was, but that was all down to the gym in the nick. There was fuck-all else to do there, everyone knew that.

'Joe. Good to see you, mate.'

Cain held out his hand and Joe Biggs shook it nervously.

'Drop of Scotch?'

Cain laughed then. 'Is the fucking Pope a Catholic, you cunt?' He sounded jovial but there an underlying threat there that wasn't lost on Joe Biggs.

Joe poured the drinks and handed one to Cain. 'I hear you've become quite the chef in the nick. Every time I see an ex-con from Parkhurst all I hear about are your fucking cooking skills.'

It was said as a joke but the intended insult was evident. Cooking was women's work as far as Joe Biggs was concerned.

'It was the best thing I ever done. I am thinking of opening a restaurant, in fact.'

Joe Biggs was a bit taken aback at that and it showed. 'I see. I wondered if you would be coming back into the Life . . .'

Cain held up his hands and the man stopped talking. 'Look, Joe, I came here to tell you first that I am out of it all now and have been for a long time. After my boy . . . Well, let's just say I've lost the heart for it. I promised my old woman that I would leave it all behind and that's what I'm doing.'

He swallowed his drink down and held his glass out for a refill. Joe Biggs obliged without even thinking about it. Cain had a way of intimidating others even when he was being the nice guy, and he was using that to full advantage now.

He continued, 'I took your brother out, and now you've taken his place down in the Smoke. You should know that I have a lot of friends here and in Manchester including your father-in-law, Graham Grange, who I have known for over forty years. Even in Parkhurst I heard that you're handy with your fists where your wife is concerned and I will tell you now: the day your wife doesn't want you any more is the day you die. Graham Grange loathes you but while his daughter is still enamoured, there's nothing he can do. Make sure it stays that way. If you ever feel the urge to avenge your brother's death, after he arranged my own boy's murder, I will rip your fucking head off with my bare hands. Without Jason and Jack, you and your brother are worth nothing. If you are after payback I will come out of my retirement and I will hunt you down like a fucking dog. I will make it my purpose in life to fucking find you, torture you and kill you. You know I am capable of it, mate. I am just trying to avoid a confrontation here. So, are we good?'

Joe Biggs knew that he had just lost the fight, the war and any respect he might have had from Cain. He nodded his head. The last thing he wanted was this cunt on his tail, especially if he was an old mate of his father-in-law.

Cain swallowed down his drink and, standing up, offered his hand in a friendly gesture. 'Let's call it quits, shall we?'

Cain held Joe's hand in a tight grip, reminding him of exactly who he was dealing with. He might be out of the Life, but he wasn't completely out of the game; there was a big difference. With that he left the offices, whistling cheerfully, and got back into the car with young David Hannan, announcing in a pseudo-posh voice, 'Home, James, and don't spare the horses.'

As they drove away it occurred to Cain Moran that he would miss the buzz of the Good Life. But it was over for him now. He had a lot of making up to do with his wife, who had stood by him through everything life had thrown at them. If he had learned nothing else, he had learned to get his priorities right. It was a mistake he would never make again.

As Jenny opened the door to her husband, her heart was in her mouth. She couldn't believe he was actually here for good. Cain walked into the flat and looked around, noting the place where his son had died. In spite of everything, Jenny had not been able to bring herself to leave their home where she had so many memories of her son's life.

'Come in, darling. Come through.'

After all this time they were both a little nervous of each other. He could have cried.

'I redecorated throughout, Cain. I thought it would be nice for us to start afresh, you know . . .'

Throwing down his bag, he picked her up in his arms and carried her towards the bedroom saying, 'Give us a quick flash and a bacon sandwich! I have waited a long time for this, girl.' He kissed her hard and she responded as he knew she would.

Suddenly the door to the lounge opened, and his little grandson, Cain, threw himself against his legs.

Eileen, who was standing behind him, said archly, 'You have waited long enough, you two, another couple of hours won't fucking kill you.'

With that they walked into the room where all the people they loved had gathered together to welcome Cain home. He knew that, no matter what, they would be all right. They had a great love that had survived the worst life could have thrown at them. Even Molly was grinning her head off, and Linda was also there with her mum and dad. It was a real homecoming. What more could a man ask for?

As his son Michael came over and hugged him, Cain felt the first real sting of tears. They had lost and gained so much, and that was what the Good Life was all about. Looking around, Cain understood that he would never be a part of it again, and he felt content at that thought. He pulled his wife into his arms and kissed her again as everyone smiled and clapped.

Little Cain, his father and grandfather's double, shouted, 'Granddad's kissing my nanny!'

Cain Moran and Jenny Riley knew that this was all they needed for the future. The worst was over; they just had to live the rest of their lives, together on the out. They had waited long enough for this, now it was time to enjoy it.

'I think anyone who grew up on or near a council estate like I did understands my books, the background.'

Read on for more about Martina Cole . . .

> *'I've always been a book fanatic from when I was a little kid...'*

- Martina is the youngest of five children.

- Her nan taught her to read and write before she went to school.

- She secretly signed her mum and dad up to the library and borrowed books in their name.

- Her dad was a merchant seaman, away on the boats for long stretches. He'd come back for Christmas and bring the books that were big in America at the time.

- She used to bunk off school to go and read in the park.

- She was expelled from school – twice – and left school for good at 15: 'They said, don't come back.'

- She was expelled from a convent school for reading *The Carpetbaggers* by Harold Robbins ('They were nuns, how did they know what was in it?!')

- Her first boyfriend was a bank robber. He was really handsome, he had a Jag. 'We're still really really great friends.'

- The first book she remembers reading is Catherine Cookson's *The Round Tower* – she borrowed it from her nan.

- She reads on average two or three books a week.

- Martina wrote her first book when she was 14. It was about a girl who was at a convent but secretly worked for the CIA.

- Her first paid job as a writer was for her neighbour – a Mills & Boon fanatic who paid Martina in cigarettes to write her beautiful stories where they kissed on the swings at the end. Her neighbour's son used to steal the exercise books from school for her to write in!

- Her books are the most requested in prison – and the most stolen from bookshops.

- She sells hugely in Russia, and sometimes thinks it's because the Russians think it's a handbook to the London underworld.

- She has her own Film/TV production company with Lavinia Warner, the woman who produced *Tenko* – the first TV series with really great female characters.

- Alan Cumming did his own hair and make-up and singing for his part as Desrae in the TV adaptation of *The Runaway*.

- *The Faithless* made her the first British female adult-audience novelist to break the 50 million sales mark since Nielsen Bookscan records began.

- *The Take* won the British Book Award for Crime Thriller of the Year in 2006.

- Her fans include Rio Ferdinand – he was snapped with a copy of *Revenge*.

> *'I'm a great believer in anything that gets anyone reading...'*

MARTINA COLE was just 18 when she got pregnant with her son. Living in a council flat with no TV and no money to go out, she started writing to entertain herself.

It would be ten years before she did anything with what she wrote.

She chose her agent for his name – Darley Anderson – and sent him the manuscript, thinking he was a woman. That was on a Friday. Monday night, she was doing the vacuuming when she took the call: a man's voice said 'Martina Cole, you are going to be a big star'.

The rest is history: *Dangerous Lady* caused a sensation when it was published, and launched one of the best selling fiction writers of her generation. Martina has gone on to have more No. 1 original fiction bestsellers than any other author.

She won the British Book Award for Crime Thriller of the Year with *The Take*, which then went on to be a hit TV series for Sky 1. Four of her novels have made it to the screen, with more in production, and three have been adapted as stage plays.

She is proud to be an Ambassador for charities including Reading Ahead and Gingerbread, the council for one-parent families. In 2013, she was inducted to the Crime Writer's Association Hall of Fame, and in 2014 received a *Variety* Legends of Industry Award.

Her son is a grown man now, and she lives in Kent with her daughter – except when she chases the sun to Cyprus, where she has two bookshops.

Her unique, powerful storytelling is acclaimed for its hard-hitting, true-to-life style – there is no one else who writes like Martina Cole.

*'I'm not educated but I'm very well read...
I read anything and everything. I can read
a book a day. For me reading has been
my biggest pleasure all my life.'*

Martina's Top Books And Favourite Authors:

Hatter's Castle by A. J. Cronin – 'The book that stayed with me all my life'

Wedlock by Wendy Moore – 'A true story written like a novel'

The Godfather by Mario Puzo – 'The book was so much more powerful than the film'

Brighton Rock by Graham Greene – 'the book that changed my life'

Hollywood Wives and *Hollywood Husbands* – 'I was always a big Jackie Collins girl – these are two of my favourite books of all time'

The Hitchhiker's Guide to the Galaxy by Douglas Adams – 'Certain books are like old friends and this is one'

Room by Emma Donoghue – 'I thought it was so good – I read it on a flight to Cyprus and made sure we ordered copies for my bookshop as soon as I arrived'

Hermann Hesse – 'For pure beauty of writing. *Steppenwolf* had a big effect on me'

George R.R. Martin – 'He's given me back my love of fantasy'

Val McDermid – 'Love a good serial killer'

For years Martina Cole has visited and worked within prisons across the UK. A passionate advocate of rehabilitation and education within the prison system, Martina has taught creative writing classes, given talks, and, in her role as ambassador for the Reading Agency's Six Book Challenge, she's seen how important increasing literacy is for educating inmates. In fact, it always surprises her how many young prisoners, especially male inmates, who can barely read and write when they get to prison, read their first book in this tough environment.

'My main function when I go in is to try and enthuse people to want to read or want to write. I show them it's possible to do it, that anyone can do it if they want'

Martina loves opening the door to the world of storytelling and language to people who have never picked up a book before. Her favourite moment in her creative writing classes within prisons is when she sees people who have never read a book in their life suddenly discovering storytelling and wanting to discuss books with her and their fellow prisoners.

'The one thing you need to read is time, and in prison you've got all the time in the world'

Martina's books are the most requested books within prison libraries and the most stolen from bookshops, a statistic she is very proud of – stealing aside! Because, for Martina, if her books are the first a person has ever picked up she's delighted to have encouraged them to start reading. She advises new readers to find their passion and read widely within it, be that crime, romance or science fiction. The book she recommends most to prisoners is *The Call of the Wild* by Jack London, a book she read and loved when she was young.

> *'When men go to prison they leave their kids with the person they trust most: their mum. But for women it's different – they often don't have anyone they trust enough to take care of their kids while they're inside'*

Martina spends a lot of time working with women in prisons, trying to get families together, making sure these women get an education and can have the best chance of making something of their life once they've served their sentence and get out of the prison system. She's worked for organisations such as Women in Prison and she's a patron of Chelmsford Women's Aid.

> *'Prisons are tough, but the thing for us is we want to send them out better people than when they went in, right?'*

As a supporter of initiatives to improve prison conditions with the aim of encouraging rehabilitation, Martina has been pleased at the positive changes she's seen over recent years in the prisons she visits regularly. The attitude towards rehabilitation has shifted in a positive direction in many institutions with better libraries and education programs in place. And Martina will continue to work tirelessly to support rehabilitation and education within prisons, as well as writing books that inmates and people everywhere will read and love.

> *'She felt that all her Christmases and Birthdays had come at once...'*
> *(Get Even)*

Keep your eye on Facebook
f/OfficialMartinaCole to be the first to
hear when the next Martina Cole
is coming out.

And if you don't want to wait, treat
yourself to a nice bit of vintage Cole.
Here's a reminder of those blinding bestsellers
that have made Martina Cole the undisputed
matriarch of crime drama – and some quotes
from the lady herself to help you choose
which one you fancy reading...

The book that first made Martina Cole's
name – and its sequel
DANGEROUS LADY
MAURA'S GAME (Dangerous Lady 2)

The only time Martina's written from the Old Bill's
perspective: her deadly DI Kate Burrows trilogy
THE LADYKILLER (DI Kate Burrows 1)
BROKEN (DI Kate Burrows 2)
HARD GIRLS (DI Kate Burrows 3)

You might have seen these on TV – but that doesn't
mean you know what happens in the books!
THE TAKE
THE RUNAWAY

*'I love the fact that my books are the most requested
books in prison and the most stolen books in bookshops,
I love the whole concept of that!'*

Martina writes brilliantly about what it's
like on The Inside. For gripping novels
that tell the truth about prison, try
THE JUMP
FACELESS
TWO WOMEN
THE GOOD LIFE

'Your family is either the best thing that ever happened to you or it's the worst thing that ever happened to you.'

Family life is always at the heart of Martina's storytelling: loyalty, protection and how the ties that bind us can also sometimes choke the very thing we want to protect...

FACES
THE FAMILY
THE FAITHLESS
BETRAYAL

'I deal with the mums, the wives, the girlfriends, the sisters, the grandmothers whose children or family are caught up in this life.'

Anyone who's ever read Martina Cole knows her women are the best: strong, resilient, vengeful – nothing will get in the way of these ladies when they know what they want

GOODNIGHT LADY
THE KNOW
CLOSE
GET EVEN

'My books are very anti-violence. I say this is what happens to you if you get caught up in the violent life.'

With her unflinching talent, Martina's stories reveal a world that many would rather ignore

THE GRAFT
THE BUSINESS
THE LIFE
REVENGE

'I wrote what I'd like to read and as luck would have it other people liked to read them too – they either love them or they can't read them, they find them too shocking to read.'

MARTINA COLE

THE KNOWLEDGE

CELEBRATING
25
YEARS
OF RECORD-BREAKING BESTSELLERS

MARTINA COLE

IT'S IN THE BLOOD